A Sprinkle of Fairy Dust

A Sprinkle of Fairy Dust

Stories by

Elizabeth Bevarly
Elaine Crawford
Marylyle Rogers
Maggie Benson Shayne

St. Martin's Paperbacks

A SPRINKLE OF FAIRY DUST

"Ever True" copyright © 1996 by Elizabeth Bevarly.
"Magic and Mayhem" copyright © 1996 by Elaine Crawford.
"Fairy Dreams" copyright © 1996 by Marylyle Rogers.
"Fairies Make Wishes, Too" copyright © 1996 by Maggie Benson Shayne.
Excerpt from *Happily Ever After* copyright © 1996 by Marylyle Rogers.

ISBN: 0-312-96035-2

Printed in the United States of America

St. Martin's Paperbacks edition/November 1996

St. Martin's Paperbacks are published by St. Martin's Press, 175 Fifth Avenue, New York, NY 10010.

10 9 8 7 6 5 4 3 2 1

Contents

∞

Ever True

Elizabeth Bevarly

For Chet, who signed my contract,

and

for Michael, who taught me to love Shakespeare.

Now, until the break of day,
Through this house each fairy stray.
To the best bride-bed will we,
Which by us shall blessed be:
And the issue there create,
Ever shall be fortunate.
So shall all the couples three
Ever true in loving be;
And the blots of Nature's hand
Shall not in their issue stand;
Never mole, hare-lip, nor scar,
Nor mark prodigious, such as are
Despised in nativity,
Shall upon their children be.
With this field-dew consecrate,
Every fairy take his gait;
And each several chamber bless,
Through this palace with sweet peace,
And the owner of it blest,
Ever shall in safety rest.
Trip away;
Make no stay:
Meet me all by break of day.

—Oberon
A Midsummer-Night's Dream
Act V, Scene ii
As told to William Shakespeare

Chapter 1

∞

"*The* course of true love never did run smooth?"

Miranda Avery sat motionless at the head of the highly polished, smudge-free table that bisected the boardroom of her New York office, steepled her fingers together, and frowned. Instead of gazing directly at her newest associate, who sat midway down the table to her left, she studied his reflection in the sleek ebony. The only concession she made to acknowledge that she had heard him was an almost indiscernible arch to one elegant, pale blond eyebrow.

Too new to Avery Advertising, Inc., to realize what that arched brow indicated, the young man licked his lips a little anxiously and continued. "It's already a familiar phrase. It would make for a memorable slogan."

Miranda relaxed her eyebrow, tilted her head back to observe her associate more fully, and folded one perfectly manicured hand over the other atop the proposal sitting previously untouched before her on the table.

The young man swallowed with some difficulty. "We, uh, we could call Malcolm's new perfume 'True Love,' and the whole campaign could revolve around Shakespeare. It's all right there in my prospectus."

Miranda gazed at him levelly, but remained silent.

The young man tugged restlessly at his discreetly striped necktie. "The, um, the possibilities for mining Shakespeare's plays for ideas would be endless. We could easily carry this campaign into the next century, and we could include Malcolm's other fragrance products with it as well.''

Miranda drummed her red-lacquered fingernails over the shiny gray folder before her, then slowly, very gradually, she smiled. ''Mr. Harper,'' she began softly, ''did you by any chance have a minor in college?''

The young man smiled back at her and visibly relaxed. ''Yes, I did, as a matter of fact. English.''

''I see. So you must have a great love for literature.''

''Yes, I do.''

Miranda smiled again. ''Especially Shakespeare, I'll bet. Am I right?''

''You're right.''

''Well, I think that's lovely. Has it occurred to you, however, Mr. Harper, that your average perfume buyer, regardless of her education, might not be particularly well versed in her Shakespeare?''

Harper's smile fell. ''Um, no. I didn't really consider that.''

''Consider it now.''

The young man's eyebrows arrowed down in a deep V as he followed her instructions. He stared at his own reflection in the table for some moments, then looked up again when he seemed to reach a conclusion.

''Well?'' Miranda asked.

''I suppose that if a consumer wasn't familiar with Shakespeare, then . . .''

''Then what?''

''Then a campaign that relied on his works might potentially be . . . um . . .''

''Yes?''

''Completely ineffective.''

Miranda nodded. ''Yes. It would.'' She arced her gaze around the table, scanning her nine remaining associates. ''Any other suggestions?'' she asked idly.

A wave of silence was her reply.

She sighed heavily, pressed her fingers to her forehead in an effort to thwart an oncoming headache, and muttered, "Fine. Well, we have until next week. Keep working on it. Harry?"

Harry Primrose, her personal secretary, snapped to attention in the chair to her immediate right, and she tried not to flinch when he did so. Although he had been with Miranda for nearly two years now, she still wasn't used to his very proper, very British demeanor. Even though at five-four he stood eye to eye with her, he seemed in no way diminutive. His lively eyes were more black than brown, his complexion smooth and fair and unlined. In spite of that, it was impossible for her to gauge his age. He might be twenty-six or fifty-six—she had no idea. He wore his black hair swept straight back from his forehead, and he was always impeccably groomed, favoring dark, conservative suits. His only concession to whimsy was a preference for silk neckties spattered with images of flora and fauna. And for some reason, regardless of the season, he always smelled faintly of wood smoke.

"Yes, Ms. Avery?" Harry replied quickly in the crisp, quiet tenor that always put Miranda at ease.

"Are there any other matters we need to address this morning?" she asked him.

He glanced quickly at the steno pad before him.

"Only Mrs. Parmentier's Midsummer Night's Masque."

Miranda groaned. "Oh, no. Is it already that time again?"

"May first is just around the corner," he reminded her. "And because you've kept putting this off, we now have scarcely two weeks to prepare."

Adrienne Parmentier had been a Manhattan fixture for what seemed like an eternity, a widow with far too much money and time on her hands. As a result, two decades ago, she had begun sponsoring an annual fund-raiser for the arts which she had decreed "A Midsummer Night's

Masque.'' Every head of every major corporation that claimed offices in Manhattan was invited—indeed required to the point of risking social ostracism if one declined the invitation—to attend the Masque, along with a hefty check for Mrs. Parmentier's charity, and a corporate retinue of players who created skits to provide the evening's entertainment.

"It seems like I just put away last year's costume," Miranda muttered. "Famous composers," she added despondently. "What kind of theme was that, anyway?"

"I thought you made a very fetching Franz Liszt," Harry told her.

Stoically, she declined comment. Instead, she asked, "What do I have to be this year?"

Harry consulted his note pad again, then threw her a pitying look and made a quiet *tsking* noise. "This year's theme is Tragic Lovers. Everyone is required to come in pairs. You'll need an escort."

"Terrific."

"And don't forget the skit."

As if she could after last year's debacle, Miranda thought. "All right, all right. Who wants to do the skit this year?"

Every head around the massive table dipped downward or toward the boardroom windows, where a bright blue sky outside beckoned heartily to anyone who wasn't tied to a high-powered career and overburdened with professional responsibilities.

"Oh, come on," Miranda cajoled. She turned to Harry again. "Who did it last year?"

He glanced at his pad again. "Beckley, Stuart, and Coleman."

She nodded. "Okay. Beckley, Stuart, and Coleman, you're off the hook."

Two women and one man sighed their relief. Miranda gazed around at the remainder of her associates. "Harper, Lewis, and Reynaldo, you're on the block this year."

The two men and one woman began to utter unified objections, but Miranda raised one hand, and the protests immediately ceased. "Just don't use any flares this time," she cautioned with a meaningful look at last year's skit masters. "Or cheese," she added with equal intent. "It took Mrs. Parmentier's staff six weeks to get rid of the smell. I'm surprised she invited Avery Advertising to participate again."

"More's the pity," Harry muttered, not quite under his breath.

"Harry," Miranda said, feigning a frown, ignoring the fact that she had been echoing the same words to herself.

"I apologize, Ms. Avery."

"No problem. Now, is that all?"

"Yes, Ms. Avery."

"Then we're through here."

Ten people rose at once and exited single-file through the smoked glass doors that divided the boardroom from the reception area. When they were clear, another individual entered. The man made his way toward the collection of lush potted palms lined like sentries before the floor-to-ceiling windows that looked down on Madison Avenue on the other side of the room.

"Hello, Sam," Harry said absently as the man passed.

"Hi, Harry," the man replied, turning casually to lift a hand in greeting. When he saw Miranda, he stumbled a bit, but quickly righted himself. After a moment's hesitation, he added, "Hi, Ms. Avery."

Miranda had glanced up briefly at the man's arrival, but when she had seen it was only the guy who came to water the plants every Tuesday, she dropped her gaze again. At his greeting, however, her head snapped up in surprise. "Oh, hello," she said.

She was about to return her attention to Harper's prospectus, hoping to find something salvageable in the campaign, but the man turned again to make his way to the other side of the room, and, for some reason, Miranda's gaze followed him. She had never noted how tall he was, nor how broad. His expansive shoulders strained beneath his denim shirt, tapering to a trim waist, and a truly remarkable derrière housed snugly in his jeans. His heavy boots attested to his earthy work, seemingly more dirt than leather. When her gaze wandered upward again, Miranda arched her brow once more. She noted the black hair bound at his nape in a ponytail and frowned.

A grown man with a ponytail, she thought derisively, returning her attention to Harper's prospectus. Honestly. Some people just refused to grow up.

"About Mrs. Parmentier's Masque?" Harry asked her.

Miranda leafed through the prospectus and only half-listened to her secretary. "What about it?"

"You'll need an escort."

"Mmm."

"Whom shall I telephone? That gentleman from the Sea-course Company who invited you to that Broadway première last month would probably be available."

Miranda wrinkled her nose. "No, I don't think so."

"Michael Dunbar, then."

She wrinkled her nose even more. "Ew. No way."

Harry sighed impatiently. "Jonathan Drew."

"Mm-mm."

"Noah Bernstein."

"Nope."

"Peter Gregg."

"I don't think so."

Harry issued a sound that might have indicated frustration in a less reserved man. "Ms. Avery, if I may be so bold, you really must find a nice man who would be an asset for occasions such as these."

"No, Harry, you may not be so bold."

Harry hesitated a moment, then, with much reluctance, capitulated. "Very well. The senator, then. As usual."

"My father?" Miranda shook her head. "No, he's too preoccupied with the election. He's way ahead in the polls right now. There's no way he'll risk becoming President by showing up in costume anywhere. Especially a Tragic Lover.''

"Your younger brother, then.''

"No can do. The regular season has started, so Tommy will be on the road.''

"Ah, yes,'' Harry recalled. "The boy wonder who will be taking the Mets to the . . . the . . . what is it they call that annual ritual again?''

"The World Series,'' she replied with a smile.

"Yes. That's right. The World Series: Then whom shall I call to play Pyramus to your Thisby?''

Miranda looked up, not certain she'd heard correctly. "Who to my what?''

Harry offered her a brief smile. "You'll need an escort,'' he repeated.

For some reason, her attention returned to the man on the other side of the room, who was bent over one of the smaller palms, inspecting its leaves.

"Is that really necessary?'' she asked. "Can't I go stag? I mean, 'Tragic' to me means these lovers ultimately wound up alone, right?''

"Actually,'' Harry corrected her, "I think it more implies that they wound up dead.''

"All the more reason to go alone, then. I could be Juliet, immediately following Romeo's tragedy. She outlived him by a good ten minutes, right?''

Harry threw her a chastising expression. "Mrs. Parmentier would be scandalized. You'd never hear the end of it.''

Miranda sighed. "Okay, I'll think of someone. Don't worry about it.''

"It's my job to worry,'' he countered loftily. "And as I said, it would be most helpful if you knew of someone who would be . . . convenient . . . for these purposes. I can't tell you how many times I've—''

"Harry.''

"Yes?''

"Petulance doesn't become you."

He sighed impatiently. "My apologies."

"And you know how I feel about this escort business. You've been trying to get me fixed up ever since I hired you, and—"

"I have *never*—"

"Oh, you have, too. And although you are; without question, the best secretary I've ever had, how many times do I have to remind you that matchmaking is *not* in your job description?"

"Ms. Avery, just because *you* don't believe in romance doesn't mean—"

"Harry."

"What?"

"Let me worry about Mrs. Parmentier, okay? I'll take care of an escort myself."

Obviously not satisfied by her reassurance, but clearly unwilling to press his luck—for the time being, anyway—Harry folded his notepad closed and stood. "Unless there's something else?" he asked her.

She shook her head and began to halfheartedly read over the prospectus again. "No. Nothing."

She scarcely noticed his departure, so thoroughly disgusted was she by Harper's nauseatingly sweet campaign. True Love, she repeated to herself. Ick. What woman in her right mind would wear a fragrance called True Love? The very suggestion of such a thing turned Miranda's stomach.

"Ms. Avery?"

"Yes, Harry?"

But when she looked up again, she realized it wasn't Harry who had summoned her. It was the plant waterer. She was about to apologize for her error, but her breath caught in her throat. She had never been this close to him before, had never paid attention to his face. Now that she did, she realized that his face was quite extraordinary— square and blunt, strong and masculine, with beautifully arranged features. His nose was narrow and regal and bespoke nobility, his lips turned up slightly over straight, white teeth. And his eyes . . .

A deep, sultry sigh bubbled up unbidden inside Miranda. His eyes reminded her of those belonging to a night creature she'd once seen on the cover of *National Geographic*, so large and bright were they, ringed with sooty lashes, and a vivid green color she had never seen on another human being. Yet instead of being cool and distant, as she had noticed that the eyes of handsome men generally were, this man's eyes were warm and inviting. Too warm, she decided when an odd heat began to spiral up from her midsection. And way too inviting.

"I . . . I . . . I'm sorry," she finally stammered. "I . . . I . . . I thought you were Harry."

"No, I'm Sam," he said, his mouth broadening into a roguish smile. "Sam Armado. I'm—"

"You're the guy who waters the plants every Tuesday," Miranda finished for him without thinking.

His eyes fairly sparkled with delight. "Among other things, yeah. I'm flattered you noticed."

"No, I didn't—" she began to protest before realizing her statement indicated just the opposite. "I mean . . . um . . ."

Sam waved her off. "I just wanted to tell you that you have an anthracnose on a couple of your *Phoenix canariensis*."

One of Miranda's hands flew immediately to the top button of her white blouse, while the other gripped fiercely the lapels of her dove gray suit jacket. Sam towered over her, so she pushed her chair backward and stood. Unfortunately, even in her high heels, she found herself gazing at his chest—and a rather noteworthy chest it was, she thought before she could stop herself—and still standing a good foot shorter than he. That didn't stop her, however, from wanting to slap him for the forwardness of his statement.

If she could just figure out how, exactly, his statement had been forward.

''I *beg* your pardon?'' she demanded.

Sam laughed, a rich, rumbling sound, redolent of vast lakes and sunny vistas. ''You have a fungus,'' he told her, laughing a little harder when he noted her confusion. He thrust a thumb over his shoulder. ''On a couple of your palm trees.''

Miranda relaxed. A little. ''Oh. I see.''

He scrubbed an open hand over his rough jaw. She found fascinating the utterly masculine gesture, and her gaze fixed on the long, blunt fingers that curved over his chin. His nails were clipped short, but that hadn't prevented dark crescents of dirt from forming beneath their tips. His knuckles, too, were stained with bits of black earth, and left behind a small streak of soil on his left cheek. For some reason, Miranda wanted to reach up and run her fingertips over that black smudge, so she clasped her hands fiercely together to keep herself from acting on the impulse.

''A little fungicide will take care of it,'' Sam continued, evidently oblivious to her attention, ''but you might want to avoid the boardroom for a while after I spray. I only use organic products, but the smell is still kind of strong. I was just wondering when a convenient time would be to do that.''

Miranda inhaled deeply, filling her nose and lungs with the fragrance of him, something earthy and primeval and completely outside her experience. And to her utter embarrassment, she realized she had no idea what he had been saying.

''What?'' she asked in a very small voice. ''What did you say?''

She tried to convince herself that his smile was smug and dismissing, and that she should be offended by his insolence. Unfortunately, his smile seemed anything but smug, and it made Miranda feel all warm and gooey inside. And much to her horror, she found herself wanting to smile back—smile back at a man who spoke easily of fungus, and who had dirt on his face and beneath his fingernails. How very odd.

"Is there a day of the week that you don't use this room?" he asked.

"Thursday," she replied, her gaze still lingering on the dark smudge that decorated his cheek.

"Would it be okay if I came back to spray on Thursday?"

"Uh-huh. That would be fine."

Still she stared at the soil staining his jaw, unable to look away. Sam seemed to finally notice her fascination, and he dipped his head lower to hers. "Is there a problem, Ms. Avery?"

"Your face . . ." she began softly.

"My face is a problem?"

She shook her head. "No, it's . . . dirty."

A single, good-natured chuckle erupted from inside him. "That's nothing new." He withdrew a wadded-up, faded blue bandanna from his back pocket and extended it toward her. "Would you mind?"

Without even thinking about what she was doing, Miranda took the scrap of fabric from him, noting vaguely how soft it was, forbidding herself to ponder the source of its warmth. She lifted it toward Sam's face, brushed lightly at the smudge of dirt, then reluctantly withdrew her hand. Before she could return the bandanna to him, though, he circled her wrist with strong fingers and plucked the handkerchief from her grasp.

Yet he didn't release her. For one long moment, he held her hand in his, her fingers mere inches from the mouth that so intrigued her. She realized that if she wanted to, she could reach right over and run her fingertips across his lips. Or, if he wanted to, she thought further, he could tilt his head just so and kiss those very same fingertips. Perhaps even draw them into his mouth, one by leisurely—

Miranda jerked her hand from his grasp and thrust it into

her jacket pocket. "Thursday would be fine," she repeated, her voice sounding shallow and inconstant, even to her own ears.

For one brief moment, Sam's hand lingered in the air between them, as if he wanted to reach out and touch her hair, to release the white-blond tresses from the tightly coiled French twist and bunch them in his fist instead. Then, his smile still maddeningly innocent, he dropped his hand to his side. "Great. I'll see you then."

And before Miranda could say another word, he was gone, leaving her feeling as if they had just made a date, but for the life of her, she had no idea what kind.

Chapter 2

❦

*S*am Armado glanced over his shoulder at the dark paneled door of the Avery Advertising, Inc., boardroom and smiled. Ms. Miranda Avery had been positively scandalized at the thought of him knowing she had an anthracnose on her *Phoenix canarienses*. He wondered what her expression would have been like if she'd known that while he was going on about fungicide, he'd actually been more preoccupied by thoughts of her hair. More specifically, by a curiosity about how long it was. Even more specifically, about how far it would reach across a man's bare chest. Most specifically, about how it would feel scattered over his own warm flesh.

He gritted his teeth and groaned inwardly. He had no business wondering about such things. Miranda Avery was as far removed from him as he was from the earth's core, and every bit as unattainable. Even if he had a hope in hell of finding the tiniest thing in common with her, she obviously had a string of admirers waiting in the wings, if her earlier conversation with Harry was any indication. In spite of that, Sam couldn't quite squelch the idea that had exploded in his brain when he'd overheard the exchange.

How could a human being not believe in romance? he wondered. That part of the conversation more than any other had him completely confounded.

"Hey, Harry," he called out to the man who was seated ramrod-straight behind a massive bird's-eye maple desk.

Somehow, Sam got the impression that Harry Primrose was more sentry than secretary, and the idea struck him as odd. Like such a little man could ever hope to defend even himself in a tough situation, let alone Ms. Avery. Not that Ms. Avery seemed to need defending, he thought further. Not from some outside harm anyway.

Harry glanced up. "Yes, Sam?"

Sam sauntered over to the desk and perched himself on the edge. He saw Harry frown at his action, but pretended he didn't. "What was all that about in there?"

Harry's gaze rose from Sam's knee to Sam's face, his expression indifferent. "What was all what about in there?"

"That stuff about a party. And Ms. Avery not having a date." He paused only a moment before adding, "She actually doesn't believe in romance?"

Harry dropped his gaze back down to the keyboard of the computer before him. "I'm sure I haven't the vaguest idea what you're talking about. Obviously you weren't listening while you were eavesdropping."

Sam smiled. *Touché.* "Oh, come on, Harry. You can trust me."

Harry began to type vigorously and ignored Sam.

Sam sighed. "Okay, never mind. I just thought maybe I could help her out if she was in a bind. I'm going to be at the Parmentier Masque myself, you know."

That seemed to get Harry's attention, although he did a good job of hiding it. His fingers on the keyboard only faltered for a moment. "You?" he asked.

"Don't sound so surprised," Sam responded wryly. "Not only was I invited—I am, after all, the owner of a thriving business, even if it's not one located in Manhattan—but I'm going to be doing the landscaping for the Enchanted Wood Near Athens that Adrienne always puts on her patio outside the ballroom."

Harry stopped typing and turned to look at him again, and, immediately, Sam felt uncomfortable with the scrutiny. For some reason, Harry seemed to be sizing him up for something, and Sam didn't like it one bit.

"What?" he asked. "Why are you looking at me like that?"

Harry narrowed his eyes. "Tell me again what your last name is."

"Armado," Sam answered automatically. "Why?"

The other man's dark eyes narrowed more, as if he were trying to look through Sam and into his very soul. "What was your mother's maiden name?"

Sam emitted a single, humorless chuckle. "What the hell kind of question is that?"

"Tell me your mother's maiden name," Harry insisted.

"Valentine," Sam told him, wondering why he'd volunteered the information when he'd had no intention of doing so.

Harry seemed to ponder that for a moment, but before he could say another word, the door to the boardroom opened and Miranda exited.

"Harry—" she began. But she halted abruptly when she saw Sam seated so familiarly on the other man's desk. "Oh. Mr. Armado. You're still here."

"Just leaving," he said as he jumped up again. "But I'll come back Thursday to spray."

She nodded. "Fine."

"Harry," Sam said, bobbing his head toward the secretary in farewell. "Don't forget about my offer."

Harry arched his eyebrows in what could have been any number of responses. "I shall give it all the consideration it deserves," he replied.

"Yeah, you do that."

With one final glance at Ms. Avery that inevitably became a long, lingering assessment of everything from her shimmering halo of perfectly coiled hair to the pointy tips of her doubtlessly very expensive high heels, Sam lifted two fingers to his forehead in salute and made his way toward his tools. Taking care of office plants really wasn't part of his job, but he always insisted on tending to the Avery account himself. Not just because it was one of his most lucrative, but because Ms. Miranda Avery was just too good to be true.

More beautiful than a greenhouse full of orchids, softer-looking than the velvety leaves of an artemisia, Miranda Avery was the kind of woman who seized a man's heart with both fists without even realizing her strength. For seven months, since taking on the account, Sam had tried to garner enough nerve to ask the woman out. But every time he came within two feet of her, the question dried up in his throat. Today had been the first time he'd touched her. And all he could do now was replay that one brief caress in his mind over and over again.

She had been every bit as soft as he'd thought she would be. Softer still. And now it was going to be even more difficult for him when he saw her again. Because that single, simple touch just made him want her all the more.

Trying to pretend he didn't notice that she was still in the room, he gathered his equipment and looked around for his assistant, Ivy. Unfortunately, the woman was nowhere to be found. Of course, that was nothing unusual. Ivy Pinter had a way of disappearing into thin air that drove Sam nuts.

"Oh, Sam."

Sam fairly jumped out of his skin before spinning abruptly around. As if his thoughts had conjured her up, Ivy stood immediately behind him, crowding his space. She was a tiny woman, a few inches shy of five feet, seemingly lighter in weight than a slender sapling. Her dark eyes were lively, and her black hair was cropped short. On her employment application, she had checked the box to indicate that she was over twenty-one years of age. But that didn't prevent Sam from wondering if she had lied. Ivy seemed no older than a high school senior to him.

"Dammit, Ivy, do you always have to do that?"

"Do what?" she asked.

"Sneak up out of nowhere like that. You scared the bejeezus out of me."

Ivy laughed, a rich, rousing peal of delight reminiscent of a breeze tangling with gaily painted glass wind chimes. Over the top of her head, Sam noticed Harry Primrose jerk to attention. The secretary stared at Ivy with his mouth agape, as if she had just thrown a dirt clod that hit him squarely in the back of the head. But when he saw Sam watching him, Harry quickly dropped his gaze back to his computer screen.

"Good," Ivy said when her laughter subsided, bringing Sam's attention back around. "No one should ever be too complacent."

"No chance of that happening with you around," he assured her.

She smiled but said nothing more. Together, the two of them collected their equipment, rode down to the first floor in the freight elevator, and packed everything away in the dark green van scrolled along both sides with the words *Armado Landscaping, Inc. When flowers just aren't enough, we provide a touch of magic.*

As Sam buckled himself in, Miranda Avery's words came back to haunt him, and he ground his teeth in frustration. The guy who watered the plants every Tuesday, he grumbled to himself. Evidently, that's all he was to her. Still, he couldn't quite forget the expression on her face when he'd circled her wrist with his fingers and plucked the bandanna from her hand. For someone who didn't believe in romance, Miranda Avery sure did have some starry eyes.

"So you got a thing for the Avery woman, huh?"

Sam's attention snapped to his companion, and he eyed Ivy suspiciously. "What makes you say that?"

She shrugged and gazed out at the rows of taxis and delivery trucks surrounding them. "I saw the way you were looking at her."

"What's that got to do with anything?"

"Hey, Sam, it's no big deal. Everybody needs somebody. It's only natural."

"Not necessarily."

She chuckled again, that light, lyric ripple of sound that gave him goose bumps. "What is it with people?" she muttered.

"What are you talking about?" he countered.

She sighed. "Nothing. What's the story with her secretary?"

"Harry?" Sam found Ivy's curiosity odd, but told her, "I don't really know him that well."

"Is he single?"

"As far as I know. Why?"

She smiled. "Just curious."

"Isn't he a little old for you?"

"Not necessarily," she told him, echoing his own words.

"Then why don't you ask him out?"

"Maybe I will. Why don't you ask Miranda Avery out?"

He detected a quiet, but very real, challenge in her tone. And Sam had never been one to turn away from a challenge. Well, not until Miranda Avery, he reminded himself grimly. The realization just made him grow that much more irritable.

"Maybe I will," he told Ivy as he gripped the steering wheel more fiercely. "Maybe I will."

Thursday afternoon found Sam exactly where he'd been Tuesday morning—in the Avery Advertising, Inc., boardroom, fondling palms and being ogled by Miranda Avery. Because that's the only way he could think to describe the way she was looking at him from where she stood, framed by the boardroom door. The moment he'd approached her in her office some minutes ago, her eyes had gone all dewy again, and her body, one minute all ridges and angles—which he supposed was a necessary posture for women in the male-dominated corporate world—had eased into a softer, more inviting repose. And the way she was looking at him now . . .

Sam drew in a none-too-steady breath and held it, waiting impatiently to hear what she had to say.

"Is this going to take long?" she asked.

Depends on what you mean by the word 'this,' he thought wildly to himself. But what he said was, "No. It shouldn't take long at all."

"Because everyone's on their way out now," she pointed out unnecessarily, jabbing an index finger over her shoulder. Behind her, a parade of pinstriped personnel were lined up in wait for the elevators. "I was under the impression that you were going to be here earlier."

"Well, I meant to be, but I got a little tied up this morning at the nursery. I've been running behind ever since."

"I really do need to be leaving, too," she added. "I, um, I have plans for the evening."

"I understand," Sam told her, trying not to dwell on the fact that she had plans for the evening that obviously included someone other than himself. "I'll do this as quickly as I can."

She nodded, but said nothing more. Instead, she continued to stand in the doorway, staring at Sam as if she were contemplating which pork shop in the butcher's window was juiciest and most capable of satisfying a voracious hunger. Her black wool suit, which he supposed was meant to be conservative and elegant, was actually about the sexiest thing he'd ever seen a woman wear, hugging every curve and valley her body possessed—and there were lots of curves and valleys on Miranda Avery. All Sam could do was wonder how it would feel to loose each button one by one and slip the garment leisurely away. Preferably by candlelight. Or moonlight. Or no light at all. Hey, he wasn't picky.

"Mr. Armado?"

Sam forced himself to focus once again on the task at

hand. Unfortunately, he couldn't quite remember just what that task was. "Hmm?"

"You were going to spray."

"Yes. I was."

"So why don't you?"

"Because you're still standing here, and, like I told you the other day, this is going to smell kind of unpleasant."

She stepped away and began to pull the door closed behind her. "I'll just wait out here then, okay?"

"That's fine."

Miranda closed the door behind herself and paused to catch her breath. Why, all of a sudden, did Sam Armado so fascinate her? He'd been coming to water the plants for months now, and she had scarcely noted his comings and goings. Now, out of nowhere, all she could do was relive that one brief moment when he had held her hand in his, and wonder what it would be like to have him touch her like that again.

And then there were some of those dreams she'd been having for the last two nights. Those dreams that had been some of *those* dreams. The kind that featured her and Sam Armado. Running through fields and forests. Laughing and cavorting. Kissing. Hugging. Naked. That kind of thing. Just where on earth they were coming from was anyone's guess—Miranda had never cavorted, naked or otherwise, in her life. But one thing was certain. Thanks to thoughts of Sam, she had been completely unable to keep her mind on her work lately. And that just wouldn't do.

Ever since earning her Master's in marketing eight years ago, Miranda had quickly and effortlessly scaled the corporate ladder, reaching the top rung without so much as chipping a nail in the process. She was one of the best in her field, well respected and much admired. Avery Advertising was a top ad agency, well on its way to becoming number one. It was all Miranda had ever wanted in life—to be a professional success. Nothing else had mattered at all. Men, romance, and all the accoutrements that went with them, had never been a concern for her. On the contrary, she'd gone out of her way to avoid romantic entanglements. Not only were they too time-consuming, but she'd simply had no reason to want one.

Until Tuesday morning. Until Sam Armado had curled his fingers around her wrist and gazed down at her with those impossibly beautiful eyes. Now it was all Miranda could do to remember that she had a job, let alone perform it to her fullest capacity, something that had once been her sole reason for rising in the morning. Instead, she spent her time behind her desk wondering what Sam would look like naked. Wondering what it felt like to want another human being as badly as she wanted professional success. Wondering exactly what it was that drew two human beings to a bond like that. And what it would be like to follow that wanting, to let it guide her through the process that led to its fulfillment.

And she could understand none of it. Why the sudden fascination with something she'd never been interested in before? Why, out of nowhere, had this desire for . . . well, desire . . . been born?

"Ms. Avery, you're still here."

Miranda turned to find Harry studying her with much surprise. He was shrugging into a trench coat, angling the collar up behind his neck as if he were already outside, trying to ward off the chilly spring breezes that still carried hints of winter.

"Mr. Armado is just finishing up," she said. "He and his assistant will be done shortly."

Harry's expression grew inquisitive. "Sam's assistant is here with him?"

"Mm-hm." Miranda looked around. "At least, she was here a minute ago. I don't know where she went. Oh, wait, yes I do. She said something about seeing to the plants in the Xerox room that she forgot about on Tuesday."

Harry nodded, then seemed to remember something. Pressing his fingertips to his forehead, he muttered, "Drat.

I forgot to tell you that Mr. Malcolm called this afternoon while you were out. He wanted you to return his call before the end of the day. I apologize for the oversight.''

"That's all right," Miranda told him as she glanced down at her watch. "Malcolm never leaves his office before seven anyway. I still have time to reach him."

Harry nodded again, and as soon as Miranda was out of view, made his way briskly to the Xerox room. As promised, he found Ivy Pinter tending to a long row of cacti. Even though she had her back to him, and even though she didn't move, and even though he had entered silently, he knew she was aware of his presence. And even though she was the one who had invaded his turf, as these Americans so quaintly put it, Harry decided to let her be the one to speak first.

"I think *cactaceae* are the most fascinating creatures, don't you?" she asked without turning around. "I'd never seen them before until I came to America. They seem so standoffish when you first meet them. But they're really very warm and inviting, aren't they?"

Harry nodded. "Yes. They are."

Ivy turned to gaze at him, her smile playful and flirtatious. "You, on the other hand, really are quite standoffish. You're not at all like your Uncle Robin."

"So I've been told," he replied dryly. "You've met Unc have you?"

"Once or twice."

Harry crossed his arms defensively over his chest, as he always did when the conversation turned to the subject of his relatives. "Yes, well, I can't say that I'm surprised. Even though Uncle Robin isn't the most .... respected ... member of the Goodfellow family, he certainly is the best known."

"He sends his regards."

Harry ignored that and asked instead, "What are you doing here? Who sent you?"

"You know very well who sent me."

"Why?"

"Because you're not doing your job."

"Says who?"

"Says them." Ivy stroked the fuzzy fronds of a cactus one final time, then turned to make her way across the room. When she stood nearly toe-to-toe with Harry, she dipped a finger beneath his necktie and ran her thumb over the silky fabric. "Nice," she commented. "And expensive, I'll bet. But, then, you Goodfellows have always been the favorites, haven't you?"

This time it was Harry's turn to smile. "Jealous?"

She shook her head slowly. "Not a bit. I'm not the one in trouble here."

"I suppose that's meant to be a threat?"

Ivy released his tie and settled her fisted hands on lush hips. Her blue jeans and sweater were more than a little snug, and it was impossible for Harry to ignore how extraordinary she looked in the trappings of mortals. Nor could he prevent himself from imagining her as her more . . . natural . . . self, clothed instead in the wispy wear of the forest.

"You were supposed to have this fixed by now, Harry," she told him. "Miranda Avery should have been happily married ages ago. Yet here she is, languishing on the vine, without ever having even tasted real passion."

"That's not my fault," Harry countered. "She wants nothing to do with the men I've arranged for her."

Ivy made a face. "That's because you pick yucky men."

"They've been perfectly suitable. Responsible, successful, decent, hard-working—"

"Booooorrrring," Ivy sang out. "With a capital B. They're everything *you* want and need in a mate, Harry. Not what Miranda needs. Not what she deserves, either, for that matter."

"Oh, and I suppose you know exactly what Miranda Avery needs."

"As a matter of fact, I do. Sam Armado."

Harry rolled his eyes heavenward. "Oh, please. You can't be serious. He's far too common."

Ivy gaped at him for a moment, then flattened her palm and smacked it against his forehead. Hard. "What's the matter with you, Harry? You've been living among mortals too long. Don't you know who Sam is?"

Harry rubbed his forehead and narrowed his eyes. "He's the chap who comes to water the plants every Tuesday."

Ivy sighed with obvious impatience. "He's a kinsman of Theseus and Hippolyta."

That stopped Harry in his tracks. "He's what?"

"He's the Duke's great-great-great-great-great . . ." Her voice wandered off, and she began to count silently on her fingers. But she'd gone through them all before she gave up and concluded, "Anyway, he's a direct descendant, and the only single male of marriageable age left in his generation. All the others found good fortune, complete happiness, and true love a long time ago."

"As has everyone else in Miranda's family and generation," Harry mumbled thoughtfully.

"She's the only single female of marriageable age left who came out of Hermia and Lysander's union, right?"

"Correct."

"So she and Sam are perfect for each other." Ivy's shoulders rose and fell philosophically. "It's destiny, is what it is."

"Says who?" Harry asked again.

"You know who says who. Them."

This time Harry was the one to make a face. "Oberon and Titania retired more than a century ago. They're living quite nicely on Bermuda. What could their interest in this matter possibly be?"

"Oberon's the one who started it all," Ivy reminded him. "Don't you think he's going to be concerned that his blessing hasn't been fulfilled? Don't you think he's going to do whatever it takes to make sure Miranda and Sam find the true love that's been destined for them? Sure they've had the good fortune and complete happiness part. But that true love business, Harry . . . That's serious stuff.''

"Yes. I suppose it is." Harry sighed wistfully and rubbed his eyes. "Honestly, there are times when I could just strangle my Aunt Lily for giving the Duke's history to Shakespeare for public consumption. Yes, it made for a nice little comedy. But I had no idea it would go this far.''

Ivy concurred. "Yeah, well, how could any of the Fairies have known back then that someday people would be calling Willie 'The Bard'? Everyone just thought it would be something nice to do for Queen Bess, didn't they? Everyone thought she deserved a little something special for her entertainment, that's all. Putting those ideas into Shakespeare's head . . .''

She, too, sighed before adding, "It just went farther than anyone could have known it would. But it's too late to change that now. And from what I've seen of Miranda, you're going to need some help with her.''

Harry nodded reluctantly.

Ivy grinned and took his hand in hers, twining their fingers together. "Lucky for you, Harry, I have an idea.''

He gazed down at his hand linked with hers, marveling at the odd heat that wound up his arm and through his chest, to settle heavily in his midsection. It was quite unlike anything he'd ever experienced before. For a moment, he could think of nothing to say. And finally, when he did speak, he couldn't entirely prevent the uncertainty that crept into his voice.

"Yes," he said softly, as he tightened his fingers around hers. "I suppose that *is* lucky.''

Chapter 3

∞

Miranda cradled the telephone receiver between her ear and her shoulder, nodded impatiently, and tried to concentrate on what the man at the other end of the line was saying. She had kicked off her shoes some time ago, and now leaned back in her chair with her stocking-clad feet settled atop her desk, crossed at the ankles. The five minutes she had planned on spending on this conversation had actually become twenty-five, and she was anxious to conclude her business and be on her merry way.

"We're working on it, Malcolm, honestly," she said. "Just give us another week. We'll have a campaign for your new perfume that will knock your socks off. What? A name? Well, um . . ." Miranda hated it when clients wanted to get specific before she was ready. "We, uh . . . we've been bandying around True Love," she confessed, caught off guard and unable to come up with a better idea. Hastily, she added, "But we're by no means—"

An eruption of words from the receiver halted anything else she was about to say. But where Miranda had been prepared for a string of condemnations, what she heard instead were exclamations of delight.

"You actually *like* that?" she said before she could stop herself. "I mean, of course you like that, but we have a number of other ideas we're exploring and—"

More words curbed her explanation, and Miranda sat dumbfounded, shaking her head in wonder that her client was so enamored of True Love.

"Uh-huh . . . ," she mumbled. "Okay . . . If you say so . . . But . . . What? Okay, Malcolm. If that's your decision . . . No, no problem. We'll get right on it."

With a few more requisite pleasantries, she ended the conversation and hung up the phone. Then she sat motionless at her desk, completely bemused. Yet another man who was overcome by ravings and whimsy when confronted with the suggestion of True Love. Miranda was stumped. What was going on with the masculine psyche these days?

"Ms. Avery?"

Miranda glanced up at the summons, only to be once again confronted by Sam Armado when she had been expecting Harry. Still pondering Malcolm's reaction, and once again more than a little bothered by the other man's presence, she failed to alter her posture.

"All finished?" she asked him.

He nodded. "Yeah, but that's not why I'm here."

She arched her eyebrows in silent query.

"We, um, we have a little bit of a problem."

Instead of looking at her face, as one would assume a person would do when starting a conversation, Miranda noted that Sam's gaze seem to be angled lower, at right about desk level. She turned her attention to what he seemed to be studying, only to see her feet, encased in smoky black silk, still perched atop her blotter. She also noted that her skirt, which, when she was standing, fell just above her knees, had skimmed up her thighs to a point that was really very unprofessional. And when she glanced up at Sam again, she realized that her thighs—not her feet— seemed to be the real focus of his attention.

Immediately, and as casually as she possibly could, she lowered her feet to the floor and stood, then tugged down her skirt with all the dignity she could muster. Unfortunately, at the moment, that wasn't much.

"A problem?" She repeated. "What problem?"

With the objects of his inspection removed from his view, Sam shook his head slightly and finally seemed to snap out of his reverie. He gazed levelly at Miranda's face for a brief moment, long enough to let her know he realized he'd been caught taking inventory. And he smiled, as if he wanted her to know that being caught *in flagrante delicto* didn't bother him one iota. Then he looked past her, toward the windows behind her that she knew offered a stunning vista of Manhattan, especially now, at sunset, when the weather was clear.

"Turn around," he told her.

Still puzzled, Miranda did as he asked, only to find herself gazing out not at dazzling cityscape skyline, but at a nearly opaque sheet of white.

"Snow?" she said incredulously. "*Snow*?"

"Blizzard is more like it," Sam corrected her.

She shook her head in disbelief. "But it was fifty degrees this afternoon. Twenty minutes ago, there wasn't a cloud in the sky."

"Yeah, well . . . now there's a lot more than a cloud in the sky."

"This is crazy. We've never had a blizzard in April before. What kind of meteorologists are the local channels hiring these days, anyway?"

"I don't think you can blame this one on the meteorologists. This is a freak storm if ever there was one. It came out of nowhere and looks like it's already dumped several inches of snow on the ground."

Miranda stepped back into her shoes and reached for her coat. "We'd better get out of here while we can."

"I think it's a little late for that."

"But—"

Sam shook his head again. "There's no way we're going to be able to navigate in that. God knows when the snow plows will be able to make it out. And it'll be dark before you know it. You don't want to get stranded out in something like that, even here in the big city. Hell, *especially* here in the big city. We'd be better off staying here where it's warm. And safe."

Oh, no, no, no, no, no, no, Miranda thought. *I don't think so.*

The last place she intended to find herself was snowbound with some total stranger who wore his hair in a rebellious ponytail and had eyes that made a woman want to howl at the moon. For some reason, she just didn't think it was a good idea.

Then she remembered that she and Sam weren't alone. If he was still here, Ivy must still be around, too, right?

"Okay," she conceded reluctantly. "I guess you're right. We've even got some meager provisions here. There's a fridge in the employee lounge, and people tend to keep snacks in there overnight. Yogurt, candy bars, that kind of thing. It's not Cordon Bleu, but at least we won't starve."

Sam nodded. "Good. Then we should be able to get through this night with relatively little incident."

Relatively little incident, Miranda echoed to herself. That remained to be seen.

"With three of us, though, we'd better think about rationing," she said.

"Three?" Sam repeated, clearly confused.

"Ivy's still here, isn't she?"

"No, she left with Harry about twenty minutes ago. Just before the snow started."

"Ivy and Harry left together?"

Sam nodded. "She said they were going to go have a drink together." He smiled devilishly. "Just between you and me, I think there may be a little romance blossoming there. Who knows what will happen if the two of them get stranded together out in this?"

"That's nonsense," Miranda told him.

"Why? Because you don't believe in romance?"

"No, because Harry's never exhibited an interest in any woman since I met him, and he says he can't be bothered with . . ." She halted and eyed Sam suspiciously when the significance of his question finally jelled in her brain. "How do you know I don't believe in romance?"

He shrugged. "I heard you say so."

"When?" she demanded.

"The other day. When you were talking to Harry."

"You were *eavesdropping*?"

"No, I wasn't *eavesdropping*. How could I help but overhear a conversation that was taking place a few feet away from where I was standing?"

"Maybe you could have minded your own business, that's how. Boy, the nerve of some—"

"Ms. Avery," he interrupted her tirade. He took a few steps forward, and his voice softened some as he modified his objection to "Miranda." But when she narrowed her eyes at him angrily, he immediately returned to "Ms. Avery."

"What?" she asked petulantly.

"It's going to be a long night, so let's not get off on the wrong foot."

"I'd say we're already off on the wrong foot."

"Then let's start over again."

He strode forward a few steps more, an action that left him standing directly in front of her desk. Miranda noted again his large size, his beautiful eyes, the exquisite fit of the denim that covered him from neck to ankle, and the sleek, black hair bound at his nape. Involuntarily, she drew in a ragged breath, reveling again in the scent of him, that dark, earthy, primeval fragrance that spoke to something equally primitive and barely restrained inside her.

He extended his hand slowly across the width of her desk and said, "Hi. I'm Sam Armado. I'm thirty-three years old, single and self-employed. I own and operate a landscaping company. More specifically, I sow, nurture, and cultivate things for a living. How about you?"

His introduction seemed harmless enough, but for some reason, Miranda wanted to take that part about sowing and nurturing personally. Gingerly, her eyes never leaving his, she placed her palm lightly against his and, cued by his introduction, responded, "Hello. I'm Miranda Avery. I'm thirty-one years old, single and self-employed. I own and operate an ad agency. More specifically, I convince people to buy things they really don't need at all."

Sam smiled and tightened his fingers around hers. "Nice to meet you, Ms. Avery."

Miranda smiled back, not quite able to ignore the warmth of the flesh pressing against hers. "Nice to meet you, too, Mr. Armado."

"Call me Sam."

"Call me Ms. Avery."

He bit his lip, but Miranda still detected the hint of a smile there. She knew she was probably being overly formal, but for some reason, she felt it vital to maintain some kind of distance between herself and Sam Armado, however meager.

"Whatever you want," he said as he inclined his head forward and gave her fingers a gentle squeeze. Then he added softly, "Ms. Avery."

This time Miranda was the one to bite her lip, but it was with anxiety, not humor. This was not a good situation, she mused. Snowed in, all alone with a man she scarcely knew, neither of them free to leave until . . . When? she wondered further. What if the blizzard kept up all night? What if no one could make it in to the office the following morning? What if she and Sam couldn't make it out? What if they were stuck here for days? Days that led into nights? Nights that led into . . . any number of things?

So what if? a little voice inside her piped up, a bit more carelessly than she would have liked to admit.

So they could starve to death, she immediately answered herself.

Depends on your appetite, the voice taunted.

Miranda chose not to reply to that. Instead, she looked up to find that Sam was still standing on the other side of her desk, still holding her hand in his, still smiling as if he knew something she didn't, still more handsome than any man had a right to be.

Damn him.

"Um," she began eloquently. Slowly, cautiously, she withdrew her hand from his and dropped it to her side, trying not to notice how cold it became without the warmth of Sam's rough palm embracing it.

"Um," he echoed, his smile growing broader.

"So," she tried again.

"So," he repeated.

She drummed her fingers against her thigh and sighed. "Are you hungry?"

His eyes fairly twinkled at the question, but his reply was relatively tame. "Not really. I had a late lunch. I'm okay for now. How about you?"

She cupped her hands over her upper arms. "I could use something hot to drink. They turn the heat off in the building at five o'clock and don't turn it on again until five in the morning. It could get a little chilly in here tonight."

"I wouldn't worry about that. We'll find some way to stay warm."

She gripped her arms tighter and tried not to think about the kinds of methods Sam Armado would use to keep himself—and her—warm. Instead, she told him, "Yeah, there should be plenty of coffee."

"Now *that* I could use."

She rounded her desk in a few idle steps, pausing before Sam. "The lounge is this way," she told him, inclining her head toward her office door.

"I'll follow you."

She nodded, knowing his suggestion was wisest, since he had no idea where the lounge could be, but for some reason bothered by the fact that he would be walking along behind her, instead of the other way around.

She sighed deeply. It was going to be a long night.

*   *   *

"You don't think we're overdoing it, do you?"

Ivy rattled her straw around in her Tequila Sunrise before indulging in a generous taste. She sat beside Harry at the bar in Le Cirque, the two of them the sole inhabitants of the restaurant, and stared at the swirls of white that danced in a frenzy outside the windows. The establishment had emptied of patrons shortly after the snow had begun, and the proprietors had shut it down entirely less than an hour later. That hadn't, however, stopped Harry and Ivy from enjoying Happy Hour there.

He sipped his port idly and shook his head. "These things can't be overdone, in my opinion. We can clear it away in the morning if need be. No harm done."

"Assuming, of course, that Sam and Miranda do what they're supposed to do tonight," she countered.

Harry made a wry face. "I have faith in your boy."

This time it was Ivy who shook her head. "I don't know. Miranda seems like a tough nut to crack. I've even sent her a few dreams about Sam—pretty good ones, too, if I may say so myself—but she still doesn't seem any too anxious to get involved with him."

"Yes, but if he's anything at all like his great-great-great-great . . ." Harry, too, surrendered to the generational mathematics and sighed. "If he's anything at all like the Duke, he shall win his lady fair with little fight. Hippolyta, after all, was an Amazon. And she was easily enough tamed by the Duke."

"Yeah, well, times were a lot different then," Ivy reminded him. "Women may not have the military weaponry or political power they once had, but they've adapted in other . . . less obvious . . . ways."

"Whatever are you going on about?"

Ivy wiggled her eyebrows suggestively. "Just that, in their own way, women still rule the world."

"You have no idea what you're suggesting. You weren't even born when women ruled the world."

"No, but my kinswomen have told me about it."

"You overestimate power, Ivy. It isn't all it's purported to be."

"Spoken like a man."

"Interpreted like a woman."

"What's that supposed to mean?"

He sipped his port again and smiled. "You're far too young to understand."

"Maybe it's not my youth, but your age, that's muddying the waters here. Times change, Harry. People—and Fairies—have to, too."

"You needn't tell me that. There was a time when I didn't have to work for a living. Not for a Mortal, at any rate."

"I kind of like Mortals," Ivy countered with a shrug.

"Yes, well, I suppose they're amusing enough," Harry conceded reluctantly. "And at least as entertaining as spaniels."

She laughed, and the sound of her delight rippled over him like a warm wave of wonder. He couldn't help but chuckle himself.

She sobered quickly, however. "So, you think Sam and Miranda have a chance? You don't think we ought to fetch that flower? The love-in-idleness? Just in case?"

Harry had lifted his glass to his lips again, but at her query, slammed it back down on the bar with nearly enough force to shatter it. He spun quickly around and clutched Ivy's shoulders fiercely, but stopped short of shaking her. Barely. "Good heavens, no. We're not to interfere with Destiny."

"But the blizzard—"

"Simply creates a situation. It will not be the cause of their love for each other. The juice of that flower is nothing but trouble, Ivy. We are not to use potions or magic directly on the lovers. They must find their way to each other voluntarily. Mark my words."

"Okay, but—"

"No buts. As you said, it's their destiny. Our job is to simply clear the path."

She nodded, but seemed unconvinced. As she turned to gaze mesmerized at the blizzard again, she said softly, "I had no idea we could create something like this together, Harry. It's so . . . awesome."

He released her and picked up his port once again, his thoughts a jumble of confusion. Eyeing her speculatively over the rim of his glass, he took another sip of the sweet wine, holding it in his mouth for a moment before swallowing, relishing the heat that eased down his throat and into his belly.

"I imagine," he began slowly, settling his glass back on the bar, "that there are a number of things we could create together, you and I, that would be, as you so . . . youthfully . . . put it, awesome."

Ivy turned to meet his gaze and smiled. "Why, Harry," she said coyly, "I didn't know you cared . . ."

Chapter 4

∞

"*W*ell, that's it for the Dove Bars."

"Bummer."

Miranda stared into the mini-fridge in the corner of the employee lounge, one foot settled atop the other. Sam sat at a nearby table watching her, quietly going mad. He told himself the reason he felt so wired was because of all the coffee he'd had to consume in the last several hours. But he knew caffeine was the least of his worries. What was making him feel so bewitched, bothered, and befuddled now was the sight of Miranda Avery shoeless, with his own heavy cotton gym socks covering her feet over her stockings.

They'd been in the gym bag he had tucked in with his equipment and had intended to use after finishing up his work here. He'd offered the socks to Miranda when she'd complained that her feet were getting cold. Now, as he observed the scraggly, ragged socks in contrast with the translucent black stockings and impeccable suit, he found himself entertaining ideas he had no business entertaining.

The incongruity of her footwear was yet another indication of how perfectly ill-suited he and Miranda Avery were for each other. But the realization did nothing to curb his desire for her. On the contrary, it only made him wonder wildly just what kind of sparks the two of them would generate rubbing off of each other. In a manner of speaking.

"Are you warm enough?"

Miranda's question jolted him out of his reverie and back to the here and now.

"Fine." The word was strangled when it emerged from his mouth, so he cleared his throat and tried again. "Fine. Just . . . fine. Plenty warm."

"You sure?"

"Mm-hm."

Again his response sounded a bit rough, so he wrapped his fingers around his coffee mug and raised it to his lips. *Warm* didn't begin to describe his current situation. *Hot, raging inferno of lust* might be a little more appropriate at this point. Oh, man, he thought, was there anything that could make this predicament any worse than it already was?

As if playing a very bad joke, the lights above them flickered once, twice, three times. Then they extinguished themselves completely to plunge Sam and Miranda into complete and utter darkness.

Great, he thought. This was just great.

"Oh, no." Her voice was quiet, close, and full of dread. "This can't be happening."

"Don't move," he told her. "You're closer to the door, so I'll get up and come to you."

He rose from his seat and began to move slowly and cautiously toward her, his arms outstretched to ward off any foreign object he might encounter. Within a half-dozen strides, he found her. Unfortunately, with his hands held out before him the way they were, his fingers were actually what found Miranda first, and they found a part of her that was soft and warm and pliable—a part of her that most women considered off limits to virtual strangers.

In spite of his discovery, Sam didn't—couldn't—immediately remove his hands. He was too stunned, too surprised by what he'd done, and too mesmerized by her softness to pull away from her. She smelled vaguely of gardenias, a scent that somehow seemed appropriate for her, despite the way she hid behind her rigidly restrained hair and conservatively cut suits. And the feel of her beneath his fingertips was nearly too much for him to bear. He was about to press his luck, about to curve his palms more intimately over her breasts, when her voice cut through the darkness and stopped him.

"Mr. Armado, if you don't mind . . ."

Immediately, he came to his senses and dropped his hands to his sides. But not before he noted that her breathing had become as ragged and unsteady as his own.

"Sorry," he mumbled. "I, um, I didn't mean to . . . uh . . . I mean . . . um . . ."

"There are some candles and matches in one of the drawers," she interrupted him, ignoring his apology. Even though it was dark, he could sense her stiffening and tugging at her suit. "Birthday cake candles. We, um, we normally have a little party when someone in the office has a birthday. Excuse me a minute while I find them."

He felt her move away from him, and when she did, he inhaled slowly, deliberately, trying to steady his heartbeat and hoping she couldn't sense just how close he'd come to kissing her. He wondered what she would have done if he had. If he'd followed his instincts and roped his arms around her waist, then covered her lips with his and plundered her mouth the way his libido commanded.

She probably would have popped him in the eye, he thought. And, he supposed, he couldn't have blamed her when she did.

The scratch of a match brought him around, and in a small, pale circle of gold light, he saw Miranda's face. Her cheeks were flushed pink; her eyes were round and huge. He didn't think he'd ever seen a woman more beautiful than she was. And if he didn't know better, he would almost have thought he had never seen one more aroused.

"That's better," she said, her voice scarcely above a whisper. She fumbled with a box of candles, spilling the contents out on the counter, then quickly picked up one and lit it. She dripped some wax onto the bottom of an upturned paper cup, then anchored the candle there. She repeated the action with three more, scooped up the rest of the candles and dropped them into her pocket, then handed two of the makeshift torches to Sam.

"Let's go back to my office," she said. "I think it may be a little warmer in there. Certainly there's more room to move around."

In other words, he thought, it would be easier for her to put more distance between them.

"Good idea," he conceded reluctantly.

They made their way back to her office slowly to keep the candles lit, then lined up the cups along the edge of her desk. Sam watched as Miranda emptied her pockets of the rest of the candles, noting the meagerness of their light supply—it probably wouldn't be sufficient enough to last until dawn. Then again, that wasn't necessarily a bad thing, as far as he was concerned.

Miranda seemed to notice, too, because she bent forward and blew out two of the burning candles. "Might as well make them last as long as possible."

"Mm," he said noncommittally.

He dropped to sit on the floor before her desk, leaning back against the smooth teak that almost seemed to glow golden in the scant light of the candles. He supposed he could have taken a few steps to seat himself in the chair opposite, but for some reason, he wasn't sure he could have made it without stumbling. He expected Miranda to move to the other side of the room, or at least to the other side of her desk, but much to his surprise, she knelt beside him, scarcely inches away. His astonishment must have shown on his face, because she smiled.

"I, um . . . I'm cold," she said. "Would you mind . . . ?"

Without hesitation, he lifted his arm, elbow slightly crooked, in invitation. Gingerly, as if having second thoughts, she twisted to sit on the floor beside him. For a moment, she didn't lean back against him, just continued to sit watching him guardedly. Then, evidently coming to the conclusion that he was harmless enough—or maybe just too cold to react otherwise—she angled her body against his. Sam curled his arm around her shoulder and pulled her close, half-expecting her to jerk away, pleased when he felt her relax instead. Lifting his other arm, he hooked his fingers together to draw her nearer still.

Not a good idea, he decided at once. Having Miranda this close, and being completely unable to take advantage of their position, was definitely not conducive to coherent thought.

It was, however, warmer this way. Much, much warmer.

"Thanks," she murmured. "I'm sorry. Just . . . the cold was beginning to get to me."

That's funny, Sam thought, *it's the heat that's beginning to get to me.*

"No problem," he told her, rubbing his hands briskly up and down her upper arm. "I have a jacket out there with my things, too, if you want it."

"No, that's okay. This is fine."

For a moment, neither said a word. Then, finally, Sam broke the silence by asking, "I guess this really put a crimp in your plans for the evening, didn't it?"

"What plans?" The words were out of her mouth before Miranda realized what she'd revealed. She bit her lip, hoping he wouldn't notice her gaffe.

No such luck.

"I thought you said you had plans tonight," he said as he moved his body a little to the left to facilitate a better view of her. "I mean, I thought you had a date or something."

"Um, actually," she began, "I . . . uh . . . I . . . I . . ."

"You were just going to go home and pop a cork on a bottle of wine all by yourself, weren't you?"

She nodded. "Yeah. Sorta."

He smiled. "Me, too."

She, too, adjusted her position to look at him, but said nothing further. For a long moment, her gaze locked with his, but she remained quiet and never turned away. When he seemed no longer able tolerate her silence, he shifted a little closer to her and gazed back.

Finally, he asked, ''Why do you keep looking at me like that?''

Miranda felt herself blush, felt the heat that had warmed her midsection since Sam's arrival in her office creep up past her heart, along her neck, and into her face. She hadn't meant to be caught staring. Then again, she wondered, how could she not stare? His embrace had roused something in her she'd never felt before—something from a place deep inside her she'd never bothered to explore. Some indistinct, undefined longing to be as close to another human being as one could be. A reaction to something warm, something wonderful, something beautiful. Something that simply was Sam Armado.

Scrambling for an excuse—any excuse—she panicked and uttered the truth instead. ''It's your hair,'' she said softly.

''What about it?''

''I . . . uh . . . I was just wondering . . . um . . .''

''Wondering what?''

''Um, how . . . how long it is.''

Without hesitation, and without taking his eyes from hers, Sam reached behind himself and tugged the rubber band away to free his hair. It fell in a soft cascade of black just past his shoulders, and he negligently nudged it away from his eyes.

''There,'' he told her, fingering a few stray strands into place. ''That's how long my hair is. How about you?''

Puzzled, she asked, ''How about me?''

''How long is your hair?''

Before Miranda had a chance to respond, Sam lifted a hand cautiously toward her face. He paused for a moment, as if waiting to see if she would object. She told herself she *should* object. But she didn't say a word. Her silence seemed to be all the response he needed, however, as he slowly, ever so slowly, reached behind her. But instead of loosing her hair from its coil as she had expected he would do, he curved his palm gently over her nape.

Miranda's heartbeat quickened as he traced his fingertips gently over her neck and along the smooth line of her jaw. He stroked the pad of his thumb along the slim column of her throat, halting the caress where she knew her pulse was raging wildly. He smiled when he realized how profound was the effect his simple touch had ignited in her. Then he leaned forward.

She closed her eyes and held her breath and waited. Then she felt his fingers burrowing in her hair, the warm pads of his fingertips pressing gently and methodically along her scalp in search of the hidden bindings that kept the tightly wound tresses so neatly restrained. Each time he encountered one of the hairpins, he tugged it from her hair, until the thick mass of pale blond fell down over his fingers, his hands, his wrists, his arms. In a dozen shades of white, silver, gold, and yellow, Miranda's hair spilled to her waist. When she opened her eyes, Sam was bunching thick handfuls of the silky strands in two big fists. Then, as she watched him, he lifted each sheaf to his lips.

"And you said you didn't believe in romance," he murmured when he completed his ministrations.

"I don't," she insisted. But her voice lacked the conviction she'd once felt so strongly.

"Yet you grow your hair like Rapunzel's," he countered with a smile.

"It's not. I—"

"Miranda."

"What?"

"Have you ever been in love?"

She shook her head mutely, wondering why he had posed such a question, wondering more why she was bothering to answer it.

"Never?"

Again, she shook her head, but still she said nothing aloud.

"Not even once?"

She hesitated only a moment before telling him quietly,
"No."

"So you don't know what it's like to feel that roiling,
wonderful uncertainty in your gut? That utter confusion that
clouds your mind until you can't tell up from down? That
vague, daydream state of mind that turns even the most
logical human being into a stark, raving poet?"

Again, her voice was quiet as she responded simply,
"No."

"That dizzying ecstasy that overtakes you for one brief
instant when you begin to understand that the person you
love might possibly be falling for you, too?"

"No. I've never felt those things."

He sighed and shook his head slowly, clearly disappointed by her inexperience. "That's too bad."

Miranda didn't like the judgmental condemnation that
laced his words. She stiffened as she asked him, "So I
guess you *have* felt those things before?"

He seemed to grow a little guarded as he admitted,
"Yeah, once or twice."

"You fall in and out of love a lot, do you?"

"I wouldn't say that."

"You just did say that."

"Okay," he relented. "I've been in love a couple of
times. But not—"

"Then how can you say true love exists? If true love
existed, people wouldn't fall in and out of love the way
they do." As unobtrusively as she could, she opened his
hands and freed her hair from his grasp, throwing the long
strands over her shoulders.

"I didn't say I'd ever experienced *true* love," he countered, staring at his empty hands as if she'd just branded
them with a red-hot iron. "Just that—"

"Love and romance," she told him as she tried to rewind
her hair into some semblance of its former restraint, "are
nothing but an illusion. Or, more accurately, they're the
result of good PR."

"What?"

"It's true," she insisted as she released the makeshift bun at her nape, only to have it fall in a fleet rush of blond back down around her shoulders and over her back. She sighed her exasperation and tried again. "The only reason people fall in love is because TV and movies and magazines tell them to. The reason romance exists is because major corporations spend lots of money to advertise in the media and keep it alive."

Sam expelled a rude sound of disbelief. "You don't honestly believe that."

"Of course I believe that. It's what I do for a living." She shrugged negligently, and her hair fell down around her shoulders again. She sighed once more, but surrendered to the mass. "It's essential that romance be kept alive, because without it, the economy would collapse."

Sam made a doubtful face. "So it's an economic thing."

"Of course it is. Sex sells. It's a cliché, but it's true. Romance is responsible for the sale of everything from flowers to hygiene products. Without it, no one would be buying greeting cards or candy. No one would be adding to their wardrobes with nice clothes for socializing. No one would go out to eat or to the movies or to the theater or whatever in nearly the numbers that they do now. Think of how many people would be out of a job if romance—if that promise of true love, which doesn't even exist—disappeared.

"What you feel when you think you're falling in love, Mr. Armado," she concluded, "is actually just a reaction to a really good ad campaign."

Sam eyed her warily for a moment, then scrubbed a hand over his mouth, along his jaw, and into his hair. "You honestly believe that?" he finally asked.

"Yes, I do. It's my job."

Instead of arguing, he threaded his fingers through her hair again, cupped the back of her head, and pulled her toward himself. His face hovered within inches of hers for a moment, then he covered her mouth with his.

It was an extraordinary kiss. Miranda wasn't sure she'd ever felt quite the way she did when his lips touched her own. For a moment, all he did was brush his mouth lightly over hers, then he closed his lips over her lower one and gently tugged it inside his mouth. He traced her lip with his tongue, and when she gasped her delight, ventured more deeply. Softly, gently, as if painting feathery strokes on a delicate canvas, Sam tasted her as fully as he dared. And all Miranda could do was enjoy it.

Without even realizing what she was doing, she leaned toward him, gripping the heavy denim of his shirt with hungry hands before splaying her fingers open over his chest. Beneath her fingertips, she detected raw strength and poetic beauty, something that just made her want to explore this man more intimately. Instinctively, and as if of their own free will, her hands crept higher, over his shoulders, down his arms, gripping salient biceps before curving around to his back. And with every advance she made, Sam echoed her motions.

She felt his fingers twine in her hair more fiercely, pulling the long strands forward over her shoulders. Then he curved his hand gently around her neck once more, tilting his thumb against her jaw to tip her head backward and facilitate an even more thorough kiss. Before she knew it, his fingers were working at the buttons on her suit jacket, unfastening them one by one, until the cool air in the office whispered against the thin shell she wore beneath. Only then did Miranda realize how far things had gone between the two of them, and only then did she pull away.

But she didn't get very far.

Sam's fingers were still curled around her nape, their gentle insistence keeping her from fleeing entirely. That along with the fact that Miranda just didn't want to flee. Instead, she simply sat where she was and stared into those eyes that had haunted her for days.

Why him? she wondered. What was it about Sam that compelled her in a way no man ever had before?

"Why are you looking at me like that?"

His question was the same one that had started their embrace initially, and somehow, Miranda thought, it seemed appropriate for ending it now. But she couldn't quite find the words she wanted to put him off. Instead, she covered his hand with hers, carefully removed it from her neck, and placed it back in his lap. Then she scooped her hair into her fist, and as Sam watched in silence, began to wind it back into a knot as well as she could.

"Miranda . . ." he began.

"Ms. Avery," she corrected him.

But he shook his head and smiled almost sadly. "Not anymore," he said softly. "Never again."

Finally, this time, her hair remained up where she wanted it, albeit not nearly as perfectly arranged as before. Confident that she had re-established some semblance of order with that small success, however, and with visibly trembling fingers, Miranda refastened her buttons. All the while, she was more aware than ever of Sam's gaze scanning her from head to toe and back again.

"Ms. Avery," she feebly insisted again, unable to meet his eyes.

He said nothing in response.

So Miranda, too, remained silent as she rose to her knees, then to her full height, and made her way around the desk to take her seat in her big, leather-bound CEO chair. She had hoped such a position and posture would restore her confidence completely. Instead, it just made her feel silly.

"Not cold anymore?"

Sam's voice came to her from the other side of her desk, where he remained seated on the floor. She couldn't see him from her where she sat, but she was certain he was smiling, mocking her.

"No," she replied, striving for indignation, fearing that she sounded indecisive instead. "I'm not."

"That's funny," she heard him reply. "Suddenly, I'm not cold, either."

She sighed wearily in frustration and wondered how much longer the two of them would be trapped here together.

At some point during the night, Miranda managed to doze off, and when she awoke in the morning, she was alone. She was also stretched out on the sofa that spanned one wall of her office, and couldn't recall having moved there under her own steam. She was also covered from shoulder to hip by a man's leather baseball jacket that she didn't recognize. And she was wearing a man's socks that she did.

That last realization more than any of the others caused her distress, precisely because she did remember how she had come by those. She wiggled her toes in the comfortable cotton, noting that they no longer felt numb from the cold, and wondered what had happened to Sam.

Mr. Armado, she immediately corrected herself. Where could he have gone?

She glanced over at the windows behind her desk to find that the morning had dawned beneath a bright blue sky harboring not even a trace of the previous night's storm. She could almost convince herself that the blizzard—and the turn of events that had come about because of it—had never occurred. Until her gaze fell to her desk, and she noted the stubs of birthday candles melted down the sides of a quartet of paper cups.

Then she remembered how Sam—Mr. Armado—had loosed her hair and held it to his lips. How he'd kissed her as if she were the answer to a prayer. How she had kissed him back in much the same way.

"Oh, no," she groaned, lifting a hand to cover her eyes.

How had such a thing happened? she asked herself. How could she have allowed things to go that far? Just because she'd been snowbound with an attractive man, and just because the lights had gone out and reduced them to candle lit surroundings that were more than a little romantic, and just because the way he had looked at her made her feel wanton and needful, and just because the things he had said had roused emotions inside her she'd never felt before . . . Just because all those things had happened, it hadn't given her free license to behave like an adolescent with her first crush.

Come to think of it, though, Miranda mused now, she'd never been an adolescent with a first crush. So maybe she was entitled to this bizarre, unfounded, inexplicable—and very temporary, she was certain—infatuation.

There was only one way to deal with this, she told herself. She must make sure she never had cause to be alone with Sam Armado again. Infatuations were dangerous things. They caused a person to be preoccupied and fanciful, something that detracted from what was really important—work. Miranda had a major ad campaign to arrange, and she had only a few days to do it. Idle daydreams about a handsome man with a ponytail would only prevent her from doing her job. And her job was what was most important.

Bottom line.

Her office door flew open then, and Harry Primrose entered. At first he didn't see her, but made his way resolutely toward her desk with a sheaf of papers. When he spun around, however, and saw her lying on her sofa, he halted.

"Ms. Avery," he said, clearly shocked by her appearance. "What on earth are you doing here at this hour, and looking as if you slept here? You didn't spend the night here, did you?"

She managed to fold herself into a sitting position, and automatically reached for her hair to straighten it. "Of course I spent the night here. In case you didn't notice, there was a major blizzard last night. It happened so fast, Sam . . . I mean, Mr. Armado and I never had a chance."

Harry narrowed his eyes at her. "Sam spent the night here, too?"

She nodded.

His gaze dropped to the socks covering her feet. "I see."

She detected more than a small hint of suspicion in his

comment and held up a hand to halt it. "Oh, no you don't. You don't see at all. It was perfectly innocent. And just what happened to you last night? Sam—Mr. Armado—said you and Ivy left together."

Harry's gaze dropped to the floor. "Ah . . . yes . . . well, um . . . Actually, Miss Pinter asked me to walk her to her car, and how could I refuse—you know that parking garage is unsafe for anyone, let alone a solitary woman."

"How chivalrous of you, Harry," Miranda observed wryly.

He nodded a bit anxiously. "Then, when we got down to the garage, and I noted that it had begun to snow, I decided it might be best if I went directly home myself."

"Sam said you and Ivy were going out for a drink."

Harry cleared his throat indelicately, glanced up at Miranda again, then quickly back down at the floor. "Yes, well . . . she did actually mention stopping off somewhere for a drink, but . . ."

"Yes?"

"Well, I didn't think it a very good idea. She's quite young. Not at all my type."

"Mm."

"And, as I said, by then it had begun to snow, so . . ."

"Mm."

Harry straightened, stretched his neck a little, as if his collar had become too tight, then folded his hands behind his back. "Shall I bring you a cup of coffee?"

Miranda nodded. "Please. But hold my calls for a while, okay, Harry? I need to wake up a little first."

He nodded and hustled out, closing the door softly behind himself. Miranda stood and strode to the bathroom connected to her office, moaning when she saw her reflection in the mirror. Her hair was a mess, looking as if it had been handled too playfully by someone who had no desire to see it contained. Which, she supposed, was exactly what had happened to it.

But for some reason, she couldn't quite bring herself to

contain it again. Instead, she brushed it out, then plaited it into a braid that fell nearly to her waist. She shrugged out of her suit and into a spare change of clothes that she kept at the office in case of emergency, bypassing the extra suit for a pair of pale blue leggings and matching knee-length sweater instead. For some reason, she didn't feel like working today. Lucky for her, she was the boss and could give herself the day off.

"Harry," she called out when she heard him return.

"Yes, Ms. Avery?"

She exited the bathroom briskly and collected Sam's things from the sofa where she'd left them. "I'm going to be out of the office today. Would it be a problem to rearrange my schedule?"

He quickly ticked off her agenda in his head and said, "No. There's nothing pressing. Where are you going?"

She was surprised to hear him ask. Harry was far too professional to wonder about his employer's personal life. Except when it came to fixing her up, she reminded herself. She eyed him warily. "Why?"

He shrugged. "In case something pressing does come up."

Sounded logical enough, she thought. Still, she found herself reluctant to reveal her destination. Instead, she fingered the softly worn leather sleeves of Sam's baseball jacket and felt the fabric grow warm beneath her touch. It reminded her of the way his hand had felt brushing against hers the night before, and her face grew warm.

"I need to return something to someone," she said softly. "I'll take the pager. If you need me, you can beep me."

"But—"

"Have a nice weekend, Harry. Don't do anything I wouldn't do."

And with that, she gathered her things along with Sam's and left her office, taking the first self-induced holiday she could ever recall giving herself.

Chapter 5

❧

$\mathcal{A}$rmado Landscaping and Nursery was located in Connecticut, but was in no way difficult for Miranda to find. The place was huge, sprawled across several acres of green, green grass, dotted here and there with steamy hothouses, and surrounded by softly sloping hills and valleys. Where the hills and valleys ended, groves of trees began—lush, proud evergreens, and fruit trees on the verge of bursting into full spring bloom.

Funny, Miranda thought, how the line of last night's massive blizzard seemed to have stopped right at the edge of New York City. Certainly, it hadn't touched Connecticut at all.

The tires of her car crunched over gravel and stray bits of cypress mulch as she pulled up before what appeared to be the main office. When she threw open her door and stepped outside, she was assaulted by the fragrance of pine and freshly turned earth. The aroma reminded her instantly of Sam, and not for the first time, she wondered why the owner and operator of such a large business came in person to water the plants in her office every Tuesday.

Because it was good PR, she answered herself immediately. Making the customer feel like she was number one was always the right way to do business.

Miranda pushed her way through the front door accompanied by the tinkling of a tiny brass bell, and was greeted at once by Ivy Pinter, who breezed through another door to Miranda's left. When the young woman saw her, however, she halted abruptly, and for some reason looked a little guilty.

How odd, Miranda thought. Ivy's expression was almost identical to the one Harry had worn in her office scarcely an hour ago.

"Ms. Avery," she said, bobbing her head in greeting. "Can I help you?"

"Is Mr. Armado here?" Miranda asked.

The other woman nodded. "He's out back. In the orchid house," she clarified quickly. "You want me to go get him?"

Miranda shook her head. "That won't be necessary. If you'll just point me in the right direction . . ."

Ivy gave her instructions, and within minutes, Miranda found herself standing at the threshold of what could only be the most amazing place she'd ever seen. The glass house was like a monstrous gemstone, the sunlight refracted erratically through windows that were smudged and dripping with condensation, thanks to the elevated heat inside that countered the chill in the air outside. And the aroma that assailed her was exquisite—luscious and poignant, unlike anything she'd ever encountered before. Around her were hundreds, perhaps thousands, of flowering plants, fat green vegetation splashed with delicate blooms in the most incredible colors Miranda had ever seen—vivid vermilions, cobalts, saffrons, and violets mingling with a softer palate of pinks, azures, ivories, and lavenders.

So stunned was she by the utter beauty of her surroundings, that her breath caught in her throat, and her thoughts evaporated from her brain. For a moment, she was too immersed in the stark, radiant magnificence of Nature to notice anything else. She'd had no idea such a place as this could exist on what was, to her, an otherwise pallid planet.

"Miranda."

Her name rose softly from somewhere amid that beauty, carried on a breath of wind, ethereal and enchanted, as if someone had whispered an incantation. She looked to her left to find Sam Armado emerging from behind a rich, robust flowering plant whose bright red blossoms were nearly the size of dinner plates. And somehow, she found herself wondering if he hadn't just materialized from all that pulchritude.

"Sam," she replied without thinking.

He smiled as he strode toward her, wiping his hands on a blue bandanna. "What? No 'Mr. Armado?' " His hand flew to splay open over his heart. "Why, Miranda, I'm touched. Really, I am."

She ignored both his sarcasm and her gaffe. "Mr. Armado, I need to talk to you."

He, too, seemed to want to focus on something other than their conversation, because instead of making light of the fact that she returned to the more formal version of his name, he extended his hand and reached behind her, lifting her braid away from her back and pulling it over her shoulder.

"And you wore your hair down for me, too," he said as he ran his thumb and forefinger along the length of pale blond. "Well, sort of down, anyway. More so than usual. Maybe there's hope for you yet."

Miranda curled her fingers around her braid and tugged it free of his grasp, tossing it back over her shoulder. "Mr. Armado, if you don't mind . . ."

He seemed to snap out of whatever reverie he had fallen into, and he focused his attention on her more fully. "I don't mind at all. What can I do for you?"

She nodded over her right shoulder, toward the greenhouse entrance. "I have your things out in my car. Your jacket and your socks. Thank you for loaning them to me last night."

He smiled, that maddeningly knowing smile that sent an involuntary—and not unpleasant—squirm wiggling through her entire body. "Any time," he told her.

"Yes, well, I don't think such a time will ever arise again. Because that's the other reason I've come."

"What? You mean you didn't just drive all the way out here to see me because you couldn't stand not having me so close? That lame bit about returning my things to me, something you could have done next week, wasn't just that—a lame bit?"

She sighed, drumming her fingers nervously against her side. "No, Mr. Armado, it wasn't a 'lame bit.' And neither is the rest of what I have to say to you."

"Which is?"

She inhaled a quick breath, and said as she exhaled it, "You're fired."

His dark brows shot up in surprise. "I'm what?"

"You're fired."

He leaned back on his heels, crossed his arms over his chest and smiled at her even more. "You can't fire me. I'm not one of your employees."

"No, but you do work for me, in a sense."

He nodded, made a rather large production of pretending to suddenly recall something, then slapped a hand to his forehead in mock stupidity. "Oh, yeah. How could I forget about being the guy who comes to water the plants every Tuesday? It's something you so frequently remind me of."

Miranda's reaction was as bland as his was colorful. "Yes, well, now you won't have to come and water the plants every Tuesday. You're fired."

"But we have a contract," he pointed out, the businessman in him obviously finally starting to kick in. "You signed on for a full year. You still owe me five months."

The businesswoman in Miranda kicked in then, too. "That contract also states very clearly that if I'm ever dissatisfied with your service in any way, I can discontinue it at any time without being penalized."

"You've never given me any indication that you were ever dissatisfied with my service."

"I am now."

Sam gazed at her thoughtfully. "You're dissatisfied with my service."

Miranda gazed back. "I believe that's what I just said, yes."

His eyes darkened, and his lips flattened into a tight line "Is that so?"

"Yes, that's so."

He leaned forward, bending at the waist and tilting his head toward hers until he was as eye-to-eye with her as he could be, considering the significant differences in their heights. "Gee, you didn't seem especially dissatisfied with my service last night," he said levelly. "On the contrary, I'd say you were extremely *satisfied* with my service. Or, at least, you could have been, if you'd allowed things to progress to their natural conclusion."

Before she realized what she was doing, Miranda shot her hand out to slap him, but was prevented from succeeding only because Sam, clearly expecting such a reaction, intercepted her by catching her wrist in strong fingers. She didn't know what came over her. She'd never struck a living creature before in her life, had never even been tempted to. But there she was, the evidence of her aggression overwhelming, ready to do harm to another human being.

Immediately, she tried to snatch her hand back, but Sam held onto her firmly.

"Hit a nerve, did I?" he asked.

"You have no idea what you're talking about," she assured him in a less than steady voice.

He studied her intently for a moment, seeming to weigh something heavily in consideration. Just when she thought he would never speak again, he told her evenly, "No, you know, I think maybe that's part of *your* problem, Miranda. *You* don't know what *you're* talking about."

She shook her head, confused by the turn of the tables. "What do you mean?"

"I mean you never have been satisfied, have you?"

"Of course I have. I've—"

"Don't bother to deny it. It's obvious you've never been satisfied by a man."

"How dare you—"

"It's obvious you've never experienced real passion."

She expelled a sound of disbelief, and tried again to free her wrist from his grasp. But Sam continued to hold her firmly. "I'm a thirty-one-year-old woman," she reminded him, temporarily ceasing her struggles, "not some wilting high-school virgin. I think I've had my share of passion, thank you very much."

He shook his head. "I didn't say you'd never been with a man. I said you've never enjoyed real passion. *Real* passion, Miranda. It's sort of like true love. Very hard to come by."

"Oh, and I suppose you know all about real passion," she countered. "You are, after all, the expert on true love."

He seemed to give her charge serious thought, then he shook his head slowly. "No. You know, now that you mention it, I'm not sure I've experienced real passion, either. Mind you," he added quickly, "I've had some very nice passion in my time, but . . . I don't know that it's been the real thing—pure, unadulterated passion."

Miranda took advantage of his preoccupation to give her wrist another yank, and this time she managed to free herself from his hold. She circled her wrist with her own fingers, noting that they were cool and detached and held nothing of the odd heat that Sam's had possessed.

"Well, then, now you have a goal for the future," she snapped. "A quest, as it were."

He nodded, rubbing his index finger thoughtfully under his chin. "You know, you're right. This could be interesting. What do you say? You want to come with me on the search for real passion? Be my sidekick? Play MacDuff to my Macbeth?"

She lifted her chin defiantly. "I'd rather play Hamlet to

your Ophelia and watch you float down the river after hurling yourself into it.''

"Ouch. You sound more like you're playing the shrewish Katharina to my Petruchio."

Miranda sighed impatiently. "So now that we've established that we both scored fairly well in Shakespeare 101 in college, do you think we can get back to the matter at hand?"

"Right. The fact that neither of us has enjoyed real passion."

"No, the fact that you're fired."

"I like my fact better."

"Your fact is no fact. It's fantasy."

"So you're going to stand here and tell me that real passion, like true love, doesn't exist, and that it is simply the product of great admen and -women like yourself, is that it?"

She nodded and replied simply, "Yes."

"It has nothing to do with the response of the human heart to certain, oh . . . stimuli, is that what you're saying?"

Again, she nodded and again, she offered him a simple reply. "Yes."

"So if I kissed you again right now, that wouldn't have any effect on you, right?"

Miranda felt her face coloring in irritation, felt her belly go all hot and tight inside. She cursed her fair complexion for being so damnably revealing and the two chili dogs she had hastily consumed on the way to Sam's for not sitting well in her stomach. In spite of her physical reaction, however, she assured him, "Of course it wouldn't."

"Even though our kiss last night had a pretty big effect on you?"

She dropped her gaze to study the fingernails of one hand. "What happened last night was just the result of too little sleep and too many Dove bars."

"I thought you said things like that happened because of good advertising."

Her brain was humming with disorder by now, and she wished Sam Armado would stop being so annoying and trying to confuse her with her own words. "Yes, and that, too," she said, not altogether certain what she had just agreed with.

"So like I said, if I kissed you now, you wouldn't have any reaction at all."

"Yes."

"Yes, you wouldn't have any reaction, or yes, you would?"

She narrowed her eyes in chagrin, her head still buzzing with confusion. "What?"

Instead of answering her verbally, Sam looped one arm around her waist to pull her body flush against his. Miranda was so surprised by his gesture that she didn't immediately pull away, and instead opened her palms lightly against his chest. Evidently taking her lack of struggle as an accession—which, she had to admit, she wasn't sure it wasn't— he caught the end of her braid in his other hand and began to wind the length of hair around his fingers. When he reached her nape, his fist was completely bound by the thick plait, and with one gentle tug, he forced her head backward beneath his. Then, with one final smile, he lowered his lips to hers.

Unaffected, Miranda reminded herself stoically as he brushed his mouth lightly over hers. She was to remain completely, totally unaffect . . . uñaf . . . un . . . umm . . . What was it she was supposed to remain again? Oh, yeah. Unaffected.

Yet as Sam deepened the kiss, unaffected was the last thing she felt. When he claimed her mouth with his, her traitorous hands skimmed up his chest to wind around his neck and into his hair. She pulled the rubber band from his ponytail and tangled the soft tresses in her fingers, then cupped his rough jaw in her palms, marveling at the differences in the two textures. She dragged one hand back down the length of his chest, then roped it around his waist.

He seemed to grow bolder with her insistence, because he pulled her closer still.

She felt his hands on her back, on her shoulders, at her waist, then she felt them journey around to the front of her, over her flat belly and softly swelling breasts. She tightened her fingers in his hair, drawing his head closer to hers, her mouth warring with his over who could consume the other first. So focused was she on the feel of him in her mouth, that she scarcely noticed when he took his explorations further. Not until she felt him dip his fingers beneath her sweater and drag them along the backs of her thighs and over her taut derrière. Not until that one, solitary, delirious moment when she enjoyed the warm insistence of his palm as he pressed it between her legs to urge them open, and the eager manipulation of his fingers as he traced rough, erotic circles against the heated heart of her.

Only then did Miranda realize just how far she had allowed things to progress. Only then did she understand just how utterly affected she was by Sam Armado. Only then did she realize what kind of a mess she had created for herself. And only then did she find the strength to push him away. Hard.

His surprise at her vehemence was the only reason she succeeded in breaking their embrace. He had clearly had the upper hand in the matter, and she had willingly allowed him to take it. Now, however, he was apparently willing to let her to have it back. For that she was grateful. But not for much more.

At her sudden push, he had stepped away from her, but still stood quite close. Miranda heard his breath coming in rasping fits and starts and saw that his black pupils nearly eclipsed the vivid green surrounding them. The taste of him lingered on her tongue, and the earthy, masculine scent of him filled her nostrils. Almost involuntarily, she lifted a hand to reach out to him, but quickly altered the gesture to push a few loose strands of hair away from her face. When she noted that her fingers were trembling, however, she dropped her hand hastily back to her side. Then, unable to tolerate the stark, angry look of abandonment in his eyes, she dropped her gaze, as well.

"That's . . . um . . ." Sam's voice wavered some, so he cleared his throat and tried again. "That's not what I'd call unaffected."

Miranda inhaled a fortifying breath and released it slowly. "No. No, I guess I wasn't as, uh, unaffected as I thought I'd be."

"So you admit now that there's something pretty hot and heavy burning up the air between us."

"Yes. I'll admit that."

From somewhere deep inside herself, she found the strength to glance up and meet his gaze. She was surprised to find him smiling. Smiling a bit anxiously, she had to confess, but smiling nonetheless.

"So then I'm not fired?" he asked. He had assumed a very confident pose, but the timbre of his voice assured her that he was anything but confident of her response.

She looked down at the floor again, and her heart tightened in her chest. Somehow, at some point during their embrace, one of them—perhaps both of them—had stepped on and crushed one of the gorgeous red orchids that had been growing nearby. What had once been a fragrant, vibrant, beautiful life now lay limp and broken on the floor. Tears stung her eyes, and Miranda couldn't understand why. It was only a plant, she reminded herself. It didn't have feelings. Yet, for some reason, the death of that flower sparked something dark and grievous inside of her.

"Miranda?"

She recalled that Sam had asked a question she hadn't yet answered, and she looked up to find him eyeing her curiously. "Um, no," she finally said. "No, you're not fired."

His smile at that was full of relief. "I take it, then, that you're satisfied with my service?"

"What?" she asked, still preoccupied by the dead orchid lying between them.

"Satisfied," he repeated. "You're satisfied with my service?"

"Oh, yes. Yes, I'm satisfied."

"Good. Always happy to oblige a customer. It's in my contract, after all."

Miranda shook her head in an effort to clear the cobwebs from her brain. Something had been bothering her since their embrace of the night before, and until his mention of their contractual agreement, she hadn't realized what. Now, suddenly, she understood exactly what it was about their professional arrangement that caused her to have second thoughts about their burgeoning personal one. It was exactly what was causing her distress at the sight of the crushed flower.

Her contract with Sam did in fact guarantee a union of sorts, but it also stipulated that such a union would only be for a finite period of time. In five months, their contract would terminate and come up for renewal. Why should any other relationship she might have with him last any longer than that, and was there any guarantee that it would be renewed, too? Especially when the foundation for their personal union was grounded in little more than a physical desire that would, no doubt, eventually run its course?

Yes, what she and Sam might enjoy together would be exotic, untamed, and beautiful. But even the most beautiful things in the world eventually, ultimately died. The two of them had nothing in common beyond a professional contract and a personal desire. Sam lived in the country, Miranda in the city. And his livelihood depended on his home base as much as hers did. He was comfortable amid natural elements. She was perfectly suited to boardrooms. He had dirt under his fingernails. She had heavy lacquer on hers. He was a wild creature, completely uncontained. She was bound by a specified set of societal regulations.

It would never work.

It might be fun for a while, but there was no question in her mind that in the end, there was absolutely no future in anything the two of them might create together. Undoubtedly, one of them was going to wind up getting hurt. And Miranda didn't want to speculate about which of them it would be.

"I have to go," she said suddenly, turning away.

But before she could bolt through the door, as she had intended, Sam caught her hand in his and pulled her back.

"Go?" he echoed. "Why? Where? Things are just starting to get interesting."

She allowed herself one final survey of him, starting at the mud-encrusted soles of his work boots, up along the lengths of his denim-clad, dirt-streaked legs, lingering at the taut, flat belly and truly remarkable chest. His arms, too, she recalled, were extraordinary, strong and yet gentle, capable of hauling heavy weights and warming cold women. And his hands, she mused . . . huge and masculine, nurturers of orchids.

Her gaze met his then, and she nearly lost herself in those amazing eyes. She closed her own, and freed her hand from his. "I have to go," she repeated.

"But—"

"I'll see you on Tuesday," she said softly as she turned away again. She forced a lightness she didn't feel into her voice as she added, "Don't forget your watering can."

Not wanting to see what effect her jab had on him, Miranda hurried through the door and out to her car, spewing gravel in her wake as she sped away. She completely forgot that she still had Sam's things folded neatly and primly on the backseat.

"I thought you said that orchid house was enchanted," Harry said to Ivy as the couple watched from the office window Miranda's car disappearing from sight.

Ivy shook her head as she turned toward him. "No, I said it was enchant*ing*. I could have enchanted it, but you said we shouldn't use magic on the lovers.''

"Not directly, no," he concurred. "But Miranda is behaving most disagreeably. I suppose we are going to have to take more drastic measures now."

"Like what?"

He pressed two fingers to his mouth and thought for a moment. "Hmmm . . . The Parmentier Masque is next weekend . . ."

"How could I forget?" Ivy responded. "Sam and I are designing the Wood Near Athens for Mrs. Parmentier this year."

Harry turned and eyed her thoughtfully. "The *Enchanted* Wood Near Athens, you mean?" he asked.

She eyed him thoughtfully in return. "Well, not yet it isn't—not technically, anyway. But it wouldn't take much. A few choice words from the two of us could turn it into quite a place."

"With all those people there, too. And dressed as tragic lovers, no less. How terribly appropriate."

"Sam said he refuses to wear a costume," Ivy acknowledged.

"Miranda swears she's leaving as soon as is possible without offending Mrs. Parmentier," Harry replied.

"Hmm . . ."

"Hmm . . ."

The two Fairies smiled.

"I think," Ivy said, "that almost anything can happen in an Enchanted Wood. You never know who you might run into in one."

"And people," Harry added, "particularly lovers, say and do the most remarkable things there."

"Do you remember the spell for Truth and Beauty?" she asked him.

He nodded. "I believe I do. And, if memory serves, it requires the powers of two Fairies, does it not?"

"Yes it does."

"So which would you prefer? Truth or Beauty?"

She thought for a moment. "I'll take care of the Beauty."

"Then I shall provide the Truth. Or, rather, Sam and Miranda will provide the Truth. It will, after all, be required of them, should they decide to venture into Mrs. Parmentier's Enchanted Wood."

Ivy looped her arm around his neck and pulled him close. "Oh, Harry," she said, "I do so love an honest man."

He hooked his hands at the small of her back. "And I have rather a weakness myself for a beautiful woman. Until Midsummer-Night," he said.

"By the light of the silvery moon," she added.

"All shall be well."

Chapter 6

∞

𝒜drienne Parmentier's Midsummer-Night Masque was, as always, packed. Miranda hovered in the corner of the ballroom in the elegantly appointed Fifth Avenue penthouse, amid people known as movers and shakers by all the well-known financial publications and anyone who called his or her employer a Fortune 500 company. People who were normally attired in expensive, conservative suits that revealed absolutely nothing about the moral character or personal idiosyncrasies of their individual style.

People who, tonight, looked more than a little uncomfortable dressed in apparel that ranged from fig leaf-dotted spandex to Renaissance plumage.

Miranda tugged again at the clingy bodice of her Cleopatra costume and hoped her painted-on black eyeliner didn't look as cakey as it felt. Her black wig was beginning to itch, and she wished she was somewhere—anywhere— else. Beside her, her date appeared to be equally uncomfortable in his costume, yanking as unobtrusively as he could at the pleated centurion skirt.

"Honestly," Harry Primrose whispered sharply, "there is the most frightful draft in this room. You'd think Mrs. Parmentier would complain to the superintendent about it."

"Oh, quit griping," Miranda scolded him. "At least you

have a nice metal breastplate to keep you warm. I'm freezing my asp off here.''

Harry threw her a pained expression, frowning at the rubber snake that wound up her forearm. ''I cannot believe you said that,'' he hissed. He glanced around at the other party-goers and shook his head. ''Nor can I believe I allowed you to talk me into this. Why, the last time I put on a skirt was—'' He halted abruptly and hastily sipped his drink.

Miranda found his comment more than a little intriguing. ''Was . . . ?'' she encouraged him. ''You wear skirts a lot, Harry?''

He squared his shoulders indignantly. ''Not as often as I used to, no, but . . . there have been times in the past when the occasion demanded.''

She grinned at him. ''I see.''

His expression when he looked at her again was inscrutable. ''I doubt very seriously that you do.''

She sipped her wine spritzer and gazed out at the crowd. ''Oh, look,'' she said, pointing toward the opposite corner of the ballroom. ''There's Malcolm. He said he and Roger were coming as Sappho and Phaon. He designed the costumes himself. Aren't they gorgeous?''

Harry's gaze followed the direction she indicated, and he frowned. ''Good heavens. Sappho wouldn't have been caught dead dressed like that.''

Miranda eyed him, bemused. ''How do you know?''

''She just wouldn't, that's all. She was nowhere near that ostentatious.''

''Yeah, well, if you say so.'' She decided it might be best to change the subject. ''Malcolm wound up loving Harper's campaign, by the way. He minored in English in college, too, and loves Shakespeare. Who knew?''

''It's good to have that outcome resolved at least,'' Harry replied cryptically. ''You must be very happy.''

She shrugged. ''The client is happy. That's what's important.''

"So your own happiness never comes into play, is that it?"

She turned to face her secretary more fully. "What does my happiness have to do with anything?"

"You see, that's precisely my point." He, too, angled his body to face hers. "You never consider your own happiness. You never have."

"I thought we were talking about Malcolm and the campaign for the new perfume he designed."

"Oh, I do apologize," Harry countered, pivoting on his heel to scan the crowd again. "I thought we were talking about what makes people happy."

"I'm very happy," she assured him, wondering why she was bothering to continue something she'd just tried to make clear she had no desire to discuss.

Harry responded absently, "Are you? Good for you then."

"Yes, I am."

"As I said, good for you."

Miranda tapped her foot impatiently and wondered why she was fuming about something so silly that had come up for no good reason. She had nothing to prove to Harry. She was happy. She was. Really. Truly. Honest, she was. As happy as any person could be. She had everything she could possibly ever want—a wonderful, loving family, a respected, thriving business, a substantial income, a beautiful home, lots of friends . . . There wasn't an area in her life that was lacking in any way, nothing she could add to it that would improve it.

So, dammit, why was Sam Armado's face constantly lingering in the forefront of her brain? she asked herself. Even now, as she vowed to herself that she was completely fulfilled, a not-so-hazy recollection of the kiss they had shared among the orchids rose up in her memory as vividly and intensely as if it were happening now.

She noted that Harry was still studying her from the corner of his eye, and she frowned. "What?" she demanded.

"Nothing," he replied.

"You don't sound like you believe me when I say I'm happy."

He shook his head. "No, if you say you're happy, then you must be happy."

"I am happy."

"That's fine."

"I am."

"That's wonderful."

"Harry."

"What?"

She sighed fitfully, shifted her weight from one foot to the other and then sighed again. "Did, um, did Ivy mention if Sam was coming to the party tonight?"

Again, Harry turned to face her. "What causes you to think Ivy Pinter would mention anything to me?"

"Well, the two of you have been seeing each other, haven't you?"

He colored a bit, then looked away. "On occasion," he said quietly. But he didn't elaborate further.

"So did she say anything about Sam being here tonight?"

"I believe she mentioned that he would be attending, yes."

Miranda nibbled her lip and forced herself not to start searching frantically for any sign of him. She wanted to ask Harry more, but was afraid she might seem desperate and overcome with longing. Which, she knew, she was. But there was no reason Harry had to know that.

As if he could read her thoughts, however, he told her, "Sam is to be dressed as Tony to Ivy's Maria."

Miranda narrowed her eyes as she tried to figure that one out.

"*West Side Story*," Harry supplied for her.

She made a face. "That's no costume. What's he got on? Jeans and a T-shirt? And what about his hair? No self-respecting New York street punk wore a ponytail back then.''

Harry shrugged.

Miranda shook her head and scratched the back of her neck where her synthetic black hair was tickling her nape. ''Boy, I wish I'd thought of something like that.''

''He should be easy enough to find in this crowd.''

She stopped rubbing her neck and met her secretary's gaze levelly. It really was starting to drive her crazy, the way Harry seemed capable of reading her mind all the time.

''Who says I want to find him?''

Harry sighed heavily, shook his head in what she could only interpret as disappointment, and covered her shoulders with his palms, holding her firmly in place.

''This has gone on long enough,'' he told her. ''And it's going to end now.''

She was so stunned by his action that she didn't even try to pull away from him. ''What are you talking about?''

''Ms. Avery . . .''

He made an exasperated sound, released her shoulders and buried his fingers in his hair, gripping the short, dark strands until his knuckles grew white. It was the first time Miranda had ever seen Harry display such an intense emotional response to anything. And she wasn't sure she was comfortable with it at all.

''Ms. Avery,'' he began again, a little more calmly. He released his hair and scrubbed both hands over his face, then met her gaze evenly again. ''There's something you must know about me.''

''What?''

''I'm not who you think I am.''

She shook her head, now completely confused. ''I don't understand. You're not my secretary, Harry Primrose?''

''My name is indeed Harry Primrose, and I am without question your secretary. But there's more to it than that.''

She smiled nervously, his sudden, intense demeanor making her feel uneasy. ''What? You're an international spy engaged in corporate espionage? Are you about to steal the True Love campaign for some rival Communist ad agency?''

"No. But I have been in your employ under false pretenses."

"What do you mean?"

"I'm more than a secretary. And I've been sent here, so to speak, to help guide you in ways that go beyond the professional."

"Harry, I have no idea what you're talking about. Just tell me whatever it is you're trying to tell me."

"All right. I'm trying to tell you that I'm—"

"That you're what?"

"I'm—"

"What?"

"I'm—"

Her patience at an end, she demanded, "Harry, for pete's sake, what? What are you trying to tell me?"

He drew in a deep breath and expelled it slowly. "Ms. Avery, what I'm trying to tell you is that I'm . . . I'm a . . ."

"You're a what?"

He hesitated only a moment longer before confessing, "I'm a Fairy."

Miranda relaxed and waved him off. "Is that all? Oh, Harry. That's nothing. What's the big deal?"

He gaped at her, clearly amazed at her reaction. "You're not surprised? You're not put off?"

"Of course not. Actually, I kind of suspected as much anyway."

His expression would have been the same if she had just struck him on the back of the head with a blunt instrument. "You did?"

She nodded a little sheepishly. "But, Harry, a person's sexuality is completely immaterial in this day and age. Or at least, it should be. And don't call yourself a fairy. Don't disparage yourself that way. 'Homosexual' is a perfectly acceptable word to use. It's—"

"Homosexual?" he repeated. "I'm not a homosexual. I'm a *Fairy*."

This time it was Miranda's turn to be confused. "I don't understand."

"A Fairy, Miranda. With a capital F. It's an *ethnic* orientation, not a sexual one. I'm one of the Little People."

She nibbled the inside of her jaw and stared at him. Finally, she repeated, "The little people. Mm-hm. Well, there's no crime in being short, either, you know. I'm only five-four myself, but that doesn't make me any less of a human being."

He shook his head in obvious exasperation. "Not short people. *Little People*. The ones who have traditionally lived in Enchanted Forests and spent their time frolicking about and cavorting with Nature. Okay, so we've played the occasional game with you Mortals, but it's all been in fun, honestly."

Miranda said nothing in reply. She just studied Harry idly and wondered what on earth had gotten into him.

He must have taken her silence as an indication that she was perfectly willing to buy his story, because he continued steadfastly with his tale. "But these days, with society moving in on those Enchanted Forests, we've been forced to adapt to the mortal ways in order to survive. There's no room to frolic and cavort anymore. So we've been forced out into the world at large. We've become health professionals, entertainers, scientists ... executive secretaries. Whenever anyone shows remarkable skill or acumen in any given profession, you can usually count on that person being one of us."

For a long time, Miranda remained silent, wondering if maybe she had been demanding too much of her secretary recently. She recalled that he hadn't taken a vacation in some time. Maybe she should insist that he take a few weeks off. Check himself into one of those celebrity "spas" she'd heard about. Give himself a little mental rest.

"Um, Harry," she finally began again, "just how much of that Puck punch of Mrs. Parmentier's have you had to drink tonight? I can tell you from past experience that that stuff is lethal. It'll have you thinking you can circle the globe in forty-five minutes if you drink too much of it."

He slumped forward. "I'm not drunk, Miranda. I'm speaking the truth. And that's not all of it."

"Well, gee," she told him. "Don't stop now when it's just getting good. Tell me the rest of your story."

He seemed more than a little reluctant to do so, but inhaled a deep breath and continued. "When you were a girl in school, did you by any chance read a play by William Shakespeare entitled *A Midsummer-Night's Dream*?"

She nodded. "Yeah, when I was in college. But I don't really remember it very well."

"Allow me to give you a quick refresher then. In addition to a number of Fairies, there were three sets of lovers in that play. Two of them, Hermia and Lysander, are your ancestors. You are directly descended from them."

"Whoa, whoa, whoa," Miranda interrupted. "First off, for that to be true, Hermia and Lysander would have to have been real people, and you yourself just said they were fictional characters who appeared in a play. And why am I even discussing this with you?" she added, feeling more and more confused. "You're obviously drunk and have no idea what you're saying."

He ignored that last part of her response and instead emphasized, "I never said Hermia and Lysander were fictional."

"But they appeared in a play," she insisted, still not certain why she was bothering. "They were figments of Shakespeare's imagination."

Harry rocked back on his heels. "Yes, well . . . with all due respect to young William, he was never the most imaginative of writers."

"I thought he was supposed to be the greatest writer in history."

Harry rolled his eyes. "Come now. Surely you don't uphold the notion that he wrote all those plays by himself?"

"Well, there is that theory that someone else actually wrote them," Miranda conceded. "Something about Francis Bacon or some—"

"*Bacon!*" Harry interjected. He looked positively scandalized. "Please, madam. Although he did remarkably well with his scientific and philosophical endeavors, to borrow a phrase from your generation, Sir Francis Bacon couldn't write his way out of a paper bag when it came to dramatic work. Young William had help, to be sure, but it wasn't from Bacon. It was from Fairies."

Miranda nodded indulgently. "Oh, right, like I'm supposed to believe *that*. Harry, this conversation is completely—"

But Harry was insistent. "No mortal being could have written those plays, Miranda. They're too beautiful, too exquisite, too perfect. Of course Shakespeare had help. He never could have done it on his own. No mortal could have."

"Well, I guess if you put it like that, is does kind of make sense, but—"

"*A Midsummer-Night's Dream* was put in his head by a Fairy, and the entire play was nothing more than the retelling of an actual event. Hermia and Lysander were real people. And when all was said and done, they, and the other lovers in the play, and all of their collective descendants, were blessed by the Fairies. That blessing has been maintained perfectly through the ages. Until you came along."

Miranda eyed him for some moments, wondering just how far she should let him carry on with his delusion. No farther, she finally decided. "Harry, again I ask you. Just how much have you had to drink tonight?"

"Fairies don't drink, Miranda. It isn't necessary."

She sighed again. "Then what's this blessing you're going on about?"

"At the end of the play, Oberon, then king of the Fairies, sends all the Fairies through the house to bless the lovers and their descendants, ensuring that all will be beautiful, fortunate, and successful. They will have it all—their hearts' desires. And, until you came along, they all did."

"What do you mean? I have all those things. I have a wonderful life."

"But you have no one with whom to share that life."

She blinked once and inhaled a quick breath. Then, very quietly, she said, "That's because I don't want anyone to share my life."

Harry smiled sadly. "Everyone wants someone to share his or her life, Miranda."

"I don't."

He met her gaze levelly, his black eyes shining. "*Everyone*," he repeated softly. "It's a law of nature. No living creature is meant to be alone. Solitude is a wonderful thing when enjoyed in moderation. But too many people embrace solitude as a way of life. And it isn't natural."

"But—"

"Solitude disrupts the workings of the universe, which relies on interaction between all living things to survive. Solitude is the reason for disharmony. Solitude is what prevents Utopia. It isn't natural, Miranda," he repeated emphatically. "It isn't right. Yet you've maintained a solitary existence all these years. And it's my job to see that you, at least, don't wind up alone. It's why I was sent here to begin with."

"But—"

"Miranda."

The summons came not from Harry, but from someone else. Sam, she realized before she even turned around to find him standing behind her. She would recognize his voice anywhere, not just because of the familiarity of the deep, rugged baritone, but because of the utter longing that laced it. A longing she had sensed in him that day in the boardroom, a longing she knew reflected what she felt deep inside herself.

"Oh, Sam," she said quietly, hoping her words didn't sound as shaky as they felt. "Thank goodness you're here. Harry has gone absolutely nuts. He's—"

She spun around to include Harry in the conversation, only to find that her secretary had vanished. All that was left was a puff of silvery fog reflected by the hazy light in the ballroom, and the faint aroma of wood smoke.

"Harry's what?" Sam asked.

"He's gone."

"So I see."

"No, I mean, he was right here two seconds ago, and now he's . . . gone."

"You were alone when I came up," Sam said. "Just how much of that Puck punch have you had to drink tonight?"

"I haven't . . . I—"

"Miranda, we need to talk."

"Okay," she replied absently, still searching the crowd for Harry.

Sam glanced at all the people milling around them, too, but evidently for different reasons, because he wove his fingers with hers and whispered, "Not here."

"Then where?"

When he tugged at her hand, she submitted without hesitation, agreeing that she and Sam did indeed have something they needed to address. Her thoughts on that score quickly evaporated, however, as she followed in his wake.

Some costume, she thought as she strode behind him at arm's length. His Levi's were softly worn and hugged the lower half of him with much affection, affording her a very nice vista of strong thighs and buttocks with every step he took. His skintight T-shirt had probably once been black, but was now patchy and faded to dozens of shades of dark gray. The short sleeves strained against generous biceps, and she fancied she could see every muscle in his back rippling poetically with every long stride he made. His black hair caught what little light suffused the room, throwing it back in glossy bits of silver, blue, and green. And Miranda wondered how on earth she had been able to resist him for as long as she had.

When she realized he was leading her to the Enchanted Wood outside the ballroom, she smiled. Somehow, their destination seemed appropriate. The warm evening enveloped them as they passed through the French doors and out onto the patio, redolent of springtime in the city and scores of flowering plants that made up a maze of flora. Somehow, the two scents should have clashed in disharmony, she mused. But they offset each other nicely, rounded out in a balance that left each smelling all the sweeter because of the other's influence.

Sam kept walking until the two of them had wound their way through the maze to its center, and Miranda caught her breath at the beauty that greeted her there. She was reminded of the magnificence of the orchid house, but here the greenery that surrounded her was even denser and more lush than what she had witnessed before. Only moments ago, Harry had assured her Utopia didn't exist. But now Miranda saw that Harry was wrong. Utopia was right here, right now, all around her—as long as she had Sam at her side.

Why hadn't she seen that before?

Without saying a word, Sam spun around and pulled Miranda into his arms, kissing her soundly as he wrapped her in an uncompromising embrace. He held her as tightly as he would anything he feared would flee him, caught her so close because he could no longer bear for her to be so far away. Her bare skin beneath his fingers was warm and vibrant, her mouth under his compliant and eager. For long moments, he only let himself rejoice in the feel of her, enjoyed her body's movement against his, her fingers tangling in his hair, her lips dragging open-mouthed kisses along his neck. Then he remembered that he had brought her here for conversation, not seduction, and reluctantly, he took a step away.

"Miranda, I—"

His words halted in his throat when he looked at her. He had been so happy to find her in the crowd that he honestly hadn't taken much notice of her attire. But now that he considered the form-fitting, diaphanous lines of her costume, he realized he had been remiss in his observations. Miranda looked . . . she looked . . .

"Wow," he finally managed. "You look great."

She laughed low. "You're not so bad yourself."

"No, I mean you look . . . great."

She laughed a little more, but this time sounded a bit uncertain. "Just call me Cleo."

He shook his head. "I'd rather have Miranda."

"No problem," she told him with a smile. She reached up and unpinned her wig, stripped off a stocking cap that clung to her scalp, and let the mass of white-blond and silver hair tumble around her shoulders and down her back. "How's that?" she asked.

He smiled back. "Perfect."

She seemed to suddenly grow anxious, because she took a few steps away from him and leaned against the trunk of a slender birch, its lower branches dripping with sweet-smelling wisteria. He watched her gaze dart from the fat purple flowers over her head to the rolling white moss beneath her feet, then back to the black sky overhead, spattered with stars surrounding a full moon that shone brighter than a silver dollar.

"You've done an amazing job with this place, Sam. Everything looks gorgeous."

"Yeah, it does," he agreed, his eyes never leaving her face. "But all I did was provide the greenery. Ivy's the one who suggested the design and added all the final touches." Now he did look around at the rich foliage embracing them. "I don't know exactly what she did, or how, but . . . Something about this maze is just . . . I don't know . . . unusual."

He shrugged. "Gives a person a funny feeling. Not unpleasant, just . . ." He shrugged again. "Different."

It was uncanny, really, he thought. Even though nothing around him was anything he didn't already recognize—hell, everything had come from his nursery, after all—everything still seemed different. The colors were more vivid, the fragrances more pungent, the sounds crisper, the air more alive. Ivy Pinter had some future ahead of her as a landscaper should she ever decide to go into business for herself. Sam only hoped he could manage to compete with her if she did.

"I missed you this week, when you didn't come water the plants."

Miranda's confession jolted him back, and he covered the brief distance between them to stand before her. She continued to lean against the tree, and, unable to tolerate even that small space between them, he flattened his palm against the trunk above her head, ducking his own toward her.

"Really?" he asked softly. "I thought you'd be happy to have me gone."

She shook her head and lowered her gaze to the ground. "I'm sorry. I don't know what made me say that. It just sort of came out."

"Don't apologize. I don't mind that you said it. As long as it's true."

She nodded. "It's true. I have missed you. I didn't mean what I said that day at your nursery. I was just scared."

"Of what?"

She hesitated before answering him, but finally admitted, "Of you."

"Why?"

"You make me feel things."

"What's so bad about that?"

"Nothing. I realize that now. But at the time . . ."

"What?"

She continued to stare at the ground, so he crooked his

forefinger under her chin and urged her to look at him again. "What, Miranda?"

Her brows furrowed downward, as if what she were about to reveal to him was painful somehow. "I'd just never had feelings like that before. I wasn't sure where they were coming from. They made me feel off-kilter. Out of control." Her cheeks flamed pink, and her hands flew to cover them, as if she were embarrassed by what she had just told him. "I can't believe I'm saying these things to you. I don't know what's gotten into me. You really do make me feel out of control."

"There's nothing wrong with being out of control."

"Maybe not for you, but . . ."

He leaned forward again, settling his forehead against hers. "I love you," he said softly, surprising himself. He'd never said those words to another individual in his life, wasn't sure he'd ever even felt them. But somehow, telling Miranda he loved her was the most natural thing to do. It felt good. It felt right. And suddenly, everything seemed so simple.

"I couldn't possibly have heard you right."

He lifted his head to gaze into her eyes, cupping her chin in his hand, tracing the pad of his thumb over her lower lip. Her eyelids fluttered closed, and the roses in her cheeks bloomed more radiant. Sam felt an answering warmth rise up inside himself, something rooted deeply that had lain dormant for too long. He pressed his mouth to hers again, and felt her melt into him as surely as he dissolved into her.

"I love you," he told her again when he pulled back. "You heard me perfectly. I love you."

She opened her eyes and stared at him for a long time, as if she couldn't quite bring herself to believe what he had told her. Finally, she said, "I love you, too. Honestly, Sam, you make me say and do the damnedest things."

He chuckled. "I was just going to say the same thing about you."

She glanced up at the sky overhead. "Or maybe it's just the midsummer night," she murmured. "The full moon. This Enchanted Wood." She began to laugh at that.

"What?" Sam asked. "What's so funny?"

"This Enchanted Wood business reminds me of something that Harry said a little while ago. I think he's had a bit too much to drink tonight."

"Why?"

She continued to smile as she told him, "He, um, he thinks he's a Fairy."

Now Sam wondered if *he* was hearing things correctly. "Harry thinks what?"

"Before you found me tonight," she explained, "he was telling me some cockamamie story about me being descended from some Shakespearean lovers, and about how he'd been sent by the King of the Fairies to help me find my destiny."

Sam laughed, too. "Wow. I can remember being that drunk back when I was in college, but not lately."

Miranda's laughter joined his, and she sounded oddly relieved somehow. "Yeah, me, too."

He bent forward and brushed his lips lightly over hers again. "So what's this destiny he's supposed to help you find? Did he at least tell you that?"

"Mmm," she said, though whether in response to his question or his kiss, Sam wasn't sure. Her voice grew mellow and vague as she told him, "True love."

He dropped his lips to nuzzle her neck and throat, then skimmed the tip of his tongue along her collar bone and shoulder. "I'll say it is."

"No, Sam, I mean . . . Oh, Sam . . . Harry, um, Harry said he was supposed to help me find true love."

"Why would you need a Fairy for that when you have me?" he asked before tasting the hollow at the base of her throat.

"Got me," Miranda cooed. She gasped when he shoved aside the fabric of her gown and carried his kisses lower.

"Yeah," he agreed before closing his mouth over her breast. "I do got you."

"Oh, Sam . . ."

"And you got me, too."

Miranda threw back her head as she pulled Sam's closer to her heart, and the last thing she saw before succumbing to the passion—the real passion—he roused in her was the full midsummer moon shining down on them from above.

"It worked," Ivy said as she watched the lovers from the highest branch of a nearby dogwood. "Your Uncle Robin will be so proud of you."

Seated beside her, Harry nodded his agreement. "Yes, I imagine our work here is done now. We can return to our own."

"Oh, I don't know," she countered. "I might hang around for a while. I kind of like it here. And these Mortals, though they are fools, are kind of fun. I like working with Sam."

Harry thought for a moment, then decided she had a good point. "And I honestly can't imagine how Miranda would manage without me. Good executive secretaries are very difficult to come by these days. I'd hate to have to train someone new. Explaining the filing system alone would be horrendous."

Ivy turned to look at him. "So, Harry . . . you thinking of staying in New York for a while?"

"I suppose I could. It is a rather interesting place, isn't it?"

"You, uh, you maybe need a roommate by any chance? My apartment building is going co-op."

He gazed at her incredulously. "Are you suggesting we move in together?"

She nodded. "Sure."

He laughed. "Now that I consider it, the idea does have some merit. Although you do realize you really are far too young for me."

"I'll be three hundred and twelve next month," she informed him haughtily.

He scoffed at that. "You're still a child."

"And you're irresistible."

He smiled at her. "Yes, I suppose I am. It's that Goodfellow charm."

"No, actually, it's your cute butt."

"Ivy . . ."

She pointed down to the blissfully entwined lovers. "Besides, look at the good work we do together, Harry. I think we're needed here."

He thought for a moment more, then decided that she had another good point. "We'll have to get approval from the others."

"No problem," Ivy said, standing. She extended her hand to him. "We can be basking by the pool at Oberon and Titania's place in five minutes. I'm sure they have a spare room open for the night."

Slowly, gingerly, Harry reached up and settled his hand in hers. "Just promise me you don't snore."

She grinned at him. "How about instead I promise you to be ever true in loving?"

"I suppose that shall have to be good enough. In return, my young, glorious Ivy, I shall be ever true in loving, as well."

They clasped their hands firmly together, and together, they headed toward the midsummer night moon.

Fairies Make Wishes, Too

Maggie Benson Shayne

For Krissie

CHAPTER 1

The Wish

*H*er tiny feet bare, her slippers dangling from two fingers, she tiptoed over the chilly granite floor to the arched window of her bedroom. A warm, sea-scented breeze kissed her face and lifted her hair and tugged at the gauzy thin silk of her dress. Enya inhaled deeply, and a smile pulled at the corners of her mouth.

"You're going there again, aren't you?"

Enya stiffened, but relaxed almost immediately. It was only her older sister, Lena. She turned, leaning back against the stone sill, and fixed her face into an expression she hoped was all innocence. "I don't know what you're talking about, Lena. Goin' where?"

"Don't try to fool me with those big brown eyes, little sister. You disappear every time our isle passes this way. Whenever we're in reach of that giant mainland where they wouldn't know a unicorn from a dragon. You go there. I know you do. You've been doing it for years."

Swallowing hard, Enya lifted her chin. "Don't be silly. 'Tis forbidden to leave the enchanted isle. You know that." She realized that she was nervously fiddling with the miniature conch shell suspended from a thong around her neck, and took her hand away.

"And so do you," her sister went on. "If the Fay Queen ever finds out what you've been up to—"

"She won't find out!" Enya hurried across the room, catching her sister's shoulders and holding them tightly. "Queen Ciarnán can't know, Lena. She'd stop me from going anymore. I know she would. You won't tell, will you?"

Lena's blue eyes narrowed.

"Please," Enya said, and she touched the shiny black shell her sister wore, the one that matched her own. "Mother would have approved."

"That isn't fair," Lena said, but she sighed and lowered her head. "But I'll keep your secret. *If* you'll tell me why you go there."

Enya relaxed, her shoulders slumping a bit. "I've always gone there, Lena. 'Tis simple as that. From the time I learned to use my wings, I'd flit to the mortal world whenever we drifted within reach. It fascinates me." She let her hands fall to her sides, and paced slowly back to the window, staring out through the thin mist at the barely visible shape of a vast continent's coastline, deep purple on the horizon.

"There's more, Enya. I know there is."

Leaning her elbows on the stone windowsill, Enya stared at the world she longed to be a part of but never could. "Yes. There's more. There's . . . there's a man." She heard her sister's sharp gasp, and turned quickly. " 'Tis not like that. He's a friend. I was only a girl the first time I saw him, and he a mere boy. But there was something about him . . ." Her eyes fell closed as Devon's beautiful face appeared in her mind's eye. His black satin hair, always wind-tossed and wild. The sea-deep blue of his eyes.

"This man has *seen* you? *Spoken* to you? Enya, how could you reveal us to a *mortal*! You've put us all in danger of—"

"Oh, don't be foolish, Lena. He's no threat to us. He's sweet and gentle and . . ." She gave her head a shake. "And besides, he hasn't seen me, except in his dreams. I know the laws of secrecy as well as anyone. I only go to him when he's sleeping. Just so I can look at him . . . and smell his hair . . . and touch him . . ."

"Touch him? Oh, Enya, this is bad. This is very bad. You shouldn't even be entering the mortal realm. You know it's deadly to us. All that negativity is poison to—"

"Sometimes," Enya said in a whisper. "When he was still a boy, I'd join him in his dreams, and we'd run and play . . . But he grew up. He lost his belief in magic."

" 'Tis just as well," Lena said, tossing her head. "You keep going there, you'll take ill."

"Nonsense. My short visits don't hurt. I once heard Queen Ciarnán say a fairy could survive several days there before she suffered ill effects."

"All the same, Enya, you're breaking the rules. You'll be in terrible trouble should the queen ever learn—"

"Aye, but she won't, because you are going to keep my secret. You promised."

Lena nodded slowly. "But Enya,'tis said Queen Ciarnán knows everything that happens on this isle. She's bound to find out."

"Were she going to find out, she'd have found out by now," Enya insisted. "And she obviously hasn't, or she'd have done something about it." She hopped up onto the windowsill, and swung her legs over the edge. Before her the rolling green hills of the enchanted, floating island, sloped downward to kiss the midnight blue of the sea. And far, far beyond the white-capped water lay the land and the mortal man that had called to Enya all her life. She gave one last glance over her shoulder at her sister. "If anyone asks, I've but gone walking. All right?"

Lena hesitated, frowning, but nodded at last. "Oh, all right. But we must talk about this when you return."

Enya only smiled, and pushed herself off the ledge. She let herself plummet nearly to the crystal cliffs below the castle, and heard her sister's squeak of alarm, before flexing her wings and catching an air current.

"Of all the mischievous fay-folk on this isle," her sister

called after her, "I vow, Enya, you're the worst!"

Enya sent her sister a wink, and then fluttered away.

She rode the wind out over the ocean, frowning a bit at the dark clouds she saw gathering, and the deep rumble in the distant sky, and the nervous response of the sea below. But she cast off her concerns over the approaching storm when her wings took her into the night skies of the mortal world, and she flew faster, right to Devon's bedroom window.

It was not the same bedroom window he'd had as a boy. But the house was the same. A broad, white, motherly home, with a wide front porch that looked to Enya like a pair of open arms. Black shutters, and the rocky beach beyond them. And a few hundred yards away, the big, barn-like structure where Devon worked. He built sailing ships, her Devon did. He'd always loved the sea.

These days, Devon slept in the master bedroom, as he had since his father had died several years ago. Until recently, his brother Bryan had occupied the room across the hall. But she hadn't seen Bryan during her last couple of visits. She supposed he'd married and moved away.

It gave Enya a twinge of pain to think of Devon's brother leaving him. They'd been as close as any two people could be, for as long as she could remember.

Enya hovered outside Devon's bedroom window, peering through. But the tall four-poster bed lay empty and neat. And she didn't feel a hint of Devon's presence there.

The creak of a screen door drew her attention. Then voices, below. Someone on the porch. Enya flitted over there, and landed on the porch roof, peering over the edge to see the people below. Belle and George, who were technically employees, but, at the heart of it, were more like family. Belle had been far more than a housekeeper to Devon and Bryan. More like the mother they'd never known, Enya suspected as she tilted her head to listen.

"... never should have taken it out on a night like this,"

Belle was saying. She shook her head and stared worriedly at the white-capped sea not far away.

"Now, sweetie, no one can handle a sailboat like Devon can. He'll be fine."

"I'm not so sure about that. Georgie, it seems to me he's asking for trouble, going out alone with this storm brewing. Seems to me he's . . ." Her voice trailed off as she shook her head.

"Tempting fate," George finished for her. "Still blamin' himself, I guess."

"We ought to call the Coast Guard," Belle said. "He should have been back by—"

Her words were cut off by a blinding flash of lightning, rapidly followed by a boom of thunder so sharp Enya felt it vibrate in the center of her chest. A gust of wind came charging off the sea, sending her hair out straight behind her. Enya faced the wind, staring out at the roiling ocean. Devon, alone in a sailboat, in this?

She sprang from the rooftop, taking to the air with furious speed, closing her eyes and whispering her will to the fates. "Take me to Devon. Take me to him now." The wind lifted her and swept her along, and she let it, praying she wasn't too late.

Devon stood braced against the vicious wind, sea spray razing his cheeks, lightning ripping the sky apart overhead. He stood there, and he taunted it. Dared it. Faced it down. "You want me . . . well, here I am," he shouted, his voice swallowed up by thunder. "Here I am, you bastard. Come and get me!"

Anyone looking at him now would think him insane. But it wasn't madness that had driven him out here tonight. It was regret . . . regret so deep it ate at his soul. And remorse for a mistake that had proven far too costly.

The darkness was relieved only by the flashes of white foam appearing and vanishing on the angry sea, and the increasingly frequent lightning strikes that left him blind and blinking. But he was used to darkness. There'd been very little other than darkness in his life for over a year now. He was angry with the sea, and the skies, and the fates. But he was even more angry at himself. He was not depressed or suicidal. He was furious and reckless and wild.

"Come on," he taunted. "Come and get it!"

As if in answer, a monstrous wave of black water rose like a serpent in front of him. The way it paused for just a moment reminded Devon of a king cobra preparing to strike. He braced himself, and the wave swept down over him. Her heard its roar, and the splintering of wood, and the tearing of fabric. Felt the chill of its wet embrace. And that was all.

There was an odd, floating sort of sensation. He felt as if his lower body were still in the water, but his upper half seemed to be floating above it. And he thought for a moment that his recklessness had got him killed, and that he was about to discover what really awaited him on the other side.

But then there was warm breath on his face, soft lips touching his cheek, and a hauntingly lovely voice, singing in a language he didn't know. It held a lilt that might be Gaelic, and the resonance of a bell. And gradually he knew there were delicate arms encircling his chest from behind, pulling his body upward, skimming him through the sea at remarkable speed. Her hair hung down around his face. She was behind and above him . . . as if she were . . . were *flying* or something, for heaven's sakes.

And then his body was slipping over sand, farther and farther from the water, until he lay on a raised bit of beach where the waves didn't reach.

And the woman knelt beside him, her small hands running over his face and through his hair, and her voice, still with that lilting magical accent, whispered, "Don't you die on me, Devon MacKenzie. Don't you dare die on me."

He felt her lips covering his mouth then, and his starving

lungs slowly filled with the sweetest air he thought he'd ever inhaled. Her hair tickled his neck and his chest as she lifted her head away, only to lower it again a moment later, pressing those succulent lips to his once more. And Devon thought it wouldn't have mattered if he'd been dead for a month, those lips would have brought him back.

She lifted her head away, and when she lowered it again this time, he slid his hands into her hair, and held her face to his, and he kissed her. Her sweetness filled him, and she didn't pull away. In fact, it seemed to Devon that she kissed him back. God, she tasted good. But there was more. There was this sensation of warmth and . . . and light. Yes. Light, filling him right to his soul, where it had been dark for so long.

And he didn't want to let her go. Not ever.

She sat up slowly. Devon forced his eyes open. He was dizzy, weak. His lungs ached, and his vision was blurry. But he hadn't thought himself delirious. Now, though, he wasn't so sure.

In the pale but growing light of the rising orange sun, he saw a woman too beautiful to be real . . . a woman he knew . . . from somewhere. Soft sable and auburn curls, twisting and winding all the way to the sand on which she sat, and pooling there. Who knew how long it might be? Huge brown eyes like doe's eyes. Slanting upward at the outer corners and making her look impish. Her eyes were deeper and more mysterious, and more heavily fringed, than any eyes·he'd ever seen. And he knew those eyes. Her lips were as full as ripe plums, and every bit as sweet, and he knew them, too. She wore a powder-blue dress of something thin and sheer, and he could see her slender body beneath it. And for a long time the tender pink centers of her breasts held his attention. But then something moved beyond her, and his gaze shifted. And he saw the all but transparent wings, and his heart tripped to a stop.

" 'Tis all right," she whispered. It was Irish, her accent. "Don't be afraid."

"Are you . . . an angel?"

Her smile was so bright and so lovely he wanted to kiss her again. Was it a sin, he wondered, to be overwhelmed with desire for an angel?

"No," she whispered. "I'm no angel. If you remembered me at all, you'd not be asking." A soft giggle, a gentle hand touching his face again, stroking him like a favorite pet. "I'm a fairy—though I'm not s'posed to be telling you so."

He blinked, and looked at those wings again. "Are you real? Or am I dreaming?"

A sad expression overcame her. "Alas, I'm only a dream. Everybody knows there's no such things as fairies, don't they, Devon?"

She couldn't be real. No, of course not. She didn't exist, except in this odd, vivid dream. Still, she seemed so familiar. Her face . . . it was one he'd seen before, in other dreams. And it didn't hit his conscious mind until now, but he'd dreamed of her often, on and off, when he'd been a small child. A younger version of her, but her all the same. For several years, going to sleep had been his favorite thing to do, because in his dreams, he could romp and play and get into mischief with her. His own, personal fairy. God, she'd been his best friend.

And now . . . just look at her, now.

A damned shame he'd outgrown those silly dreams. Or . . . he'd thought he had.

"If you're only a dream," he told her, lifting a hand to cup her cheek, "then there's no harm in my kissing you again."

"No," she said softly. "No, I can't see that there is." And she let him pull her closer this time. Until her body laid atop his, and her small breasts pressed tight to his chest. She was light as a feather, and full of fire. He wrapped his arms around her waist, and felt the touch of those mystical wings against the backs of his hands. He kissed her deeply, parting her lips with his tongue and probing inside her mouth, tracing its shape, tasting her. Wanting her. Needing her. It was a sensation like nothing he'd ever felt before. Not just physical desire. This was a hunger of the soul. A hunger only she could assuage. He ran one hand down to her buttocks, and pressed her tighter to him as he feasted on the drugging nectar of her mouth.

And then, very gradually, he felt himself fading, slipping slowly into a sleep that must rival heaven.

Enya lifted herself from the man's wet body, taking her lips away from his, though it broke her heart to do so. She sat for only a moment, knowing she had to leave right away, before he became lucid and realized she wasn't a figment of his imagination. But leaving him was the last thing in the world she wanted to do.

She gazed down at him, stroked his beautiful raven hair and his lovely face. And a single tear fell from her eye, to land right there on his cheek. There had been a sadness lingering in Devon's eyes. A deep hurt. He was haunted, and she had no idea why.

"I do believe I love you, Devon MacKenzie," she whispered. "And my only wish . . . my only wish is that I might have you for my own. I could heal those wounds you're hidin' inside. I'd give anything . . . anything at all."

But it was a foolish wish, she knew. As a fairy she couldn't survive in his world. And as a mortal, he couldn't live in hers. It simply wasn't to be. She kissed his mouth once more, and then she flitted away, back to the enchanted isle where she belonged. But she'd never be happy there. Never.

CHAPTER 2

The Risk

∽

The tap on his bedroom door was rapidly followed by Belle bustling through it, laden tray in hand. He smelled her homemade biscuits and melting butter as he yanked a sheet over himself and sat up in bed.

"Belle, you didn't have to do that. I told you, I'm fine."

"Hmmph. I'll be the judge of that. Washed up on the beach like so much seaweed, barely conscious when we found you. That's far from fine, boy. If you were in better shape, I'd tan your hide for foolishness."

She settled the tray on his lap, and stood back, hands propped on ample hips, eagle eyes narrowed. She wouldn't leave until he ate, so he figured he might as well take a stab at it. He wasn't hungry in the least. Not for food, anyway. The soul-deep longing gnawing away at the pit of his stomach was for the mysterious woman he'd dreamed about. The one he'd held tight to him for all too short a time, the one he'd kissed as if there would be no tomorrow.

God, it had seemed so real!

Real. Right. A real live fairy right here on the coast of Maine. Yeah, and pigs could fly, too. But she was one hell of a hallucination. He'd gone to sleep last night eagerly, hoping against hope he'd dream of her again. But it hadn't happened. And he woke this morning feeling more empty than he had before. And that was saying something. Better that she remain a fantasy. There would be no chance for them if she were real. Those eyes. They still lingered vividly in his mind. So deep and brown and big and filled with . . . with wonder or magic or something.

"You're looking awfully pale, Devon. Are you sure you're feeling all right?"

He blinked twice, shook himself, and glanced up at Belle. "Fine. Really, Belle, I'm just fine." Dutifully, he picked up a still-warm biscuit and bit off a healthy portion.

Only then did Belle nod in approval and leave him in peace. And the second she closed the door. Devon got out of bed and pulled on some clothes. He gave Belle five minutes for good measure, before he slipped into the hallway, walking softly. He headed down the stairs and paused at the bottom. Pots and pans rattled from the kitchen. The coast was clear. He hurried across the foyer and out the front door, and he never slowed his pace until he was on the beach with the cool, frothy water washing up over his bare feet and lapping at his ankles.

He dragged his feet through the surf. Bits of the sailboat had washed up here and there, jagged broken parts of what represented months of work. Yet he felt oddly calm, almost disconnected. And he realized it wasn't the wreckage of that boat he was looking for as he walked slowly along the shoreline.

It was her.

He was remembering that feeling that had washed over him when he'd held her in his arms. That feeling of . . . of peace. His pain had vanished. "God," he whispered. "I wish I could get that feeling back again."

Enya waited her turn in the gilded hall outside the Fay Queen's chambers. She paced nervously back and forth beneath glimmering crystal prisms, and rehearsed again and again what she would say. She'd thought long and hard about this. She'd made her decision, but only Queen Ciarnán had the power to make her wish come true.

She'd given it time. Night after night, she'd waited for the yearning in her heart to fade away. But it had only grown stronger. She'd committed an unforgivable sin. She'd fallen in love with a mortal man. And she was about to compound it with this unprecedented request. But he needed her. She couldn't shake this feeling that something was terribly wrong with Devon, and that he truly needed her.

The doors opened. She heard her name on a voice that tinkled like bells. "Enya. Come forward."

Swallowing hard, Enya stiffened her spine and stepped through the doors. Queen Ciarnán sat upon a throne entirely carved of glittering amethyst. She wore no crown. There was no need. One need only look at her to know she was the Fay Queen.

"You have a request?" Ciarnán asked, and her voice was calm, her blue eyes kind.

"Yes." Enya licked her lips, searching for the lines she'd rehearsed.

"Don't be afraid, child. I already know what it is you wish."

"You do?"

She nodded, her red-gold locks moving magically as she did. "You want to be made mortal. To forsake all you are—your magic, your heritage, your home—for the love of a mortal man."

Enya blinked in surprise, but nodded. "Aye. Aye, that's what I want. 'Tis the only way I can exist in his world. And I have to be with him. I must."

"And if he doesn't feel the same?"

She felt her eyes widen. "I . . . I hadn't thought of that."

Ciarnán smiled gently. "I don't believe you've done much thinking at all, child."

"Oh, but I have—"

"You're young. The first gentle breeze of attraction seems to you like the tempest of true love. But only time will prove whether these feelings are true."

"They are true," Enya said, stepping closer and thrusting her chin up in her zeal. "I love him."

"You can't be sure. You're far too young to know love. Would you have me take such drastic action only to learn later that you were wrong? Once you leave the isle, you can never return, you know."

"I know! And I'm willing to do that! I love him. Ciarnán. I'm empty without him."

Ciarnán nodded, her eyes filled with understanding. "All the fairies in my realm share similar qualities, Enya. Impulsiveness and boldness, daring and mischief, and boundless courage. They're bubbling with emotions and passions. But in you, child, those things seem multiplied a thousand-fold. Of patience, however, I fear you have a small supply."

Enya lowered her head, and already tears filled her eyes to brimming.

"Come back to me in a year. If you still feel the same, I'll grant your wish then."

"A year! Gods, Ciarnán, anything might happen in a year. He might be dead, killed by his own recklessness or buried so deep in his despair that I cannot save him. I *can't* wait that long. Something is wrong with him, Highness. Terribly wrong. I sensed it. I cannot wait—"

"You have no choice, Enya. Please, I make this decision for your own good. It's only because I care for you that I—"

But Enya had heard all she cared to hear. She turned and ran from the queen's chambers, and through the great hall and out of the castle. All the way down to the rocky shore she ran, and she flung herself down among the quartz boulders, crying as her heart shattered.

She wasn't sure how long she remained there, half out of her mind with grief. But at some point, a harsh, deep voice interrupted her crying.

"Such a pity, a beautiful fairy child like you, so sad. Such a terrible pity."

Her head came up fast and she dashed the tears from her face with the back of her hand. He was short, and powerfully built, as all trolls tended to be. His face had that pugnacious quality, with the long, narrow nose's tip pushing down to his upper lip. His hair was wild and blue-black, and his wide-set beady eyes, pale, pale blue.

Enya scrambled to her feet and took a step backward. Trolls were tricksters and powerful magicians. Yet they lacked the power of flight, and were envious of the fairies' wings. They were dangerous. Queen Ciarnán herself often warned her subjects to steer clear of them.

"Don't be afraid," he croaked in that deep, bullfrog's voice. "I can help you with your problem. And unlike that stubborn despot in the castle, *I will.*"

"Don't talk that way about my queen, troll."

The troll smiled, very slightly. "No offense meant. If you're not interested in becoming mortal, then I'll just be on my way. I was only trying to help." He turned, his short legs moving quickly away from her.

Enya bit her lip, grated her teeth. "Wait."

The troll stopped and stood waiting.

"I . . . I am . . . interested. I mean, at least I can hear what you have to say."

"Such a reasonable child," he said, turning to face her once again. "It's quite simple, really. I can make you mortal. I have the power. But I want something in return."

Feeling her heart swell in her chest, Enya whispered, "What?"

"Your wings."

Enya blinked in shock, immediately shaking her head from side to side.

"Oh, silly child, once you become mortal they'll disappear anyway. What harm is there in giving them to me in advance . . . just in case the spell doesn't work?"

She swung her gaze down to the marble eyes of the troll. "There's a chance it won't work?"

"A small one. Surely this love of yours is worth a small risk?"

Narrowing her eyes, Enya said, "What *kind* of risk?"

"Sit down," said the troll, waving his stubby arm and broad hand toward a quartz boulder the size of a foot stool. "And I'll explain."

Enya bit her lip, wondering if she should be running away from this prankster as fast as she could. And yet, she sat.

"This is the way it works," he said, pacing back and forth in front of her with his hands clasped behind his back. "You give me your wings, and I'll give you a boat that will take you off to the mortal realm. You'll be able to live for three days and three nights there, with no harm to your sensitive fairy's body. In that time, you must make this mortal man fall in love with you. And you must do it without telling him your secret, and without using your magic. If you do either of those things, you will die at once. If he falls in love with you before the three days are up, you will become mortal, and be free to live a mortal lifetime with him there."

Enya swallowed hard. "And what if he *doesn't* fall in love with me in three days?"

The troll shrugged. "You'll still be fay. You'll suffer the same effects any fairy would who tried to exist more than three days in the mortal realm."

"I'll die like a mortal."

He stopped pacing and nodded. "But look at you, Enya. You're as beautiful as Ciarnán herself. Why, any man would have to be insane not to love you instantly."

He was wrong, of course. No one was as beautiful as Queen Ciarnán.

"And you did tell the queen you were willing to give up your magic for this man, didn't you? Surely you wouldn't have done that unless he'd shown some signs of a budding affection for you?"

She lowered her head to hide the blush that crept into

her cheeks. It was true, Devon had kissed her with a passion that had set her soul on fire. But he'd been delirious at the time. And probably thought he was dreaming.

"I suppose the only question is, do you believe this love is worth the risk? Will you be content moping about this isle pining away for him for the rest of your days? How will you feel if you lose him, when you had the chance set at your feet and you turned away from it?"

Enya drew a deep breath, squared her shoulders, and faced the troll. "You're right," she said. "I'll do it. I'll risk anything to be with Devon."

"That's my brave girl."

"What must I do?"

The troll opened his hand, and a sheet of vellum, folded and sealed with wax, appeared in his palm. "Take this. Do not look at it yet. Go to the beach by the light of the full moon, and recite the words on this page. That's all."

She blinked in shock that it was so simple. "But . . . tonight is the full moon."

"I know," said the troll, and he turned and lumbered away.

Enya clutched the vellum in her hands and stared at it until her eyes watered. Finally she tucked it into the folds of her dress, and turned to walk back home. It would be her last evening with her sister. And she wanted to make the most of it.

She stood on the deserted beach, beneath the light of the full moon. Midnight. The perfect time for magic. With trembling hands she broke the seal and unfolded the vellum sheet. She thought of Devon, of that soul-shattering kiss they'd shared, and the pain that haunted his blue, blue eyes. She read the words in a loud, strong voice that was caught up by the wind and carried out to sea.

"Earth, Air, Fire, Sea.
"To Nánraic's terms I do agree,

"I vow by magic, great and small
"For true love I will venture all!"

The wind sharpened and angled downward, and for a moment she felt it pounding her, yet she stood still, arms uplifted. Odd that it should be so simple. A spell so similar to one a fairy might use herself. But would it work? Was it some kind of trick? The blasting wind slowly died away. And when it was gone, she realized with a startled glance over her shoulders, her wings were gone with it. Her back felt oddly bereft without them. A chill raced up her spine and into her nape, and she saw a small rowboat resting in the sand where none had been before.

Enya drew a deep breath, whispered a prayer, and went to it.

CHAPTER 3

The Reunion

$\mathcal{D}$evon sat in the sand, staring out at the gentle, rolling waves, and trying to find some peace in his mind. But he couldn't. Night after night, he'd come out here, and pondered and puzzled over the woman from his dream. He'd never been so moved by a dream before, and he sensed his inability to let go of this one might indicate that it meant something. But for the life of him, he couldn't figure out what.

The full moon held no answers. The sea only whispered more questions. Why would he even have a dream like that? He had no interest whatsoever in women. And even if he did, he'd never find one like her. Not anywhere. And even assuming the impossible—that he *was* interested in, and *could* find a woman like that one—she wouldn't give him a second glance. The way Devon saw it, that kind of love only came to those who earned it, and he certainly hadn't. He didn't deserve or desire the love and trust of another human being. Not after what he'd done.

Absently scooping a handful of sand and letting it sift through his fingers, Devon stared out at the reflection of the full moon on the gentle swells. And for just a second, he thought he saw something there. A small rowboat. A slender form bending to the oars. A flag of sable, auburn-tinged hair, sailing in the wind. He blinked and rubbed his eyes, but when he looked again, the apparition was gone. Vanished.

Damn, it was bad enough he'd dreamed of this fantasy woman. If he started imagining her when he was awake as well, he'd be *really* worried. Nonetheless, he got to his feet, brushed the sand off his jeans, and walked a little closer to the water's edge, squinting and trying to see beyond those ever-growing swells.

Funny, now that he thought about it, the way the waves were picking up in size and strength all of the sudden. There was no wind, to speak of, and not a cloud in the sky. Yet each wave rolled farther up the beach, and with more force pushing it. If there *had* been any little rowboat out there, it would be a small miracle if its occupant could beach it in one piece. For crying out loud, he could even hear the change in the surf. The waves growled low and deep now, a menacing sound.

Fortunately, there had been no rowboat. Only a flash of Devon's usually docile imagination. He scanned the waves one last time, then failed to dodge a huge, vicious breaker that exploded around his shins, soaking his jeans. Damn. Another followed rapidly, and then another, as Devon high stepped his way back up the beach. Shaking his head in self-deprecation, he turned toward the path that would lead him back up to the house.

"Stupid, worthless bit of wormwood!"

Devon went still at the voice that seemed to come from nowhere. From the darkness, or the sea, or . . . or his own imagination. It was all but drowned out by those crashing breakers, but he heard it all the same, and even thought he detected a faint Irish accent.

There was a coughing, sputtering sound. "Wretched little troll, giving me that lead-bottomed sieve!"

Devon battled the chill that raced down his spine, told himself it was not the same voice he'd heard singing to him in his dream, and that when he turned he would not see that same beautiful woman. And then he turned around.

And he tried to adjust his vision. Her hair was wet, and dripping straggles clung to her face. It looked nearly black, though he knew that could be a trick of all the water it held. It wasn't curly as he remembered, and most of it was twisted up in a knot in the back, so he couldn't determine its length. Okay, so her resemblance to his dream woman might not be complete. Might not even be all that strong. It had been awfully dark in his dream, after all. He quickly glanced above her shoulders and sighed in relief. She didn't have any wings. Well, then, maybe he hadn't totally lost his mind just yet.

She slogged out of the surf, wringing bunches of the long white sundress as she went. Coming right toward him, though she hadn't seen him yet. "I'll break that long nose of his when I see him again. I'll take his short little arms and tie them up in knots, and then—" Her eyes found his, and she stopped her tirade.

Even in the moonlight, he knew they were brown. Deep and dark and as round as any eyes he'd ever seen. He almost fell into them as he stood there, staring at her. And when he finally found his voice, he couldn't think of a thing to say to her. What *could* he say? *Hi. Remember me? We were making out on this very beach the other night, right after you pulled me from the water. Only you had wings then.* She'd probably run screaming for the nearest cop. Or psychiatrist.

He cleared his throat. "Whose arms are you going to tie in knots?"

She blinked, her eyes widening a bit farther. "The horrid little . . . man who gave me that rowboat, is who."

"What rowboat?" Devon sent a pointed glance beyond her, but saw only the dark indentations her tiny, bare feet had made in the sand.

"The one that disintegrated before it got me to shore." She came closer to him, dropping the hem of her dress and gathering up another section, twisting it mercilessly in her hands. Water trickled from the cloth and ran down her legs.

She stopped when she stood very close to him. Devon couldn't stop himself from reaching out, and picking a bit of green seaweed from her hair. "Are you all right?" he asked her.

She only stared at him and nodded.

He stared back, blown away by the urge that over-whelmed him. The urge to pull her right into his arms and begin again where they'd left off the other night. Only . . . that had been a dream. Hadn't it?

"Do I know you," he attempted. "You seem so . . . fa-miliar."

For the first time, her gaze fell away from his. "I only just arrived here in your country this evenin'," she told him.

Devon's shoulders slumped. "Then I couldn't have met you before, could I?"

"I don't suppose so."

He had to touch her. Didn't matter that she was a stranger and had nothing to do with his dream. He had no choice in the matter. His hand clasped hers, in what he hoped seemed like a friendly shake. "I'm Devon MacKenzie."

She lifted her eyes again, even smiled a little. "I'm called Enya."

No last name? That was interesting, wasn't it?

"Enya," he said softly, and saying her name was almost like kissing her again. The way the soft syllables caressed his tongue as they passed.

He shook himself, and added, "If you'll tell me where you're staying I'll give you a ride back."

She bit her lower lip. "I'm not sure where I'll be staying, Devon MacKenzie. That rowboat ride was a kind of a spur-o'-the moment decision. I did it before I'd made any other arrangements."

"Impulsive, aren't you?"

Her grin was quick and stunning. "Aye, so I've been told."

"It doesn't matter." He took her shoulders—yes, just an

excuse to touch her again—and turned her in the direction of his house. "That's my place, up there," he said, pointing. "Come home with me. We'll get you dried out, and then we'll find you a place to stay. I can take you to wherever you left your luggage, and—"

"Oh, my," she said on a breathy sigh.

He tilted his head. "What is it?"

"My luggage. Everything I own was in that wretched rowboat."

"Jesus," he muttered. "Everything?" She nodded. "Cash?" he asked her. "Credit cards?"

"Everything, Devon." She said it with downcast eyes and a sad shake of her head that seemed a little bit exaggerated. But then she brightened, casting a glance toward the house again. "Oh, but it looks as if you live in a giant of a house. Surely you have room for one soggy female."

He blinked, stunned, only just beginning to hear the warning bells that had been sounding in his head since she'd walked out of the surf. Her story made no sense whatsoever. She was obviously lying, or at least not telling the whole truth. And she hadn't even given him her last name.

"I'm not sure that's such a—"

She faced him, her hands fluttering lightly up to his shoulders, and her eyes boring into his. "Please, Devon. I won't impose for long, I promise. Three days is all I'll be askin' of you. Just three days."

His brows drew together as he studied her face. "What happens in three days?"

"I won't know until they've passed," she told him. "But whatever happens, I won't require your hospitality beyond that."

He shook his head, still baffled. God, was she running from something? Some one? Was she a criminal or a witness or a victim or what?

Since her hands had taken the liberty of resting on his shoulders, he didn't think he was stepping out of line when his rose to clasp her tiny waist. "Are you in some kind of trouble, Enya?"

"I very well might be, at that, Devon MacKenzie. And you're the only one who can help me."

Damn. She was trouble with a capital T. And the last thing he wanted to do was to let her waltz into his life for three days and then disappear again. Vanish into the sea as quickly as she'd appeared from it. There was an ominous feeling writhing around in the pit of his stomach, telling him to run for his life.

And then she pressed her small hand to her forehead, and whispered, "Oh, my," and closed her eyes. Her knees bent, and her body sagged toward his, and the next thing he knew, Devon had a bundle of sopping wet beauty in his arms. And he was left with no choice but to carry her back to the house.

Holding her this way, despite the circumstances, felt incredible.

CHAPTER 4

The Challenge

Enya had known a sudden burst of panic when it had seemed Devon would turn her away. So she'd done the first thing that came to her. She'd fainted in his arms. Oh, it wasn't very nice, and certainly wasn't playing fair, but for heaven's sakes, her life was on the line, here. She couldn't afford to be subtle.

She opened one eye as he carried her up the porch steps and through the front door, and she saw his proud, strong chin, and his corded neck. She wanted to trace both with her lips, but of course, it was to soon for that. Oh, goodness, three days! She had three days to make this man fall in love with her! She'd thought it would be easy after the way he'd kissed her on the beach. But this time, he hadn't even wanted to bring her home. It might not be as simple as she'd anticipated!

Devon carried her through the house and up the stairs. The place was dark. Belle and George must be sound asleep, it being the wee hours and all. He kicked a door open, and carried her into a room, and a second later he was lowering her into a bed, and straightening away from her. Oh, bother. She didn't want him away from her. Having his arms around her had been much better.

She moaned a little, and affected a shiver.

"Dammit, you'll catch your death in these wet clothes,"

he muttered. And then he was bending over her again, and she felt the warmth of his breath, and the slight tremor in his hands as they moved over the long row of buttons down the front of her dress. He slipped one arm beneath her shoulders, and lifted her off the bed slightly. With his other hand, he pushed the dress down over her right arm. His warm palm skimmed over the bare skin of her shoulder . . . and stilled there. For the barest instant, he paused, feeling her skin against his. His head bent a little, and she heard him inhaling the scent of her hair.

"Damn," he whispered.

He lowered her back to the bed and moved away. A second later, a blanket was tossed over her, and then he was gone.

It was Belle who came to her in a short while, and undressed her and gently rubbed her down with a heated towel. Belle who dressed her in a warm flannel nightgown, and took the pins from her hair, and brushed it and toweled it dry. Belle who didn't ask questions. Just coddled. And who brought hot chocolate, and a down comforter, and who tucked her into bed.

Enya didn't want to sleep. She wanted to be with Devon for every possible moment of her three days here. She needed that, if she were going to succeed. But more than likely, Devon was asleep now, too. So she might as well rest, she decided, the better to put her plan into action tomorrow.

He sipped the scalding coffee, burned his tongue, swore.

"In a fine temper this morning, aren't you, Devon? I'd never have guessed finding a lost beauty would put you in a bad mood."

He scowled at Belle as she bustled around the kitchen, then shifted his gaze when he heard a muffled chortle from George. George, however, only gave the morning paper a firm shake and remained hidden behind it.

"A stranded woman is the last thing I need around here, Belle. Especially one like her."

"One like her?" Belle set a platter of steaming blueberry muffins on the table and propped her hands on her hips. "You mean beautiful? Young? With brown eyes you could drown in and hair like silk, and that lost, needy look about her? Is that it?"

"Hmmph." He helped himself to a muffin, split it with his thumb and pulled it open as blueberry-scented steam escaped its prison. "Dishonest, is what I mean. Wouldn't give more than her first name. Refused to say where she came from. Trouble, Belle. You mark my words, that girl is trouble."

"You could do with an awful lot of that kind of trouble, my boy." Belle sent him a wink and all but skipped into the kitchen.

Devon buttered the muffin and took a bite, sending a sidelong glance through the archway into the living room and the staircase beyond. No sign of her yet. Good. He wasn't sure he could handle seeing her in the daylight . . . seeing the embodiment of the dream he'd had as he'd lain near death on the beach. Minus the wings, of course. Holding the muffin in one hand, the coffee mug in the other, he pushed his chair back and got up.

George lowered the paper when the chair legs scraped the floor. "Not rushing off, are you, Dev? Wouldn't be polite."

"Polite, hell, I have work to do."

He stalked around the table and through the archway. Escape was within reach. The front door stood just to his left. But she appeared, just like magic, on the stairway at his right.

She paused there, tilting her head slightly and studying him with those unnaturally large brown eyes, and he thought he detected a twinkle of gold in them when the morning sun danced over her face. And she smiled, and something fluttered in his chest.

"Good mornin', Devon."

" 'Morning." He sent a longing glance toward the door. "Did I oversleep?"

His gaze snapped back to her again. She wore a long flannel nightgown of snowy white that billowed and floated just above her bare feet. Something Belle had dug out for her, no doubt. And her hair, all those long, burnished curls, surrounded her like a cloak.

"Uh . . . no. No, not at all," he managed, and then he cleared his throat.

"That's good," she said, smiling again and coming the rest of the way down the stairs. "There's nothing worse than eating breakfast alone. I'm glad I won't have to." She came right up to him, stood directly in front of him, staring up into his eyes. Her smallness made him feel big and awkward. "Unless . . . ," she said, glancing at the coffee mug in his hand, "you were leaving."

He looked down at the coffee mug himself, then back at her. She was doing something to him with those eyes of hers. He could swear she was. "No, I'm not leaving." He nodded toward the dining room, and she turned and preceded him through the archway.

George shot to his feet, his newspaper landing in his oatmeal, and pulled out a chair for her. "Ma'am," he said dipping his head as she sat, just as graceful as an angel.

"You must be George," she told him. "I'm Enya."

"Pleasure's all mine." Before George made it back to his own seat, Belle was calling for him. She stood in the kitchen, holding the door open, and smiling like a cat with feathers in its fur. George grumbled, but excused himself and headed into the kitchen.

Leaving Devon alone with . . . with *her*.

Fine. He could deal with this. It had been dark that night on the beach. He'd probably dreamed it all, anyway. And so what if he'd dreamed of a woman who looked a good deal like this one? Didn't mean anything. Maybe it had been a premonition or something—not that he'd ever believed in that sort of nonsense. Still, he supposed it was possible. Happened to people all the time, he'd heard.

"Did you sleep well?" He asked, just to kill the heavy silence.

"No, actually. I didn't sleep at all well."

He squirmed in his seat. It was not the polite response he'd expected. Nonetheless, that lilting brogue of hers had a way of putting a spell on him. Didn't matter what she said. It was the sound of her voice. Like music.

Like that creature in his dream when she sang to him . . . Devon shook himself. "Sorry to hear that. Was the room all right? The bed—"

"Oh, no, the room is fine. Lovely. And that mattress, soft as eiderdown."

Now there was a term you didn't hear every day. Eiderdown. "Then why didn't you sleep?"

She shrugged, reaching for a muffin without taking her eyes from his. That was what was so disconcerting about her, he decided. The way she looked at him. So intensely, and so deeply, and with that soft longing he couldn't identify lingering beneath the sparkle in her eyes.

"I don't know, for sure. Perhaps 'twas just loneliness keepin' me awake."

Loneliness. A shiver worked right up his spine.

"Why did you leave me to Belle's tender mercies, Devon? Why did you not stay, and tend to me yourself?"

He choked on the muffin, reached for the coffee, and sloshed it over his hand in his haste to bring the cup to his mouth. His eyes watered. But the coffee had cooled by now, and it washed away the muffin blockage. He set the cup down and took a few calming breaths, while trying to cover his momentary lapse by pretending to concentrate on wiping the coffee from his hand with a napkin.

"Now I've gone and shocked you, haven't I?" The mischief in her eyes glittered brighter that a pagan bonfire. When she smiled, her cheeks dimpled.

Devon got to his feet, battling a sensation of something

that seemed ridiculously close to fear. "I have to go," he muttered, making no apologies.

"Where?" she asked, and to his horror, she rose as well.

"Nowhere you'd be interested in," he assured her. "Just to my workshop."

"Oh, aye, the big building I saw from my bedroom window."

"Yeah, that's the place." He turned toward escape.

" 'Tis there you build your ships, then?"

Frowning, he faced her again. "How did you know . . ."

"I'd love to see it, Devon," she whispered. "I've always had a passion for the sea."

"P-passion?"

"Aye, the wind whipping my hair, and all that salty spray soakin' right through my clothes. The sun, kissin' my skin dry again like a devoted lover." She sighed, her eyes dreamy. But still twinkling.

Devon's jeans were getting a little too tight.

"Can I come with you, Devon?" That intense gaze bored into his for a long moment. And as if reading his wayward thoughts, she smiled and added, "To the workshop, I mean."

His palms were damp. The nape of his neck, prickling and itching. "I . . . uh . . ." He glanced down at her attire, gripping the excuse like a lifesaver. "You're not dressed . . . and I'm in a hurry."

"Oh, that's all right. I can find my own way." Her bright smile was one of victory. She'd won and she knew it.

"Whatever," he muttered, and hurried out of the room.

It would seem Enya had an ally. Perhaps even two. Belle heartily approved of Enya's plan to walk down to the workshop and make Devon give her a tour. And George, though silent on the matter, did smile encouragingly.

Enya's dress of the night before had been cleaned and pressed, and was ready for her to slip on again. She'd brought no others, and she knew now that had been bad judgment on her part. Oh, but she'd been so eager to be with Devon that she'd forgot about being practical.

She did love him so!

And she'd make him love her, too. She would. Enya had never set her mind to something and failed to achieve it. So she'd be forward, if that were what it would take. She'd tempt and she'd tease, and she'd hound the poor man to madness if need be. But she would succeed. Her life depended on it, after all.

She strolled along the well-worn path to the giant of a building, which sat along the top of the slope that rolled gently downward to the sea. It was a long, narrow, one-story structure with the same white clapboard siding and black shutters as the house. Neat as a pin, but lacking the touches that would make it perfect. No flower boxes on the windows, she noted. Nothing green and growing around about it, save the grass, and that needed tending.

The rear of the building faced the sea, and there were stacks of lumber off to one side. A well-worn path led to the shore, and she saw a dock there, with small sailboats tied up along either side of it. She continued along the path to the front door, which looked out on a flagstone walkway that led to a winding, ill-paved road. Above the front door was a hand-tooled sign that read "MacKenzie Brothers Shipyard."

Brothers. Ah, yes. Again, she recalled Devon's younger brother, Bryan, and she wondered where he'd been hiding himself.

But she quickly brushed that thought aside, and without knocking, she opened the door.

Devon crouched at the bow of a small boat, patiently sanding what appeared to be a stubborn rough spot in the wood. Other boats, in various sizes, shapes, and stages of construction, littered the building from end to end. And there was a long, narrow table with complex electrical tools laying strewn over it, and big, boxy metal machines scattered about in no order. As if the sky had opened up and rained the contraptions. Sawdust coated most of the floor.

She closed the door behind her and stepped forward. "She's very beautiful."

He looked up fast, as if she'd startled him. "Thanks," was all he said.

"I've never seen the building of a sailboat before. But I can see you're gifted at it."

"Years of practice," he said, resuming the slow, circular motion of the sandpaper in his hand. "This was my father's business before mine."

"And your brother's," she put in. At his dark glance, she added, "The sign says MacKenzie Brothers."

He only shook his head, which further ruffled his always mussed raven hair, and turned his attention back to his work.

"I've said something wrong, then?"

"No. Look, Enya, I have orders to fill. Work to do. Do you mind?"

She lifted her head with a snap to send her hair flying back away from her face. "Yes, Devon. As a matter of fact, I do." At his astounded expression, she moved closer, slipped around behind him, her hands slipping over his shoulders—oh, and they felt so strong and hard to her touch—and she bent her head down so she spoke close to his ear. "I told you last night, I've only three days to spend here. The least you can do is keep me comp'ny."

His body was all stiff. She felt the way he tensed beneath her hands. And he rose slowly to his feet, but didn't turn to face her. "You say that as if I owe you something."

"Now that's an odd thing to say, Devon. 'Tis not as if I saved you from a shipwreck, now is it?"

He whirled, his eyes wide and angry. *"What?"*

She gave him what she hoped was an elusive smile. The troll had said she couldn't tell him who she was. But not that she couldn't drop a few hints. "I was merely pointing out, Devon MacKenzie, that it was you who rescued me when I washed up on the shore, and not the other way 'round. Indeed, if anyone owes anyone a thing here,'twould surely be I owing you.''

He blinked, eyes narrowing as he apparently sought hidden meanings beyond her words.

"So I suppose I ought to leave you be, if that's what you wish. You might well have saved my life. And when someone saves *my* life, I figure the least I can do is show them gratitude. Spend time with them, should they ask it. Or leave them alone, should that be their desire. So I'll return to the house now, Devon.''

His Adam's apple made a swell in his throat when he swallowed. And she knew he was getting her meaning. She'd saved his life and he knew it . . . or, perhaps, he only suspected it. Or maybe he only knew it deep down inside, where you knew the things too strange to be kept on the surface with the mundane. Still, her barb seemed to prick his conscience, as intended.

"It's all right,'' he said softly, still looking as if he'd just been dealt a blow. "I'll show you around.'' He reached out to take her arm, but she danced a step away so his grip closed on her hand instead of her elbow. And she twined her fingers with his and squeezed tight.

Devon's eyes fixed on their joined hands, and he stared as if in wonder. And then he returned her squeeze, and led her through the building.

CHAPTER 5

The Enchantment

She danced with words, making them spin and leap and do her bidding. Making him think maybe it had been her after all, that night he'd nearly drowned in the shipwreck. Maybe she'd been there, somehow, on the shore, and his mind had only conjured the rest: the wings, and the way she'd seemed to hover above the water as she pulled him to shore.

And the way he'd kissed her?

Damn, had that been real, or a dream? Had *any* of it been real at all?

He held her hand like a schoolboy with a crush as he led her through the building, showing her the various stages of shipbuilding, and explaining the process. Her hand nestled in his . . . so small and warm, and sending shivers of awareness up his arm and straight to his libido. Especially the way she kept occasionally moving her fingers, just slightly. Enough to gently rake a nail across his palm, or rub her forefinger along the side of one of his own, or twist her palm back and forth over his. He'd never dreamed holding hands could be so erotic.

He didn't want this. Even if he had kissed her on the beach, he'd been delirious, only semi-conscious. It hadn't meant a damn thing. He didn't want to want her. And he damned well didn't deserve for her to want him.

But she did. And she was doing precious little to hide it.

"What beautiful work you do, Devon."

"Thanks."

She used her free hand to stroke a newly varnished bow, her touch light, and smooth, and arousing to see. He couldn't help but imagine what it would be like to *feel*.

"She looks ready to sail," she observed.

"Yeah, just about. One or two finishing touches and she'll be ready to test on the water."

She faced him, grinning and wide eyed. "Oh, Devon, let's take her out today! It's been so long since I've been sailing."

Devon's heart sank to his feet. "No, Enya."

"But why? 'Twould be such fun. And it's a perfect day, no less."

He swallowed hard, willing her to drop it, but knowing she wouldn't, just by the disappointment he saw in her eyes. "I only sail alone."

Her brows drew together, auburn brows, so fine he wanted to smooth his fingertips over them. "Sounds as if it's a rule you've made."

"It is."

"Aye. The question is why?" Her fingers tightened on his, and she turned to look up at him, to scrutinize his face intensely. "I see in your eyes the subject pains you."

"I don't discuss it," he said, but it didn't carry the none-of-your-damned-business tone he'd intended.

"You can discuss it with me, Devon. I'm not like the others, you know."

"No, I *don't* know. I'm not even sure I want to." Her eyelids fell suddenly, and he knew he'd hurt her somehow. Odd, since she barely knew him, but . . . "Tell me, Enya, why it is you think I'd be comfortable sharing confidences with a stranger? A woman who refuses to tell me her last name? Who won't say where she's come from or why she's here? Tell me that, if you will."

"Ah, sweet Devon, I would if I could," she whispered. And then her chin lowered to her chest.

Devon couldn't help himself. He was compelled to hook a finger beneath that porcelain chin, to lift it until she looked into his eyes again. "Tell me . . . tell me *something,* Enya."

"Look at me with your heart, Devon, and not just your eyes. Your heart will tell you all you need to know. We're not strangers, you and I."

Damn. The tone of her voice, the look in her eyes . . . he was damned if he wasn't believing her. She was so familiar, and she had been all along. Even the night of his near-death experience, the night he'd dreamed of her. Even then he'd sensed he'd known her before. He'd likened her to the fairy enchantress of his childhood's fondest dreams.

Narrowing his eyes on her face, he whispered, "Who *are* you, Enya? What is it you want from me?"

" 'Tis not so much I'm wanting of you, Devon. Only your heart."

She said it with a little smile, as if she were making a joke. But Devon believed every word. He caught her other hand in his, so he held them both now, firmly, in his own. "Don't pin your dreams on my heart, little Enya. My heart died a long time ago. The thing beating in my chest now is more like a machine than that tender organ could ever be. There's no more feeling left there. You understand?"

"Aye, Devon. I understand."

"Good."

"If I can't have your heart, then, I'll ask a good deal less. A simple ride in one of your sailboats."

"I told you—"

"You only sail alone, I know. So I'll be forced to borrow one and set out to sea all by my lonesome." She shook her head sadly. "And me, not knowing all I should about sailing. Ah, well, I'll manage, I suppose."

"You can't do that," he told her.

"I can and I will. I've three days in your world, Devon, and I intend to savor them."

In your world. Now what the hell . . .

No time to analyze it now, she'd whirled around and was heading out the door, and he had to rush after her. She raced around the building, that white dress of hers like a sail in the breeze. Down the slope to the water's edge, where several small vessels were docked. Her bare feet made prints in the sand as she dug in, hair flying madly behind her, Devon rushing after her. Tough to get traction in loose sand. She beat him to the dock and leapt onto the wood like a dancer, snatched the lines of the tiny boat on her right, untied them.

"Dammit, Enya, you can't just take one. It's grand theft." He jumped onto the dock just as she jumped off it, and landed in his boat.

Her hands braced on the side, she smiled at him tauntingly. "So have me tossed in the dungeons, then," she shouted, and quickly turned to work the lines. The sail unfurled; midnight blue, with a brilliant yellow cradle moon. Wind filled it and the boat skimmed the water. Devon ran full tilt to the far end of the dock, and then gave a mighty leap. And he made it, just as the boat cleared the dock.

He lay on his back, where he'd wound up after his ungraceful landing, blinking at a clear blue sky, and surrounded by the sound of her delighted laughter. Sitting up, he gave his head a shake.

"Now, don't be lookin' so angry, Devon. I daresay you'd be laughin' too, if you could have seen the picture you made. Flying through the air like a wounded duck, if ever I saw one. Lord a'mercy . . ." And she doubled over, laughing harder, and holding her waist.

Devon's lips twitched and pulled at the corners. The anger he tried to cling to melted like butter at the sound of her laughter, and in a moment, he was smiling fully. "Glad you find my *grace* so amusing," he told her, looking up, meeting her eyes, and freezing there as his smile—and hers—slowly died.

"I love when you smile," she told him. "You don't do it very often, you know."

She was beautiful, this way. The wind and sunlight playing tag in her hair. The light in her eyes. The wonder. And still, that longing.

A gust came up and the boat rocked, reminding him painfully of the last time he'd taken anyone besides himself out on the fickle sea. He intended to turn back, but she sat down close beside him, covered his hands with her own.

"Just a short sail, Devon, please. We needn't venture far from shore. And I'm a strong swimmer."

"I—"

He broke off, because there was something in her eyes that made it impossible to refuse her. He reached to the floor and snatched up a life vest. "All right, a short ride. But put this on."

She held it up, looked it over, wrinkled her nose. His stomach twisted with longing. "And just how is a woman supposed to entice the man of her dreams wearin' something like this, Devon MacKenzie?"

He swallowed hard. "Just put it on."

She did. But those hot, heavy-lidded brown eyes never left his, and when she settled down again, she sat still closer. Her hip touched him, and her thigh and her knee and her shin. Her shoulder. And as he guided the boat into deeper, calmer waters, she lowered her head to rest it on his shoulder, and Devon's heart skipped a beat.

We're not strangers, you and I.

No, they were not strangers. Not when he felt this . . . connected to her, this drawn. The questions remained. But Devon let them fall by the wayside as he maneuvered the boat and manipulated the winds. He relaxed beside her, just a little. Let himself enjoy her nearness. But he went utterly stiff all over again a second later. Because that was when she began to sing.

*   *   *

She sang an entire verse before she saw the look of wonder in his eyes, and when she did, the Gaelic words of the song trailed off into silence.

"You look as if you've seen a ghost," she told him.

"That song . . ."

"Aye, 'tis lovely. An old Irish love song, I'm told."

"I've heard it before."

She blinked in surprise, and then bit her lip. Lord, but she'd let herself get carried away in the moment then, hadn't she? Let the touch of the wind and the feel of the sea beneath her and the man beside her overwhelm her common sense. Of course he'd heard the song. It was the same one she'd sung to him that night when he'd nearly drowned. She wondered for a moment, if she'd pushed the limits of the troll's rules too far. She closed her eyes, braced herself, and waited. But she didn't die as the seconds passed, and could only breathe a sigh of relief and whisper a prayer of thanks.

"That night . . . the night of my accident . . ."

"Oh? You had an accident, you say?" She averted her eyes as his probed and sought.

"You know perfectly well I did. You were there. You . . . you were singing that same song and then . . . and then I kissed you." He shook his head hard as if trying to shake water from his hair. "But I thought it was just a dream."

"Perhaps it was, Devon. And perhaps it wasn't. And perhaps you ought to kiss me again. Just in case."

Devon looked at her, and she saw his gaze dip to her lips as if against his will before he turned away. He stood abruptly, furled the sail and dropped the anchor, his every movement harsh and quick. He was angry. She couldn't seem to do anything right, she thought miserably. When the boat bobbed in the sapphire waters, he knelt in front of her, gripped her shoulders, bored holes in her eyes with his probing stare. "I have to know what really happened that night."

"And I'll tell you. When my three days are up, 'twill no longer matter, and I'll tell you everything, Devon." She lifted a hand to his face, stroked his hair back, away from his forehead. " 'Til then, can't you simply enjoy my comp'ny as I'm enjoying yours?"

He continued staring, but the anger faded. Something else replaced it in his eyes. His hands on her shoulders kneaded, and his gaze focused once again on her lips. She ran her tongue over them, hoping she saw what she thought she saw in his eyes. Lust wasn't love, but it was a powerful good start. He leaned forward. Closer, so slowly it was as if he were being pulled there involuntarily. His lips hovered a hair's-breadth from hers. And then a nasty little wave slammed into the small boat, rocking it sideways, and Devon's hands fell away, his eyes widening in something like panic.

"Damn!" He turned to weigh anchor, and again set the pretty sail flying. And this time, she saw with a heavy heart, they were heading toward shore.

"I'm not ready to go in yet, Devon."

"Then you're a fool."

She winced at his words, but felt something dark and hurtful lingering beneath them.

"The waves are kicking up," he added in a much gentler tone, sending a glance over his shoulder at her. "You have no idea what can happen out here, how suddenly a pleasure cruise can turn into disaster."

She tilted her head, narrowed her eyes. "But *you* do, don't you, Devon?"

"Yeah. I sure as hell do."

She waited, but he said no more. Just guided the boat back to the waiting dock, secured the lines, and stalked back to his workshop, leaving her alone once more.

CHAPTER 6

The Mystery

∞

*H*e didn't come in for dinner, and Enya was too sick to her stomach to eat. Nearly twenty-four hours now, since her arrival. An entire day wasted, with not one hint of progress made. Lord, but she didn't want to die. For the first time, she wondered if she'd made a terrible mistake by bargaining with her life.

And then she thought about the shivers that had rushed up her spine when he'd kissed her that night on the shore, and she knew she hadn't. She must try. She had to reach him somehow.

"Odd, that Devon is working so late," George observed between healthy bites of his pot roast. "It isn't like him to skip meals."

Belle only looked worried. Enya sipped her water, which seemed to be the only thing that didn't set her stomach to rebelling, then replaced the glass on the table. "I'm afraid it's my fault," she said softly. "I made him take me sailing this morning, and—"

"He took you out in one of the boats?" Belle's graying eyebrows rose high, puckering the skin of her forehead.

"I . . . er . . . didn't give him much choice in the matter, I'm afraid."

"I see. Well," she said, and a knowing look passed between her and her husband. "Well."

"Good for you," George said. "About time he got over this nonsense. Isn't good for a man to isolate himself the way he has since—"

"George!"

George looked up, bit his lip. "No man is an island, sweetheart. That's all I'm saying."

Enya sat a little straighter, thinking she might have stumbled onto something, here. Something that would help her understand Devon better, a clue as to what haunted his blue eyes so. "Then," she said carefully, not wishing to appear nosy. "Devon is of a mind to live his life all alone?"

George nodded, his lips forming a thin, disapproving line.

"But why?"

"Punishing himself, is my guess. But then, I'm no head shrinker."

Belle patted Enya's hand with her own. "It's not our place to tell you Devon's secrets, dear. Besides, it would do more harm than good if he found we had." She gnawed her lower lip, seeking her husband's gaze as if in search of approval. He nodded almost imperceptibly. And Belle nodded back before she went on. "Still, Enya, if you could get *him* to tell you—"

"Get me to tell her what?"

Devon's deep voice came from the archway, and all three of them jumped like children caught doing something they oughtn't. Belle and George quickly returned their attention to their meals, but Enya held Devon's inquisitive stare, lifting her chin, determined not to be less than honest with him. Three days left no time for lies.

"I was askin' Belle what haunts those sea-blue eyes of yours, Devon, and what makes you such an ogre to me. But she wouldn't tell me."

"Wise of her." He came the rest of the way into the room, yanked out a chair and sat down. He reached for the bowl of baby vegetables all mingled together and swimming in broth, and ladled some into his dish.

"I agree. 'Twill be far more meaningful when you tell me yourself. So, Devon, why *are* you such an ogre to me?"

His eyes narrowed as he looked up at her, ladle still in his grip. "This is me, Enya. You don't like it, you can always leave a couple of days early."

Enya held his gaze, and she could feel the energy zapping between her eyes and his. Anger, yes, there was that. He was certainly less than pleased at her prying. But there was more, too. A pull. A magnet that nearly drew her right out of her chair and into his arms. And he felt it, too. He *must*.

"I'll not leave you, Devon. Not until the fates force it."

"Funny, I could have sworn you told me you were leaving in two more days."

"Same thing," she whispered, and she lowered her eyes to the dish of food as her stomach twisted.

"The sooner the better, as far as I'm concerned."

"Devon, really!" Belle threw her napkin on the table as she rose to her feet.

"No, 'tis all right," Enya told her. Though her suddenly tight throat made the words come soft and coarse. Belle shook her head slowly, but sat back down. Enya rose, though, pushing away from the table. "I believe I'll go on up to my room now, if you'll all excuse me." No one said a word. They just watched her as she turned and moved through the dining room. But something stopped her, something made her turn and step up to Devon's chair, despite that his spine went rigid at her approach. He didn't turn. So she leaned over him, until her lips were very close to his ear, and she whispered, "I'm beginnin' to think you need me as much as I need you, Devon MacKenzie. I only hope you realize it, before it's too late." She brushed a gentle kiss across his cheek, and then she turned and hurried away.

Belle and George glared at him after Enya's footsteps died away. They couldn't have heard what she'd whispered to him. He had, though, dammit. He still heard it. Her heartfelt whisper breezed through his mind over and over, making him grate his teeth and order it silent.

He met their accusing stares. "You don't know what she did today," he told them. "Listen, she deserved it. Dammit, she took a brand-new boat, after I told her not to, and left me with no choice but to . . ." Sighing, he shook his head. "Never mind. Why the hell am I explaining myself, anyway? I'm a grown man."

"You're a grown fool," George said. "Any blind man could see that girl's falling for you."

"Yeah, well I don't want her falling for me. I don't want anyone falling for me."

Belle shoved her plate away. "Maybe it's time you did! And even if you're too damned stubborn to admit that, there was no call for you to go and make her cry."

His eyes widened, first at Belle's use of a cuss word, which was so out of character he almost choked, and then at the final phrase. The one about Enya . . . crying. It made his stomach turn over. "I didn't . . . she wasn't . . ." He glanced over at George, not sure trusting a woman's version of things was a good idea at the moment. "Was she?"

"What, crying? Oh, yes indeed, Devon. Tryin' hard to hold them back, you know, but those big tears managed to slide right down her cheeks before she turned to go."

"Hope you're proud of yourself," Belle snapped, getting up and heading into the kitchen with her hands full of dishes, apparently not realizing—or more likely, not giving a damn—that Devon had yet to eat.

George turned his attention back to his food, cutting Devon's presence off like snapping off a light switch. He couldn't believe these two who'd practically raised him were siding with her.

And he couldn't believe he'd made her cry. It wasn't her he was angry with. It was himself. Because he was wanting her more with every breath he drew, and he knew it wasn't just physical. He didn't want this. She was forcing it on him, making him feel things he'd decided he'd never feel. Things he didn't deserve to feel. But it would pass, because he sensed she'd been honest when she'd told him she had only three days here. He knew, instinctively, that she wouldn't stay longer. He thought she might want to . . . and at the same time, he was almost certain she'd stay longer if he asked her to. But he wouldn't ask. He'd wait it out, stick to his guns, protect himself from the lure of her, until her time was up. And then it would be over, and things could go back to normal.

No beautiful face across the table in the morning. No curious questions and childlike enthusiasm. No one pestering him in the shop. No one making his heart beat for what felt like the first time in two years. There'd be no one, once she left. No one at all.

"I'm going for a walk," he said, and to his own ears his voice sounded grim. Lifeless. He got up and left without having touched a bite of his food.

He walked, and walked, and walked. He found himself in town a few hours later, and stopped in at a diner for a burger and fries. All the nutritional value of cardboard, he thought as he consumed the salt and grease. He took his time, because he was in no hurry to get back to her. To have to see her again and try again not to feel what he was feeling in every cell of his body. He ate slowly, and then ordered more fries, and nibbled on them, and then ordered a slice of cherry pie, and he managed to make that slice of pie last through three cups of coffee. But it did no good to stay away from her. Because he was thinking of her anyway . . . or of someone very like her.

Those dreams he'd had as a child . . . God, it was uncanny how vividly he recalled them. She would come, that fairy child. She'd take his hand, and twinkle those big brown eyes at him, and dare him to come with her, and he'd always accept. Together they'd explored rain forests, watching lions or elephants from amid the greenery. They'd explored castle ruins, and rolled down lush green hillsides.

Jesus. She'd been so important to him. She'd been an imaginary friend, yes, but she'd also been his best friend. And he was damned if he could shake the feeling that she'd come back to him now, all grown up and more beautiful than ever.

He ordered another piece of pie, and started on a second carafe of coffee.

It was after ten p.m. when he finally left the diner, and by the time he'd walked the eight miles back home it was pushing midnight. And he was safe.

Or . . . he thought he was safe.

He went up the front steps, reached for the front door . . . and the wind picked up, just enough to carry her voice right to his ears. Singing again. A different song, this time. Something plaintive and unspeakably sad. Coming from the beach.

And her song might as well have been a siren's, because it worked the same way. It lured him, called to him, tempted him, until he turned away from the house and stared down to the white sand dunes standing at the lip of the blue-black sea. And she was there. Her white dress billowing like an angel's robes, her ankles surrounded by froth and foam. She walked along the shoreline, slowly, her steps keeping time with the song, and she tipped her head back and sang as if her heart were breaking.

And maybe it was.

Stupid thought. Why would it be? She barely knows me.

Wrong. She knew him. Maybe too well.

Her song tugged, and he went like a man sleepwalking. Knowing he was going, but somehow unable to stop himself. One foot dropped in front of the other, and he felt as if he were just an observer, watching some poor fool sailor stupid enough to submit to the lure of the sirens.

CHAPTER 7

The Revelation

She felt him before she saw him. Fay sense. It wasn't magic, really. Just a part of who she was. She wondered whether she'd lose it, if she won this battle, passed this test, and became a mortal woman. And then she decided she might never know, because so far, she was failing.

And for some reason, that bit of knowledge wasn't the most important thing on her mind. The thing that was, was Devon's pain. She could see it, so very clearly. It shone from his eyes and cried from his soul. It was in his walk, his voice, his very essence. A hurt that enveloped him like a shroud, refusing to let him feel pleasure or happiness or love ever again. And suddenly, her own life and death didn't seem nearly as important as removing that funereal shroud from Devon's vibrant soul.

Her song died away, or was carried off by the sea breeze. And Devon stood close behind her, not saying anything, just standing there. She turned, looked at him, but he was staring past her, out to the rolling whitecaps and foamy waves. Lord, but his eyes were haunted.

"Ah, Devon," she whispered, and her hand cupped his face, fingers slipping into his hair. "Don't you know I'm here for you? Can't you see me here?"

"I see you. I can't stop seeing you."

"I've come to make it better, Devon."

He blinked the moisture from his eyes, but continued staring at the sea.

"I didn't realize it at first, of course," she went on, rubbing a lock of his hair between thumb and forefinger as the wind whipped the rest. Like satin, his dark hair. Black satin. "I thought I'd come for such selfish reasons. But perhaps I was wrong. Because there's no such thing as coincidence, Devon. So 'twas not pure chance I chose that night to visit you. And 'twas not longin' alone that told me I must come to you now. You need me, Devon. You wished for me, and that's why I'm here."

He dragged his gaze from the sea, and finally locked it with hers. "There's nothing you can do."

"Aye, so you believe. But you have to let me try. Otherwise, your wish will be wasted."

He stared at her for a long moment, unblinking, searching.

"You've nothing to lose, have you, Devon? An' if telling me about what troubles you does you no good, well you've lost nothing. I'll be gone soon, and you can pretend you remained stolid and solitary straight to the end. You can pretend I was never here, make believe I was a dream, the way you've done before."

He blinked at her in astonishment, but Enya only smiled. She took his hands in hers, and pulled him with her to a dry patch of sand where the tide didn't quite reach. "Sit," she told him. "And talk to me. You know you want to."

He sat. She did, too. And she pulled her dress over her knees and hugged them close, and waited for him to begin. And when he didn't, she said, "Your brother Bryan used to live here, with you. He was your partner, and your friend."

"I loved him."

Enya nearly sighed in relief. He was talking, at least. "How did you lose him, Devon? Was it to the sea?"

Devon nodded. "But it wasn't just him. He had a wife,

Sarah. Young and shy and beautiful . . . and expecting their first child.''

Sadness poured over her soul, making her heart feel heavy all of a sudden.

''She wanted to sail down the coast. I argued, but Bryan . . . well, he never could say no to her. I insisted on going with them. I knew . . . something inside me knew they shouldn't go. Why the hell didn't I listen to it?''

''Most men wouldn't even have heard it, Devon. You tried.''

''Not hard enough. We ran into weather, not fifty miles south. Sails ripped to shreds, that little boat foundering like a guppy, fighting twenty-five-foot swells. Radio bringing nothing but static. I put out an S.O.S., but damned if I knew whether anyone received it. And about that time the mast came down. Sarah never even knew what hit her.''

Enya bit her lip. ''She . . . she died?''

''Before she hit the deck,'' he said.

''And your brother?''

''He lost it. He just lost it. Fell down on top of her, there on the deck screaming, shaking her, begging her to wake up . . . God, it was a sound I'll never forget. It haunts my dreams.''

She closed her eyes and closed both of her hands around one of his, squeezing gently.

''When he realized he couldn't bring her back, he . . . I don't know, he went wild. Picked her up in his arms. Knocked me on my ass when I tried to stop him. And then he just . . . he just went over the side. Sank out of sight. I went in after him, but it was as if the sea just swallowed them both whole. I couldn't find him. I was still diving and searching when the Coast Guard arrived. They pulled me out of the water, tranquilized me. Hell, if they hadn't, I'd probably still be out there.'' He shook his head slowly.

''Perhaps you're thinking you ought to be,'' she whispered.

He blew a sigh. ''Why the hell not? Why should I be

here, safe and sound, while my brother and his wife and their baby . . .'' The hand she held curled into a fist before he pulled it free. ''Fate got it backwards, Enya. It should've been me hit by that mast, not her.''

''That isn't true, Devon.''

His head jerked toward her. ''How can you say that? How can it not be true? They had so much to live for, the two of them. A baby on the way, a new marriage . . . God, Enya, they were so in love.''

''Aye,'' she whispered. ''I imagine they were. But Devon, every soul knows when it's time to move on.''

His brows drew together.

''You've no way of knowing what lay ahead for them. You imagine they would have had long lives filled with unending bliss. But what if that wasn't what fate had in store, Devon? Suppose only heartache and pain awaited them, instead of this bliss you've imagined? Suppose one was bound to leave the others, or two were bound to leave the one, alone and grieving? Suppose on some level—not a conscious one, mind you—they simply decided to move on together, rather than to remain and be separated?''

Devon gave his head a shake, blinked, searched her face. ''What kind of a notion is that?''

''The only kind that makes sense, Devon. Souls move on when they're ready. Rarely before.''

''How can you know that?''

She shrugged. ''How can you not?''

He stared hard at her for a long moment, then shoved himself to his feet and began pacing toward the water. She rose as well, keeping pace.

He walked rapidly, right to the water's edge, and stared out at the dark horizon as waves lapped over his feet. And finally, he shook his head hard. ''No. No, I don't believe it. It wasn't part of some grand scheme, there was no meaning, no reason. It just happened.''

''And because it happened to them instead of you, you feel you've no right to a life. Since their happiness ended, you won't allow yourself to feel any. Instead you go about in your tiny boats on nights when the worst sorts of storms murmur their dire warnings in your ears. You shake your fists at the black night sky, and you challenge it. And part of you wishes the darkness would win. It nearly did, the last time, Devon.''

"It wasn't like that.''

"No? How was it, then?'' Her hands curled over his shoulders, felt the tension there.

"Not suicidal,'' he told her. "That kind of thing isn't in me, Enya. I was angry when I went out that night. Furious. Raging, just as I've been since they died. Going out in that storm . . . I was lashing out at the sea and the sky and maybe even God Himself, I guess. Daring Him, yeah, but I never had any doubt I'd survive. Beat Fate. Petty vengeance, at best. At worst, I suppose you could call it a temper tantrum.''

"But it wasn't the first time you've taken such a risk.''

He bent low, scooped up a small, perfectly formed shell and pitched it into the waves. "Probably won't be the last, either.''

"Suicidal or not, Devon, you could be killed. Last time . . .''

"Last time I probably would have drowned, if not for you.'' He turned slowly and stared into her eyes. "I don't know how, but I know you were there. You were, weren't you?''

She averted her eyes. "I . . .''

"Don't lie to me. If I need anything from you right now, Enya, it's the truth.''

"What you need from me, Devon, is healing.'' *And magic,* she thought. Her magic could help him see the truth. But she wasn't allowed to use it here. Only . . . maybe she could let *him* use it.

"Nothing can give me that. Healing. It's never gonna happen.''

Enya bit her lip. "I used to feel the same way,'' she

whispered. "When my mother left my sister and me, it seemed I could never be happy again. But she left me something." Slipping one hand into the vee of her neckline, she closed it around the tiny black conch shell, with the bright pink inside. She thought it over, and made her decision, nodding once, firmly when she did. If she were to die here two short days from now, she'd have no more need of the shell. And if she were to live . . . it would mean her every wish had come true. And she wouldn't need it then, either.

She couldn't use her magic to help Devon. But she could give this shell and the magic it possessed to him. And let him help himself. She took the thong from around her neck, and cupped the shell in her hands.

He only frowned at her.

Bending down until her dress pooled in the froth that surrounded her feet, she dipped the shell into it, filling it with water. And then she straightened again, turning round until the moonlight from above flashed on the water in the shell, turning it to liquid silver that winked and shone.

"Hold out your hands, Devon."

"What . . ."

"Just do it, just like this."

Slowly, Devon's hands rose, palms cupped to receive the shell, and closing her eyes, Enya placed her shell there. Not a drop of silvery water spilled. A good sign, she thought.

"The magic of this shell works only for its owner. Therefore, dear Devon, I give it to you."

He frowned at her solemn tone, glancing down at the shell, and then up at her again. "I don't know what you're—"

"Open your heart, Devon," she whispered. "Look. See the truth that eludes you, and put an end to this torment."

He frowned hard, his narrowed eyes studying her face, as he stepped closer to her, then, almost hesitantly, dipping lower to focus on the shell, and the suddenly gleaming water it held.

"The shell is a doorway. It only opens when the need is strong, as I believe your need is tonight," she explained. "It will show you what you need to see."

He looked down at the glistening water as it took on a brilliant white gleam, so bright the light touched his face and sparkled in his eyes. Suddenly his frown vanished. His eyes widened and his jaw fell. *"Bryan . . ."*

Enya looked down at the apparition, the face of Devon's brother floating in the shell where the water had been, emitting that white light.

"Bryan," Devon said again. Enya touched his face with her palm. And then she turned and moved silently away, leaving Devon to see what he needed to see, praying it would be enough to save him from the darkness of his soul.

Devon had no idea what was happening, much less *how* it was happening. But there, in that shell that had suddenly become a miniature television screen—or, a tiny doorway of some kind—he saw a scene unfold before his eyes. He saw his brother, Bryan, looking happier than Devon had ever seen him, running through a lush green, wildflower-dotted meadow beneath a white-hot sun, with a giggling little girl on his shoulders. Devon blinked, but the vision remained. At the edge of the meadow, Sarah sat in the deep grasses with her legs curled beneath her, watching her husband and child romp. There was a look of utter peace on her pretty face. There were wildflowers in her hair.

And even as Devon gaped, and shook himself and tried to make sense of this, his brother stopped playing and turned. And it was as if he were looking straight into Devon's eyes. Devon's throat swelled, and his eyes burned, and he gulped in a mouthful of salty air.

You don't have to understand it all, Dev, Bryan said, though his lips didn't move. And Devon didn't actually *hear* his voice. It sort of floated into his mind, rather than his ears. *Just know that I'm where I need to be right now. We all are. And none of it was your fault. We're okay,*

Devon, but we can't be completely at peace until you get past this. Get rid of the guilt. Find your own happiness, brother.

"I can't. Jesus, Bryan. I should have been able to find you, to pull you out . . . I should—"

Love us, Devon. Think of us with love, not guilt.

"I do! I do love you!"

I know. The apparition smiled, the crooked grin that was so familiar it made Devon's heart twist. *I've always known.*

The vision in the shell rippled, and faded, and became crystalline water once more. Devon stared at it, tears clouding his eyes. "Bryan! Wait, don't go!" He shook the thing, but that only resulted in the water it held slopping over his hands. "Bryan . . ."

Devon began to shake. He let the shell fall at his feet, and he hugged himself as unearthly chills raced through him, and he lifted his head to search the night sky as if the answers might be found there. "Bryan!" he yelled, and it was a cry of anguish.

A cry that died away as three shooting stars cut a glowing arc through the night, one after another, all following the same path.

Devon sank into the cool, damp sand, the shock and the wonder of it all making his knees too weak to hold him. And slowly, he drew his gaze away from the sky, and looked toward the house, just in time to see Enya as she fluidly mounted the steps, crossed the porch, and stepped inside.

How had she done this . . . this magic?

He remembered the way she'd appeared to him the night of his accident, the way she'd appeared to him in his childhood dreams. The wings. And he remembered the word that had flitted into his mind the first time he'd seen her, the word she herself had used that night as he lay half-conscious, clinging to her. *Fairy.*

CHAPTER 8

The Dawning

Cool water washed over his fingertips, and Devon opened his eyes. He saw the sea, its foamy waves rolling ever closer to where he lay, coated in sand. The fiery orange upper curve of the sun rested on the horizon, big as the world, ascending slowly to take possession of the sky.

He'd fallen asleep on the beach. And the rest had been a dream. A dream, that's all it had been. A very strange, very vivid, utterly ludicrous dream. He hadn't spoken to Enya out here last night. And she hadn't given him any magical seashell, and he hadn't talked with his dead brother.

He'd eaten too much junk food, and he'd done too much vigorous walking in the hot sun, and he'd slept on the beach and he'd dreamed. Period.

He sat up and scrubbed the sand from his hair with both hands. And then he stopped. Because lying beside him in the white sand was a pure black conch shell, small enough to fit in the palm of his hand. It was bright pink inside, and there was a tiny hole bored through one end, where some-one had strung a leather thong. A now familiar chill raced up his spine, but his mind refused to believe . . .

No, Enya must have been walking out here, and lost this thing. That was all. He snatched it up and ran toward the house with it, determined to return it to her, and prove to himself that nothing had happened.

The screen door banged shut behind him, and Belle looked up from her dusting of the mantel in the living room, to smile at him. "My, but it was a beautiful night last night, wasn't it, Devon? Enya said you'd decided to sleep on the beach. Did you see that wonderful display?"

He halted in his tracks, halfway to the stairs. "What display?" he asked without turning.

"Why the shooting stars, of course! Three of them, right in a row. I've never seen the like. Come, Devon, you couldn't have been out there and not seen it."

He blinked, pressed his lips tightly together, swallowed hard. *It was real.*

Bullshit.

"Where is Enya?"

"Oh, that one! Insisted on preparing breakfast, the imp, though I daresay she doesn't know her way around a kitchen any too well. Still, she was so eager, I couldn't say no to her."

Yeah, well that made sense. He'd been having a hell of a time saying no to her, himself. He changed direction, heading through the archway into the dining groom, and through the door at the far end that led to the kitchen.

And then the questions, the confusion, the mystery—all of it—just faded away. And Devon MacKenzie laughed.

Enya stood at the counter with her back to him, elbow-deep in gooey dough. Her arms and hair sported sprinkles of flour and smudges of shortening. To her left, the gas range's front burner blasted full force beneath a smoking skillet full of charred sausage links. To her right, the coffee maker churned in protest as streams of thick-looking brew coursed down its sides.

He saw her back stiffen, and tried to stifle his laughter. He was almost successful, in fact, but then she turned to glare at him, and she pulled her hands from the dough that didn't seem quite willing to relinquish its sticky grip. He

held on, right up until she lifted a hand to push her hair
out of her eyes, and smeared a glob of the stuff across her
forehead. But that was his undoing. He nearly doubled over
as the laughter burst from somewhere deep in his gut. He
crossed his arms around his belly, fought for breath, and
laughed all the harder.

"Of all the rude and ill mannered hosts I've ever heard
tell, Devon MacKenzie, you take the cake." She tried to
wipe the dough from her one hand with the other, but since
both were well coated, the effect was minimal.

"I'm . . . s-s-sorry. If you . . . could *see* yourself . . ."
And that was all he managed, because he got lost in the
laughter once more.

It only died when he realized they were no longer alone
in the kitchen. Belle had stepped in from the dining room,
and stood stock still in the doorway, staring at him, wide-
eyed. For some reason her lower lip was trembling. George,
too, seemed to wonder at the commotion. He came in
through the back door, and then stopped, still holding it
open and blinking at Devon as if he'd suddenly sprouted a
second head.

"Lord be praised," Belle whispered. She folded her
hands to her breast, closed her eyes. "He's laughing."

She looked across the room at George, and both of them
turned toward Devon, with canary-eating grins on their
faces. Damned if Belle wasn't a blinking back tears.

Devon choked back another round of mirth, cleared his
throat. "Of course I'm laughing. *Look at her.*"

Belle did just that, only instead of laughing at Enya's
gooey hands and flour-splattered face, she beamed at the
woman. And then she shook her head, dabbed at her eyes
with the hem of her apron, and crossed the room to grab
George's elbow and lead him back outside. As they left,
Devon noticed, Belle leaned her head on George's shoulder.

Enya had moved over to the sink and was trying to turn
the knobs with an elbow, while keeping her dough-encased

hands up like a freshly scrubbed surgeon would do. He almost lost it again, but bit his lip and moved up beside her, turning off the burner as he passed. He leaned past her to crank the faucets, adjusted the water to a tolerable warmth, and then leaned against the sink while she washed the dough from her hands and forearms.

"So," Enya said, squirting a bit of dish detergent into her palm for good measure. "You think this is funny, do you?"

"Hilarious." Even now his lips were quirking at the corners as he watched her. And it was quite by accident and totally unintentional when he reached up to brush a bit of flour from her cheekbone with his thumb. And then his smile died, and he thought that even in bread dough, she was the prettiest thing he'd ever seen.

"I suppose it serves me right," she said in her magical Irish brogue. "Tryin' to impress you with my domestic skills was not the best idea I've had of late."

He blinked, surprised yet again by her blunt honesty. So she'd been trying to impress him.

"Cookin' is not somethin' I've had much call to do."

"Apparently not," he said, and he glanced at the box from which she'd taken the sausage links and chuckled all over again. "Those sausages are supposed to be nuked, not fried."

She frowned at him, and he nodded in the direction of the microwave. But she only tilted her head, still looking puzzled.

"It's a microwave, Enya. Haven't you ever seen one before?"

"No," she admitted, and sent him a worried glance. "Does that make me frightfully ignorant in your eyes, Devon?" When he only stared at her, his mind refilling itself with all those questions he'd forgot about, she turned off the water and wiped her hands on a towel, lowering her head. "I guess it must."

He took the towel from her, lifted it to her face. "If I

wanted a woman who could cook, I'd work on stealing Belle away from George.''

"Oh, that you could never do, Devon. It's deep in love, those two are.'' She closed her eyes and let him clean her face. But all of a sudden he was more interested in kissing it. He grated his teeth and finished the job, dabbing the sprinkles and spatters from her neck, running his fingers over that lean, smooth flesh as he did.

"Tell me, Devon,'' she whispered as he traced the curve of her neck again and again. ''How long has it been since you've laughed aloud like that?''

His hands stilled, fingertips poised over the fluttering pulse point. He hadn't thought of it before. But of course, that was it. That was why Belle and George had seemed so blown away. ''I can't say for sure,'' he told her. ''But it's been awhile.''

"Since your brother died, I suppose.''

He closed his eyes. Here it was, the confirmation he'd been both anticipating and dreading. ''So it really happened. I really did tell you about that trip.''

"Aye, Devon, that you did.''

He pulled the shell from his shirt pocket, letting it dangle from the cord. ''And this?''

She took it from him, and gently lowered it over his head. ''I gave this shell to you last night. And I hope you'll keep it always.''

He swallowed the sudden lump in his throat, and fingered the shell that hung around his neck. ''I saw my brother in this shell. I know that's not possible, but—''

"Everything's possible, Devon.''

He narrowed his eyes, studied her. ''Who are you really, Enya?''

She averted her big brown eyes, and he knew just by looking at them that she wasn't going to tell him. ''Who do you think I am?''

"I'm not sure. I think . . . I think you're not . . . like other people. I think you're maybe . . . not even . . . mortal.''

"Oh, I'm mortal, Devon. A bit too much so, at the moment."

"You're magic."

"Everyone is magic, deep down inside. They only need to realize it to make it so."

"You're not of this world, are you? You're composed of . . . of something else. Some mystical stuff not found in the rest of us."

"I promised you once that I'd tell you the whole truth before I left here. But I can't tell you just yet, Devon. You must be patient."

She started to turn away from him, but he caught her shoulders, held her eyes. "Tell me this much. What I saw last night in the depths of this shell . . . was it some trick, some kind of spell you cast or whatever it is you do? Or was it . . . was it real?"

"Oh, 'twas real, Devon. As real as your hands on my shoulders right now, and the way they make me feel. As real as your breath on my face, and your lips so close I can almost taste them. That's how real it was. Your brother is fine. His family is fine. You're the one in agony, love, not them."

He stared down into her eyes, and he saw that sparkle, that twinkle that had never lived in the eyes of a human being. And he whispered, "I've known you all my life, haven't I?"

And she nodded.

"You used to come to me . . . somehow . . . in my dreams. We played together . . . we—"

"We explored ruined castles and mysterious caves and virgin forests. Aye, Devon, 'twas a special time. But you grew up. You stopped believing in your fantasies, and I couldn't visit you in your dreams any more. But I couldn't stay away, either."

"Why?"

"Oh, surely you don't need to ask me that! I've crossed worlds to come to you here, but I can't stay. I can't stay unless you get past your foolish regrets and open your eyes.'' She threw the dishtowel down, turned, and left the kitchen. He heard her go upstairs to her room, heard the door slam. He gave his head a shake to clear it, but of course, it didn't work. She was real. She was here, the object of his childhood fantasies. And she needed something from him, something too scary for him to think about too deeply right now.

Work, he needed to work. And maybe, eventually, all of this would make some kind of sense. He headed out to the shop, leaving Enya to the house for a while.

CHAPTER 9

The Flame

*H*e threw himself into his work, though all day he was distracted, constantly glancing toward the shop door, half expecting her to come through it and insist he take her sailing, or begin another round of questions.

And when he wasn't doing that, he was wondering about her, wondering whether she were real or a figment of his imagination, wondering whether he'd dreamed the past two days and would wake up to find they'd never happened. And though that theory was the one which made the most sense, he found it to be the one hardest to believe. Enya was real, as real as he was. And she was here, for a little over one more day, she was here. So what was he doing out here in the shop?

Well, that was a stupid question. He was out here because he didn't want to get involved in a relationship with a woman.

Why?

Because he couldn't. He couldn't go about his life as if nothing had happened. Christ, his brother was dead. *His* life was over. How could Devon pretend that didn't matter? How could he?

But Bryan's okay. You know that now.

Yeah. He knew that now, as little sense as it made. He'd never thought much about life after death, but there seemed

no other explanation for the vision he'd seen in the conch
shell . . . or those three shooting stars. No matter how much
his practical mind rebelled at the idea, in his heart, he knew
his brother was okay. And as he let that knowledge settle
in, he realized he hadn't been feeling the same way since
last night. The bitterness, the anger . . . they'd faded. In
their place there was some kind of . . . of peace. Some kind
of knowing that left him . . . better.

Enya had given him that.

And he was left with no further excuse for avoiding her
like the plague. He was left wondering what man in his
right mind would deliberately keep his distance from a
woman like her. But of course, he knew the answer to that,
too. A frightened man, that was what kind. And he was, he
admitted a little reluctantly, afraid of her. The feelings she
aroused in him were too intense not to be frightening. And
beyond all that, was the mystery of her. Who she was,
where she'd come from, how she could do the things she
did. And why in hell she'd never heard of a microwave
oven, for Christ's sake.

*She said she'd tell you. She said to be patient and she'd
explain everything.*

True enough. And who was he that he couldn't wait another—he glanced at his watch; nine p.m.—another twenty-
seven hours for his answers?

He'd been a fool. A coward. And when he really let
himself explore his reasons for that, he found one more.
Probably the biggest one of all. He'd lost his brother, and
it had hurt beyond measure. He didn't want to let himself
feel anything at all for Enya because she was going to leave
in the end. He might just lose her, no matter what he did,
and he wanted to be damned sure he didn't suffer when it
happened. He'd been guarding his feelings like a greedy
dog with a bone. And despite his best efforts, the imp had
carved a place for herself in his heart.

He wanted her. He knew she wanted him. He had to ask
himself which would be worse. To relish the little time he

had left with her and then be forced to let her go? Or to let her go, and never have taken the chance. Never even have known what it might have been like to hold her, to kiss her, to . . .

The soft creak of the shop door alerted him. But he'd have known she'd come in even if it hadn't. There was a lightness to the air when she was near. A warmth that permeated every molecule she touched. She glowed somehow.

He rose from his squatting position beside the bow he'd been sanding, dropped the sandpaper, and turned to look at her. Her white dress stood out in the dimness of the shop, making him again think of angels.

"I'm sorry to bother you, Devon. Belle asked me to check on you. You missed dinner again, and she's worried . . . Devon?" She glanced down at her dress and then back up at him again. "Why are you looking at me that way?"

He shook his head in self-deprecation. "Enya, would you like to come sailing with me?"

Her brows rose in perfect arches above wide, round eyes. "Do you really need to ask, Devon MacKenzie?"

He smiled, and it wasn't forced. Fully natural, completely without effort. "Good. Come on." He moved forward, and took her small hand in his much larger one, and stared down at the picture that made. Her hand nestled in his. Something yawned and stretched inside him. Some part of himself that had been asleep for far too long. Coming awake now. Fully awake.

He held her hand that way as he led her through the shop, and out the back door, the one that faced the beach. And she didn't say a word as they walked through the sand, or as he untied a small vessel and helped her aboard. She sat, waiting, watching him with those deep brown eyes, and she seemed expectant and wary and half afraid.

As Devon unfurled the sail and the boat began skimming the waves, further and further from shore, she seemed to relax a bit. Enough to question him, he discovered, when she softly asked, "Why now, Devon?"

He angled the boat in a southward direction and let the wind push them along. And then he relaxed, one hand on the rudder. "I don't know if I can tell you why," he said slowly, giving it a great deal of thought. "Maybe because I've realized it's time I said good-bye to Bryan. And this is where I have to come to do that. Or maybe it's just that it's been too damn long since I've actually enjoyed sailing . . . the way I used to."

He turned his face to the wind, because he hadn't realized how true those words were until he'd spoken them. He hadn't enjoyed this, not since Bryan's death. But now, the sea's breath in his face and the spray dampening his clothes, and the moonlight glittering on the water reached deep inside him. All those old feelings returned. His love of the sea, of sailing, of becoming one with the waves and the boat. Those things were still there, alive and well. He'd foolishly believed them dead.

"But you're enjoying it now?"

Her voice came to him softly, like part of the breeze in his ears, and he nodded. "Yes."

"You could have done so without me along, Devon."

"Maybe. But you're enjoying it, too, aren't you?"

"That I am."

Something in her tone made him turn to look at her. She stood with her hands braced on the rail, hair whipping in the wind, face beaded with spray, eyes closed. And his heart contracted in his chest. It was a crying shame he couldn't give her what she seemed to need from him. It would be one lucky man who finally did, though.

"I've been living dangerously near the edge," he said to her, because he felt she deserved at least this much from him. "And creeping closer all the time."

"I know, Devon. I was frightened for you."

"But you came to me. I'll never understand how . . . or why, but you did. And somehow, Enya, you gave me back my soul."

"No, Devon. 'Twas never really gone. You only needed a bit of a nudge to help you see it again."

He nodded, wondering—and not for the fist time—how a woman so young could seem to possess the wisdom of the ancients. "You helped me find peace," he said. "And I'll always be grateful for that." She looked at him, smiling in that serene way she had. Making him feel guilty as hell for taking so much and giving so little.

"I owe you. I really do. I only wish I could give you what you need from me."

Her chin lowered fractionally. "You mustn't feel guilty for that, Devon. You can't force yourself to feel something that isn't in your heart. Even if you tried, 'twould never pass. You couldn't even fool me with such a farce, to say nothing of . . . anyone else."

He frowned at the hesitation, felt like a heel. "I care for you, Enya. And God knows . . . I want you."

Her head came up sharply, eyes sparkling with liquid fire for the briefest instant before she bit her lip and looked away. " 'Twould not be right," she whispered. "You don't love me."

He closed his eyes in anguish. "It's just too soon. Enya, if you could stay, give me a chance to get used to this new peace that I'm feeling . . . I've been living too long with the idea that I'd never love anyone. I can't just leap from that to undying devotion overnight. We've only had two days—"

"Ah, Devon, you know that's not true. We've had a good deal more." A tear shimmered on her lower lashes, but she rapidly blinked it away. "No matter. If you don't love me now, Devon, you never will. An' even if you might, my time is nearly up. Tomorrow at midnight I'll be gone." She came to him, lifted one hand to cup his cheek. "But I must tell you, Devon MacKenzie, that I've not one regret. If my coming here has helped your broken heart to heal, then 'twas well worth the price o' the trip."

She stood on tiptoe, and very gently brushed her lips

across his. And when she stepped away, her tears had finally spilled over.

"What price?" he asked her, skimming her cheeks with his fingertips, absorbing her tears into his skin. "What did you mean by that?"

She only smiled and shook her head. "I thought we came out here to enjoy the sea, and not to talk on such dire matters as my leaving. Come, Devon. Let's float awhile, and look at the stars, and forget who we are."

Devon nodded, and turned to furl the sail, while Enya dropped anchor. And then he sat in the boat's cushioned stern bench, and she sat close beside him. Her scent caressed him. Her hair tickled his cheek when the wind blew. He slipped an arm around her shoulders, and she relaxed against him, closing her eyes. His arm tightened around her. Her head fell gently to his shoulder. Turning just slightly, he pressed a kiss to her forehead, and then he thought, what the hell, and turned still more, hooked a finger beneath her chin, lifted her face and fitted his mouth over hers. He kissed her, and something kicked his heart into overdrive the second he touched her lips with his own. But there was no response. It was only when he lifted his face away that he realized why. Enya had fallen asleep.

Water awakened her. Tiny droplets of it, splattering on her face in time with the rocking motion. Not the rocking motion of the sea. Nor were these droplets like the ocean's warm kisses. This was different. Colder and less dense, wetting her skin, her arms where they were linked around . . .

She opened her eyes to look straight up into Devon's face. Wet with raindrops like her own. And her arms were linked around his neck, and his were holding her firmly. He was carrying her. Carrying her along a jagged, rocky bit of shoreline, higher and higher, away from the sea. A rumble of thunder muttered in the sky. A flash of lightning, and the rain came harder.

"Where are we, Devon? What's—"

He looked down at her, gave her a reassuring smile. "It's all right. You fell asleep on the boat, and I got so wrapped up in the sailing I lost track of the time. I saw the storm clouds rolling in and decided we'd better come ashore to wait it out. Too far to go back home."

The wind picked up. Devon stopped walking and set Enya on her feet. "I see lights in the distance." He pointed. "Let's hurry. We can get to a phone and—"

"But why?"

Enya tipped her head back, letting the strengthening rain-fall pummel her face, feeling the wind caress her. Standing perfectly still, arms out at her sides.

"Enya, what the hell are you doing?"

"Feeling, Devon."

"You're going to catch your death."

She almost laughed aloud when he said that. Death was something she couldn't help but catch. Not tonight, though. Tonight, she was alive. And she would enjoy every minute of it.

"Enya, come on."

"No." She opened her eyes and looked around her, smil-ing when she spotted the perfect spot from which to enjoy the storm, to fully relish the magnificence of nature. "You go on," she told Devon. "Go find shelter, dry yourself off. When the storm passes, I'll be right up there." And without giving him another glance, she ran from him, clambering up the stony slope to the large flat ledge that protruded out over the sea like the staff of Moses. And when she reached that ledge, she stood upon its very lip, arms outspread, fac-ing the storm that rolled in from the sea. And she let it batter her, let it do its worst. She wanted to feel everything she could, before tomorrow night when she would feel no more.

Devon's hands closed on her shoulders from behind. "Enya . . . ," he whispered.

And she turned to him. And she looked at him. His raven

hair, plastered to his forehead, streams of water running from it, down over his face and his corded neck. Raindrops beading on the soft curling hairs of his forearms. The water purling on the skin of his chest, where his soaking wet shirt was open just a bit. She felt his body's heat. She smelled him. And she realized all over again that she had only one more day to live. To *feel*.

"I'm sorry, Devon," she whispered. "I know 'tis terribly wrong."

"What is?"

She didn't answer. Instead, she curled her hands around the nape of his rain soaked neck, and she kissed him. Not the gentle, timid kiss she'd given him before, in the boat. A real kiss. A woman's kiss. Devon's response was swift and sure. His arms encircled her waist like satin chains, pulling her body hard and tight against his own. His lips parted hers, and his tongue pressed inside, licking and tasting every part of her mouth. A deep moan seemed torn from the depths of him. And Enya felt a fire she'd never felt before. Heat sizzling through every part of her that he touched, and then engulfing her utterly.

Devon's mouth left hers to trail a warm path over her jaw, down to her throat, and suckled her there, as if hungry for the taste of her skin.

"Aye, Devon," she whispered, though her voice had become coarse and raspy. "Aye, 'tis wrong. But it doesn't have to mean anything. Just let me have this. Just this. Just ... this ..."

He pushed the strap of her dress down over her shoulder, kissed her there, nipped her skin gently, playfully. And when he sank to his knees, he took her down with him.

CHAPTER 10

The Ecstasy

*H*e was lost. The instant her arms twisted tight around his neck, the moment her mouth sought his in obvious hunger, and the second her body arched against his, pressing tightly to him as if she felt this same strong yearning, he was lost. He'd wanted her this way from the moment she'd fainted in his arms after her boat broke apart in the tide. No, even before then. He'd wanted her this way since his own accident, when she'd kissed him on the beach just the way she was kissing him now. And deep inside, he knew he'd wanted her even longer than that. Maybe forever. Maybe even beyond forever.

His body responded to her in a way his heart could not. And that he'd denied these feelings release with everything in him, only made them stronger and more furious now that they'd broken free. He knelt, and she knelt, and he held her pinned to his chest, and she pressed even closer. He plumbed her mouth, and she tilted her head and opened it wider and silently begged him for more. So he gave her more. He kissed the rain-wet skin of her shoulders, where he'd already pushed the dress away. He pushed the material still further, sliding his sensitized palms down her slender, slick arms, and then closing his hands on her forearms and pulling them free of the garment. And it fell. It simply fell to pool around her knees, because it could fall no further.

Devon withdrew his hands from her arms, so he could clasp the warm, soft skin of her waist, and slowly slip around to the small of her back. He ran his palms up her spine's enticing curve, and rubbed circles over her shoulders, and then leisurely slid them downward again until her buttocks filled his palms, and he could squeeze and massage and pull at them while feeding on her luscious mouth.

He felt her swift intakes of breath, the startled gasps that seemed to come each time he moved or touched in a new way. It set his heart to beating even faster and harder. He drew his hands around her body again, to the front of her, never breaking the contact as he did. He slid them between his chest and hers, and he captured her breasts. Her response was to shiver, and back away just slightly, giving him more room to work her. And he did. When her nipples responded to his calloused palms by stiffening and pressing against them, he drew his fingers forward, slowly, tauntingly, until he held her only at the very tips of her breasts. They pulsed against his fingertips. He squeezed. They became pebbles, and he pinched them, and heard her exquisite cry of pleasure.

She was panting. Shaking. He was revelling in it. God, it had been so long . . . and even then it had never been like this. Never. It was as if he could feel every ripple of pleasure he sent through her body. He pulled his mouth from hers, and his lips were moist from the touch of her tongue. He pressed her backward, and she went, lying down on the cold stone. The clouds seemed to part then, and the storm came in torrents. Rain pummeled her face, and spattered off the rock around her body. He sat astride her, upright, watching in an unbearable agony of desire as the raindrops pounded down on her breasts and flat belly with little smacking sounds. And when he could bear the watching no longer, he bent his head to those succulent mounds, and he sucked and licked and drank every drop from one, and then the other. And then from her waist, dipping his tongue deep into her navel to drink the rainwater pooling there. And as he moved lower, he pulled the soaking wet dress with him. He tossed it aside, pressed his palms to her knees, parted them. And he stared at the feast that awaited him as the driving rain added to the wetness already there. And then he pressed his face to her. His first taste of her was drugging. Narcotic. Maddening. So that he pressed closer, and drank more deeply, striving to reach the very depths of her for more. He used his teeth and his tongue, parted her with his fingers so his tongue could force itself further inside. Her fists clenched handfuls of his hair, and her hips worked rhythmically, and then she screamed aloud, shattering the very power of the storm with the sound of her cry. It was the most beautiful sound Devon thought he'd ever heard.

He sat up, never taking his eyes from her wide, awe-stricken ones. And giving her time to relax, he peeled the wet shirt from his body, and kicked free of the jeans he'd been wearing. And then he returned to her again, joining her there on their rain-soaked stone bed.

As soon as he lay down upon her, her arms locked around him, and her legs parted for him. She kissed him desperately. Devon eased himself inside her, biting his lip as he fought the impulse that made him want to drive deep and hard and fast, right now. He took his time, sensing her inexperience, knowing the same way he knew so many things about her—things he had no way of knowing, and yet knew all the same.

Her body was tight around him, caressing every inch of him as he entered. She seemed to squeeze him from within. And the wet stone beneath his knees was cool and hard. The pounding rain beat down on his back and shoulders, his buttocks and the backs of his legs from thigh to ankle, icy cold. And her rain-slick body pressed tight to his was warm. Everywhere. Warm. Soft. Pliant. Responsive. Ready.

He moved deeper, withdrew in agonizing slowness, and entered again. This pace, he kept, though he thought he'd explode. She breathed faster, clung more tightly, and he began to shake. She moaned deep in her throat and locked her legs around his waist, and he felt cold sweat pop out on his forehead. She moved with him, and his entire body went rigid. And finally she convulsed around him, drawing him into the depths of ecstasy with her, and Devon groaned and tensed, and surrendered. His body shuddered its release into hers. They clung, they held, and then gradually, they relaxed.

Enya let her head rest back against her stone pillow. Devon rested his upon her chest.

"I love rainstorms," she whispered.

"Yeah," he said softly, with a brand new wonder dawning in his heart. "Yeah, so do I. I just never knew it until now."

He walked to the nearest house and called a cab, and then while he waited for it, he secured the boat as best he could, hoping it would still be there in the morning, when he came back for it.

When he returned to the spot where he'd left her, Enya had gone quiet, pulled herself into an invisible shell of some kind. She'd put on the soaking wet dress as if it were an everyday thing, and just sat on that stone where he'd made love to her. Her knees pulled tight to her chest, arms wrapped around them. Eyes wide and glittering, but her gaze was turned inward. She was deep in thought. And damned if he knew what she was thinking. He wasn't even sure he wanted to know. Because the look in her eyes . . . it scared him.

Something had happened between the two of them on this ledge tonight. Something that had never happened to him before. And he wished to Christ she'd stick around long enough for him to find out exactly what it had been.

But she wouldn't. She'd made that clear enough.

He touched her shoulder. "Enya, there's a cab waiting down by the road."

She blinked and glanced up at him. Her smile, very slight, and wavering, and unspeakably sad. She got to her feet and walked at his side along the path to the road, and she never said a word. Not a word. He didn't know if she regretted what they'd done tonight, or relished it. Whether she wished she'd never met him now and detested him for having taken advantage of her, or whether she'd changed her mind about leaving so soon. He didn't know anything.

In the back seat of the cab, she fell asleep. By the time they arrived home she was shivering. Goosebumps rose on her arms; he felt them when he touched her. And she was sleeping so soundly she didn't even stir when he scooped her out of that cab and carried her into the house.

Belle stepped into his path, between the front door and the stairway. She wore a flannel nightgown and opened her mouth to ask what had happened, concern in her eyes.

But Devon spoke before she could. "Shshh. It's okay, Belle, she's only sleeping." He whispered the words. But his eyes were on the woman in his arms, not on the woman he spoke to. "We got caught in the rain," he explained, and his gaze skimmed the still damp column of her throat, and the place where the dress dipped low on her chest. His throat went dry. "But it's okay. I'll take care of her."

Belle muttered a reply, but he didn't hear what she said. He moved past her and up the stairs, easily carrying Enya to her room. He laid her on the bed, peeled the wet dress from her chilled body. And yes, he looked at her as she slept. He couldn't not look at her. She was, quite simply, the most beautiful woman he'd ever known. And he did know her. He knew her as well as he knew himself, though how that could be possible was beyond comprehension. He'd always known her. He knew that her physical beauty was but a dim reflection of the beauty she held inside. Her heart, her soul, they were blinding in their beauty.

With a warm, fluffy towel, he gently rubbed her dry. And then he tucked her beneath the covers. Bending low, he kissed her forehead. And there was a pang of regret that twisted his insides into knots when he turned to leave her.

So powerful that he turned back once more, to look at her as she slept.

"I don't know, Enya," he whispered. "I don't know what the hell this is . . . what the hell *you* are. I don't know if I'm ready for it, and I damned well don't know what to do about it. I need time. Dammit, why can't you just give me some time?"

Pushing both hands through his hair, Devon forced himself to turn away, to stop thinking about crawling into that bed with her and pulling her into his arms. Dammit, he'd gone too far. He knew what she wanted from him, and now she probably thought she was going to get it. She probably thought the frantic, desperate way he'd made love to her tonight meant something . . . something more than it truly had.

He'd have to make her understand that wasn't necessarily the case. He'd have to tell her. And that wasn't a blow he looked forward to delivering. He felt like the world's biggest fool as he slowly closed her bedroom door and moved down the hall to his own, lonely room.

He barely slept. She, on the other hand, slept as if comatose. He lingered in the house all morning, dreading the moment when she'd come down those stairs and look into his eyes and see the truth there. That it had been only physical. Passion, yes. An incredible passion between them. But that was all. It had to be all. A man couldn't spend years incapable of feeling love, and then feel it overnight. Even a man with a normal, undamaged heart couldn't fall in love so quickly.

But you've known her a lot longer than that.

He ignored the voice in his mind, his heart, and he waited for Enya to come downstairs. But she didn't come down. And Devon could no longer stand the tension building in him as he awaited the moment when he'd look into her eyes again. So like a coward, he ran. He could talk to Enya later. Much later.

"You're not leaving . . . ?"

"Yeah, I am," he told Belle, wishing for once she'd mind her own business the way George had been doing all morning.

"But suppose she takes sick? She was soaked to the skin last night, Devon. She might have caught her death . . ."

"She didn't." He knew, too well, didn't he? Hadn't he crept into her room several times during the night, and at least twice this morning, just to look at her? Just to run his hands over the satin skin of her face and her silky hair? There'd been no fever. No reason to worry. But he'd kept returning anyway. He'd kept touching her. Like a drug he couldn't resist.

He had to get the hell out of here. He couldn't think.

"I have to get the boat," he explained to Belle. "I can't just leave her, Belle, or I'll go back and she'll be gone."

"Exactly," Belle said, scowling at him. "You'll get back and she'll be gone. And then what will you do?"

He frowned. "I'm talking about the boat and you know it. I spent months on her. She's worth—"

"She's priceless. Any stranger passing by could tell that much at a glance. Any fool would snap her up in a second."

He held Belle's gaze. She stared right back at him, eyes blazing until he finally looked down first. "I have to go, Belle."

And he turned to head out the door before she could say another word.

She slept like she'd never slept before. She barely remembered the ride back to Devon's house or the way he'd carried her up the stairs and tucked her into bed. She knew it had happened, but it had happened while she'd been asleep, contented, cozy, all wrapped in a soft pink glow. She'd never known love could be as it had been between the two of them. And while she knew he didn't love her . . . she had no regrets. She'd have a precious memory to take with her when she left this life. And perhaps Devon would remember last night as well. Perhaps, once in a while, he'd think of her, and smile.

She came more fully awake, sat up in bed, and blinked at the brilliant sun shining down from high in the sky. "Crimey! It's so late!"

"Well, good morning, child. You look . . . rested."

She swung her gaze around, facing Belle, a bit self-consciously, she supposed. It was silly to think Belle could see everything that had happened last night just by looking into Enya's eyes, but that was the way she felt. "I slept like the dead. But Belle, what time is it? 'Tis my last day here, I cannot waste it lying about in bed!"

Belle smiled gently, and came further into the room. Enya noticed the tray she carried. "Nearly noon," she said, as she lowered the tray to Enya's lap. "But settle down. Here, have some breakfast. It will—"

"Oh, but I can't, Belle. You don't understand, 'tis my last day." She pushed at the tray so Belle couldn't set it down, and reached for the robe someone had left lying across the foot of the bed. "Where is Devon?" she asked. "I must talk to him."

Belle bit her lower lip and lowered her chin.

"What is it, Belle? Is Devon all right?"

"Of course he is, darling. It's just that . . . well, he had to leave."

Enya blinked in response to what felt like a blow. "He . . . he's gone?"

"Oh, he waited around as long as he could, dear. I know he wants to see you. But he was concerned about leaving the boat unattended so long. So he went off to bring it home. He'll be back soon, though. Don't worry your head about that."

A sick feeling took shape in the pit of Enya's stomach. She battled a wave of tears, though they made no sense. It wouldn't take more than a few hours for Devon to go retrieve the boat and bring it back home again, surely. So why was she feeling such a bleakness of the soul? Such a certainty that this was it . . . over. The end.

"Here, Enya. Please, try to eat."

"No. Thank you all the same, Belle, but I . . . I've no appetite this 'forenoon.'"

Belle frowned hard, but took the tray away. Shaking her head and muttering to herself, she left Enya alone.

Enya blinked and swallowed hard. She would be gone at midnight. Devon knew that. How could he leave her on her last day here? Especially after last night, and . . .

Oh. Well, maybe that was it. He was realizing what he'd done last night. And maybe thinking she'd have expectations of him now. Perhaps he thought she'd be awaiting his declaration of undying love. And this was his way of avoiding her. He didn't want to have to look her in the face when he told her that it wasn't forthcoming. That last night had made no difference, had meant nothing to him. That he still didn't love her.

Lord, what a fool. She already knew all of that. She hadn't expected one night of passion to change the man's heart. She'd only wanted to know physical love, only once and only with him, before she died. But she couldn't very well have told him that, could she?

No. So now he had everything mixed up, and thought he had to avoid her. And she'd end up spending her last day in this world all alone. She battled her tears, but they came anyway. So she turned her face into her pillow, and she cried.

CHAPTER 11

The Revelation

The further he drove, the more certain he was that he was making a terrible mistake. Stupid notion, that. He could get to the boat in a couple of hours, have it loaded on the trailer within a third, and make it back home two hours after that. Five hours. He'd be back home by dinnertime.

He was a jackass, wasting five hours away from her on her last day here. But, dammit, he needed to be away from her. He couldn't think straight when he was looking into those velvety brown eyes. His mind got all clouded with emotions and longings, and practical wisdom took a powder.

So, the way he saw it, he was doing the only thing he could do. Hell, it wouldn't be any good at all to wait and do his soul searching after she left. Suppose he decided there was something here after all, and then couldn't find her again? No, he had to sort his feelings out now, before she left. And he had to do it alone.

The drive down the coast didn't do a hell of a lot to clear his mind, though. All he kept doing was picturing her face. Wondering if she was hurt that he'd skipped out before she'd awakened this morning. Wondering if she thought he hadn't wanted to see her again. He should have left her a note, explaining why he had to go.

And when he wasn't thinking about that, he was remembering every nuance of her, the way she'd been in his arms last night. The way she felt when he touched her. Wet with rain and hot with desire for him. A bit mind-boggling when he thought about that. A woman like her, burning up for *him*. And he remembered the way she'd sounded. Those little cries that seemed to come from the depths of her soul. The ones he'd learned just how to instigate. A touch here, a kiss there. Those cries were like music. Like angels singing. He wanted to hear them again. And there was the way she'd smelled. Her scent filled his mind again now. Rain-wet and musky. The mingled aromas of sex and woman and something else, something that was purely Enya, so exotic and rare it was unidentifiable. And the way she'd tasted, drugged honey. Some sweet nectar he couldn't believe he craved now the way he did. And, God in heaven, the way she'd looked! Eyes heavy-lidded, passion-glazed, mesmerizing. Long, curling auburn hair, dark with moisture and plastered to her face and her shoulders. Her lips, parted and wet and inviting. The way the raindrops beaded on her skin.

He nearly hit a stop sign, and jerked the wheel to the left just in time to avoid it. Only he jerked a bit too hard, and slammed the brakes when he shouldn't have. He smelled hot rubber, and heard the squeals of the tires, and saw the trailer swinging up beside like a jackknife folding together. He skidded sideways, wrenched the wheel into the skid, but it was too late. He felt the cessation of the friction when the vehicle became airborne. The bone-jarring impact when it became earthbound again. And then he was rolling, rolling, rolling. His body being hammered, pummeled, slammed into one hard barrier after another. And then he sank into darkness. The last coherent thought he had, was of Enya.

She went swimming. She built a sand castle. She listened to music on the portable radio George had loaned her, and she had her first slice of pizza for lunch. She walked. She sat. She thought . . . about Devon. She was pretty sure her coming here had helped him to get past the guilt he'd been suffering since his brother's death. For that she was grateful. This whole adventure was worthwhile if Devon could just go on with his life.

She decided to write a letter to him, explaining everything. She had promised him she would tell him the truth before she left him, and as the hours sped past and early afternoon became late afternoon, and late afternoon became evening, she realized that he might not make it back in time for her to tell him in person. So this letter might be the only way. She spent a long time on the letter. She described the isle where she'd come from, and told him all about the kinds of people who lived there. Even the trolls. She told him all about the beautiful Fay Queen who was said to know all, and who'd refused to use her magic to help Enya become mortal. She told him about her deal with the ugly troll, and how she'd given away her wings for three days with Devon. And then she told him that she loved him, and that she had not one regret. She'd traded a lifetime for a few days with him, and given the chance, she'd do so again. And she asked him to please find a way to be happy now that he knew his brother was all right.

She lowered the pen to the desk in her room, drained. She had no more to say. She'd poured every feeling, every emotion into the letter. It was done. She looked up from the sheet of lined paper, through the window at the darkened, star-dotted sky above, and she knew this would be the last night sky she'd ever look upon. The last star-gazing she'd ever do.

She lifted her chin, resolved to face whatever awaited her without fear. And she took the note into Devon's bedroom. She laid it upon his pillow. And then she lowered her palm gently to the spot where his head would rest later, as if she could feel him there.

A jolt shot through her palm, up her arm, straight to her heart, and her eyes widened. "Something's wrong," she

whispered. "Sweet Mercy, something's terribly wrong."
She turned and ran from the bedroom, sick at heart, shouting to George and Belle as she raced down the stairs. "We
must go after Devon," she cried. "Something's happened
to him! I feel it in my bones."

Devon came around to see stars dotting the sky above him.
And gradually pain came creeping in on the heels of con-
sciousness, until he was fully awake, and in agony. Every
part of him from the waist up, screamed in pain. He
couldn't move. He could barely breathe. The car lay tilted
on its side, neatly across his midsection. He couldn't feel
his legs . . . nothing below the waist. Which might be a
blessing, when he thought about what he might be feeling
if he *could* feel.

Dammit, what time was it? How long had he been lying
here? Was it too late? Was Enya already gone? The thought
of losing her this way, before he'd even made sense of his
feelings for her, was as painful as the knife-sharp hurts
raging through his body. Jesus, it couldn't end . . . not like
this.

But it could. A glimpse of the lopsided, waning moon
told him that it was nearing midnight. He'd never make it
back to her in time. He'd lost her. And having lost her, his
mind cleared and his feelings became perfectly understand-
able to him. He grimaced in a pain beyond anything so far.
Why had he been such an idiot?

A light flared in his eyes. And then a shout. Her shout.
Enya's voice, floating to him through the barren night like
an Irish blessing.

"Devon! Devon, where are you?"

"Here," he called out, and even as she ran closer he
wondered if he were dreaming . . . or hallucinating. Until
she dropped to her knees beside him, sobbing enough to
break a heart, kissing his face and wetting it with her tears.

"My darlin' Devon . . . How badly are you hurt? Are
you—"

"I love you!" He summoned every ounce of his strength and put all of it behind those words, so they emerged as a shout. "I love you, Enya. I want you to know that, in case—"

"In case nothing, you stubborn man. You're goin' to be fine."

"No. No, I'm not. But it doesn't matter. I've been lying here with a car on top of me, and my only thoughts have been that I didn't realize it soon enough. That I didn't tell you, and that now it was too late. You'd leave me . . ."

"Ah, but I don't have to leave you now, Devon. Not if you love me. Not if your love is true." She stroked his face, his hair. "I'll become mortal now. I'll be able to stay with you, my love."

He blinked. She couldn't stay with him. He was dying. And he didn't know what the hell she meant . . . okay, part of him knew. But it was so farfetched . . .

"I kept to the rules, Devon. I didn't once use my magic, for if I had, I'd have died. And I never told you the conditions of the deal I made. And you love me all the same, and . . ." A frown creased her brows as she stared down at him. "Devon?"

He swallowed hard. "I'm sorry, angel. I . . . I can't . . . hold on . . . much longer . . ."

Her eyes widened. She shouted in the direction of the road, far above. "Belle! George! Where is the ambulance?"

"On the way," came the answering echo. "Fifteen minutes! Is he all right?"

Enya didn't answer. She pressed her hands to either side of Devon's face, and closed her eyes. "No," she whispered. "My darlin', you're dying. You're dying."

"I love you," he whispered, and he knew he wouldn't draw too many more breaths. "I'm sorry it took . . . me so long . . . to realize . . ."

He lifted a hand toward her. Weakly. But she didn't take it. Instead she rose to her feet. She stood above him, straight and strong, and the wind suddenly picked up strength. Her hair sailed out behind her and her dress snapped and billowed. "I'll not allow it!"

He frowned, staring up at her, wondering who it was she was shouting at. She stood with feet planted shoulder width apart, and lifted her arms to the sky. "If the price of using magic in this realm is death, then so be it!" she yelled. "Better my death than his!"

The wind whipped harder, blasting gusts of hurricane proportions down into the valley where he and his car had landed.

"Enya," he whispered. "What are you—"

"Ancient Spirit of Earth, lend me your strength," she said, her voice deep and resonant and commanding. Her eyes closed. She couldn't see, Devon thought, the way the wind was suddenly launching spirals of brown dirt all around him, around her.

"Ancient One of Air, grant me wisdom," she said, and the wind currents changed, seemed to become a whirlwind with Enya at their center.

"Sacred Guardian of Water, give me your magic, your power!" Before Devon's eyes, clouds skittered over the moon, and within seconds a gentle rain began falling. And it seemed to Devon that it only fell here, in this gully, and nowhere else.

"Age Old Spirit of Fire, your passion!" Lightning split the sky, nearly blinding him.

Devon laid there on the ground while the elements seemed to join forces. The rain and wind, the dust and lightning, all swirling around Enya in a clockwise circle, and he knew he must be dreaming.

But Jesus, hadn't she said she'd die if she used magic?

"Burden, remove thyself from this man! Injuries, be gone! As I will it, so shall it be!" As she spoke, her eyes flew open and her arms swung downward, straight and so stiff they trembled, fingers pointing straight at him.

And he had to be hallucinating, because the wind and

the dirt and the rain and the flashes of lighting seemed to blend together into one blur. A rainbow flash, green, yellow, red, and blue, dazzled him as it seemed to rush from her fingertips to engulf him. The car that laid on him vibrated, and suddenly became lighter. He blinked in utter shock as it hovered briefly above his body, then moved off to one side and crashed to the ground again. But the laser show wasn't over yet. Because those light beams engulfed *him* now. And the feeling was coming back into his hips and his legs, even as the pain faded from the rest of his body.

And then the light retracted, back into her fingertips. Enya sank to the ground as limp as a rag doll, whispering something he couldn't make out. Words of thanks or something. The wind died and the rain stopped, the lightning vanished and the dust settled. He tried to sit up, and it worked. Tried to stand, and found he could. No problem. Nothing even hurt. He shook off the shock of that, and forced his eyes to stay away from the ton or two of scrap metal this tiny bit of a woman had somehow lifted off his body. Instead he went to Enya. He gathered her up into his arms and he held her, scooping her right off her feet, and he kissed her, thanked her.

"Enya, angel, you're so weak! You're shaking."

" 'Tis only because 'twas such a mighty spell, Devon. I've never had call to harness quite so much energy before."

"But . . ."

She lifted a hand to his cheek, caressed him there. "I'm of the fay, Devon. A fairy. I could become mortal only if you fell in love with me, and you did. But I broke the rules I agreed to. I used my magic, Devon, and now I'll pay the price. But I've no regrets, my love. No regrets at all, exceptin' that we hadn't more time together before I had to leave you."

He closed his eyes, held her tighter. "No. No, dammit, you didn't give your life to save mine! Tell me you didn't."

But she said nothing, only closed her eyes to prevent her tears spilling over. "Baby, why?"

"Because I love you, Devon. More than life, I love you. Always have. Always will, darlin', wherever I am."

She lifted her head, kissed him. And he kissed her back, deeply, showing her everything he felt for her.

"I won't let it happen," he whispered. And then he tipped his head back, shouting at the sky. "Who the hell made these rules anyway! Take me! Dammit, let Enya live and take me!"

"No, Devon!"

A shimmering blue-green light appeared before him, and gradually took on a human form. In seconds a glowing woman stood there. Her hair was like spun gold, and her eyes gleamed exactly like twin diamonds, refracting rainbows of light that danced on everything they touched. Enya tugged at him, and Devon set her on her feet. She tucked her hand into his, and he immediately closed his around it. He wouldn't let her go, no matter what.

Enya bowed her head, and whispered, "Your Majesty."

"Hello, Enya," the woman said, and her voice was like tinkling bells.

"Majesty, I'm sorry I went against your wishes . . . but only sorry for the offense doing so caused you. I'd do nothing differently if I had the chance again."

"I know, child. And it's for that reason I've reached the decision I have."

Enya frowned, tilting her head. "I'm afraid 'tis too late for that, Your Highness. 'Twas a terrible troll who gave me this chance, 'twas to his terms I agreed. I broke the rules. I used my magic—"

"You willingly gave your life to save Devon's. And he only just now offered his own in exchange for yours."

"Aye," Enya said, lowering her head. "You've been watching, then."

"I'm always watching, Enya. Oh, child, I cannot grant whimsical wishes to every young fairy who fancies herself in love. I first must know that love is true. I would have been delinquent in my duties had I allowed you to give up your immortality and your magic, without first seeing proof that it was truly what was best for you.''

Devon glanced at Enya, saw the puzzled expression she wore.

"I don't understand, my queen . . .''

The woman smiled. "I was the troll.''

Enya gasped, eyes going wide. "My Lady . . .''

"I had to learn how strong your love for this mortal was, and also, to see for myself the purity of his love for you. And my dear child, I find both to be worthy. More than worthy.''

"You . . . you mean . . . ?''

"Yes, Enya. You're mortal now. A human woman, with a mortal lifetime, to spend as you wish. Bright blessings, little one. I'll be watching over you, always.''

The halo of light that surrounded the woman flared brighter, and then she was gone.

A siren wailed from the road high above, then stopped abruptly. Voices rose in a clamor, and then the sounds of tumbling rocks and dirt came as people made their way down the steep slope.

But Devon paid no attention. He was lost in sensation as he wrapped his delicate prize up in his arms and held her there. God, to think of how close he'd come to losing her! How very nearly he'd let this precious woman slip right through his fingers. Never again, he vowed, and he kissed her as if he'd never stop. Enya clung to him, smiling beneath his kisses, and salting his lips with her happy tears.

The clambering footsteps halted close by.

"Merciful heavens,'' Belle whispered. "It's about time.''

Magic and Mayhem

Elaine Crawford

Chapter 1

∞

June 1778

$\mathcal{T}$he bump and shudder of the ship against the soft wood of the pier pilings didn't begin to match the drum of Shawna O'Shea's heart. In the first hush of dawn, she stood at the railing of the *Kilkenny Bride*, viewing the silhouetted waterfront buildings of Philadelphia—this city in the New World to which she'd been so carelessly, callously, banished.

Aye, but to the New World!

She'd heard much talk aboard ship about the American rebellion and their stubborn bid for freedom. Mayhaps, if the Colonists broke the yoke of the English, she, too, could break free . . . as free as she'd been in the Shillelaugh Forest before she was taken to live at Drayton Manor.

Aye, God willing, she'd find her own freedom in America.

Filling her lungs, Shawna wanted to shout in celebration, but didn't dare. Other passengers stood on deck, and they already considered her a bit odd. Instead, she reached up to the hood of her heathery tweed cloak and jostled her diminutive companion, Misty Dawn, who reclined in its folds.

"Oh, let me die in peace," the seasick fairy moaned, then snuggled deeper into the woolen nest.

Shawna tucked her chin so others wouldn't see her lips moving and whispered softly. "But we're here, Misty. We've arrived in the new land."

In a whirring flurry and tinkle of bells, the fairy soared past Shawna's nose. " 'Tis just like ye, Shawna O'Shea," she cried as she flew up and off the ship. "Leaving the important telling for last." Within seconds the streak of gold and green had disappeared from sight.

Shawna smiled with resignation and shook her head. Why the devil had she let that feather-headed excuse for a fairy come with her to America?

The gangplank slammed down onto the dock.

Shawna's heart began to race again. Time to go ashore . . . to meet her new destiny.

Shawna hadn't taken into account, however, the long wait at the customs house. The officials didn't arrive until well past noon, and by the time they rifled through her two valises, the waterfront was teeming with activity. Screeching seabirds and hawking vendors vied to be heard over freight wagons that rumbled across the landing while their drivers shouted at passengers and dockworkers, alike, to make way. It was all very exhilarating after six weeks aboard ship.

Stepping away from the customs house door, she found herself passing between two sentries. Then she spotted more, a patrol of soldiers, suited out in their bright red coats and arrogant British swaggers. *The king's currish cutthroats*, her grandmother had always called them.

Had they quashed the rebellion? With disappointment crowding her lungs, she walked in the opposite direction, her arms weighted down by her hefty bags.

And where was that unpredictable fairy?

Shawna walked off the wharf and started up a cobbled street to stop in front of a ship's outfitter. She had not the least idea which way to go, and it had grown quite warm.

Setting down her valises, she removed her cloak and folded it across the bags, then, marveling as she always did at the luxuriant day gown she now wore, she straightened the lace flounces coming from the nut-brown velvet sleeves. And, she reminded herself, she had two more of equal elegance in her traveling bags, clothing given to her by the three young ladies before they put her aboard the ship.

For the life of her, she couldn't figure why they'd been so eager to rid Drayton Manor of her presence . . . so eager they'd been willing to part with such grand gowns.

Standing on the street wondering which way to go, Shawna saw two fellow passsengers having their trunks loaded onto the back of a wagon. Moments later, a carriage pulled onto the wharf and picked up another man. The city must be larger than she'd imagined—no one was leaving the waterfront afoot.

How she wished she was being fetched by someone. Anyone. But the Radcliffs couldn't have been notified of her coming on such short notice.

At the thought, she allowed herself to muse for a moment about the possibility of simply walking away. To simply pick up her bags and start walking until she'd left the city behind—no matter its great size, no matter the soldiers, or the Radcliffs. Find a lovely glen to live in the same as the one she'd been taken from.

But there'd be none of that. She'd given her solemn oath to go straight to the Radcliffs. Emily Drayton had even brought out the Holy Bible and made Shawna place her hand on it to swear. And, the saints only knew, what terrible calamity would befall her if she broke the vow . . . *She'd heard tales*.

The day was wasting. *Where was Misty Dawn?* Aunty Gwynedd, the wisest of all the wee folk, had advised her against letting Misty come, since no fairy with an ounce of sense would trust a ship to take her thousands of miles across the great sea. But, oh, how Shawna wished the plump little Gwynedd had come in Misty's stead. She felt so alone.

The morning Shawna made her last visit to the Glen of Shillelagh had been a day of the saddest farewells. At the thought, Shawna's hand went to her throat to touch the precious gift from her dear wee family . . . a fancy gold chain and filigreed locket studded in its center with an emerald of many facets. She had never possessed anything so wondrous . . . this remembrance of the golden-haired folk who wore the greens of the forest. But even more precious was what lay hidden inside—a lock of silky black hair so like her own. Her mother's, who'd died giving her life. Dear Aunty Gwynedd had saved it for her all these seventeen years.

The wise and gentle fairy had been much more of a mother to Shawna than her grandmother had. As Gwynedd always said, fate had gnarled Granny's spirit worse than her hands.

Shawna raised the locket to her lips and kissed it before returning it to nestle against the ivory lace ruffling of her bodice. Then, growing most impatient, she searched the sky one last time for the thoughtless imp . . . *the last time*, she determined.

"Miss." A sentry, bayonet-tipped musket in hand, came walking in her direction. "You seem in need of assistance."

Should she answer the soldier? It was the light of day, she reasoned. Not the darking hours of night. Despite the fact his companion winked boldly, she decided to chance it. "I've a need of directions to the home of Thresham Radcliff."

Both king's men sobered instantly and straightened their stance. The nearest one put fingers to his mouth and whistled sharply off to the side, then motioned for someone to come.

"Begging your pardon, miss, for leaving you to wait.

The lad coming with the cart will take you there with swift dispatch.''

The mere mention of Thresham Radcliff had brought such an immediate response, Shawna knew he must be a very important man in the Colonies. Very important, indeed. '' 'Tis a true kindness, ye'll be doing me,'' she said as the pony cart drew alongside.

The soldier rested his lethal-looking weapon on the wagon wheel and tossed her bags into the back. "It would be a kindness to me if you would inform the Radcliffs that Corporal Starling came to your assistance,'' he said, helping her up to sit beside the skinny young driver, whose eyes were hooded by an oversized tricorn.

"Aye,'' she said to the corporal, "rest assured, your praises I'll be singing.''

He grinned unexpectedly, then shifted his attention. "Boy, take the lady to the Radcliff mansion out toward the end of Vine Street.''

The lad, about fourteen, stared straight ahead in what Shawna thought was a surly manner. "I know the way.''

The sentry stepped closer, appearing larger than he already was in his tall hat. "See you take her safely there, or you'll answer to me.''

The threat didn't faze the lad. Without a flick of his eye, he slapped the reins across his white pony's rump, and the cart lurched into motion.

The soldier's musket, propped on the wheel, clattered onto the cobbled street.

Glancing back, she heard him curse as he retrieved it.

The redcoat's discordant words were quickly followed by the lad's chuckling as he pushed back his hat.

She saw a twinkle of mischief and the grandest smile as the cart boy drove them up a street lined with stately brick buildings and slender elms. At least for this lad the revolution was not over.

Shawna settled back to enjoy the ride along the busy thoroughfare . . . so many people walking to and fro. So many different places to go. Until this trip, the farthest she'd been from Shillelaugh Glen had been when her grandmother died and she'd been taken to the Drayton manor house sitting in the valley below the ancient oak forest. Most months of the year the only other people on the estate had been the household servants and, of course, the wee folk who'd taken turns coming to keep Shawna company. The lord of the manor and his family were English, born and bred, and usually preferred the grandeur of London to rural Ireland.

"I told ye this would be an amazing place."

The tiny yet piercing voice in her ear startled Shawna. Misty Dawn was back.

Just as quickly, Misty darted from her shoulder to perch on the front board of the cart, spreading her filmy moss-green gown about her. My, but didn't she look saucy compared to the sick fairy who'd disappeared hours ago.

Shawna would have loved to give the tardy imp a good tongue-lashing, but the lad beside her would think she was as loony as everyone else did whenever they overheard her speaking to what appeared to them as vacant space. No one else could see the fairies save Shawna and an occasional child.

"I heard that soldier call ye, *lady*," Misty said, running a tiny mother-of-pearl comb through her glorious array of golden locks, hair so much more striking than Shawna's straight black tresses plaited against the sea breezes and fashioned into a coronet. "I told ye 'twould be wonderful. In America anyone can be a lady." She stretched and fluttered her transparent wings. "Even me."

If not for the lad, Shawna would've said the soldiers had mistaken her for one because of the fine clothing she'd been given. Instead she fanned the hem of her brown velvet skirt past Misty's pert nose and sent her a meaningful look.

"The clothes, ye think. Aye, probably so," Misty answered in agreement. She leapt to her feet, the bells on her sleeves tinkling as she pursed her lips. "Ye know, I heard that spoiled Emily Drayton and her *lady* friends talking. 'Twasn't kindness that made each of them give ye one of their dresses. *And not their prettiest ones*, ye can be sure. I can hear that Babington girl's nasal whine now. 'It *simply* won't *do* to send the *girl* to my American cousins in *nothing* but *rags*,' '' Misty mimicked to perfection. " 'A gift must *always* be *properly wrapped*.' Miss Emily and that other one bawled like the cows they be, but they finally agreed that an anniversary gift shouldn't be sent in faded homespun. That anxious they were to rid themselves of ye.''

Aye, Shawna thought, recalling how awed she'd been by the gaiety of Miss Emily, her lady friends, and their three young gentlemen when they first arrived at the manor on what they'd called a spring holiday. Such life they'd brought to the dreary stone halls.

But Shawna's awe was soon replaced by a stab of pain that had yet to dull. To be given away as if she were no better than a goat or a dog had been humiliating enough, but to later see the young ladies tittering into their embroidered hankies over their grand scheme to rid themselves of what one termed, *too distracting a wench* had been shame upon shame . . . and her greatest torment. Shawna had been sent off to the Dublin docks before she'd worked up the courage to ask the housekeeper what the words, *too distracting a wench* actually meant.

"Flying does play havoc with me beautiful hair," Misty said. As vain as she was lovely, the fairy changed the subject without any thought of the disgrace Shawna had suffered. She tugged at a knot, setting her bells to chiming while she floated down to sit again. "Fay, what grand sights I've seen. This is a city of perfect order. Every street is straight as an arrow. Can ye believe that?" She gave a pert tilt to her dimpled chin. "All the houses and lawns and gardens are set precisely so. Then just that quickly the city turns to meadows and woods. Oh!" she piped high, her green eyes wide with excitement. "Deep in the woods

I found a fairy ring. I told ye there'd be other fairies here. Valiant, handsome fairies who braved the great sea just like meself.''

"Did ye see any?''

"See what?'' the lad asked.

Shawna realized she'd forgotten herself and spoken out-loud. "Did ye see . . . any ships sail in after the *Kilkenny Bride*?'' she managed lamely.

"Nay. With the bloody redcoats occupying the city, 'tis a rare day when more than one merchant ship makes port.''

"I see. Aboard ship I'd heard that thousands of people had risen up in a great rebellion here in America. Is it over? Have they been defeated?''

"Sometimes I think so. But, no, the Continental Army is never more than a day away from the British. They're camped at Valley Forge only twenty miles from here.''

"Blood and oons!'' she cried, unable to decide whether she was more frightened or thrilled.

The lad shot her a large-toothed grin as he guided the pony to the right, down a quieter street lined on either side by smaller shops and homes. "Our boys don't have enough gunpowder or trained soldiers to meet the king's army on an open battlefield. We gotta bide our time and pick our fights with care. And plenty of time is what we got, 'cause we ain't never giving in.''

"Ah, then ye're one of the rebels.''

He glanced from side to side. "I didn't say that.'' But she knew it was true as he clucked his tongue and sent the pony into a faster trot.

Within a few blocks they turned again, and on this street the homes sat farther back in grand style with wide horseshoe drives cutting gravel or cobblestone swaths into the lush lawns.

"Is this Vine Street?''

"Aye, where a few of our wealthiest merchants live. To-ries for the most part,'' he added in clipped tones.

"Tories?'' She thought that was merely a political party.

"Those loyal to the Crown." The annoyance in his voice as much as told her he thought she was quite stupid.

"Ah, 'tis certain, I have much to learn."

Beginning to feel uncomfortable, Shawna was grateful when the lad pulled up before a tall wrought-iron fence, jutting up between stands of brick. Wide gates stood open, framing a large three-story home fronted with elegant white columns.

At the sight, Misty Dawn perked up, then darted away to investigate while Shawna parted with one of the coins in the purse chained inside her pocket.

The lad smiled brightly when she put it in his hand.

She'd most likely overpaid him, but she knew nothing of that coin's worth anymore than any of the others in the purse Emily Drayton had given her when her mistress rid Ireland of her.

With great energy, the boy hopped down, then helped her. He even carried the bags all the way up the circular drive to the doorstep.

Shawna followed more slowly, taking in the tidy splendor of brick trimmed in white, trying to determine what kind of people would preside here. Whoever they were, she would be at their beck and call for the next two years.

High above on the top floor a window banged open and a girl child leaned out. "Did you see that?" she called down.

"What?" Shawna asked, though she had very strong suspicions about what the child had seen.

"A tiny person! Flying! Maybe it's an angel!"

There was a child in the house innocent enough to see the wee folk, yet Misty flitted past her without the sense God gave a goose.

What a way to start the first day here.

At a wild clattering of hoofbeats, Shawna turned to see a raven-haired man gallop through the gates on a great black steed.

She leapt to the side.

The horse reared, nearly unseating the rider.

Regaining control, the man swung down and strode toward Shawna, wearing nothing but an open shirt and fashionably tight breeches that came to the tops of his boots. "Miss?"

She only vaguely heard him speak, because standing before her was the most striking figure of a man she'd ever seen in all her born days. *And the most imposing.*

"Miss?" Long tanned fingers reached out and raised her chin. "Did I frighten the words from your mouth?"

And his eyes were the darkest, deepest blue, fringed with thick sooty lashes.

Misty Dawn pulled on Shawna's ear. "Say something, you ninny." She darted off and flew with the swiftness of a hummingbird around the man's head.

Shawna managed to curtsy, though she could not tear her gaze from the perfectly tanned planes of his face . . . the squared jaw, straight nose, the wide brow. And black hair, she decided, could be most becoming on the right person. The casual cap of ebony curls framed his face, giving a gentleness to its stronger angles. Altogether, he was nothing short of knightly.

Misty Dawn dove back to Shawna and treaded air madly just shy of Shawna's nose. "Say something!" she hissed. "Don't let him get away."

"Shawna O'Shea of Shillelagh Glen is me name," she managed in a breathless rush.

"Shawna O'Shea." Her name coming from his lips sent a strange shiver from her breast all the way to her very finger tips. Then more of his words poured over her like hearth-warmed honey. "Do all the ladies of Shillelaugh Glen have eyes that can see forever?"

"Jeff!"

The child's cry ripped into the magic moment.

"Don't just stand there, Jeff. *Catch it*!"

Chapter 2

∞

"*G*et back inside!" the man shouted up to the child, yet his compelling gaze never left Shawna. He raised her gloved hand to lips that appeared quite firm, but upon brushing the backs of her fingers, their feathery touch surprised her. "Jeffrey Radcliff, at your service."

Shawna's legs threatened to melt like candle wax as he lifted his head to behold her again with eyes which had now deepened almost to violet.

He'd called her a lady, kissed her hand, and offered to serve her. If Lancelot had had a Christian name, surely it would've been Jeffrey.

"*What a man*," Misty said, sighing, in enthusiastic agreement as she landed on Shawna's shoulder. "If only he could see me, me milk-white skin, me glorious hair . . . Oh, well, I suppose I'll have to get him for ye instead. So stop standing there like the village idiot and say something intelligent. Tell him about the letter."

"Oh, aye." But it was so difficult to think with those eyes stealing her every thought. She pulled the envelope from her skirt pocket and handed it to this knight of Philadelphia.

His gaze left hers for no more than a second. "It's addressed to my parents."

"Aye. 'Tis across the great sea I've come to bring it to ye."

His lips curled with an instant smile, causing the dearest dimples to soften his strong features. "Then, by all means, come in. I think after such a long voyage refreshments are in order. Then you can tell me all about the magical kingdom from whence you came. For no mere mortal could be born with eyes that reach into every recess of my soul."

At once, she realized she hadn't taken her eyes from his since their gazes first collided. Abashed, she lowered her lashes . . . and saw that he had never released her hand.

He exhaled mightily, then placed her fingers in the crook of his arm and escorted her up the wide steps. Turning the large brass knob of the entry door, he ushered her inside.

And the grandest place it was! Prisms of light spilled down from a glass dome high above them and onto marble tiles veined with the same soft pink that glowed from the walls. Shawna felt as if she'd stepped right into a lovely seashell. Sweeping down from a landing above came a wide staircase.

Then, suddenly, down those stairs, raced the child of seven or eight, her dark auburn ringlets bouncing as wildly as her hooped skirts. "Jeff, did you catch it?" she yelled without slowing.

"*Catch what?*" The impatience in his voice was unmistakable.

The little girl reached the bottom, but didn't stop until she crashed into him. Shoving off, she planted her fists on the waist of her plaid taffeta frock. "Have you gone daft? The tiny person with the butterfly wings."

Shawna held her breath, hoping desperately that Misty Dawn had the good sense to stay out of sight, yet she did not dare look for her.

Jeffrey Radcliff narrowed his gaze at the child. "Have you been in Mother's sherry again?"

"Mr. Radcliff, you're home." A portly man, he entered the foyer, wearing a long gray waistcoat of many buttons.

His beetle stare missed nothing as he looked at Shawna from beneath a shelf of thick gray brows.

Mr. Radcliff turned to him. "Yes, Peterson. Would you please ask Cooky to prepare tea for us in the parlor." Then his gaze returned to Shawna again, along with his friendly smile. "And, Peterson, there are some bags out on the porch. Oh, and I left my horse standing out front, too."

"Munching on the lilac bushes, no doubt." The man sounded perturbed, but Mr. Radcliff didn't seem to notice as the servant strode away to do his bidding.

"*Jeff-rey.*" The child tapped her black satin slipper on the marble. She had no intention of giving up.

He cut her a glance. "Amy, can't you see we have a guest? Run along. We'll discuss your ghosts and goblins later." Extending his arm to Shawna, he left the child standing as he ushered Shawna into a room just to the left.

In the parlor, pink again reigned, but this time in deeper shades of rose. The wallpapers and fabrics were in florals and stripes, bringing out the graceful elegance of the wooden pieces. It was so unlike the smoke-darkened stone walls and bulky centuries-old furniture of drafty Drayton Manor. Here there was no dreary gray or rust. Everything was so much cozier . . . and friendlier, she thought as Jeffrey Radcliff sat her on a cushioned wing chair and took its companion. Only a small table separated them. For a servant like Shawna to be welcomed in such a fashion— this certainly was a new world.

The child, Amy, had followed. She scooted onto the settee a short span from them, her feet left to dangle as she stared across the tea table at Shawna with a winning smile. "Please, Jeff, be a good brother and let me stay. I'll be quiet. Cooky made cherry turnovers. I poured the icing on them myself. Then, before she threw me out, I—"

"*I thought,*" her brother interrupted, "you said if you could stay you'd be quiet."

The child clasped both hands across her mouth, but her

eyes continued to grin in that deepest of blues . . . so like her brother's.

Shawna couldn't help returning little Amy's smile. She added an understanding wink for good measure.

Then, before she could turn back to her host, the clatter and rumble of an approaching horse and carriage came from the open front window.

Amy sprang up and ran to look past the lace panels. "Blast, it's Mother and Pris." Her round face scrunched with disappointment, she skipped back to Shawna. "Pleased to meet you, Miss O'Shea. I have to go now." She bobbed into a curtsy, then made a dash for the hall.

Jeffrey called after her. "I'll steal a turnover for you, squirt." He then chuckled. "Needless to say, Mother has yet to allow her to join us for afternoon tea."

How sad, Shawna wanted to say. Instead she ventured, "Childhood can be a lonesome thing."

His face took on a tenderness, and for a few precious seconds, Shawna was alone again with the most handsome of men, yet one who seemed a bit too rugged for this flower garden of a room.

Too soon, she heard female voices in the foyer.

Jeffrey rose to his feet. "I had hoped we could have tea in private, but alas . . ." He shrugged his shoulders, their breadth most apparent beneath the loosely tucked garb, and went to the doorway. "Mother, we have an unexpected guest. From abroad."

"Oh, la." The words were followed by two women breezing into the room while they removed feathered bonnets with generous under frills. Delicate-looking ladies, they might have been spring's first pastel blossoms. Both with hair as fair as cornsilk, the mother wore petal pink over gathered lace and her daughter looked most fetching in lilac.

Shawna, feeling suddenly quite tall and awkward, came to her feet. She bobbed into a curtsy as the dainty mistress of the manor came to her, lace-gloved hand extended.

"How do you do?" Mistress Radcliff said, just as Peterson, the butler, entered with a silver tea service and golden turnovers on the side. "Marvelous. Your timing is perfect." She turned back to Shawna. "Do let's sit and get acquainted while I pour."

The two ladies settled on the settee across from Shawna and Jeffrey, and Mistress Radcliff smiled at Shawna as if she were a dear friend.

The lad who'd driven Shawna to this home had been so wrong . . . the Radcliffs couldn't be like the English if they would treat a servant with such kindness.

Her hostess then began to pour from the pot into delicate rose-painted china. She glanced up briefly. "Now, my dear, what might your name be?"

Before she could answer, Jeffrey spoke. "Miss O'Shea. She's brought a letter for you and Father from across the sea."

"Oh, la, hand-delivered from so far. One lump or two, dear?" she asked, looking at Shawna.

"Only one, please." She preferred two but didn't want them to think she had too much of a sweet tooth.

Once everyone was served and Mistress Radcliff had taken a sip from her own cup, she set it aside. "And now, if you please," she said, hand extended to Shawna. "I'll have my letter."

Shawna turned to Jeffrey.

He pulled it from inside his shirt. The instant after he'd handed it to Mistress Radcliff, his attention returned to her.

Shawna sensed his presence so strongly while Mistress Radcliff broke the seal and pulled out the missive . . . became so utterly aware of him, it seemed as if they were the only two in the room. In her entire life she'd never felt so alive.

Abruptly, Mistress Radcliff came to her feet, her pleasant smile gone. "Well, Jeffrey, I can't imagine what you were thinking, inviting a servant to tea."

Shawna sprang up, the blood draining from her face. She was sure she'd told him. Hadn't she?

The daughter, too, looked Shawna up and down. "Impossible. Not in such fine clothes?"

"Yes, darling. It seems my English cousins, the Babingtons, have sent us this girl as a thirtieth wedding anniversary gift. With the rebellion and all, they thought, and rightly so, we might be having servant problems."

The letter wasn't exactly true—she'd been sent away for that mysterious fault of being distracting. But she wasn't about to correct the error.

"But, Mother, you've been married only twenty-eight."

Her mother clasped her hands. "Never look a gift horse in the mouth, darling."

Miss Priscilla's hazel eyes moved to Shawna. Then, suddenly, her mouth fell open. "A new servant! I want her for my personal maid. Please, Mama, give her to me. You know how important it is for me to be at my best right now, with all the British in Philadelphia. Just last eve I learned that Lieutenant Burke is cousin to Lord Camden."

"How marvelous." Mistress Radcliff's humor improved immensely as she snatched her older daughter's hand. "Isn't he the one who asked you to dance three times at the send-off party for General Howe?"

The cart driver had been right. The Radcliffs were Tories. Utterly disappointed, Shawna had to force herself to concentrate as the daughter continued.

"Yes. And he's aide to General Clinton, himself."

"Then, darling, by all means, you may have the girl."

Jeffrey stepped toward them. "I saw her first. And I am the eldest. And," he added with a baiting grin, "you always did say I couldn't match my colors worth beans."

What he suggested was unheard of! Shocking! Shawna closed her mouth over a gasp.

"A personal maid to a man!" Misty Dawn was back, sitting on the windowsill. "*That man.* What a titillating idea."

Shawna groaned.

Oblivious, of course, to the fairy's presence, Jeffrey's mother arched a thin brow as she glared at her son. "I do believe we've already had enough of your brand of humor for one day."

"Oh, poo." Misty Dawn soared up and flew out the window again.

But Shawna couldn't let the flighty fairy's comings and goings concern her. Had Jeffrey been making sport of her all along? Dismayed, she turned to him. To her relief, she saw an apology in his expression. But was it for causing her the embarrassment of being out of place or for making that unseemly suggestion . . . or was he sorry for telling her she had magical eyes?

"Forgive me, Miss O'Shea," he said quietly, as if it were just the two of them. "And you're right, Mother, that was in poor taste." Though speaking now to his mother, his eyes didn't leave Shawna until several heartbeats later. "But, seriously, I would make one request. Have Miss O'Shea sleep up in the nursery wing with Amy. She and the squirt took to each other right away. Ever since the nursemaid left, Amy's been sneaking down to my bed-chamber, often as not."

"*Mama.*" Priscilla's fair face puckered as if she'd just taken a bite of lime. "If the girl stays with Amy, she'll end up doing more for the brat than me."

"Darling, do try to have charity for your younger sister. Yes, Jeff, it's an excellent idea. The girl can attend Priscilla days and be Amy's companion at night. Perhaps, then, I can stop looking for another nursemaid. Amy *is* seven now."

"Eight," Jeff corrected.

"Yes, of course. Do be a dear and take . . . What's your given name, girl?"

"Shawna O'Shea of Shillelaugh Glen, Mother."

Shawna's heart leapt like a deer in her chest. There was

something special about the way he said her name, even if he was a Tory.

However, Mistress Radcliff didn't appear all that pleased as she stared at her son with thinning lips. "An Irish lass. Now I understand why you wouldn't let her speak for herself. Oh, well," she huffed. "Take the girl upstairs and have Amy show her where to put her things. Then I want to speak to you. Alone. I'll be waiting right here."

"Another of our little chats?" With a wink at Shawna, he reached down and plucked two turnovers from the serving tray and wrapped them in a napkin. Then, taking Shawna's arm, he swept her from the room.

As they started up the grand staircase, Shawna heard Miss Priscilla. "I swear, Mother. You'd think he was raised down on the docks."

Shawna was sure most of the blame for his fall into disfavor was hers. "Forgive me, Mr. Radcliff. I must have forgotten to tell ye I was sent here to be your servant."

He stopped midway up the stairs. "You've nothing to apologize for. It's we Radcliffs who owe you one." He grinned then, showing off his dimples before starting up with her again. "I'm afraid you'll learn we're all a bit of a handful."

It was an unraveling sort of thing, the way the man always said just the right words. But she'd have to stop putting so much stock in them. After all, he was a master of the manor and she the hireling, he a Tory and she a freedom-loving Irisher. But, for the next two years . . .

A secret thrill spiralled through her.

At the second-floor landing, he pointed down the hall to the right. "Those are the stairs leading to the servants' quarters on the third floor." However, he led her in the opposite direction, walking past doors on either side of the hall. Just before reaching a narrow staircase at the other end, he paused. "This is my room."

Shawna stared at the paneled door and froze in place.

The Drayton Manor housekeeper had warned her against accepting a man's invitation to his bedchamber. The woman had said in a most sinister manner that *men sometimes forget themselves*, though she never would say more.

"*If* you and Amy should have need of me," Jeffrey added with emphasis as he squeezed her hand crooked in his arm, then he pointed to the dark stairwell leading to the next floor. "These go up to the nursery rooms. You two will be the only ones in that section of the third floor."

Shawna peered up the steep steps. "Your little sister has been staying up there all alone?" In her own early years, she and her grandmother had lived in the deep shadows of the woods, but she'd always had the wee folk and especially Aunty Gwynedd.

"Yes, for the past several months," he said, as they started up. "Her nursemaid left when the British occupied the city, and we opened our home to four officers."

Shawna stopped dead. "Ye have the king's men living here?"

He took both her hands, now, as they stood in the unlit passage very much alone. "Again, I say, if you need anything, and, particularly, if any of the soldiers bother you in the least, come to me at once. They aren't always the gentlemen we'd like them to be."

She stared at him in the faint light, her Philadelphia knight. They were so close, she heard him breathing, heard her own heart beat . . . felt his thumbs making tiny circles in her palms. The scant space between them seemed to come alive, drawing her. She wanted . . . something she couldn't put a name to.

His eyes were almost black now as they held her in the silence. He lowered his head, their breaths mingling, his lips . . .

Abruptly, he jerked back. Exhaled in a ragged rush. Then, he started up the stairs again, tugging almost roughly on her hand. "Come on. I'd better get you up to Amy before . . ."

"Before what?"

"Before?" He stopped again and stared at her, then shook his head. "Never mind."

Chapter 3

∞

All Shawna O'Shea saw of Amy when she and Jeffrey entered his sister's room were the ruffles of her hooped petticoats. Amy was again leaning out a front window.

"Squirt," Jeffrey called. "Come see what I've brought you."

"A turnover!" She squealed and flung herself around, looking rather silly with an oversized powdered wig on her head. She stopped short and stared at Shawna.

"Turnovers *and* Miss O'Shea." Grinning, Jeffrey held out the napkin-wrapped treat.

"Oh!" Leaping across a clutter of clothes and playthings, Amy ran to him as she clutched the excess length of a silver ball gown.

Jeffrey lifted the turnovers above the child's reach. "I do hope that dress you have on is one of Mother's old ones."

The child's eyes went wide. "I would *never* wear a new gown of Mother's."

"Very well." He handed her the treat. "There are two. One I'll expect you to offer to our new friend. Miss O'Shea will be staying up here with you in Miss Crumb's old room."

"You will?" Turning to Shawna, the child's rounded features glowed with gratitude.

"Aye, 'twould be me pleasure."

"I like the way you talk. It sounds like music." Amy's happy expression then turned serious. "We have ghosts, you know. I hear them talking sometimes. Eerie sounding. Like they're close and far away all at the same time."

"Did I mention that Amy has a vivid imagination?" Jeffrey asked.

"*I did, too, hear them.*" She pointed across a room of no particular color scheme, past mismatched child's chairs and wardrobes to a fireplace. "Just last night. The voices came from out of there. I slid under my bed real quiet. I was too afraid even to come down to you, Jeff."

Poor baby, spending the night under her bed. Shawna had been sent to this house none too soon. She took the child's hand. "Don't ye worry about a thing. I'll not be letting any old ghosts have their way with ye—ye can be sure of that. Now, where is it I'll be sleeping?" she asked, turning to Jeffrey.

"I'd better leave Amy to show you to your room," he said, his gaze roving Shawna's face as if he were trying to memorize it. "I have to change clothes. I'm meeting friends at the Merchant's Club at five."

Watching him leave, Shawna could hardly restrain herself from following . . . so much had she grown to treasure his presence in this short time.

"So, this is where we'll be staying." Suddenly, Misty Dawn was back. She flew to perch on a top knob of Amy's canopied four-poster.

"She's here! She's here!" The child ran to the bed and awkwardly climbed upon the quilted counterpane, her fancy gown in one hand, turnovers oozing jam in the other.

Misty dove down in front of Amy, scowling at her, then flitted to the top of the chintz valance above the window. "Ye'd best get one thing into that busy little head of yours, child. Ye'll not be grabbing hold of me."

"Did you hear that?" Amy cried, her eyes as round as plates of blue china. "She talks!"

Shawna walked to the window and held out a hand.

The fairy hesitated a moment, then dropped down onto it. "This doesn't mean I'll be letting her maul me with those sticky fingers."

Shawna took Misty and sat beside the dazzled child. "Amy, I'd like ye to meet Misty Dawn of Ireland's wee folk."

The little girl stared in amazement while Misty fluffed out her flaxen hair to the accompaniment of the softly tinkling bells dangling from her flowing sleeves.

"And, for certain, ye must never grab for her. As ye can see her wings a very fragile."

"And more beautiful than any butterfly's I ever saw."

"Of course," Misty sniffed. "I'm a Shillelaugh fairy. Me hair's been spun from gold and my wings from liquid pearls. What manner of fairies live here in America?"

"I've never seen one." Amy put out a tentative finger.

Misty deigned merely to tap it with one of her own. "How sad. I suppose this house is too far from the woods."

"I suppose." Amy brightened. "But we do have ghosts."

The fairy arched a delicate brow. "No. I've been from top to bottom. There's not a one in the place."

"But I heard voices in the fireplace."

"Probably just echoes from below. If ye hear them again," Misty said, cocking a shoulder, "I'll be here to spirit out the culprits."

"You will? Are you going to stay here with us, too?"

"Aye, for now. 'Tis sure, ye're in need of me guidance as much as Shawna. Will ye look at that gown. Lovely and sparkly as it is, it's way too big for ye. And speaking of this guidance business . . . I'm surprised a man of your brother's advancing age and powerful good looks doesn't have himself a wife. Or does he, now?"

"Jeff?" Amy fell back on the bed giggling. Just as quickly, she sat up again. "You should see the way the girls are always dropping their fans and handkerchiefs in front of him. Louise Pomeroy even swooned once, right into his arms. But Jeff said he won't settle on a wife till he finds one as pretty and lively as me.''

Not only was he not married, he wasn't promised to anyone. Shawna reveled in the thought, although she'd somehow already known as much.

"Interesting." Misty tapped a finger on her chin. "The gentleman is an eluder of women. All the more sporting. 'Tis plain, Shawna lacks me golden beauty—that black hair of hers is straight as a waterfall. But when it's brushed out it has a nice shine to it. So, Amy, tell me everything ye know about your brother.''

"*Misty.*" Shawna brought the fairy up closer to her face. "I don't want any man I have to trap."

"Shawna, me girl, ye don't know the first thing about men. Just leave it to me."

"And me!" piped in Amy.

Shawna groaned. She had the terrible feeling her troubles had just doubled.

Without warning, the door swung wide, banging into the wall. Through it stormed Miss Priscilla. "*I knew it. You little scamp.*"

Amy tried to scramble behind Shawna.

Priscilla caught her arm and dragged her off the bed, then ripped the wig from the child's head. "If there's so much as one smudge on my gown, you'll be locked in here for a week. *With nothing but bread and water.*" She snatched the turnovers from Amy. "Now, get out of my gown this instant."

By this time, Shawna had also risen from the bed. She stepped behind Amy and lifted the heavily draped skirt over the child's head, then shook it out. A thousand dots of light sparked with the movement, created by sequins so artfully sewn among the silver threads they could scarcely be seen. She offered the dress to Amy's older sister.

"No," Miss Priscilla commanded. "Take it down to my room." She laid the wig on top of the garment. "I want every inch of it checked over. But first, go to the kitchen and bring up bath water.'' Eyes still snapping, she turned back to Amy. ''As for you, young lady, I'm telling Mother on you this minute.'' That said, she blew out of the room on the same storm that brought her.

Amy made a face at the door, then turned back to Shawna with a look of contrition. ''I'm sorry I made extra work for you. I'll go down and help you carry up the water.'' Her expression brightened. ''While we're there, maybe Cooky will give us some more turnovers. ''For you, too, Misty Dawn.''

Shawna reached past the gown to catch Amy's hand. ''Perhaps I'd better explain a bit about Misty before we go.''

Amy took the lead, skipping down to the second floor, then pointed out each of the rooms of her family until she reached two at the far end. ''Captain Stewart and Major Pitcairn have those,'' she whispered. ''And the two lieutenants have rooms up with the servants. I'm not allowed to bother them. But that's easy enough. They're usually gone all day.''

Shawna hoped Misty Dawn would be obedient as well, and not follow them—an eight-year-old couldn't be expected to always ignore a fairy while in the servants' company. Didn't she forget sometimes, herself?

At the top of the stairs leading to the kitchen, Amy put a finger to her lips and started tiptoeing down.

Sure that Amy's mother hadn't meant for the child to be that quiet, Shawna, nonetheless, followed on silent feet.

A few steps before reaching the bottom, Amy stopped and raised a hand for more silence yet.

Then, Shawna realized what she was up to . . . listening in on the kitchen conversation. Among the bustle and clatter, the servants engaged in an easy banter.

''I saw Tilden Case sniffing around the Wilson girl at church Sunday,'' came one woman's voice.

"With a nose like his," another said, "that wouldn't be much of a task. Hand me that knife."

"I don't know how Annie Wilson can abide him. For all his fine patriotic talk, I don't see anything more deadly in that baker's hand than a rolling pin."

"Aye, but mayhaps what Annie likes most is that she *can see him*. It's been months since I've seen my Ben. I wish General Washington would hurry up and make his move."

Shawna felt herself leaning farther down the stairs. *Patriot servants in a Tory house?*

"Now, Maybelle, you wouldn't want him coming in here shooting up our city, would you?"

"Hortense is right," a third, older-sounding woman said. "I'm sure British soldiers will take to the field again now that Clinton has replaced General Howe. And you can wager our boys will be ready and waiting."

Knowing for sure now that the women were Patriots caused Shawna to feel less than honorable about eavesdropping. She tapped Amy on the shoulder. "Go."

As Shawna and Amy entered, the three women, in white dust caps and aprons, were busy preparing food on every table of the big kitchen. The back door stood wide open, letting out the heat as well as the savory aromas from the hearth and ovens. Shawna's stomach growled, reminding her she'd had only a few crackers since early this morning. Odd how she'd had no appetite till now.

The oldest servant, rounder than the other two combined, eyed Shawna. "You must be the new girl. Miss Priscilla informed me that you're to be her own personal maid. That you'll be taking orders from her only," she added with a huff.

Shawna certainly didn't want to get off to a bad start. "I'm sure she didn't mean I'm not to help ye after I've done me work for her."

"Oh, and, Cooky," Amy added, "Miss O'Shea will be sleeping up with me nights, and she brought a fair—"

Shawna nudged her. Hadn't she just explained to Amy that she mustn't mention the fairy to anyone?

"Oh—uh—" Amy stammered, then asked instead, "Why did you say you were making all this food? I forget."

Cooky pursed her lips, plumping her fleshy cheeks. "I doubt that. But for Miss O'Shea's sake . . . Tomorrow afternoon, Miss Priscilla and some of her friends are having a last play practice. Then in the evening they'll give their performance in our ballroom. We're expecting more than a hundred people."

"Ah, 'tis a goodly number," Shawna said. "As soon as Miss Priscilla has no more need of me, I'll come back down." At the pleased expression on the women's faces, Shawna felt obliged to also confess, "Amy and I overheard ye talking on our way downstairs."

The servants exchanged disturbed glances, then Cooky eyed Amy.

"If I were ye," Shawna added before the cook could reprimand the child, "I'd be keeping the stairwell door shut at all times, with the king's men staying in rooms just above ye."

"Yes, we've become careless," Cooky said. "I thank you for the reminder. Is that an Irish brogue I hear?"

"Aye."

"Another place that's known the heavy hand of the—" Cooky glanced at Amy.

"For more years than we care to remember," Shawna said, answering the unfinished sentence.

"You're talking about the redcoats, aren't you?" Amy glared up at them with her hands on her hips.

Cooky wiped her own on her apron and sat down, pulling the child close. "If you repeat anything we've said to your family, we'll all be fired." She tapped Amy's nose. "And you do know I'm too old to start sleeping out in the woods."

With a most tender smile, Amy wrapped her arms around

the graying lady's neck. "The fairies would take care of you, wouldn't they, Shawna?"

At the child's inability to keep a secret, Shawna was surprised the staff hadn't already been dismissed. Quickly, she changed the subject. "Where do I fetch buckets for filling the young mistress's bath?"

"Next to the door, dearie," the taller maid said, pointing a finger white with flour.

"Oh, one other thing," Amy said as Shawna crossed the slate floor. "*And nobody tell Mama about this for sure.* We've decided to get Jeff for Shawna. You know, make him fall head over heels in love with her."

Chapter 4

❧

Shawna peered out her window.

Again.

Where were those two?

The sun had gone down and still Misty had not returned with Amy. Someone in the household should have noticed by now. But no one had bothered to check on the child, not once all day. Not even Jeffrey, who had seemed so genuinely interested in his baby sister's welfare yesterday. Truth was, Shawna hadn't seen him since he delivered her to the nursery.

But then Amy had as much as told everyone in the kitchen that Shawna was sweet on him.

Shawna cringed.

Had one of the maids informed him?

No, none of those women would have been that cruel. She'd worked with them all day, preparing for tonight's gala and had found them to be as kind as they were helpful.

Yes, most likely Jeffrey was merely occupied with the family's enterprises since his father, the senior Radcliff, was away in London. But with this evening's affair being the Radcliff's most important contribution to the summer's entertainment, Jeffrey, no doubt, would be in attendance.

Tingles of anticipation shot through her at the very thought of laying her eyes on him again. She was beginning to understand why Misty Dawn was always searching for a fairy king of her own.

No doubt that's where the wayward chit was off to right now, out looking again.

After a last probing scan of the grounds, Shawna swung away from the window and strode toward the door of her simple but comfortable room. Smoothing a crisp white apron over her dusty rose uniform, she couldn't help but smile. Mistress Radcliff most assuredly favored pink—even her maids wore one of its shades to serve parties. But Shawna didn't mind. While donning her ruffled dust cap earlier, she'd noticed in the looking glass that the muted rose brought out the color in her cheeks, and even the almost transparent blue near the center of her eyes.

Reaching for the door handle, she remembered that the wee folk had called them, *old eyes*. They'd said that even as a small child her gaze had come from some wisdom deep within. Just an old fairytale, though. Not once in her seventeen years had she felt overly gifted.

But, clearly, Jeffrey had been as captivated by her eyes as she had been by his.

She started out the door . . . and found Amy sneaking past with Misty riding on her shoulder.

From their I've-been-caught expressions, it was certain they knew exactly how tardy they were.

Shawna stepped in front of them. "Well?"

Amy glanced at Misty who, in turn, busied herself, smoothing the ermine trim of her gossamer shawl.

"*I'm waiting.*"

Misty swept a petulant gaze up to Shawna. "Ye know, it's not as if we weren't trying to help your cause, too. I stationed Amy in the woods outside of town at that place where I found the fairy ring of mushrooms. She was to wait there for any of the wee folk to appear. And don't ye be accusing me of not checking on her throughout the day," she added with a wagging finger. "I did. Often. Isn't that so, Amy?"

The little girl nodded. "Still, I *am* kind of hungry."

Shawna hugged Amy closed as she scowled at Misty. "I'll fix ye a nice tray and bring it up." She then knelt before the child. "*If* ye'll promise never to leave the grounds again without telling me where ye're off to. Ye had me that worried." As Amy returned an affectionate hug, Shawna glared again at Misty, this time, eye to eye.

Misty lowered her gaze. "She was always safe. And, ye'll be happy to know, your handsome prince spoke to nary a young lady all day."

"Ye've been following him?"

"For pity's sake. Beside looking for me own fairy king, what else would I be doing? All Jeff did the livelong day was meet with merchants and ships' captains and talk about buying and selling stuff, and all that rebellion nonsense that has everyone in such a stir. Dull, dull, dull."

As Misty Dawn rattled on, Shawna's mind drifted to thoughts of Jeffrey's cobalt blue eyes and the unspoken promise that had been in them . . . a promise so true, she knew he would not, could not, break it. "Where is he now?" she heard herself asking.

"Where else?" Misty answered. "In his room, dressing for this evening. In fact . . ." She sailed off Amy's shoulder and flew toward the ceiling. "I'm going to go watch. His muscles do flex in the most interesting manner, wouldn't ye say?" Tittering, she spiraled past Shawna and out the bedroom window.

Shaking her head, Shawna turned Amy toward the child's bedchamber. "Go wash up. I'll be back with your supper before ye can sing a song of sixpence."

Passing her handsome knight's door a moment later, Shawna slowed, sorely tempted to tap on it, to see for herself his stalwart body, the manly character of his face. She stared at the door, knuckles poised. If only she could come up with a plausible reason to go knocking on a gentleman's bedchamber. She could ask him if he had need of something. Water? Fresh towels?

At the other end of the hall, another door opened, and a man in a heavily braided red uniform stepped out.

Quickly she moved on as if she'd never paused, and walked toward the officer.

The man pulled on white gloves as he, too, came forward.

Passing him on her way to the servant's stairs, she noticed his face was as hard and rigid as the rest of him. Those weasel eyes missed nothing. They inspected her from head to toe. As she began to descend the back stairs, she had yet to hear him start down the central staircase. He still watched her.

Shawna shuddered. If her grandmother knew she was living in the same house with the English devils, she'd roll over in her grave. Worse yet, on this night, Shawna would be serving refreshments to no less than thirty or forty of them. She crossed herself at the thought.

Peterson, the butler, had stationed Shawna in the foyer where she now offered the arriving perfumed and powdered guests drinks from her tray while Hortense took any unwanted wraps. Her additional duty was to direct them past the grand staircase to where the foyer opened into a ballroom which spanned the rear of the house. Of course, it, too, was pink.

This afternoon when Miss Priscilla and her friends had been rehearsing scenes from *Romeo and Juliet*, the glass doors and windows across the back had been open to a fragrant garden in full bloom, and, with potted flowers and ferns surrounding the stage, the huge room had been quite lovely. But now that all the sconces and chandeliers were lit, reflecting off the glass panes on the one side and the gilded mirrors lining the remaining walls, it was a fairy land, indeed.

Yet even in the midst of all this beauty, her thoughts strayed. At any given moment, Jeffrey would walk down the stairs, looking far more handsome, she was sure, than any other man who'd come through the front door. How thrilling it would be if she, herself, were attending the play with him, and the following ball. If she alone glided in his arms across the polished floor to the strains of a dozen graceful minuets.

But, alas, she would instead be gliding over that floor with a tray of drinks.

While Shawna now offered one of those refreshments to an older gentleman and his lady, she found herself pretending she wore the lavish silver and peach confection she'd helped Miss Priscilla into earlier.

As he took two goblets and gave her a coin with his thanks, the man, dressed in conservative maroon velvet, smiled graciously as if she truly were in evening finery.

Oh, yes, it would have been grand, so grand.

Then from the corner of her eye, she caught sight of Jeffrey. At last! He hurried down the stairs, adjusting the ruffled silk stock at his throat. More beautiful, he was, than she had remembered. His bronzed skin, the blue of his eyes, were a magnificent contrast to his powdered wig. An ivory satin frock coat with scrolled gold braiding over a brocade waistcoat only made him appear more powerful, bolder. But the fit of his tight breeches and the stockings that smoothed over his calves held her attention longer. Yes, she sighed, he truly was magnificent.

Misty Dawn soared around Jeffrey, wearing a dreamy smile. The shameless chit must have even glimpsed him bathing. Shawna had an almost uncontrollable urge to pinch her wings off, she was so envious.

Then Shawna forgot everything save Jeffrey. He reached the bottom, and a dimpled smile played about his mouth. He touched his fingers to his brow in a salute for her alone. Then, alas, he strode off toward the ballroom.

Disappointment sliced through her like a sharp knife, even though she knew he couldn't consort this evening with a lowly lady's maid. He was, after all, the lord of the manor, particularly since his father was in London. Sighing,

she watched him greet a red-coated officer, favoring him
with another of his easy smiles before disappearing around
the corner.

After that, time dragged. Then precisely when the hall
clock struck eight times, Mr. Peterson, the butler, gave her
a long-handled snuffer and instructed her to accompany
Maybelle into the ballroom to extinguish the candles for
the performance.

Trying not to show her excitement at the thought of seeing Jeffrey again, Shawna followed Maybelle to the back
of the house and started snuffing the sconce candles on the
inner wall. Using the large mirrors in between each pair,
Shawna searched the room's reflections for Jeffrey. But, to
her dismay, every single man and woman in attendance
wore a powdered wig, and clothing of whites, silvers, and
golds seemed all the vogue. Aside from army red and navy
blue only a few of the older men wore darker colors.

It wasn't until the room grew dim, and the guests began
settling into the rows of chairs before the stage that Shawna
finally spotted him . . . *with a very fetching young woman.*

The beauty, wearing one of the most elaborately plumed
wigs Shawna had ever seen, strolled toward the seats on
his arm. Chatting gaily, fanning herself and batting her
lashes shamelessly at him.

Not only did he laugh at everything she said as they
settled themselves, he leaned close and gazed upon her with
that same smile he'd had for Shawna, those same inviting
glances . . . *he was probably even saying the same words
he'd spoken just yesterday to her.*

How could he?

Yet she could not take her eyes from the scene.

Another belle dropped into the chair on the other side of
Jeffrey and took his hand.

Now he turned his rapt attention on her. Amy had been
right. The man really was a bounder.

Unable to bear anymore, Shawna willed herself to turn
away and extinguish the final flame. Then she realized

she'd have to walk all the way back facing the audience through a room still far too light to go unnoticed—facing *him* and this evening's ladies. Oh, fie, she'd been such a fool yesterday. As experienced with women as he was, he'd surely seen the adoration in her eyes, had secretly laughed at her unworldly ignorance. No doubt he'd caught her mouth agape as well. Her cheeks began burning as hot as the flames she'd snuffed. Saints preserve her, she'd rarely stopped ogling him.

Desperate to save what little dignity she had left, she started marching, chin raised, eyes straight ahead.

Not a second later, she caught a flash of green and gold swoop past Jeffrey's first companion and pluck away a large lavender plume from the lady's wig. Then, as the woman grabbed the top of her head, Misty Dawn dropped the feather. It floated down several rows ahead.

At the lady's insistence, Jeffrey went to fetch it.

Before he returned, Misty repeated her mischief, this time taking the other lady's red plume.

That woman, too, felt around on her wig, then, seeing the feather sailing away, called out. "Catch mine, too, darling." She then turned on the other woman and gave her a tongue-lashing.

The lady in silver and lavender rose to the challenge, and before Jeffrey returned the women were engaged in a heated, albeit, very politely spoken argument that didn't cease until a hush fell over the audience.

Miss Priscilla had stepped onto the stage. In the glow of a low row of oil lamps, Shawna's young mistress looked as fragile as a porcelain figurine in her swagged skirts over silver-shot lace. Spreading her beringed hand with studied grace, she announced the first scene they would perform.

Shawna took advantage of the distraction and sped along the side wall and escaped toward the rear.

To think she'd actually thought a rich merchant's son would be interested in a lowborn Irish orphan. She had no inheritance, not even the smallest of dowries, only the few coins from Emily Drayton and those so generously given this evening.

Reaching the safety of the foyer, Shawna fled out the door. Once safely alone, she leaned against the nearest portico column and took several deep breaths until, gradually, her thoughts cleared.

From now on, she determined, she must never forget what she'd vowed before she ever stepped on the dock . . . to gain her freedom from this house as soon as possible. She'd heard land in the west was cheap. With the tips she might accumulate before then, added to the coin already in her purse, perhaps she'd save enough to buy a small parcel.

Aboard ship, it also had been said that on the frontier a man was valued for nothing except his hard work and honesty. Perhaps it would be the same for a woman. For her.

Yes, she must put this place, *that deceptive man*, behind her as soon as possible.

Chapter 5

∞

*S*hawna woke the following morning to the sound of excited whispers . . . whispers coming from high thin voices. She rolled over to see the door joining her room to Amy's standing wide open and a clear view of the child's bed beneath its canopy.

In the middle of it, and still in her ruffled night rail, sat Amy.

Misty Dawn, always such a nervous sprite, flitted back and forth in front of the little girl whose face was as animated as the fairy she watched. They continued to speak in hushed, and very suspicious tones.

Shawna rose and slipped quietly to the door. That bothersome fairy was not to be trusted.

"Then," Misty piped, treading air directly in front of Amy, "I saw Maybelle sneak out the back door, and the way she looked back to see if anyone was watching, I knew she was up to something, so I followed her. She went around to the front where the carriage drivers were and called one off to herself."

The child sucked in a breath and rose to her knees. "Maybelle's married to Ben, our gardener, who went off to join the Patriots. She better not be spooning with someone else."

"Oh, no,'tis nothing like that. She's spying. Isn't that

thrilling? Told him, she did, that she'd just heard some general had written to King George that unless he sends simply *thousands* and *thousands* more troops, he wants to quit and go home.''

"The British already have thousands of soldiers here," Amy said.

"Ah, 'tis a wonder anyone would waste a glorious summer night on such boring talk. But I heard this General Clinton say he wants more men because . . ." She looked skyward. "Oh, yes. *Because of the immense geography,*" she mimicked with a strutted chest. "*And the rebels fixed resolve on nothing less than independence, and because of the absence of active support by the Loyalists.* That he said while he cast an *evil eye* around the room."

"But what does it mean?"

"It means," Misty explained, "that men loyal to the Crown, like your brother, are not joining up, becoming soldiers to help the British.

At the mere mention of Jeffrey, last night's awful revelations slapped Shawna in the face, and she started to turn away. But Amy's next words stopped her.

"Well, I don't want Jeff to become a soldier. What if he shot Maybelle's husband? Maybelle worries too much about Ben already. Poor man. He spent all last winter and the one before camped out in the snow. And now that the weather is good, General Clinton will send out some of those mean lobsterbacks to shoot at him. I want them to go back to England where they came from.''

The small child's passionate words reminded Shawna of the price these Colonials were paying for their freedom—the same freedom she, herself, so desired. Yet she was surprised that Amy, a child of Loyalists, would favor the Patriot side.

Shawna stepped into the room. "Good morning to ye, me little early birds. Such serious talk I'm hearing at this hour.''

Amy slid down from the high bed and ran to her without

so much as a smile of greeting. She placed her finger to her lips. "You must never tell Jeff what we just said. Or anyone."

Misty Dawn flew to Amy's shoulder. "I wouldn't worry overmuch about that. Not if Shawna wastes her every opportunity playing the fool as she did last night." She stared hard at Shawna and sniffed. "Not a single one of his heart-strings did ye try to pluck, no matter how many advantages I gave ye."

"What's she talking about?" Amy asked, looking from the fairy on her shoulder to Shawna.

"Don't be asking *her*," Misty said. "Why do ye think I braved the great sea to come here? The girl is so slow-witted she can hardly put one foot in front of the other. I mean, odds bobs, have ye ever in your born days heard of a grown maiden who could still see the wee folk? May Goibniu boil me like black pudding if she has a single cunning bone in her body. Not once last night did she make the teensiest effort to attract your brother, no matter how many clumsy accidents I caused the other ladies to have."

"Well, ye can quit wasting your time. I don't want the man." Shawna turned back to her own room. But spurred by her anger at the twit, she swung around again. "And, I'm pleased to announce, *ye are growing dimmer by the moment*. Any day now, I may lose my vision of innocence altogether. Then I won't have to put up with ye ever again." She slammed the door behind her for added effect. But it didn't stop her from hearing the high buzz of their voices as, she was certain, Misty plied Amy with every single detail of last evening's embarrassing follies.

Shawna walked to the tall oak wardrobe across the room to fetch her clothes. She doubted Priscilla would arise before noon, but she could find plenty to occupy herself, restoring the house after the party.

The adjoining bedchamber door swung open again, and in pranced Amy with Misty still riding on her shoulder.

"I know ye're in a nettle," Misty said, flying straight

toward Shawna, "but Jeffrey's flirting with those other females doesn't mean a fig. If ye'd a come off your high
horse long enough, ye'd a seen him making Angus
MacBrugh eyes at ye every chance he got."

"Who's Angus MacBoog?" Amy asked.

Misty flipped over and flew back to the child. "Ye've
never heard of him? Why, he's one of me very own ancestors. His very kisses turned to doves, and them doves
sang nothing but words of love."

"No doubt," Shawna snapped, "he was the fairy king
of Blarney Dun." Whirling away, she pulled from the
closet another of the fine dresses she'd been given at Drayton Manor, a summer linen costume the color of creamy
butter trimmed with flaxen lace. To protect it she also withdrew a full-length apron. "If the two of ye will excuse me,
I'll be dressing now."

"Please, don't be mad at Jeff," Amy pleaded in wide-
eyed sincerity.

The sound of her voice melted Shawna's anger. With a
sympathetic smile, she turned back to the child. "Sweeting,
I'm not angry. But ye'd be doing me a great service if ye
would'na be trying to match me with your brother. That
goes for ye, too," she said to Misty *without the smile*.

Undaunted, the chit now sat innocent as ye please on
Amy's head, powdering her wings with sparkly fairy dust
as if she had nothing in this world she'd rather be doing.

Ha! And when the sky falls she'll be catching larks.

"Shawna! Shawna O'Shea!"

Miss Priscilla's summons went through Shawna like the
screech of a snared badger—that from one who appeared
so fragile. Priscilla had slept well past noon, but in the
hours since she'd awakened, she'd been keeping Shawna
running, readying yet another ball gown for a house party
this evening. But, thank the posies of Ballylee, this one
would be elsewhere. Only a few hours more and the Radcliff servants would be left to enjoy a peaceful evening.

Balancing the tray of food she brought from the kitchen, Shawna hurried up the back stairs. "Coming, Miss Priscilla. Coming."

Upon entering the young woman's room, Shawna saw that she was in a high temper, her face flushed and blotchy.

"I don't know where you got that locket around your neck, and I can't accuse you of stealing that expensive linen gown you're wearing," she said, her small breasts heaving against her chemise. "But when I took my pink sapphire ear bobs out of their case not twenty minutes ago, they were perfectly fine. Now look." She opened her hand. "Look at what you've done."

"Me?" Keeping a safe distance, Shawna peered into her palm. The large transparent jewel no longer lay in its pronged setting. "Oh, fie, a disappointment that surely must have been. Perhaps Mister Peterson could fix it."

"That old curmudgeon? I think not. You'll have to take care of it *and within the hour.* Take it to the jewelers at Fourth and Mulberry. Don't let him put you off because of your common Irish brogue. Tell him straight away you're there on my behalf."

Shawna was still seething as she walked out of the jewelry shop with the repaired ear bob tucked safely in her small purse. She couldn't decide whether to be more angry at being accused of stealing, of malicious mischief, *or* because Miss Priscilla had acted as if Shawna's speech was so common nothing of worth came from her Irish mouth.

And this was only the third day of a two-year sentence.

Rounding the corner onto Fourth Street, Shawna very nearly crashed into none other than Jeffrey Radcliff, himself.

He caught her arms. "Whoa, there. Not so fast."

Misty Dawn, the chit, sat pertly on the front lip of his tricornered hat, looking more smug than ever.

Suddenly it all became as shining clear as the sapphire in Priscilla's earring. Misty had plotted the entire thing, from breaking the piece of jewelry to arranging this meeting. Shawna stepped out of Jeffrey's hold. "Good day to ye, Mister Radcliff." She sidestepped to pass him.

He caught her arm, then turned to a companion whose features seemed particularly stern when compared to Jeff's ... but, then, who else had Jeffrey's rakish good looks, even in his somber business suit of dark brown?

"Mr. Cullen, it would seem I've been gifted with a most pleasant task. So I bid you good day. If there is anything further you wish to discuss, you know where to find me."

With a thin smile, the man tipped his tricorn and moved on down the street.

As he did, Misty flew to Shawna's shoulder. " 'Tis a lot of trouble I went to, getting the two of ye alone, so the least ye can do is put out one tiny smidgen of effort. A smile. Anything would help."

"You shouldn't be out here on the street alone," Jeffrey said as he tucked Shawna's arm within his. "Since the rebellion, our town is crawling with ruffians. If you need to go out, ask me to take you, or ask Peterson."

"Needless to say, ye were not at home and Peterson is running errands for Mistress Radcliff, and Miss Priscilla had to have her ear bob repaired before this evening. So, if ye'll excuse me, I'll be on me way."

Misty tugged hard on a hair at the nape of Shawna's neck. "*Smile.*"

Shawna barely resisted the urge to swat the pesky gnat.

Jeffrey, however, gazed at her with the same sincerity as he had on their first meeting. "Have I offended you? If I have in any way, I'm truly sorry."

"*Smile!*"

"*No!*"

Jeffrey reared back with a surprised grin. "You say that as if you meant yes."

That did it! Shawna slapped at the twit.

But the fairy was too fleet. She lighted on top of Jeffrey's tricorn again—out of reach.

Shawna returned her attention to Jeffrey and was once more caught in the wonder of his utterly blue eyes. Her heart was no less affected as it leapt in her breast. " 'Tis meself who should be apologizing," she murmured. "In such a hurry I am, I must have left me manners behind."

"Then we'd better get to stepping along."

Too rude it would have been to refuse to walk with this man who had never been anything save kind to her. And, Shawna hated admitting as she strode by his side, she thoroughly enjoyed being squired down the tree-lined street in the company of such a fine figure of a man, and she in a lovely dress of her own, no less.

Passing folk tipped their hats or smiled in a most pleasant manner. Cities truly were agreeable and fascinating places, contrary to all of her reclusive grandmother's warnings.

"Slow down, fool!" muttered Misty Dawn. " 'Tis a lovely stroll I arranged, not a bloody horse race."

Misty would not let her enjoy anything. Oh, how she'd love to take a cudgel to the squawking kit of a shrew. Yet on one so scrawny, the back of a hand would do just as well. "Pardon me, sir," she said to Jeffrey. "I'd be stopping a moment, if ye don't mind. There's something in me shoe."

Gentleman that he was, he appeared sincerely concerned. "May I assist you?"

To Shawna's delight, the gentleman knelt before her on the brick paving . . . and brought the fairy riding his hat within perfect dispatching distance.

But, drat, Shawna must have given herself away—before she even raised her hand, the fairy's eyes rounded, and she flew away.

"Ungrateful wretch," Misty railed as she soared upward. "Don't be holding your breath, waiting for me to help ye again."

"This one?"

Remembering the man at her feet, Shawna felt rather foolish. "Aye." She hesitantly held out a kid slipper.

Ever so gently and slowly, he removed the shoe from her stockinged foot and gave it a shake, then slipped it back on, all the while one warm hand held her ankle aloft in a most stirring manner. She found herself experiencing the same tingly feelings she'd had the other day, but this time they started at her toes and reached upward to her most intimate regions.

She didn't realize her hand was on his shoulder until he began to rise, and she found herself ever so close to him, felt the warmth of the manly scented space barely separating the unsheathed upper swells of her bosom from his chest. Lifting her gaze from the heated shadows, she found his own lifting to meet hers. Dark as the shadows they'd just left, yet luminous, his eyes held a desire for things she, too, so fervently wanted, needed . . . things she still didn't understand. Yet instinctively she knew this was what she'd been born for, this thing so sacred, others spoke of it only in whispers.

"Jeff! Jeff Radcliff," a man called from behind Shawna.

Jeffrey's head jerked upward. "*Blast*," he muttered, then smiled broadly as he moved Shawna to the side.

A raw-boned redheaded man and a female version of him bore down on them. He held out a hand in greeting. "How fortuitous. We just arrived from London yesterday. And Martha, here, was saying we simply have to throw the biggest party this town has ever seen. We missed everyone terribly."

The young woman looked at Jeffrey with the same devouring gaze as all the ladies had last night.

Shawna wanted to scratch her eyes right out of her head.

"It has been a long while. You and your sister have been gone for what? A year?"

"Almost to the day," the woman said, her voice a cat's purr as she held out her hand gloved in peacock blue to match the rest of her summer costume.

Jeffrey took it and lavished the utmost regard upon it before returning his attention to the gentleman. "Ashton, I see no reason to wait until another time to catch up on the latest. If you have no pressing engagement, may I invite you and your sister to the coffee house down the street. There's so much to talk about. No doubt you've seen the preponderance of red uniforms since your return. They've been with us since last fall. Too, I suppose you have no end of news of your own.'' He tucked the lady's arm in the crook of his.

Shawna stood off to the side, totally ignored by Jeffrey. Today was even worse than last night. At least then she'd been overlooked because of her servant's attire.

When was she going to learn that she was a mere diversion for him until something better came along?

Yet, this Ashton person looked at her with an appraising eye, and seemed most pleased with what he saw.

''Shawna,'' Jeffrey said, finally remembering her. ''You'd better run along before Pris calls for your head on a platter. But I don't want you walking.'' He dipped into a waistcoat pocket, then handed her a small coin and pointed up the street. ''Tell Wilkie at the livery that I said to see you safely home.''

She whirled away and strode off as fast as her feet would carry her. *Now, with a frizzy haired peacock for company, he had no more time for her.*

Never again would she be tricked by him. Never. Never.

Chapter 6

∞

Shawna's mood had improved very little by the time she was dropped off at the gate of Radcliff manor. Noticing the low slant of the sun only made it worse. The jeweler had taken much too long, resetting the sapphire.

"The fury of the Scald-crow will be in Miss Priscilla's eyes for sure."

Risking a reprimand from Mr. Peterson, Shawna decided to go in the quickest way, the front entrance. To her favor, no one was about when she stepped into the pink glow of the foyer. But there was no time to enjoy it. She lifted her skirts and raced up the sweeping staircase.

Another color caught her eye. Red. She looked up to find two British officers at the top.

And they viewed her with uncommon interest.

Nearing them, she veered to the left, giving the soldiers a wide berth.

To no avail. The closest, sidestepped and rudely grabbed her arm.

"Please, unhand me." She wrenched away.

He snagged her from behind and yanked her flush against the scratchy wool of his uniform, clamping both arms across her breasts. "So, this is her, you say."

Alarm stiffened her spine. "I'm not that sort. Let go!" She attempted to break his hold.

He tightened his grip. A short man, he jutted his pocked face to within inches of hers.

The other, long of tooth, stepped directly in front of her. "Don't make a fuss, dearie." He'd cut off her escape, and the evil intent in his bulging eyes turned her to ice. "Now, isn't she the tasty morsel I said she was?"

"And being served up to us right here on our very own plate." The one behind seared her ear with his hot breath. "The Radcliffs truly are *the most generous hosts*."

Lunging to the side, Shawna tore frantically at his fingers. "*Release me. Now*." She prayed her voice didn't betray her fear.

"Spirited, too," he said. "Waltzing up the front stairs as if she owned them."

"And I wonder what interesting things she must have done to earn these fine clothes." The one blocking her uncurled a long bony finger. Slowly, deliberately, he traced the ruffled edging of her scooped bodice.

Revulsion added to her panic. A shudder ran through her. Then rage. "Release me at once or I'll scream the roof down."

A hand did release her—only to slam across her mouth. Hard. Forcing her head back against the man's chest, cutting off her breath.

She bucked, kicked, her heart near bursting.

The man in front pressed closer. "I think we'd best partake of this little treat in the privacy of my room."

Shawna rammed her heel into her captor's shin.

He grunted. "Grab her feet, Fred." The soldier started dragging her backward, down the hall toward the officers' rooms while the other chased after trying to catch her flailing legs.

Unable to breathe, her lungs burned. Her eyes began to lose focus. With a last mighty effort, she lashed out a foot, catching the horseface at the base of his long nose.

"Shawna O'Shea!"

Instantly she was dropped.

Taking in great gulps of air, she saw the villainous culprits sidling toward the stairs, straightening their jackets. Staggering to her feet, she spotted Miss Priscilla standing in her doorway.

"Come here, you worthless slut," her mistress railed, shaking a hairbrush at Shawna. "Small wonder the Babingtons got rid of you. Have you even bothered to take my ear bob to the jewelers?"

Her mistress had grossly misinterpreted what she'd seen. But at the moment Miss Priscilla could think anything she pleased. She'd saved Shawna from being ravished by those two barbarians. "Yes, miss, I have it right here." Starting toward Priscilla on legs as weak as willow switches, she couldn't quite picture the horrors that would have befallen her, but from hearing the old Viking tales, she knew it was 'the fate worse than death' . . . this fate that Jeffrey had left her to.

Shawna breathed a grateful sigh as she watched Miss Priscilla fairly float down the stairs on a cloud of shiny pink ribbons and ruffles to join her mother in a waiting carriage. Despite her unpleasant nature, when all decked out, the spoiled young woman rivaled a fairy princess.

Something thumped just above Shawna's head.

Her own not so princess-like fairy came to mind. And, come to think of it, Shawna hadn't seen Amy, either, since early this afternoon. She started up to the nursery to see if the little girl had eaten supper yet and prepared for bed. Since the Radcliff women had nothing but their social calendar on their minds, she doubted either of them had taken time to check on the child . . . no better than a poor orphan, she was.

Upon reaching Amy's room, Shawna stepped in and, to her surprise, found the child in bed fast asleep and Misty Dawn, looking just as cherubic, nestled in Amy's dark ringlets, her own gold-spun tresses swirling among them. Shawna's frustration at the imp melted away. In Misty's rare still moments it was hard to stay angry at her.

Shawna blew out the bedside lamp and quietly closed the door behind her and repaired down the stairs. A relaxing cup of tea was in order after such a disturbing and stressful day.

Opening the stairwell door to the kitchen, she saw Cooky sitting at the table with a sturdy young man. After the harrowing encounter with the redcoats just a few short hours before, her first instinct was to turn and run back upstairs. But the sight of his big calloused hands clumsily holding onto a fragile teacup stopped her. She could easily see those same hands at home in Ireland guiding a plow down a straight furrow or swinging a scythe in a field of ripe wheat . . . good honest common man's hands. They put her at ease.

Seeing her, he stood, an expectant expression beaming from his kind brown eyes.

"Get yourself a cup, lass, and join us," Cooky said, motioning to a shelf of stacked dishes. "I'd like you to meet my nephew, Barney. Barney Hanks."

After introductions, she'd fetched her cup, and the polite man helped her with her chair. These Americans did have a way of making a servant feel like the lady of the manor.

His generous smile erased any remaining trace of Shawna's distrust as he took his own seat across from her. "So, you've just sailed in all the way from Ireland."

"Aye. That I did, to this grand new city." She poured herself a portion of steaming brew from a china pot on the table, noting that Cooky was entertaining her nephew with next to the best service. "Have ye always lived here?"

"Barney don't live here, at all," Cooky said, patting his ruddy hand with one of her pudgy ones. "My brother, his pa, has a place on the post road to Reading. But Barney, here, is—" She looked behind her and lowered her voice. "He's a corporal in General Washington's army."

Shawna, herself, glanced to and fro, though she knew everyone except Amy was gone for the evening.

"Don't fret yourself," Barney said, lounging back in his chair. "Whenever I can get leave to come check on Aunt Cora, I hitch a ride on a farm wagon coming in for market day. Ride right past the lobsters with hardly no questions at all. But why would a young Irish lass like yourself hire into this den of English dogs?"

"Leave her alone. Shawna had no idea what she was walking into, did you, girl?"

" 'Twas a place where a body could have their own land, I'd heard. So when Miss Emily, the daughter of me manor back home, wanted to—to send me here, I agreed."

Barney burst into laughter. "I'll wager she did want that. She's probably as scrawny as a wet cat and didn't want her suitors to see what they would be missing."

"Oh, no, 'twas nothing of the kind." Being a 'distracting wench' had been her sin. Perhaps she'd one day ask Cooky what it meant, but not yet, not with a man sitting there. She changed the topic. " 'Tis pleased I am that ye're fighting the English to set this land free. I only wish I could help."

"Leave this house, then," he said. "Come with me out of this lobster cage of a town." He must have seen her astonishment, for he quickly added, "Nothing dishonorable intended. I would merely see you settled with a good patriotic family."

Realizing what a suspicious person she was rapidly becoming, she relaxed. "There's nothing I'd like better, but I vowed to work two years for the Radcliffs in payment for me passage across the great sea."

He scoffed. "They aren't worthy of your good faith."

"Me vow was given on the Bible."

"Oh, I see. Well, if you do change your mind. Go across the river to the township of Haddonfield. Tell the proprietor at the Indian King Tavern that Barney Hanks sent you. Can you remember that. They'll see you safely resettled."

"That easy, is it?"

"Aye. With so many men off to war, folks are begging for workers of every kind."

"That's a pure fact," Cooky said. "Mr. Peterson hasn't been fit to be in the same house with since Ben, our gardener, left to enlist, and he had to add Ben's duties to his own."

Barney turned his friendly grin on Cooky. "Why, Aunt Cora, I thought you was sweet on the butler."

"Pshaw!" Cooky gave his shoulder a playful slap. "That old man? Go on with you."

Barney winked at Shawna. "Methinks you protest too much, Cooky, love." Then his expression grew sober again. "Seriously, Miss O'Shea, if you want to rid yourself of the Radcliffs and this vipers' nest, come with me."

At that moment, the door to the stairs flung wide and banged against the wall, setting the dishes to rattling.

Amy stood on the threshold. "You're going away? Leaving me?" Her eyes shone with unshed tears. "And taking Misty?"

Shawna left the table and hurried to Amy. "No, sweetings," she cooed and held her close. "I'll be here for ye. I promise."

"Looks like this would be a good time to get going," Barney said, coming to his feet. He grabbed his wide-brimmed hat off an empty chair and escaped toward the back door, then paused. "But do keep in mind what I said to you, Shawna O'Shea."

At his words, she felt the tighter clutch of Amy's hands. "Thank ye, Mr. Hanks, but for now I'll be staying right here with me little sweetings."

Turning to Amy, Shawna noticed Misty Dawn, her legs dangling from atop the stairwell door, her nose in an obvious snub. Nonetheless, the fairy knew to keep a safe distance. Especially since this afternoon's business outside the jeweler's.

Glowering at the fairy, Shawna brought Amy back to the chair. She sat down and found herself level with the child's eyes. "Don't ye worry. I'll be here for ye. But there is something ye must promise me." Shawna shot an including glance at Misty. "This trying to match me with your brother must stop. It can never happen. He's of the wealthy merchant class, and I'm but a poor servant girl."

"But—"

Shawna put a finger to Amy's lips. "There's more. I sympathize with the Patriots, and your family is loyal to the British."

"Not me. That's why we came down here."

"Who's with you?" Cooky asked, a frown adding more creases to her brow.

Caught, Amy glanced away. "No one. But, look!" She whipped a paper from the pocket of her blue striped play dress. "It's an order, telling Major Pitcairn to prepare his command for . . . evac-u-a-tion. It's a big word, but I sounded it out. Doesn't that mean he's leaving?"

Cooky took the document. "Does it say how many troops he has? Doesn't he lead a battalion of light infantry? They're the best trained and fastest." After scanning the lines, she looked up. "There's no mention, at all, of where they're being sent."

For a moment, Shawna forgot everything save the fact that both the small child *and* the cook had been taught to read. America truly was a land of opportunity.

"No mention at all?" Amy said as if reading were a natural-born gift. The child glanced up to Misty on the door ledge. "But we can find out quick enough."

"Oh, no, you won't," Shawna cried, regaining her senses. "You are to stop this dangerous snooping at once." Then she faced Cooky with resolve. "This child is not to be used to go against her family no matter how urgent the information is."

"I agree. Child or no, they might hang her for spying." Cooky took Amy by the arms. "Scoot yourself upstairs this minute and put that paper back exactly where you found it, right down to the way it was folded and turned. Now, get on with you," Turning the child toward the door, the older woman gave her a swat for good measure.

Before Amy reached the doorway, Misty Dawn flew away, up the dark passage. For once the imp had known better than to say a single word.

Shawna noted, too, the shimmering aura that always surrounded the fairy had disappeared *How odd*. Was she actually losing the vision of innocence she'd earlier threatened? Small wonder, considering the day this had been. Then the realization struck, swamping her in a great wave of sadness. She'd always known she might never see her wee folk of Shillelagh again. But now the certainty of it loomed before her. With a sigh, she started to follow after Amy to make sure the child did as she was told.

Cooky placed a staying hand on Shawna's shoulder. "I'd have a moment alone with you." Her roll of a face remained deadly serious. "Mr. Peterson overheard two of the officers talking about you when they were out in the stable saddling their horses."

She could easily imagine what Mr. Peterson had heard. Would this day never end?

"Watch that you don't let any of them catch you alone. Lock the door to your rooms at night. Ever since the war started, those lobsters have been treating our women like fair game, if you know what I mean. Particularly pretty housemaids with no man to stand up for them. In fact, child, you might reconsider taking up my Barney on his offer. He's a good honest lad, and he appeared real taken with you. You could do a lot worse."

It would seem Cooky, too, had seen the way he'd looked at her . . . and with almost as much promise as Jeff had. But well set-up as Barney Hanks was, Shawna had not felt a single tingle race through her, no leap of her heart. No magic. "I'll think on it," she said and turned to go, wishing desperately she understood all these new feelings.

If only Aunty Gwynedd had come to Philadelphia with her instead of Misty Dawn.

Chapter 7

∽

Life had been much simpler in Ireland, Shawna thought the next morning while making Amy's bed. Here everything was so much more . . . more everything. So much so, her head and heart were near to bursting with the plethora of confusing thoughts. Some quite painful. She picked up a pillow to fluff, but hugged it close instead. Then, catching herself, she quickly started shaking it. She didn't want Amy to question her behavior.

The child lay belly-down on a large braided rug, reading a newspaper to Misty who sat on her outstretched arm. To Shawna, the fairy seemed much fainter now than yesterday. She tried not to dwell on its portent.

"I would sometimes lie down," Amy read from the printed page, "and let five or six of them dance on my hand."

Five or six dance on my hand? Shawna tossed the pillow on the bed. "So 'tis true? There be fairies living in the New World?"

Amy looked up, bewildered for a moment, then tossing back her ringlets, she laughed. "No. I'm reading this week's installment of *Gulliver's Travels*. It's the story of a man who is shipwrecked in a land where there's nothing but wee folk. They're called Lilliputians."

"Lilliputians, ye say. Sure, it must be grand to simply

pick up a broadside and read all the wondrous things on it.''

Misty flew up and landed on the child's head. ''Amy has promised to teach me. Then 'twill be no end to what I can discover.'' A sudden glaringly guilty expression crossed her face, and she quickly added, ''Maybe then I'll find out where the American fairies are.'' Then she gazed off into space, and her voice became wistful. ''If there be any.''

Shawna found herself sympathizing when a stern reprimand was in order. She straightened. ''One thing I know for sure, if ye endanger this child again, I'll pluck your wings off.''

The sprite's lower lip jutted out in a pout, and she sailed off Amy's head and landed on a spot next to the child that was out of Shawna's view.

Amy's demeanor no less guilty, the child swiftly looked down at the newspaper and began reading aloud again.

Obviously, this spying game was much too tempting for them both. Turning away to pick up the other pillow, Shawna knew she'd have to keep a very close watch on those two.

''Hi, squirt,'' came an exceedingly male voice from the doorway.

Shawna's heart banged in her chest.

''Jeffrey!'' Amy squealed and sat up.

Turning, Shawna filled her eyes with the sight of him. He wore a simple collared shirt beneath a gold-trimmed navy waistcoat and breeches. It seemed there was no color or style that didn't look splendid on him.

He shot her a fleeting smile before plucking Amy to her feet. ''Missed you the last couple of days,'' he said to the child. ''I had too much business to take care of.''

His behavior yesterday came swiftly to the fore, and Shawna very nearly retorted, *Yes, redheaded business*. But then, he wasn't apologizing to her.

''So, to make amends,'' Jeffrey continued to Amy, ''I bought you a little present.''

In a whir, Misty flew to Amy's ear.

Amy's eyes brightened, and she grinned. "I bet I know what it is."

"How could you?" he said. "I just bought it yesterday afternoon."

"A locket. It's a locket. Is it as pretty as Shawna's?"

He frowned. "I hope you'll think so. *Have you been snooping in my room?*"

"No. Promise. I guess I'm just magic sometimes."

Jeffrey obviously wasn't satisfied with her answer as he withdrew a tiny box from his waistcoat pocket and offered it.

Greedily, she opened the container and pulled out the gift while letting the box fall to the rug. A heart-shaped locket dangled from her hand. "Oh, Jeff, it's prettier than anything Pris gets from her suitors."

"I'm pleased you like it, but I had more of a reason for choosing it. From now on, no matter how long we're apart, you'll always have my heart with you."

As he hugged her close, Shawna could see why the child adored him so. He was the only member of the family to come up here since Priscilla had stormed in looking for her ball gown. And Amy's father wasn't even in the Colonies.

Amy gave Jeffrey a quick kiss, then ran to Shawna, holding out the necklace. "Put it on me. Please."

As Shawna complied, she felt the heat of Jeffrey's gaze, causing her fingers to fumble with the clasp. When she'd finished, her eyes betrayed her again by meeting his.

"I have a token for you, too," he said, his voice as mellow as it was warm. "For deserting you yesterday."

Determined not to let him know the pain he'd caused her, she shrugged. " 'Twas of no consequence. I scarcely took notice."

"I did," he said in close to a whisper. Then his voice strengthened. "I know it didn't seem so, but I had urgent business with Ashton Carlisle that couldn't wait. Please." He pulled another small box from his pocket and taking her hand, he pressed it into her palm. "Accept this with my sincerest apology."

The touch of his hand cupping the back of hers . . . the velvet box, warm from being next to his body . . . His eyes . . .

"Open it!" Amy cried, rattling Shawna out of yet another fog.

Shawna took a breath and stepped back. Never in her life had she received a single present. Now, in a matter of weeks, she'd been given the dresses, the Shillelaugh locket, and, today, this gift of apology. How could she not forgive him? She lifted the jet velvet lid.

A cry caught in her throat. It was another emerald, much larger than the one in her locket, set in a filigreed band of gold . . . a ring as elegant as the rich ladies wore.

"I noticed you always wear your locket. I thought this might go nicely."

Her hand went to the pendant. " 'Twas a farewell gift from me dearest friends. I could never take it off."

He stepped close again. "I pray you'll feel the same about the ring."

The promise with which he beheld her confirmed the sincerity of his words. He spoke the truth. She sensed the strength of it. His lips drew her with equal force. Dare she kiss them as Amy had? Should she?

"Do it!" Misty shouted right into her ear. "Kiss him."

Another spell shattered. Hastily, Shawna returned her attention to the gift. "I—I don't know how to thank ye," she whispered. " 'Tis a fine ring. A thing of grand beauty."

She saw his chest expand and heard him sigh. "Well," he said, turning away. "I'd better get downstairs. With Father gone, I have to go to the warehouse early every morning."

"Ha!" Misty exclaimed as soon as Jeffrey left the room. She soared up to the floral chintz valance. "Now I'll be expecting your apology and gratitude. That ring proves his undying love for ye."

"His love?"

"That's right!" Amy started twirling around the room,
her petticoats chasing after her. "A ring has no beginning
and no end. It's forever."

Shawna felt as if she were floating on her own glowing
pink cloud the rest of the day in spite of the fact that Miss
Priscilla cast suspicious glances at the ring all the while
Shawna prepared her toilet and helped her into her afternoon attire. And every time Shawna walked into the kitchen
she barely heard Cooky bragging on her nephew. Her spirit
couldn't be daunted, either, by the necessity to check every
hall and stairwell for the redcoats until the last devil had
left around noon.

Tomorrow was soon enough to face the hard realities of
being a servant in a Tory household . . . and the reality of
Jeffrey's fickle nature. For this one day, at least, she was
determined to revel only in the glory of the *forever* gift.

Walking the length of the second-floor hall, Shawna
paused at the center and let the glow from the glass dome
reflect off the emerald stone. She turned her hand this way
and that, so each facet could catch the late afternoon light.
Before continuing on to the kitchen stairs, she smoothed
her finger across the gem as she had so many times today,
polishing it, making sure she wasn't dreaming.

Passing Major Pitcairn's room, she noticed the door was
slightly ajar. Had he returned home? What about the other
officers? Tension gripped her. She'd been too preoccupied.
Glancing around, she listened for male voices.

Instead, only small high whispers came from the narrow
opening. *Amy and Misty Dawn.*

That Misty was at it again. If her own neck wasn't in
jeopardy, she cared not a whit about the danger into which
she'd placed young Amy's. Nothing mattered to that fairy
as long as she, herself, was having a gay old time.

Shawna shoved wide the door and marched into what
turned out to be the officer's study. Her nose flared at the

stench of stale tobacco as she looked about. Heavy velvet drapes covered the window, making even more dreary the furnishings and Oriental rug, so reminiscent of Drayton Manor. For certain, the decor had not been pink-loving Mistress Radcliff's choice.

But where were Amy and Misty? Had she been wrong? *Not bloody likely.*

Shawna moved past two upholstered arm chairs and on around the desk. Several drawers had been pulled out. Papers scattered on the floor. And inside the leg well, huddled Amy, her hooped skirts bunched close to her.

"Hi, Shawna," she squeaked.

"Get yourself up from there this instant." Shawna took Amy's arm and pulled her to her feet.

Standing before Shawna, the child clutched several sheets of paper. The incriminating evidence. But where was the instigator?

Shawna searched the upper half of the room, the top of the curtains, the wall sconces, to no avail. She turned back to the child. "Where's Misty? I know ye didn't come in here on your own."

Amy's eyes and mouth became three round holes in her face. But she said nothing.

Then her ringlets stirred slightly.

Shawna flipped back Amy's locks, and lo and behold, there cowered the culprit.

The instant Misty knew she was caught, she sprang to her feet. "Ye can say anything ye want. But we found exactly what Cooky needed to know. And we were just about to put everything back. *Until ye came charging in.*"

Shawna spread her hand to encompass the over-flowing drawers. "Do ye really think ye can set this mess to rights again? Major Pitcairn is no fool. He'll know someone has been in here rifling through his things." She took the papers from Amy. "Where did ye get these?"

"*From the bottom drawer on the right.*" The words came in clipped authoritarian tones.

The major loomed in the doorway.

Chapter 8

∞

 $\mathcal{M}$ ajor Pitcairn strode into the room, his gloves making a sharp sound as he slapped them against his leg. His gaze, lethal as any weapon, missed nothing . . . except that miserable coward of a fairy escaping out the door.

He stopped in front of Shawna, his body taut with rage. A vein stood out at his temple.

Shawna fought the urge to shrink back. But for Amy she had to be brave. And clever.

He ripped the papers from her hand. "What have we here?"

Amy clung to the back of Shawna's skirt, cowering from the fierce presence.

" 'Tis not what you think, sir," Shawna said, hoping to come up with an inspired explanation.

"And who are you to presume to know what I'm thinking? From the expensive cut of those clothes you're wearing, it's obvious you're nothing but thieving Irish trash." He snatched her wrist. "And from whom did you steal this?"

She jerked free. "The ring was a gift, sir. Never in me born days have I stolen a thing."

He wheeled past her and grabbed Amy's arm. "A pity this one can't say the same."

The child gasped and flung up an arm to block any forthcoming blows as he dragged her from behind Shawna.

"Release her at once," Shawna railed. "Or I'll call for her mother."

"You will, will you?" Her threat did not faze him. "By all means. I relish the opportunity to have a word with the silly pink froth." He glowered down at Amy. "She's allowed this ragamuffin to run amuck ever since I moved in here. And now that the child's schooling has stopped for the summer, the situation has become unbearable. But this time the little heathen has gone too far."

"Aye, I've seen how true that is, meself," Shawna said, hoping to pacify him. "But Amy is not to blame. A lamb is not at fault for wandering if the gate is left open."

"So they would have me believe. But there's much more to this than a bit of idle peeping. Isn't there, child?" He picked up Amy and thrust her into one of the arm chairs. "Who are you spying for? Who told you to pillage my desk? What do they want to know?"

Shawna moved to stand behind the chair. She placed protecting hands on Amy's shoulders. "Surely you're not saying anyone would tell a mere child to spy on you. No one would do such a thing."

"Leave the room, wench. You just landed here. You know nothing of what we're faced with in these godforsaken colonies."

"Tell him, Amy." Shawna squeezed the trembling child's shoulders. "Tell him you were merely looking for different colors of paper to make your fans."

"I said, get out. I will have some answers from this urchin." His red-faced menace left no room for contention.

But she couldn't abandon the child. She ignored her racing heart. "I will not leave Amy to the mercy of your dragon's fire. Not even for the time 'twould take to fetch her mother."

His eyes of dull iron flared wide, then narrowed. He raised his hand against her.

Shawna braced for the strike.

"*Pitcairn.*" Jeffrey stood in the doorway, his own expression no less dark and fearsome.

Turning on his heel, Pitcairn inflated his chest. "I am fully within my rights. Someone has set your sister to spying on me. I *will* have the name of that person."

"That's preposterous." Jeffrey strode into the room and confronted the major. "Amy rarely leaves the grounds. Therefore, if you accuse her, you accuse a household that out of loyalty to the Crown rid itself of rebel sympathizers months ago. And, I might add, a household that sees to your every comfort. I resent these charges almost as much as I resent your terrorizing my baby sister." He switched his attention to Amy. "Squirt, go on up to your room. I'll be there in a few minutes. It's time you and I had a serious talk."

Amy, white with fear, bolted from the chair and out the door as if she'd been catapulted.

"You, too, Shawna. I would have a private word with Major Pitcairn."

Relieved to be dismissed, herself, yet concerned by the violence in the men's expressions, Shawna started for the door. The realization that Jeffrey could be as dangerous a force as this hardened officer was shocking. As she passed, she silently begged Jeffrey to be cautious. She prayed he could see her fear for him.

But he gave no indication as he followed her to the door and, grim-faced, closed her out.

Something terrible was about to happen, she knew that as surely as she knew she could not leave them to it. She knelt and pressed her ear against the keyhole.

"There are only two ways this can be resolved." Jeffrey's voice came through only slightly muffled. "Either you admit that Amy was merely up to some childish prank—for which I intend to deal with her forthwith. Or we'll take this insane accusation of yours to the field of honor. I will not have you besmirch my family's good name with such treasonous slander."

A duel! Jeffrey was challenging him to a duel!

"You are a fool if you think you can trust your servants."

A gaping silence followed.

"Regardless of what you think"—Jeffrey's voice was tight, measured—"the choice is still yours."

Shawna knew the major was too proud to back down. She charged into the room. "Sir."

Simultaneously, the men swung toward her. "*Yes*?" both grated, venting their rage on that one word.

She had to say something. "Mr. Radcliff, your mother . . . Amy. Your mother said to come at once. Amy is hysterical, and she can't handle her."

Jeffrey's expression softened for but a second.

"*At once*," she repeated. "Amy's nose is bleeding buckets."

Jeffrey turned back to Pitcairn. "We'll finish this later." And there was no doubt he meant it.

The major gave no ground. He still stood ready to strike. Then he exhaled a long slow breath. "Go to your sister. I'll let it pass. This one last time."

Jeffrey didn't appear satisfied. "There will be no further talk of this. To anyone." It was a demand, not a question.

Pitcairn waved him off. "This time."

Shawna's relief was beyond measure as she followed Jeffrey out of the major's room.

Jeffrey's face was still dark with anger. "Where are they?" he asked, his voice harsh.

"Uh . . . up in the nursery?" She lengthened her stride to keep pace as they traversed the distance of the hall.

He took the stairs two at a time.

Lifting her skirts, she did the same, her chest knotting. How could Amy's spying ever be explained away?

At the top, Shawna placed a hand on his arm. "Don't be too hard on her. You know how children are. The more I warned her against it, the more adventurous spying seemed to be."

He halted. "*She actually was spying?* The devil be damned!" He glanced back down the hallway. "Had I known . . ."

"Would ye have acted any different?"

He exhaled. "I reckon not. *But you.* You knew, yet didn't tell me." Wheeling away, he strode through Amy's door.

Across the room next to her bed, Amy was stuffing her night rail and a green-checked dress into a valise. Seeing them, she worked all the faster.

Jeffrey swung back to Shawna. "You said she was in hysterics."

" 'Twas all I could think to say."

"I see. To get me out before I learned the whole truth."

"Nay, to prevent a duel."

His jaw muscles bunched.

Nothing she said helped one whit.

He returned his attention to Amy. "And where do you think you're going, young lady?"

"I—I'm leaving before Major Pitcairn fetches the hangman."

"We don't hang children in this colony. Yet."

"Then he'll surely have me put in chains."

The tension left Jeffrey's shoulders. "Don't you know your big brother will always protect you, no matter what?"

"You will?" That look of worshipping wonder returned. Amy turned from the bed. But instead of going to him, she ran to her marble-topped commode and grabbed her brush and a handful of ribbons, then sped back to her valise.

"If you believe me, why are you still packing?"

"Because I'm a Patriot, and I have to go find General Washington. This is much too important to trust to others."

Jeffrey plucked her up and sat down with her. "Stop being such a whirligig and tell me what in heaven's name you're talking about."

The little girl stared up at him with searching eyes. "Can I really trust you? Really, truly?"

He placed a hand over his heart. "Really, truly."

She looked away, toward the window valance.

Shawna did the same, but Misty wasn't there. In fact, where was the miserable schemer?

"The whole British army is leaving Philadelphia on June 18th and marching back to New York."

Jeffrey's mouth dropped open. "The entire force? That's only ten days from now."

"Aye. I counted." Amy slid off his lap and shoved her brush down the side of her valise. "So you see, I have to hurry."

"I can't believe General Clinton could be so callous." Jeffrey shook his head, still stunned. "Abandoning the city without notice?"

"That's lobsterbacks for you." Amy swung away from the bed again.

Jeffrey caught her as she passed and held her in front of him. "Are you certain this is true?"

"You know what a good reader I am. The word on the paper said, evacuate, and I know what that means."

"Yes," he said scarcely above a whisper. "It will be Boston all over again. The Loyalists forced to ship out with scarcely more than their lives." He pulled Amy close. "I've got to get you and the family out of here with as much of our property as possible. Before the panic starts, *and* before there's a run on the counting houses."

Amy's whole face puckered with determination. "You're not listening to me, Jeffrey. My country is depending on me. I have to go find the Continental Army. Now."

This time the ridiculousness of her statement struck Jeffrey funny. His mouth slid into a lopsided grin. "And just how do you propose to do that?"

"Don't you worry, I'll have all the help I need."

Shawna had no doubt whose help. She searched again for Misty. She had some wings to pluck.

"I'm sorry, squirt." Jeffrey pulled her close in a hug. "The *Bristol Lady* is sailing tomorrow on the evening tide, and you have to be on it. Father would never forgive me if I didn't seize the moment.''

Amy wrenched away. ''I will not be stopped. Just like Mr. Franklin's postal service, *this message shall be delivered.*''

Lines creased Jeffrey's brow. ''You're being very stubborn about this.''

Amy stepped back, out of his reach and thrust her fist high into the air. ''I only regret I have but one life to lose for my country.''

There was no doubting Jeffrey's amusement this time. All his teeth flashed and his dimples dug deep. ''I see you've been given lessons in more than reading and sums. But I'll make a deal with you. If you board the ship tomorrow night without breathing another word of what you know to anyone, I will personally take the message to Washington for you.''

Astounded by his words, Shawna stared, mute.

Amy, however, was not the least fooled. ''I'm not some five-year-old baby, you know.''

Jeffrey now held her in a steady gaze. ''Have I ever lied to you? I give you my solemn word.''

''Your word's not good enough this time. I hear the bad things you say to your friends about the rebels.'' Abruptly, Amy turned and looked at her shoulder as if she were listening to someone else.

Misty Dawn must be there. Yet Shawna couldn't see her. *Had Shawna fully lost the vision of innocence? Was it really gone?*

Amy turned back to Jeffrey. ''We agree to go on the ship across the great sea *if* Shawna goes with you to tell General Washington.''

Invisible or not, the chit of a fairy never gave up. Danger at every turn, and Misty Dawn was still trying to be a matchmaker.

Before Shawna found her tongue to protest, Amy continued. ''You see, when Shawna gives her word, she never goes back on it, no matter what. Misty says she doesn't even know how to lie."

That was no longer true—she'd just lied to stop the duel.

"Misty? Who's Misty?"

Shawna closed her eyes against Jeffrey's question and Amy's next words. If the child started talking fairies, no explanation would suffice.

"Misty is someone who came on the ship to America with Shawna. She knows her better than any of us do."

Vastly relieved, Shawna raised her lashes and started to breathe again . . . until she found Jeffrey glowering at her.

"It's a deal," he said, his anger reviving full force. "I'd be most interested in having a nice long talk with Miss O'Shea. But first things first."

Chapter 9

∞

It took very little persuasion from Jeffrey to have his family packed and on the docks by the next evening. When Mistress Radcliff heard the dire news, she'd been most anxious to set sail for London and her husband before the rest of Philadelphia's Loyalists learned of General Clinton's plan and pandemonium set in.

Shawna stood on the pier alongside the *Bristol Lady* on that balmy night, amazed so many details had been managed without a single soldier in the house becoming any the wiser. Despite the servants' differing politics, they truly were like family.

Jeffrey had insisted that Shawna accompany him to see the Radcliffs off, and, from the look of him, she knew it wasn't for reasons of companionship. Out of the corner of her eye, she watched as he stood in the glow of a lantern, wrapped in his chiffon-swathed mother's embrace while a teary Amy clung to his arm.

Miss Priscilla, thrilled by the prospect of a season in London, had blithely boarded the vessel accompanied by an attentive ship's officer. She strolled with him toward the stern.

In the distance, Shawna heard a bell tolling the hour. A lonely sound, considering it was time for the departure of dear little Amy . . . to be closely followed by the reckoning

Jeffrey had waiting for her. Her gaze returned to the threesome as the gongs echoed across the Delaware River.

"I simply hate that we're not going together," she heard Mistress Radcliff say in her cultured voice.

"As I've explained, when the panic starts, it will be much easier to book passage for one than four. And there are still so many details left undone. With you safely on your way, I'll arrange tomorrow to have the furniture crated and shipped."

"I know, I know," she said, looking up at her son with a sad smile. "Oh, that reminds me." Mistress Radcliff stepped away from Jeffrey and came toward Shawna.

As she did, he slipped a note to Amy and gave her an enormous hug, then whispered something in her ear.

Reaching Shawna, Mistress Radcliff pressed a coin into her own hand. "You've been such a big help today. I wanted to reward you. Are you positive you don't wish to return with us to where it's safe?"

Shawna bobbed into a curtsy. "I couldn't be surer, ma'am. The agreement was for me to serve here, in America, in exchange for me passage."

"Then I'll leave you to help Mr. Peterson and Cooky to pack up the rest of our things."

"Last call to board," the purser announced from above.

Shawna stepped back to allow Mistress Radcliff's wide skirts to sweep past.

Then Amy hurled herself into Shawna's arms, her eyes red-rimmed, her cheeks wet. The child clung fiercely for several seconds before reaching up and pulling Shawna's face close. She whispered a fast stream. "Misty is going with me, and she knows you can't see her anymore."

Shawna's anger flared—to lose her vision when the sprite needed a good thumping. Some fairies had all the luck.

Just as quickly, her ire was engulfed by sadness. With that loss went her lifelong friends, as well as so much of herself.

"Misty wants me to tell you something more," Amy said, wiping an eye. "She says she's learned her lesson this time. From now on she promises to take very good care of me."

Shawna swallowed hard. "Ye tell Misty that—that I love her. But I'd better not hear of any more mischief, or Aunty Gwynedd will be told about it, if I have to go all the way back to Ireland, meself." Her threat rang hollow, for soon even her memory of the fairies would fade as surely as gloaming into night.

"What's this about more mischief?" Jeffrey had moved directly behind Shawna.

Amy spun away and fled up the gangplank, waving wildly as she ran. "Farewell. Farewell."

"Godspeed." Shawna waved back, lonesome already for the tyke . . . And for her wee folk. Even Misty Dawn. Her eyes began to blur as dockworkers unlooped the ship's moorings and tossed the ropes aboard. The workmen then walked off the pier, leaving only Shawna and Jeffrey to watch the Radcliffs' departure.

Silently, the *Bristol Lady* slipped away, moving with the current, a current that would take the ship to the river's mouth and out to the great sea. The vessel's lanterns flickered across the black waters, and soon the threesome waving from the stern were lost in the darkness.

Yet Shawna and Jeffrey continued to wave until the last dots of light disappeared around the bend.

Then she felt his hand at her elbow.

He gripped firmly. "Come along. We have some traveling to do of our own tonight."

She sought his face in the glow of the nearest pier lantern. "Then ye *are* going to keep your word to Amy."

"Of course. I wouldn't lie to her. Not about something so serious. But I can't tell you how disappointed I am in you. To endanger my sister with your silence."

"That I did. I can't deny it. So there's nothing for me but to come out with the whole truth." She took a fortifying breath. "The one who led Amy down that dangerous path is still with her."

Jeffrey's gaze shot to where the ship had disappeared behind the bend.

" 'Tis the one she spoke of. Misty Dawn. She's aboard with Amy. The willful chit has promised to be good from now on, but—"

"That's impossible. My family were the only passengers."

"Aye, one might be thinking that. I hesitate to tell ye what I'm about to, because I've never been believed before. But Misty is one of Ireland's wee folk. A fairy."

"Miss O'Shea, this is no time for fairy tales."

"Please, I beg ye. Remember the day I arrived, and Amy was calling for ye to catch the flying creature. That was Misty Dawn. Amy was the only one in your house who could see her. The only one with the vision of innocence."

Shawna saw the same disdain in his expression that she'd seen after her previous tellings. Defeated, she turned away. "I'll have me things packed within the hour. Ye needn't bother going to this Washington fellow. Just point me in the right direction."

His hand clasped her shoulder. "Wait. There's something I must tell you. When Major Pitcairn was interrogating you and Amy, I was nowhere near enough to hear what was happening. But I had a very clear, very distinct sense that you were in danger in his room. It was as if this tiny voice was right in my ear. And as unbelievable as it seemed, I knew I couldn't ignore it. I even thought it might be Amy's guardian angel. My busy little squirt certainly needs one."

"Misty didn't just fly away like the coward I took her for? She came to ye, made ye hear her wee little voice?" Shawna glanced downriver. "Mayhaps she *has* learned the dangers of playing such reckless games." With a tender smile she recalled the imp's myriad expressions and poses, and that last look of horror when she'd been caught. "I'm sure she'll keep our Amy safe now."

Jeffrey took Shawna's hand, then, and ran his thumb over the emerald ring. "And I believe my baby sister was right about you all along. So was I . . . from that first moment I looked into your incredibly pure, incredibly guileless eyes."

Turning from the lamplight, Shawna avoided his gaze. "That's not completely true. I've more to confess. 'Tis not merely Amy who sympathizes with the freedom fighters. I, too, believe in their cause."

Jeffrey didn't so much as blink at her confession. Instead, he untied her bonnet and let it fall away. "Do you realize, for someone who accepted my ring, I've never seen your hair unbound."

Had it been a *forever* ring for him, too?

Her wonderment soon faded, for Shawna could think of nothing, nothing save his touch, the feel of his fingers removing one pin after another, of the weight of her hair falling to her waist. Of him filling his hands with great handfuls, then brushing the strays from her brow.

"I knew your hair would feel this silken. It's as black and shiny as a China girl's. And with those transparent eyes . . . Do you have any idea," he whispered. "No, I see you don't." Lifting her face with gentle fingers, he feathered a kiss on one of her eyelids, then the other.

Shawna had no breath left as she raised her lashes and saw in his loving gaze that same promise . . . *That same promise she'd seen when he'd looked at all those other women.*

"*No.*" She thrust him away. " 'Tis not the same innocent fool ye'll find as when I first arrived. Ye'll not trick me into thinking ye care again, just to cast me aside when one of your lady friends happens by."

He blinked and lowered his hands to her shoulders. "Yes, I'd been wanting to explain that. Now that the British are leaving, I can. You see, I have a confession of my own to make." He took her hands. "I didn't agree to take the message to Washington merely for Amy's sake. I am an agent for the Patriots. A professional spy. It's been my duty to ferret out information any way I could—including being charming to the ladies, if that's what's needed."

"But there were so many. And all so beautiful."

"Beauty is so much more than glittering clothes and fancy wigs, my darling, my innocent. Lasting beauty comes from within. Beauty knows when a little girl is lonely . . . and cares. It's faithful and brave . . . Beauty is what I see whenever you look at me with love in your eyes. But I've seen the pain there, too." His hand smoothed along the side of her cheek. "It was rude of me not to introduce you to the people on the street the other day. But I hated the way Ashton looked at you. He has a shabby reputation, especially where pretty young servant girls are concerned. Still, sending you away so callously, just so I could glean some information from them, was the hardest thing I've ever done." He raised one of her hands and pressed it to his chest. "The hurt in your eyes pierced my heart."

He had known . . . and cared. Her pain had been his. Shawna lifted her gaze. "Me own heart has been acting fiercely strange since I met ye." She took his other hand and held it flush to her breast. "See how it pounds." Even as she said the words, she felt his breath catch, and no doubt remained. He loved her as truly as she loved him.

Jeffrey's eyes darkened, and he caught her to him, so close she didn't know whose drumming pulse was whose. He lowered his head until their shallow breaths mingled one into the other. Then his mouth claimed hers. Urgently. Careening across in a passion so swift, it was as frightening as it was thrilling.

She felt his hands in her hair again, and on her face, roving . . . his thumbs tracing her temples, her closed lids. All the while his lips, his teeth, his tongue did such wonderous, exciting things, her heart truly would burst if he didn't stop soon.

Much too soon, he did stop. He broke away from the kiss, his breathing as harsh and ragged as her own. Then slowly he began to explore her face with eyes that had become midnight dark yet warm as noon.

She discovered her own hands around his neck, her fingers woven among his curls. And her legs, weak as water.

''Shawna O'Shea,'' he rasped on a longspun whisper. ''My fairy-tale love.''

Then, with a deep groan he stepped back and held her at arm's length. ''Tonight there's a message to be delivered, and I'll be going to join the fighting soon. So I know this is crazy, but, Shawna O'Shea of Shillelaugh Glen, before another hour passes you've got to marry me.''

Her heart contracted at his look of desperation. But his words . . . ''I—I—''

''It could be done. I know a judge who, for a small price, would have the banns waved.''

She touched his cheek. ''I don't know about that.''

His breathing stopped. He froze, his grip tightening on her arms.

She stared directly into his eyes. ''An hour. That's a fearsome long time.''

Fairy Dreams

Marylyle Rogers

Chapter 1

∞

"*I* beseech Thee, Heavenly Father, send Thy humble child deliverance from this brutal storm." The desperate prayer rose on gasps of breath visible in frigid air while Maevis struggled upward despite impeding drifts of white. "Elsewise this freezing cold will see me dead."

Surely, Mae reasoned, Sister Heccabah's lonely passing was contrition enough for the folly of a poorly timed pilgrimage to the shrine of St. Finnian. . . .

Guilt struck.

As an acolyte in the Abbey of St. Hilda's Heart since childhood, Mae knew well the sin in questioning God's will and promptly added penitent words to her forlorn plea for divine intervention.

"As Thou wills it in this as in all things."

Lifting legs so unnaturally heavy they must have become unwieldy blocks of pure ice, Mae at last reached the crest of a hill she'd been climbing for what seemed an eternity. From here Mae had earnestly hoped to glimpse some sign of human habitation, some promise of haven. But, despite sunshine unexpectedly breaking through dark clouds to turn the snowy countryside's soft blanket into a shimmer of blinding light, the view brought only bitter disappointment.

Mae had expended a final burst of desperate energy to reach this high point. Now, thoroughly disheartened, she sagged against a sturdy tree growing from the hilltop's center. Clearly rescue was not to be the answer to her prayer. Rather, bleak reality would see her earthly time cease amid the harsh, white beauty of this land in which she was a stranger.

Mae cast her Reverend Mother a rueful thought. St. Hilda's abbess would've been gladdened to learn that at last a solemn matter had succeeded in dampening Maevis's shameful yet irrepressible humor. But, no, Mae found the image of the abbess's relief amusing, and despite this wretched cold could feel chapped lips curling into a faint grin.

Lacking strength to press onward, Mae sank down atop the frigid pillow of snow piled up beneath a winter-bare oak's limited shield. Her nose, fingers, and toes were numb but still she courageously fought to keep her lashes from closing in the final sleep that would end a life two years short of a full score.

Then, even while struggling to defy the seductive call of a deadly weariness, Mae visually stumbled over a wondrous sight . . . flowers reaching upward to bloom despite the weight of winter's icy blanket.

Mae concentrated on the unbelievable circle of flowers. They were a miracle. Yes, a blessed miracle of hope.

Slowly, so slowly Mae initially thought it a further sign of fast-fading life, her vision of the amazing blossoms blurred as they were enveloped by a moonglow brightness far different than the blinding glare of sunlight on snow. Blinking against this inexplicable brilliance, Mae's changeable hazel eyes went all to deep brown as she gradually focused on the stunning, golden man at its core.

"Are you an angel?" Mae asked in awe as the powerful figure reached out to lift her. "Have you come to carry me to my eternal rest?"

Although a faint, enigmatic smile was his only response, Mae found confirmation in her certainty that there could be no other explanation for a being so incredible. Prayers thus answered, she relaxed into the circle of strong arms and surrendered her battle to keep her hazel eyes open.

"You brought a *human* here . . . a human *female*?" Setting scarlet robes rippling like a flag of emphasis, the speaker motioned toward the unconscious creature whose delicate form left but a gentle outline beneath the wide bed's silken covers.

In response to words more a hiss of disapproval than simple whisper, the mockery behind Gair's wry smile deepened. Ardagh hadn't arrived by invitation. Yet, despite their race's distaste for predictability, Gair had expected this ever disapproving elder to appear—he always did at the very moment when least welcome.

"Permit me to rid you of her company's taint." Even the most earnest of Ardagh's smiles failed to hide his insincerity.

Hair the shade of sunlight reflected through honey rippled as Gair shook his head. "I didn't carry this near-frozen creature here only to see you return her to a peril none among her kind could survive."

"Then you share your older sister's weakness for humankind?" Ardagh made no attempt to shield his disdain as he flicked dismissive fingertips toward surrounding walls. "Or is it some malady spread by the air in this isolated abode?"

"Lissan was not ill, nor was love for Killian, her human mate, proof of weakness but rather of a strength lent by their bond."

"Hah! So, to honor your elder sister you not only live in the hill-home she abandoned along with her powers but also follow her example in rescuing another pitiful mortal best left to die?" The angle of oddly winged brows slanted more deeply with the scowl Ardagh focused on the damsel laying unaware of the restrained yet fierce conflict being waged over her safety. "You turn your back on the Tuatha de Danann to whom you owe loyalty and tend not merely any mortal but a female devoted to service of the long-dead Patrick's single God."

Though rarely surprised, emerald eyes widened as Gair wondered by what arcane trickery Ardagh had come to know something so specific about this member of a race despised.

Gair discounted his unwelcome visitor's implication that an intentional slight of their kind had been intended by the rescue of this damsel. They both knew how unlikely *he* was to have planned any deed with a potential for harming his brother. In truth, by the mercurial nature of fairy, few of their kind would waste time laying advance plans to accomplish any purpose.

Reading in Gair's expression the unspoken question for the source of his knowledge, Ardagh sneered, "The style of her odd garb is unique to women of that faith's calling."

Gair's reaction to Ardagh's contempt was a bright grin. Despite the intervening passage of human centuries, this poor being had yet to accept revered Queen Aine's decision to leave control of the Faerie Realm to a lesser branch of her distinguished family tree. Ardagh had devoted vast periods of his life to Queen Aine's service for the sake of proving himself worthy of that honor, and still deemed himself betrayed by her naming as heir Gair's older brother Comlan.

The next instant another issue drove every hint of emotion from Gair's face. How could Ardagh possibly know anything about this frail human's clothing? Gair had rid the damsel of a pair of satchels and the whole of her cold, sodden garb in the same moment that he'd whisked her into the privacy of his hill-home. And, *before* Ardagh's arrival, with warm blankets he'd covered the complete length of her shivering form save for a piquant face framed by masses of brilliant red hair.

"If you leave coarse cloth moldering on the floor, your guest will have naught of her own to don when she awakes." Much older and more experienced in sensing the thoughts of others, Ardagh took delight in exposing what the other would have to accept as an error in his silent reasoning.

Gair's attention followed Ardagh's gaze to drenched garments cast into an untidy heap at the foot of the bed. Yet rather than a rueful grimace, he gave a broad grin. "I'm sure I can deal with that challenge . . . and handle it better *alone*."

"No doubt," Ardagh hissed. "But now while the petty wars of these mortals begin to boil anew with long simmering hatreds, beware. . . . Humans are ever imbibing of a deadly brew and their bites inevitably hold the poison of adders."

The unwelcome guest disappeared just as it flashed across Gair's mind that no human venom could be as lethal as Ardagh's own. Acknowledging that fact led Gair to question the visit's odd timing as he turned to glance down and meet solemn eyes no longer probing brown but a soft and grateful moss-green.

Although Mae had feigned an unnatural sleep, she'd overheard much but understood depressingly little of the conversation filled with ominous undertones. Bewildered by contemptuous references to humankind and mortals, she'd been left with another inescapable revelation: Despite the incredible beauty of both, neither was this place heaven nor was her rescuer the divine being that he had at first appeared.

Confused and struggling to make sense of the irrational sights and sounds enveloping her, Mae had stolen glimpses of her unspeakably beautiful rescuer's gaunt, narrow-faced opponent. The discovery that beneath abundant hair more silver than gold, he looked less an angel than a bright demon with winged brows, long nose, and sharp chin had sent her attention fleeing back to the one who held it still.

"Don't take Ardagh's unpleasant words to heart." Gair's emerald eyes sparkled with warm humor. "I've been their target for more time than you could possibly conceive and yet have survived unscathed . . . as I promise you will."

Although completely irrational, Mae found herself reassured by this deep voice containing tones of gentle thunder.

"Where . . ." Mae embarked on a surely rational question while sitting up—only to abruptly drop back and jerk an unbelievably soft coverlet tight to her chin.

She was nude, as completely bare as on the day of her birth! This fact was terrifying to a female who had never before in her life been alone with a man. It left Mae feeling vulnerable and utterly mortified with this stranger so close.

"You were nearly blue with cold when I brought you here." Gair calmly announced, practicing wise restraint in not sharing with this amazingly shy rabbit how beautiful he'd found her lovely body despite its chill. Though well acquainted with intimate charms belonging to the willowy females of his own race, Gair had never before encountered curves as generous and warmly hued.

"I meant you no disrespect but in order to see your health restored, it was necessary to rid you of sodden clothing."

His arguments made perfect sense, yet Mae clenched hazel eyes shut while her cheeks burned ruby-bright. Unfortunately, even the truth that his actions were logical could in no way lessen her embarrassment. Mae's head, like a shy butterfly returning to its cocoon, was soon completely hidden beneath the coverlet, save for the few fiery ringlets that escaped to trail across pale sheets.

Golden head tilted to one side, Gair studied the curious sight created by the clearly embarrassed human. In his world such extremes of modesty were unknown—a fact which left him to fear she found some lack in his hospitality.

"Do you find this abode unpleasant?" Gair questioned his guest, although it was most improbable. And, yet, he knew so little of humankind. . . . "Are you still cold? Or too warm? Is the bed too firm for your liking? Perhaps you simply find my company objectionable?"

"Oh, no—" The hasty response was a squeak muffled by the luxurious bedclothes which dainty fingers tightly clutched over a head of bright, unruly hair.

Mae's rescuer had plainly misunderstood her awkwardness in the face of too many new and difficult situations. And yet being a pigeonheart was one sin for which Reverend Mother never had reason to find fault in her. She must refuse to fall faint now when that courage was most needed.

Moreover, proud of being honest in all things, it was necessary to rectify an erroneous impression. And it would be wrong to let him think she found anything here worthy of less than the highest praise. She'd learned that truth by her few glimpses of this chamber's unearthly beauty (a just background for her devastating host who, despite her inexperience in such matters, even she realized was a model of superb masculinity).

Mae went still, barely breathing while seeking the perfect words to fulfill the deed. Then, before she could speak, her companion did.

"Surely by rescuing you from an icy fate I've proven that I would not harm you, nor allow your ill-treatment at the hands of another?" Gair focused an unwavering emerald stare on the motionless figure. Unfamiliarity with her kind was playing havoc with his rarely shaken poise. "After giving my oath that you'll be safe in my company, I must ask if I am so hideous, so fearsome that you can't bear to look upon me?

"You're beautiful!" Startled by his misconception, the words flew from Mae's lips as she sat bolt upright, coverlet instinctively clasped to her breasts and sparks of irrepressible laughter dancing in the depths of her eyes.

As one among a host of exceptional beings, Gair had never before been gifted with such honest praise and it immediately healed the breach in his confidence. He responded with a slow smile of devastating potency while claiming one of Mae's hands to brush a whisper-light kiss across its back.

Despite shyly averted eyes, a quick grin of delight put dimples in Mae's cheeks.

Anxious to see the unexpected beauty at ease in his company, Gair busied himself fetching and serving her a light repast. It included fine wheaten bread, honey-butter, and fresh berries whose amazing presence on a winter's day Mae didn't think to question until much later.

While Mae nibbled, Gair settled on an oddly shaped stool drawn near to the bed. Seeking to engage his bright-spirited visitor in light conversation, he posed a question about the only subject they seemed to have in common.

"How is it that you came to rest in the center of my sister's fairy ring on a day and during a season so unwelcoming?"

"Not by my choice." Sensitive about the folly of its poor timing since the ill-fated journey's outset, Mae completely missed Gair's reference to an unfamiliar term—fairy ring.

"Truly—" To smooth over the unfortunate brusqueness of her answer, Mae hastily explained. "The Reverend Mother of St. Hilda's Abbey in Northumbria assigned me to accompany elderly Sister Heccabah on a pilgrimage to the Shrine of St. Finnian."

"Pilgrimage?" Although Gair knew little enough about the Christian religion, the meaning of this term he had learned. " 'Tis a very poor time of year to embark on a travels of any sort."

"Reverend Mother Edwina warned us of the dangers." Mae nodded. "But because Sister Heccabah's days were rapidly dwindling, she gave her blessing and chose me (the abbey's youngest and, yet unconsecrated, the least likely to be missed) to guard and tend its eldest on a final mission."

From early in his life, Gair had chosen to learn little about either the religion foretold to bring an end to the De

Danann's days in the mortal world or its practitioners. Now he regretted the lack of such knowledge.

"How long have you lived in the abbey?" Gair asked, trying to understand.

"Near as long as I can remember." Mae's shoulders lifted in a slight, uneasy shrug. "Though I have vague recollections of my mother and, I think, several brothers."

A slight frown drew Gair's bronze brows together. "Then you were not raised by your own kindred?" To one of his background this was an utterly foreign and most unpleasant concept.

Her host's disapproval was clear and something with which Mae agreed. Still, she found herself defending the path taken by a mother and father all but unknown. " 'Tis the custom for parents to contribute a tithe of their children to God's service."

"You were given to the abbey?" Gair mused aloud before shifting a penetrating emerald gaze back to the flame-haired woman. "Is this a common practice?" Not waiting for an answer, he said, "I hope that leastways there were other young ones present to share childhood joys."

"Nay." Memories of past unhappiness momentarily clouded Mae's ever-cheery expression. "I was the last thus given to be accepted by St. Hilda's Abbey."

Watching Mae struggle to replace bleak thoughts with a determined smile, Gair wielded a fine blend of sympathy and laughter to calm a guest still absently clutching the coverlet to preserve modesty.

Also by virtue of such subtle tactics Gair soon recognized the generosity of spirit radiating from the lovely damsel and realized that Mae's innate beauty was as bright as the vivid hair unmatched even in his shining realm. All in all, Mae was revealed as that rarest of humans worthy of trust, admiration . . . and his promised protection. Toward that goal, there were actions to be taken.

"I beg you to pardon me," Gair began as he rose to his

feet. "I'm expected in my brother's court and must leave you for a time . . . a brief time."

While his powerful figure towered above, a deep awareness of the devastating man swept over Mae, and her gaze dropped to the coverlet edge again tightly grasped in both hands.

"But I promise you'll be safe in my absence and that I will soon return." With that oath, to Mae's amazement, he simply vanished. Startled, she blinked against the impossible—a stunningly handsome figure very much present one instant, gone in the next.

Shaking her head in a vain attempt to restore some semblance of rational thought, Mae abruptly recognized an unhappy truth. While she had babbled on and on (doubtless boring him with trivial details about her uninteresting life) she'd discovered less than nothing about him, had failed even to learn either what manner of being he was or where—

Without the nearness of a man against whose magnetic presence all else faded, Mae paused for the first time to carefully study her surroundings with eyes widening in awe. Neither small nor large, this was the most amazing chamber she had ever seen. It was filled with objects of rare beauty and a making unknown to her while tapestries in stunning hues covered the walls. Though strangely lacking windows, doors, fire, or any observable source of light, it was fully illuminated . . . as if an invisible sun were shining inside.

Utterly overwhelmed by inexplicable events, beings, and objects, Mae made to slowly lay back, the better to ponder odd matters for even the faintest thread of logic. As she turned her head to sweep a dense mass of fiery curls to one side, her gaze fell on a delicate gown in an incredible silver-green hue. It was draped over plumped pillows directly behind her—a place she would swear it hadn't been earlier.

*   *   *

"Betray our pact at your own peril—" Ardagh's nearly colorless eyes burned with dangerous lights as in an ominously quiet voice he issued a warning to the seated conspirator revealing unsuspected signs of weakness. "Without my aid, your mighty boom would not stretch now across the Shannon."

Sechnaill jumped to his feet, unwilling to cede even a superior viewpoint to this capricious being. No member of the De Danann could be trusted. For a millennia and more mortals had known that steadiness of purpose was an anathema to the fairy natures of such creatures. That being so, how could Ardagh expect from him a trust that was plainly not returned?

"Ah—" By the experience gained in having existed beyond a great many human lifetimes, Ardagh nearly heard the other's thoughts aloud. "But our alliance is not a matter of trust, rather one born of a desire for mutual gain. You wish not to be a king of powers reduced by the sovereignty of Munster's Brian Boru while I, too, desire the thwarting of that man's attainment of Erin's high kingship—though for reasons no mortal could possibly comprehend."

Sechnaill gave a grudging grimace that passed for a smile yet argued the truth of his guest's initial point. "But my men and I would have succeeded in spanning the Shannon without your aid."

"Eventually . . . perhaps. . . ." Absently nodding, Ardagh wondered anew if the mortal's greasy hair were truly brown or merely the product of an apparently permanent layer of grime. Then with an expression he doubted the human was sharp-witted enough to recognize as a sneer, he added, "But it will not long survive without the protection of my spell."

Sechnaill desperately wanted to disagree with the unpleasant boast yet couldn't be certain he would be justified. Besides, though lacking the magical race's knowledge, he assuredly knew better than to provoke this undeniably powerful creature into proving his claim. Thus, to safely evade the dangerous issue completely, Sechnaill pursued a more important matter.

"Have you retrieved critical items?" As if fearing that the mere sound of these words might have caused walls to sprout prying eyes and ears, Sechnaill glanced nervously over his shoulder.

"Nay," Ardagh responded, eyes unaccountably dancing with glee. "But, fear not, for I shall!"

By abruptly spinning with arms wildly waving, Ardagh set scarlet robes to fluttering in wide arcs. And in that dramatic instant he disappeared.

Chapter 2

∞

"*N*o!" Mae shouted as loudly as a panic-constricted voice allowed. Desperate to escape the bright demon's reach, she scrambled wildly across a bed seemingly become vast and treacherous. "Stay away!"

Heart thumping in dread of whatever unknown horrors this despicable creature meant for her, Mae flung herself over the soft mattress's far edge. She landed on the floor—hard.

Wasting no moment, Mae struggled to her feet. Then, in quick succession, she energetically threw crusts of bread, a spoon, and a bowl snatched from the tray Gair left behind after serving her. Still the vilely grinning Ardagh, ducking and dodging, drew dangerously near. Undaunted by the discovery that she'd depleted her source of worthy missiles, Mae gripped the heavy oak tray with both hands and smashed it over his head.

As her assailant collapsed into an inelegant heap, Mae's burst of strength deserted her. Whole body trembling, she sank down on the same stool her devastating host had earlier occupied. A crooked smile was inspired by the absurd hope that sufficient traces of Gair's powers lingered to revive her flagging spirit.

"'Tis undeniable, brother, your guest *is* as exceptional as you claimed."

Startled, Mae jerked around while the unexpected voice continued.

"Had I not seen it for myself—" A thread of warm affection laced words together. "I would never have believed any human female capable of taking such courageous actions."

Certain that following Gair's departure she'd been alone until the frightening Ardagh abruptly appeared, this sudden discovery of yet others present cast Mae adrift on a sea of illogic. Still, with uptilted chin she faced the giver of unexpected praise. . . . And she initially chose to interpret the speech as praise despite a dubious wording to his last statement.

" 'Struth—" Standing beside the first speaker but gazing at Mae, Gair's expression was a curious mixture of admiration and amusement. Were it less likely that she'd be embarrassed by the compliment, he would've told Mae how lovely she looked in the gown he'd provided. Instead he offered approval of a less personal nature.

"You've managed not only to thwart but to wreak retribution on a wily foe as precious few of even our kind have done."

"Despite your promise of protection—" Off-kilter since discovering them present, Mae misinterpreted Gair's words and, like a rasp across iron, unpleasant thoughts struck sparks in hazel eyes. "You left me here alone for the sake of proving to your brother the rightness of some childish claim?"

"Nay," Gair's own gaze softened to the comforting hue of a summer meadow while he brushed fingertips over the warmth of her flushed cheek. "Our purpose was nothing so trivial."

"But there *was* a purpose?" His physical closeness and touch fostered an ever deeper awareness which hastened Mae into unwary speech. Shaken by the renewed confusion born of inexplicable deeds and incredible beings, she'd already turned deaf ears to their peculiar manner of speech—

"our kind" versus the humans or mortals plainly viewed as inferior—but was unwilling for this issue to pass unexplained.

Gair grinned. He had wanted her to ask necessary questions and yet, sharing his race's distaste for anything of a certainty one way or another, gave no direct answer. "Though unable to see us, you were alone for only the briefest of moments and never truly in danger."

Despite the brevity of their acquaintance, Gair found more in this bright beauty's quick temper and even quicker mind to attract him than anyone or anything else had in a very long time.

Bemused by the discovery, Gair shared more than first intended. "At best I hoped this evening's tactic would prove my suspicions of Ardagh unjustified. At worst I expected that a frail mortal damsel captured without harm would be as easily and safely retrieved."

"You expected me to meekly submit?" Hollow disgust echoed through Mae's words.

Gair gave a rueful grimace and brief shake to his golden mane. "I confess my utter folly and assure you that never again will I underestimate the brave defenses of the fiery woman you've proven to be."

A fiery woman? Mae bit firmly down on her lower lip. This succinct description she perceived not as praise but as damning confirmation of the wrongful attitude which Reverend Mother often admonished her to control. Taught from childhood to quietly endure all difficulties (even assault) with patient forbearance and charitable forgiveness, she'd learned that physical defiance was as unforgivable as irrepressible laugher. Thus, rather than taking pride in her feat, a fresh tide of disgusting color burned Mae's cheeks with shame for the complete loss of temper that had ended in an attack on Ardagh.

"Mae," Gair quietly called, anxious to ease the unfathomable distress of the woman gazing determinedly downward. "I want you to meet my older brother, Comlan."

Wanting to be as gracious, Mae forced dark thoughts back, allowing the cheerful nature rarely dimmed to reassert itself. Dimples peeked as Mae glanced up to be struck again by how uncannily alike were the golden-haired, emerald-eyed brothers. "The head of your family?"

Gair nodded, adding, "And first among all sharing the blood of the Tuatha de Danann."

"What . . . ?" Mae's slight frown betrayed to her companions that she had no vague notion what these succinct words meant nor how rare was a statement so direct from any among their kind.

"What that means"—Comlan welcomed the damsel's abbreviated query since, by the laws governing contact between their worlds, fairy answers were forbidden without human questions first posed—"is that while I am king of our realm, my little brother is a prince and the heir apparent."

"Ah, but—" Gair caught Comlan's teasing glance. "What isn't as clear is that I possess no driblet of ambition to play any role in the unpleasant intrigues constantly waged in struggles for power."

Mae's eyes glowed with approval. That this rescuer already admired recognized how easily politics, whether in court or abbey, curdled the fresh milk of human relationships lifted him even higher in her opinion.

Gair felt the warmth of a hazel gaze resting on him and looked her way.

Disconcerted to be caught staring, Mae's attention immediately dropped to the floor.

"He's gone!" Mae gasped, pointing to the bare spot where Ardagh had fallen. "How could he depart without being seen or leastways heard?"

The two males exchanged wry smiles so alike one seemed a reflection of the other before Gair offered Mae a gentle reminder.

"You saw Ardagh silently vanish this afternoon and were here when he arrived tonight. . . ."

Yes, of course. That was true. And, having observed both inexplicable events, with a faint grimace of self-disgust Mae acknowledged the ridiculousness of her question.

"There's a more important answer to seek." Comlan reentered the conversation to direct the others' attention toward a hazy goal that must be brought into focus. "Believing Gair absent, why did Ardagh return here?"

Having no answer, Mae could only wish that she did. While she steadily met two pairs of probing eyes, to the growing confusion experienced since first arriving, an uncomfortable sense of helplessness was added.

"Lady Mae—" Comlan gently continued pursuing the same line. "You must know something of great value for Ardagh to risk abducting you from my brother's home. Can you tell us what that is?"

Mae solemnly shook her head but irrepressible dimples soon peeked. She'd never before been titled *lady* rather than *sister* . . . and, though doubtless a sin, she liked the sound.

Gair took up the quest. "If you carry no secret knowledge, then something you possess must be what Ardagh seeks. Think on it. Are you transporting anything unusual, anything that might hold a hidden meaning?"

Again Mae ruefully shook a head of vivid hair. "Sister Heccabah and I were dispatched from St. Hilda's Abbey with naught but the barest of necessities—a change of clothing, rosary, and foodstuffs sufficient to feed us for little more than a single day."

The damsel's basic honesty was obvious to both men, making it plain that further questioning of Mae would be fruitless.

Sensing her companions' growing frustration, Mae settled on a plan of her own. "Come," she invited, "let's look through my satchel. Perhaps there's something with a meaning I don't understand; maybe it's a part of the bag itself.

Having earlier separated bags from the sodden pile of discarded clothing, Mae turned to fetch hers from where she'd carefully placed it at the end of the bed.

Vanished! Her satchel had vanished along with its thief. . . .

Crash! A precious goblet suddenly smashed to the floor sending shards of crystal out in a wide arc while a low thundering reverberated through the walls of King Sechnaill's great hall.

"Ardagh," Sechnaill roared, thumping both hands palm-flat on the high tale. "I am wearied to the bone by the ridiculous tricks of your dramatic comings and goings. Is it not possible for you to simply arrive and depart in a normal manner?"

"Tsk, tsk. . . ." Ardagh mocked as he appeared in a swirl of scarlet robes. "Without me, how would your boring little company amuse itself?"

Lips clamped so firmly together that they went white, Sechnaill refused to reply. However, his eyes burned with enough venom to strike cold terror into the many warriors and servants gathered in the hall to share a new day's first meal.

"Asides"—Ardagh's brittle laughter was an intentional assault on the atmosphere of silent tension filling the chamber—"I've brought you a gift . . . something I know you've long coveted."

Sechnaill warily leaned across the high table toward his untrustworthy protagonist as with a flourish Ardagh tossed a satchel down to land between his host's tensely clenched fists.

Never one to waste attention on niceties, the keep's lord wielded a dagger and sliced through the bag. Once laid open, his rough hands dug wildly through its contents, flinging useless items aside until nothing remained but coarse cloth, now shredded, that had once formed a satchel.

"Gift? Miserable gift!" Once thrown the bag made an

awkward missile that dropped at the giver's feet. "You thought that I might covet an impoverished nun's miserable belongings?"

While Sechnaill raged, for nearly the first time, his visitor cooperated with an earlier demand.

Fuming with repressed fury roused by the mortal who had tricked him, Ardagh vanished without either fanfare or drama.

Chapter 3

∞

"Something was said, odd and likely of no real importance, but mayhap...."

With these hesitant words Mae instantly reclaimed the attention of two devastatingly handsome brothers. After the theft of her satchel was discovered, the males had fallen into a solemn discussion, trying to identify the reasons for Ardagh's belief that a human female possessed something needed.

"From the moment that approval of our pilgrimage to the Shrine of St. Finnian was granted, Sister Heccabah was effusive in her gratitude to the abbess. Because of that I paid little heed when with the dawn of our departure, to her fervent thanks, Sister Heccabah added more...."

Mae prayed she could keep the implied promise by identifying or leastways pointing the way toward the item besought.

"Sister Heccabah assured the Reverend Mother that she would fulfill the blessed mission with a grateful heart; pay penance with restoration."

While rising from her seat on one side of the bed, Mae was all too aware of the emerald eyes watching. The desire to show herself worthy of Gair's approval deepened Mae's shame for an oversight foolishly allowed in the mad whirl of unexplainable matters. However, the white flash of

Gair's potent smile overcame Mae's hesitation and encouraged her apology.

"I'm sorry for failing to immediately recognize a hiding place that should've been obvious by the fact that anything of value—temporal or divine—would be entrusted to Sister Heccabah."

To emphasize the sincerity of her regret Mae moved to where, only moments before Ardagh's assault, she had placed still damp but folded clothes. She lifted that neat stack to reveal below an unintentionally hidden satchel almost a duplicate of the one stolen.

Carrying the bag heavier than her own had ever been, Mae it placed gently atop a long table inlaid with precious metals. Then, with Gair on one side and Comlan on the other, she opened and began deliberately laying out its contents. All was as expected until she reached the bottom . . . and the final item. It was heavy, the length of her forearm, and carefully swaddled in white linen.

Heart pounding, Mae steadily unwound strips of cloth in a process so long that the tension of anticipation became almost tangible. At last a dark ebony and richly bejewelled cross lay in stark contrast atop soft piles of discarded swathing.

"Ah," Gair wryly observed. "I see Sister Heccabah was blessed with wealth."

"Oh, no." Taking the words literally, Mae promptly denied a suggestion which this amazing being apparently didn't know was impossible for one of their calling. "Nuns take vows of poverty as well as chastity."

The issue of mortal riches meant nothing to Gair but the last word instantly caught and diverted his attention from their important discovery.

"But if you take vows of chastity, how is possible for the human race to be perpetuated?"

Blush burning and gaze downcast, Mae choked back a nervous giggle to venture a delicate explanation. "Such vows are spoken only by the few who freely give them-selves into God's service.''

"And have you?" Gair asked while a gentle forefinger urged Mae's chin upward.

"I recognize this prize." Comlan's calm announcement sundered the tender moment with a summons for the pair's attention.

" 'Tis the Cross of St. Finnian.'' Comlan trailed finger-tips lightly down the well-cared for article. "Centuries past it was claimed as booty and hauled away by the invading king of Northumbria.''

With this explanation for the holy symbol, Mae under-stood Sister Heccabah's parting words to the abbess. Plainly the Reverend Mother had entrusted the elderly nun with the duty of seeing St. Finnian's Cross restored to his shrine.

"A Christian cross." Gair quietly acknowledged an ob-vious fact, grateful that his curious brother had investigated this new religion. "But of what imaginable use could such a thing possibly be to Ardagh?"

"To Ardagh alone, none." Comlan's lips tilted in faint mockery. "But to any mortal king the Cross of St. Finnian is a treasure of immeasurable worth.''

By his steady gaze Gair wordlessly demanded a further explanation.

"The saint blessed it with a prophecy: Until all men of this isle submit to the Cross, no human king can rule over the whole of Erin.''

Bronze brows arched dubiously above Gair's emerald gaze. "Then, according to Finnian's prophecy, to know peace this isle must be Christian?"

"Seems the literal meaning." Comlan nodded, though his wry smile deepened. "However, the prophecy was soon more loosely interpreted to mean that only a king possess-ing the Cross will successfully establish sovereignty over all Erin.''

While her companions debated the prophecy's intended

message, to Mae it was clear. Till all mankind accepted the unconditional love and salvation provided by Christ on the Cross peace would not rule. Still, despite their various views, they all three recognized the political value making this lovely piece dangerously important.

"Plainly," Comlan continued, "Ardagh and his unknown confederates are anxious to insure that St. Finnian's Cross won't fall into the hands of their foes."

"I agree." As Gair firmly nodded, his golden mane glowed. "And only wish I hadn't discounted the warning Ardagh issued when he came to reproach me for rescuing Mae. Though tainted by his prejudice against humans, I should've recognized his hints of coming battles as proof of his involvement in their planning.

"Now if only we knew with precisely who Ardagh colludes. . . ."

"Because we have what Ardagh wants, he'll return." Mae pointed this fact out with soft deliberation. . . ."

Assuming Mae feared another assault, Gair immediately responded. "I promise to guard you more carefully this time. . . ." He gently brushed his hand over the fire of her unruly curls.

"Nay," Mae instantly shook her head. " 'Tis exactly what you must *not* do!"

Comlan grinned, recognizing a strategy which the frowning Gair would doubtless try to thwart.

"Don't you see," Mae earnestly argued, eyes now brown and pleading with Gair, "by taking me, Ardagh reveals more than he learns."

"Your aid in this matter will be greatly appreciated—" Exercising his rights as both king and older brother, Comlan issued a decision that left the other two's discussion moot. ". . . and rewarded."

Gair would've continued to argue the wisdom but dainty fingertips pressed to his lips prevented the words from being spoken.

"I offered—" Hazel eyes danced with the joy of having

outflanked this man doubtless well versed in winning tactics. "And now the bargain has been struck it cannot be so easily broken."

Gair couldn't bear the thought of Mae purposefully courting danger. True, he'd allowed her to *think* herself alone when Ardagh attacked but she hadn't been. Now. . . .

In a fine example of his race's mercurial moods, Gair's frown vanished beneath a brilliant smile. Now, Mae no more needed to face danger alone than she had then.

Gair teasingly nipped at her fingertips for a moment before turning her hand over to press a kiss into its palm. "I'll agree, if you will agree to do one thing for me."

Mae instantly nodded. It was easily done since there was no decision to be made. She had already realized that for Gair's sake she would do anything.

"Wear this for me." Gair pulled a simple gold ring from his little finger and with another slow, potent smile slid it onto her right thumb. "Though you won't see me, so long as my ring remains on your hand, I will always be near."

Though rarely timid, for once Mae's courage wavered. She wanted but failed to ask if his promise was literally meant.

Incredibly, an instant later Mae found herself standing in deep snow beneath the same oak from which Gair had rescued her. Her bubble of pleasure in realizing that this time she was bundled in a pale rose cloak both incredibly soft and warm was shattered by the assault of harsh voices.

"There she is! Seize her!"

Mae spun around to see a small army of mounted warriors galloping toward her.

At the great hall's far end, Mae was bound to a thick column that had once been the trunk of a tree. She silently scrutinized her captor—not the bright demon she'd expected but rather a crude soldier plainly come to power by violence not birth . . . and badly in need of a bath. Having just proposed yet another toast lauding his own feats, he was standing, albeit unsteadily.

"Aye, 'tis me, King Sechnaill, who's succeeded where that untrustworthy sorcerer failed." Though his endless boasts imparted the same news, they'd grown steadily louder with the draining of successive horns filled with bitter ale. "Strange creature couldn't even capture a nun. But still Ardagh would have us believe 'tis only by his power that our boom survives. Hah!"

"Success?" Ardagh materialized within a hand's span of Sechnaill's flushed face. "You deem this capture of a *nun* success?"

Sechnaill stumbled a step back and abruptly landed in his own fortunately wide chair.

Gliding forward the brief distance necessary to send an intimidating glare down into the befuddled king's face, Ardagh demanded, "Where is our goal—the Cross of St. Finnian?"

"Search her." Sechnaill blustered out an order although there wasn't a man in the hall sober enough to obey. "Find the wretched cross."

"Don't be a fool." Ardagh's never hidden disgust for humankind seethed. "The Cross of St. Finnian is too large for the nun to carry on her person."

"No matter." Never sharp, and with his mind further blunted by abundant ale, Sechnaill mentally flailed about for some tactic to silence the sorcerer. "We'll barter the nun for the Cross."

Ardagh cackled with vicious glee. "You'll barter with *who*?"

Not so sotted that he didn't know himself on the losing side of this battle, Sechnaill simply hunkered down and went mute while Ardagh continued alternately gloating and raging.

"Your foolish action has likely roused slumbering powers the might of which you can noways conceive, powers able to threaten our mutual goal."

This last was enough to prod Sechnaill back into the fray
with a surprising measure of his senses restored.

"After telling me so oft that 'tis *your* powers which hold
the boom in place, now you'd have me believe in even
greater though unseen forces able to upset that barricade?"

"Why not," Ardagh sneered. "You actually believe St.
Finnian's Cross can empower a high king to rule over all
Erin."

"But—" The bullheaded Sechnaill rose to his feet again,
determined to continue the argument face to face. "*We* built
it to foil Boru's campaign to extend his authority over all
the kingdoms of Ireland and spread the religion of Patrick
... which by your lights is the only force able to harm the
Tuatha de Danann. How can these unseen powers possibly
threaten to destroy our work?"

Ardagh slowly shook his head in feigned regret while
disgust burned in nearly colorless eyes. "No human is capable of comprehending. . . ."

The attention of everyone, including Mae, was centered
on the two figures locked in a fierce verbal battle. Then
suddenly Gair appeared at her side with a reassuring smile
and silent laughter in his gaze.

Gair swirled his black cloak out to envelop Mae and in
a twinkling whisked her to safety.

Though doubting it possible to ever be less than startled
by such amazing feats, Mae refused to question this welcome miracle. One moment bound as captive in an enemy's
hall and the next amid the comforts of an incredible hill-
home alone with the devastating being twice her rescuer.

Chapter 4

∞

"*I* understand," Mae tentatively began, casting a searching, sidelong glance to the handsome face a brief distance away. "Ardagh is working with Sechnaill to thwart Brian Boru's ambitions. But why? What will he gain?"

" 'Tis simple." Though Gair's bright smile flashed it ended with a wry tilt to his lips. Again he sat atop the oddly shaped stool while Mae was perched primly on an edge of the wide bed. "Ardagh will count it a personal victory if by assisting Sechnaill, he can claim an important role in seeing Brian Boru fail to establish himself as high king."

"And, of more import to Ardagh"—Gair took Mae's dainty fingers into his much larger hand, lightly squeezing to emphasize the point—"this he believes will in turn impede the spread of Christianity."

A deep, rumbling laugh escaped as Gair saw by Mae's slight frown that his words had provided not answers but more questions.

"No doubt," Gair continued while his slow smile both held her attention and offered silent admiration. "Ardagh would then feel justified in claiming that by his feats he'd proven himself more worthy than Comlan to rule the Tuatha de Danann."

Lowering her gaze from the bemusing lure of his, Mae took a deep breath and tried to make sense of all that had been said. One question rose to the top of a bubbling mental caldron containing many.

"Why does Ardagh . . . why should anyone fear the spread of Christianity?" Raised in an abbey and believing to the depths of her soul in Christ's love for all, such a concept was utterly incomprehensible to Mae.

"I don't fear Christianity," Gair promptly stated. "I don't, even though an ancient prophecy was clear in pointing to this new faith as the end to my kind in the human world."

Mae frowned. There it was again, *my kind* as opposed to the *human* world. And now added to that puzzle was this mysterious reference to an ancient prophecy.

Wanting to ease the sweet damsel's distress, Gair quickly shared the seer's message. "The return of Patrick, a former slave, was foretold as was the religion calling humans to worship only his God and to turn against all previous beliefs."

Though Gair's words had lessened the haze, Mae still saw no clear answer and tried to learn more by rewording the question. "But how can belief in Christ put an end to the Tuatha de Danann?

Despite his nature's distaste for anything of a certainty one way or another, the unexpected but very real emotions inspired by this fiery damsel drew from him a direct and simple answer.

"Because when humans cease to believe in us, we become invisible to them."

Wondering if Gair were teasing or serious, Mae's brows met in a suspicious frown. "Then how is it that I can see you when I'm not even certain *what* you are?"

Golden head falling back, Gair's deep laughter filled the chamber before mirth was sufficiently restrained to permit an explanation.

" 'Tis my fault. Without allowing you the opportunity to disbelieve, I whisked you here where such proof of my existence abounds as will make it near impossible for even your faith to make me invisible to you."

Anxious to deny him any reason for guilt, Mae earnestly argued. "By whisking me here, you saved my life."

" 'Struth." Gair gave a slight, deprecating shrug. "And a deed I will never regret."

Feeling released from restrictions governing exchanges between their two worlds by Mae's welcome curiosity, Gair attempted to help her understand the Tuatha de Danann, their powers, indeed, the whole mercurial nature of fairy-kind.

It was a chore of immense proportions, and at length Gair chose to give Mae time to assimilate all that he had imparted by changing the focus.

"Now I have question for you." Gair reached out to brush the damsel's soft cheek just as he had when earlier posing the same query. "Have *you* given vows of poverty and chastity?"

Mae gasped, knocked completely off-kilter and certain her inquisitor must feel the flaming heat of her immediate blush beneath his fingertips. The feel of him so near, his warmth reaching out to enfold her, threatened to overwhelm Mae with forbidden sensations. To forestall its power, she stared with unequaled fervor at hands tightly clasped in her lap and hastened to answer.

"Save living in and working with the sisters of the abbey, I've taken none of the requisite steps to formally join their number."

An emerald gaze narrowed on vivid curls clustered atop a nervously bowed head. Though hers was clearly an honest response, it wasn't the complete answer he sought.

"Is becoming a nun what you wish to do with your life?" Gair probed further while threading a hand through the silky fire of her hair. "Do you long to spend the rest of your days in the abbey?"

These questions were even harder to answer than his first.

Refusing to yield to a gentle tugging meant to tilt her face upward, Mae dithered.

"The Reverend Mother dispatched us from the abbey knowing full well that Sister Heccabah, elderly and ailing, wouldn't survive to return . . . and likely hoped I wouldn't either."

Green sparks glittered in Gair's eyes. Not anger with the innocent Mae but with the vile creature who seemed to have wished ill on a sweet bundle of spirit and laughter.

"Mother Edwina rightly despairs of me." Mae hastened to atone for her wrong in criticizing the abbess. "I giggle during prayers, nap during mass, and have never been properly submissive or attentive to her counsel. In truth, I live in the abbey but have never truly belonged there . . . or anywhere."

The mournful droop of Mae's lips was the more pitiful for being so uncommon on a usually cheery face.

"Perhaps 'tis a quirk of my contrary nature," Gair began with a tentativeness foreign to him. "But from where I stand you seem a welcome and natural part of my world."

Wonderment glowed in Mae's wide eyes while a shy smile bloomed. Raised where material goods were banished along with the sinful pride they caused, Mae had never been given a gift. Now she felt as if the magical prince had plucked a star from the heavens and presented it to her.

Lacking experience in such matters, Mae had no notion how to respond yet. . . . She drew a deep breath and offered her gratitude in a statement awkward but sincere.

" 'Tis the nicest thing anyone ever said to me."

And it was true, Mae inwardly acknowledged. With soft words Gair had gently unwrapped and opened her secret vision of an enchanting future. It was a wishful fantasy that she hadn't acknowledged even privately for fear that a deed so bold might rip the fragile web of her fairy dream.

Beyond gratitude, Gair heard in Mae's poignant speech further proof that she deserved better treatment than her humankind had given. That fact, added to his relief that she neither had nor apparently wanted to take distasteful vows and join the abbey, was oddly pleasing.

Gair wanted and would gladly treasure Mae here in his world where she already seemed to belong. *Wanted.* His lips tilted in self-mockery. 'Struth, he desired the beguiling damsel, but not merely for the physical delights he'd no doubt could be theirs. He longed as much for her to be his companion in sharing both life's joys and inevitable sorrows.

Gair abruptly realized, by Mae's faint frown, that she was concerned by his lengthening silence. With a flashing smile, he calmed his love's distress, and yet the easily repaired confusion emphasized the importance of not rushing Mae into an intimate relationship before she fully comprehended the vast differences between their races. It would be all too easy but unjust to wield fairy powers and influence the sweet damsel's choice when the decision was one she alone must make.

Mae nibbled her lower lip. With an emerald gaze focused steadily upon her and its source so near, increased awareness played havoc with rational thought. The instinct to flee was strong, but stronger still was the wish to be closer yet.

Possessing experience aplenty, Gair had been aware of Mae's admiring response to him from near the moment after her rescue when she'd awakened in his bed. Having promised to protect her against harm, he had . . . even to the extent of taming his own instincts. But now, despite noble sentiments about not rushing her, he fell to temptation.

Gair moved to sit beside Mae on one side of the bed— the better to drink in a tempting sight it would've been wiser to postpone. It was folly, utter folly to test his willpower's limits by close proximity to a piquant face framed in a wealth of fiery curls and eyes melted to soft brown velvet by helpless longing. Sweet lips of tantalizing promise were slightly parted as if in anticipation of a lover's caress.

Mae stopped breathing beneath the intensity of emerald eyes. Not even to save her soul from perdition could she have broken the visual bond with this source of thrilling currents jolting from his vibrant body to hers.

Although Gair had yet to touch her with passion, he had in her dreams—leaving Mae to ache with nameless wanting. During waking hours she could strive for purity of thought as admonished by the Reverend Mother. But at night. . . .

Feeling almost as if he were caught in the daze between sleep and full wakefulness, drawn by powers as strong as his own, Gair leaned closer to Mae. . . . In the last instant turned his mouth from hers to brush a far less dangerous whisper-kiss across her cheek.

This damsel with a temper to match her fiery hair but a sweet core of concern and constantly changing eyes seemed created to perfectly suit one of his mercurial nature.

Despite his questions and her answers, somewhere in her depths Mae suspected that this incredible being who'd easily claimed her heart would not lightly take from her the one possession he knew she'd been raised to regard as most precious—chastity. But if this were to be her only chance for love and pleasure shared, she would seize the prize no matter the cost.

Willfully closing her mind to thoughts of the abbess's dire warnings against sins of the flesh, Mae mentally lashed her courage into supporting bold actions. Nearly as much to her surprise as Gair's, Mae's small hands slowly slid up over a tunic covering the powerful contours of his chest, explored the dip at the base of his sun-bronzed throat, and brushed across a bristled cheek to twine into golden strands.

Gair felt Mae tremble, heard the tiny catch in her breath, and his blood caught fire, racing through his veins with the speed of windswept flame. His bright head turned the whisper of distance required to bury his mouth against the satin curve of skin between her throat and shoulder.

Mae instinctively arched her throat into the heat of Gair's kiss. Then, sensing tantalizing pleasures just beyond reach, she nestled closer until powerful arms wrapped her within a fierce embrace.

A soft moan would've escaped but for Gair's hungry mouth brushing repeatedly across hers, enticing her lips to part. When they opened to the heat of joining, the kiss immediately deepened, whirling Mae into a chasm of fiery delights.

Reveling in the sweet assault giving life to dreams. Mae arched deeper into his hold while tingles of hot pleasure rippled through her. She closed her eyes and willfully sank into a welcome sphere of unthinking sensations.

Soft lips pressing curious little kisses against Gair's throat curled into a delighted smile with the discovery of a rapidly beating pulse. Tongue venturing out, Mae tasted the flavor of skin vibrating with a groan rumbling from his depths as she moved her mouth slowly down to nuzzle the laces holding the neck of his tunic closed.

Gair tangled the fingers of one hand in the wealth of fire-bright curls falling in a wild riot past the base of Mae's spine. Gently, insistently he tugged her head back until he could recapture her teasing mouth and teach her all the devastating pleasures a kiss could contain.

Time seemed to melt into an unpredictable sea of pleasure and fiery sensation until the moment when Gair pulled completely free of Mae's arms. A small whimper escaped from her throat but became a sigh of admiration as he stripped off his tunic in a single smooth motion so rapid that her first sight of a bare masculine chest was a brief glimpse of rippling muscles. Only after Gair turned full attention to ridding her of clothing with even greater haste, was Mae able to focus curious, unblinking eyes on the stunning male beauty of his form.

Gair immediately lowered himself to lie at Mae's side and pull her into the hungry cradle of his arms. Smoothing her hands over the strong muscles of his back, she clung to him while he savored the complete yielding of her deliciously soft body to the hard contours of his own. Breath caught in Mae's throat only to sigh out in little gasps as his mouth trailed fires of tender torment over her ripe curves and gentle valleys.

Driven by this shocking delight into a fiery sea of need, Mae writhed with innocent abandon against Gair, wanting to be nearer, wanting something more. The tiny, inarticulate sounds welling up from her core were more than he could resist. Gair turned her full into his embrace, hands sliding down her back, caressing and cupping her derrière to mold her tempting form ever more tightly against his need.

Lost in a dark vortex of wicked delights, Mae pressed even closer, twisting with enticing, inciting motions, pushing Gair to the edge of his control. He began to rock against Mae in a magical rhythm born with the dawn of time but when his passionate virgin instinctively matched the motion, he abruptly pulled free of to dispense with a last piece of clothing, the last physical impediment.

Desperate to lure him back, Mae reached out to wrap her arms about his neck and arched up to brush generous curves across the width of his chest, reveling in the sweet rasp of its wiry curls across sensitive tips.

With trembling gentleness Gair urged Mae to lie back. Then, sliding one leg between her silken thighs, he shifted to lie atop her slender length. Resting on his forearms to spare her his full weight, he gazed down into eyes dark with wanting, watching for the first hint of discomfort as he pressed intimately nearer.

Aware only of the gentle abrasion of his skin against hers, Mae moaned with erotic delight and with yearning desperation surged upward. The sudden stab of pain was quickly lost amid a myriad of stinging pleasures.

With hard, sharp movements and a rhythm that grew wilder and wilder, Gair rocked them both deeper into the delicious torment and anguished hungers at the pinnacle of the fiercest flames. Incredible pleasures seared every nerve until the blaze impossibly sweet exploded in unfathomable ecstasy.

"I love you—" Amid glittering sparks of satisfaction Gair's words were a barely intelligible growl yet to Mae a gift so precious that this avowal was the greatest pleasure of all.

"You're crying." Gair was distressed by teardrops he feared were proof of a greater pain than he'd realized.

"But in joy," Mae softly explained, "joy for the miracle of love shared." Beneath her crystal teardrops a smile of blinding sweetness bloomed. "Tears water the flowers of happiness. The intertwining of both is a habit to which we humans are prone—and surely it must be the sort of contrary experience that your fairyfolk would appreciate?"

Gair responded with a quiet laugh and such warmth of emotion in green-flame eyes that Mae melted against him once more.

"Wake up, brother."

Although the call hadn't been directed to her, Mae's eyes were the first to snap open. Instantly aware of a shameful lack of even the smallest item of clothing, she was inordinately thankful for bedcovers already drawn up to her chin.

"Good morrow, Lady Mae," Comlan said, right hand sweeping a dark cape's edge across a wide chest to be pressed against his heart as he made a gallant bow.

"Good morrow," Mae squeaked, wiggling deeper down into the bed until no more than fiery curls at the very top of her head could be seen.

"Go away." Rolling over to lay on his back, Gair irritably chided the newcomer. "You've frightened Mae."

Comlan feigned a hurt look. "Never in the whole of our vast lifetimes have we stood on ceremony with each other."

"'Struth, never before." Gair rubbed sleep from his eyes with fingertips that next combed back a tangled, gold mane. "But from this day henceforth we shall."

With a teasing grin Comlan nodded. Beyond his mocking smile was sincere delight that his younger brother, too long alone and aimless, had found someone to bring meaning to his life.

"Now, curious as are members of our kind, I doubt you left the joys of your own court for the sole purpose of prying into the most intimate details of my life."

"Hmmm," Comlan mused with a feigned innocence betrayed by the teasing gleam in his eyes. "Enough alike to nearly read each other's minds."

"Brother—" Gair's single word was both demand and threat.

"I yield," Comlan laughed, lifting hands palm-out. "I, too, have had a busy night and am here to discuss possible strategies to safely bridge an expanding bog of complications."

Chapter 5

∞

*F*rom a hilltop overlooking Athlone and the mighty river Shannon, Mae glanced up into a sky hosting rolling storm clouds, heavy and dark—an appropriate setting for this perilous confrontation. Amid piercing wind lifting swirls of stinging snow into the air she was grateful for her rose cloak but even more so for the further shield provided by Gair's powerful form.

A fortnight of strained waiting had at last passed, and the appointed hour was at hand.

On the banks at one end of a long boom, amazingly hardy for a man of silver-streaked hair, King Brian Boru thrust his broadsword into the air as a silent demand for the attention of all.

On the opposite shore Sechnaill stood at the forefront of gathered monarchs from all the northern kingdoms.

"As a leader who prizes justice, I offer you a choice. Submit and accept my sovereignty now or choose to resist and pay the price for your defiance with precious life-blood."

The response was immediate.

"Never!" Sechnaill shouted his rejection of both the offer and the man. "Never will we of the northern kingdoms yield to your rule!"

A thunderous roar of support rose from the throats of

Sechnaill's allied kings and the combined hoard of their warriors. The noise swept across the intervening river like a brewing storm.

"Your threats have no meaning." Confidence in his position buoyed to new heights, Sechnaill taunted his unmoved foe. "How could they when your advance is prevented by our unbreachable barrier."

"The obstruction you've placed across the Shannon is easily destroyed." Brian dismissively shrugged, signaling his disdain.

Sechnaill snarled, "I think *not*." He was certain that even the renowned Boru could not defeat Ardagh's unworldly powers.

King Brian moved on to the next step of a carefully constructed plan. Just as he'd first thrust a sword into the sky to demand attention, now with joined hands he lifted firmly above his silver-streaked head a far different symbol.

"Here, safe within my grasp"—Brian's deep voice easily carried across the river—"is the treasured, long-sought Cross of St. Finnian."

The gasp earned by Brian Boru's announcement was quieter but no less intense than the roar incited moments earlier by Sechnaill's boasts.

When muttered doubts passed among the northern kings and their followers, Sechnaill instantly attempted to shame them back into line with threats and repeated boasts.

"Stand steady," Sechnaill harshly demanded. "Hold your position as firmly as does our boom." Slowly spinning, the better to intimidate followers of all classes, he made an unpleasant discovery. Too many of the bloody fools had lowered their eyes to avoid meeting his gaze.

"Remember," Sechnaill snarled. "Only the most craven of dastardly cowards would yield the field to avoid honorable battle."

"Look to your leader. He is the craven fool." With no trace of hysteria in deliberate words, Brian went on to make a solemn declaration. " 'Tis I who possess the Cross of St.

Finnian and by its powers now I claim the right to over-kingship of all Erin.''

His opponent on the far shore let out a hoot of derision but Brian refused to be diverted from his goal and continued without pause.

"Sechnaill has promised that your river barrier cannot be destroyed . . . but he lies. And by his boastful deception lures you toward the slaughter. Will you sacrifice yourself for his vanity?''

Again the furious figure across the river hooted but this time added a seemingly endless litany of ever more vile curses.

Unmoved by the verbal assault, Brian steadily held the cross high, listening carefully while from the shifting masses on the far bank rose ever clearer murmurs of distrust and grumbles of resentment.

Yet still, despite their obvious uneasiness, the northern kings remained aligned with Sechnaill and kept their warriors in check.

"The lies are not mine but *his*,'' Sechnaill snarled, forced to address the treacherous issue not by his enemy but by division in his own ranks. "Boru claims the ability to breach our boom, but plainly 'tis false since he hasn't—and can't.''

Mae tightly gripped the strong arm wrapped about her waist. At last, here was the ill-considered but expected challenge they'd been waiting for the unwise Sechnaill to issue.

Although previously solemn, Boru's lips parted in a broad smile glowing with victory anticipated. Through chill air gone to the ominous stillness that precedes a storm his voice carried strong and deep.

"Will you agree to submit to whichever warrior-king whose claims are proven true?''

The response was a tangled rumble of many voices that Brian chose to accept as agreement.

Even on this heavily overcast day, jewels glittered when with a sweeping gesture King Brian swung the precious cross down and with it pointed toward the boom.

Mae felt Gair's powerful body go tense at her back just as Comlan's black-cloaked figure abruptly materialized behind Sechnaill an instant before the first snaps in the boom were heard. That faint but ominous sound quickly became a loud splintering, cracking roar. The barrier disintegrated into small pieces, allowing waters unnaturally restrained to again rush with wild currents.

Soon Boru led his army in fording the Shannon to claim oaths of homage and hostages given by monarchs of all the northern kingdoms, including a truculent Sechnaill.

Before Gair could whisk Mae from their vantage point above the river to his hill-home, a furious Ardagh confronted them.

"That cross had no power to break my spell! It was *you*—you and your brother—who thwarted my plans."

The heated accusation was plainly intended to provoke a battle of one sort or another, but Gair responded with a negligent shrug.

"Aye—" Ardagh refused to permit this critical issue to be so lightly dismissed. "It was you who destroyed the boom and with it the Tuatha de Danann's last hope for impeding Patrick's dangerous beliefs."

Approaching unseen from directly behind Ardagh, Comlan responded to the source of this acrid bitterness. "Dangerous beliefs? Only if you fear their cost." He shook his head as if to be rid of some item of no consequence.

"For myself," Comlan continued, "I think I'll welcome the change. To be unseen by humans is no bad thing. It can have only a beneficial affect on the lives of the Tuatha de Danann."

Gair agreed though his comments were pointedly addressed to Ardagh. "You erred in thinking that any attempt to halt the tide of Christianity (doomed at the outset) would induce others of our breed to depose Comlan and elevate you to the crown. But in the end you've merely underscored the wisdom of Queen Aine's choice of heir."

"King Comlan—" Another voice intruded. "Prince Gair—"

The males thus called ignored Ardagh's furious departure to immediately shift their attention toward the approaching King Brian Boru.

"I returned in the midst of important deeds," he announced once close enough to be easily heard, "to request your presence tonight as guests of honor at my victory feast."

"We will gladly accept," Comlan graciously responded. "If you'll permit us to provide both the banquet and an adequate structure to protect your celebration against the coming gale's intrusion."

Amid a magical pavilion formed by panels of nearly translucent cloth in an astounding array of hues never before seen, King Brian Boru welcomed awed guests. Though lacking any visible support, the delicate chamber stretching across a wide meadow stood impervious to howling wind and driving rain.

As guests of honor Mae sat between Gair and Comlan at a high table shared with their evening's host. Though possessing more experience of the Tuatha de Danann's incomprehensible powers than most humans, Mae was also amazed by the view below the dais.

Long lines of linen covered tables bore an abundant array of succulent dishes seemingly impossible to have been prepared without the aid of an army of servants and massive ovens. A multitude of fine waxen candles arranged on curiously designed stands provided points of light sufficient to match a star-filled sky and yet couldn't account for either the brightness or warmth of these surroundings.

Mae listened while Gair and his brother reviewed with their host the winning strategy so recently employed and then moved on to discuss others among Brian's military victories and negotiated successes. By the time the meal was eaten and the toasts drunk, she had learned that Brian

Boru was an invincible warrior, just ruler, and consummate politician. Far more surprising, though a Christian himself, he was also tolerant of other beliefs. All in all, Mae realized that the generosity Gair and Comlan had shown Boru was likely influenced by the many traits they shared.

Mingling and sipping exceptionally fine wines flowing freely, guests lingered to enjoy genial company far into the night. Having shared the table with the man, Mae was surprised when King Brian sought her out as the first glimmer of dawn glowed on the eastern horizon.

"I have only just heard the tale of your ill-fated pilgrimage," King Brian began with a gentle smile. "And to repay you for the part played in seeing the Cross of St. Finnian safely into my hand, I wish to provide you with escort back to the Abbey of St. Hilda in Northumbria."

Mae felt the smile on her lips freeze in place. King Brian's offer was generous, one that deserved sincere gratitude and immediate acceptance. But. . . .

The offer also destroyed Mae's excuse for remaining in Ireland, for staying as close as possible to the incredible beloved clasping her shoulders and gently urging her to lean back and rest against his powerful chest.

So close, Gair felt Mae tense at their host's suggestion, as if against a blow. And although he would risk much to spare his love even the slightest distress, in this single instance he perversely welcomed the poorly hidden anguish in her reaction. It provided undeniable proof that her loving commitment to him was as deep as his for her and sent a surge of relief twined with joy pouring through him.

"We give you our gratitude for the consideration and willingness of your offer." Gair nodded with a white smile as bright as his golden hair. "But 'tis unnecessary as Mae will remain here as my wife."

Brian's eyes widened for only a moment as he mused, "Interesting notion—human mate for a prince of the Faerie Realm."

"In my world"—sensing the human king's doubt that

joy could flourish in so unequal a union, Gair shattered fairy rules to calm Boru's uneasiness—"mortal time means nothing and there my human love can share with me a long and happy existence."

Brian's attention shifted to the fire-haired damsel. "And is this where you wish to remain? What will make you happy?"

Bright curls caught candlelight as Mae immediately nodded. " 'Tis the only place I've ever really felt that I belonged. And I can only be truly happy with my beloved Gair."

With this declaration, Mae turned her head and glanced up to meet eyes deepening to the hue of a shadowed forest.

From the far side of a pavilion formed by fairy magic, Comlan fondly watched as Gair unobtrusively led his ladylove to a shadowed corner from whence they disappeared in a single instant. Pleased by this success, amusement glittered in emerald eyes as he congratulated himself on maneuvering Boru into offering Mae an escort. That ploy had surely won a happy ending for two whose future contentment meant much to him.

TURN THE PAGE FOR A PREVIEW OF
MARYLYLE ROGERS' EXCITING NEW
HISTORICAL ROMANCE,
HAPPILY EVER AFTER . . .

Prologue

∞

May 1, 1900

A slight breeze teased the mass of golden curls and skirts of a white-gowned woman gazing up an Irish hillside. Lissan's attention rested on beloved parents nearing its crest, bathed in the bright pastels of dawn. Her father, remarkably fit for all his years, climbed a few paces ahead and carried her fragile mother without the slightest sign of strain.

Clearly this was the moment she and her siblings—two brothers and two sisters—had been warned to expect. Each, on their twentieth birthdays, were called into the study for a private talk during which their parents requested a solemn promise. When their mother's failing health made it clear that the end was near, her children and grandchildren were to bid their last good-byes. Lord Comlan of Doncaully was then to be left in peace to carry his wife into the Irish hills unchallenged.

Serious oaths had been given to neither follow nor question their father's action. The four older siblings, married and with families of their own, had curiously discussed this odd command but never argued against the wishes of a father both loved and respected. However, Lissan took pride in an independent nature, and her curiosity was not so easily quelled.

Days earlier as his frail Amy began sinking into an unmistakable decline while visiting a cherished retreat, the
small Irish home known as Daffy's Cottage, Lord Comlan
had summoned their descendants to her bedside. Seeing the
inevitable looming near, five adult children hadn't been surprised when during the dark hours of night their father announced his intent. Though her brothers and sisters
accepted this decision with deep sorrow, a decade younger
than the next older child, Lissan had begged that she be
permitted to accompany her parents at least so far as the
first slope's summit. A frowning Lord Comlan had agreed
only after his gravely ill wife added a whispered entreaty
to their daughter's plea.

When her parents halted at the brow of a rise beyond
which lay others progressively steeper, Lissan assumed that
they had paused to wish her a final farewell. She would
then be expected to keep a promise by returning to the
family members waiting in the quaint, ivy-covered cottage
below.

"This can't be the last time I see you, not yet, not now
. . . ," Lissan huskily whispered, embracing both her father
and the woman he cradled near.

"But it is either *now* or never," Lord Comlan firmly
stated although love softened an emerald gaze caressing the
golden hair that framed his youngest daughter's captivating
face. He loved all of their children but shared a special bond
with the ever-curious, often impetuous Lissan.

Lissan bent to press a kiss against her mother's papery
cheek before letting her arms drop and beginning to retreat.
Lady Amethyst's fragile hand restrained her.

Eyes clouding against the prospect of never seeing her
parents again, Lissan glanced down to find unsteady fingers
affixing a beautiful brooch to the tucked and daintily embroidered dimity of her bodice.

"Wear my amulet *always.*" This was an earnest appeal,
their speaker prayed Lissan would heed. "Wear it and
you'll be protected from harm."

"But, Mama—" Lissan started to protest this giving of her mother's most treasured piece of jewelry—an exquisitely carved, ivory unicorn, gold-horned and rearing inside an onyx circle.

"Hush now, my baby, my fairy-child," Lady Amethyst gently rebuked. "Do as your mama says this one last time."

Firmly biting lips to block useless pleas that the lump in her throat would strangle anyway, Lissan stepped back. Yet, rather than depart completely, she froze a short distance away, waiting to watch her parents continue the foretold journey through Irish hills.

The sight of small white teeth mistreating a full lower lip brought a sad half-smile to Comlan's mouth. Despite carrying his youngest sister's name and having inherited both his fair coloring and emerald eyes, this willful daughter was very much her beloved mother's child—likely a further reason that she held a special place in his heart.

Lissan was puzzled when, rather than continuing the journey, her father stepped into the ring of beautiful flowers encircling an ancient oak and paused.

She'd been told that her name came from this site known since the distant past as Lissan's Fairy Ring. It was her favorite place in all the world, and she had long thought that fact the likely reason her mother called her a fairy-child.

As a youngster Lissan had begged again and again to be told the magical tale of the dainty fairy damsel who'd fallen in love with a mortal warrior. To share his life in the human world, the ethereal princess allowed her mystical powers to drain into the earth and at that moment around her feet a circle of perfect flowers had sprung up—and bloomed still. During the magical days of childhood, Lissan had often wished that fairies were real and fantasized about the wondrous adventures she would have if only she were one. Then, inevitably, she'd grown up. . . .

Attention abruptly returning to the present, Lissan was

horrified at having allowed foolish memories to claim her
thoughts in the midst of this serious and sorrowful event.
Guilt joined guilt as she closely watched her white-haired
father lower his frail burden's feet to the ground. Holding
the weak woman barely able to stand close against his side,
he started to walk counterclockwise around the ring of
flowers. With each pace forward, the woman's steps became firmer, while an aura of ever brighter light wrapped
about them. Lissan's eyes widened as every completed circuit seemed to strip years from the luminous couple until
they abruptly fell into the circle's center . . . and disappeared completely!

Where were they? Lissan started forward but stopped.
Clearly this was exactly what they hadn't wanted their children to see. But *how* had they done it? What did it mean?

"Worse yet," Lissan murmured aloud—a regrettable
habit she'd yet to tame. "How in sweet heaven's name can
I possibly go back to the cottage and explain?"

Bewildered, Lissan sank to ground padded by thick
grasses. She had long since outgrown fairy tales and didn't
believe in magic. But if what she'd just seen wasn't magic,
then what . . . ? How could she explain the impossible? She
couldn't return to her waiting siblings and simply tell them
that their parents hadn't died but instead miraculously
grown young again? And then vanished.

No, that truth certainly wouldn't satisfy either her sci-
entifically minded oldest brother, Garnet, or David, a well-
respected clergyman. As for Opal and Pearl, the two sisters
determined to see her as happily wed as they were and thus
preoccupied with finding a husband for her, well—Lissan
grimaced, green eyes darkening to a forest hue while gazing
morosely into the fairy ring.

Her family was certain to think that grief had weakened
their little sister's hold on sanity and driven her back into
childhood's wild tales of fairy magic. No, she couldn't ra-
tionally expect them to accept the truth for truth. But neither would she lie and say their father had simply carried

his gravely ill wife ever further into the hills. But if not that, then what?

Perhaps, Lissan's eyes narrowed. Just perhaps she would discover a rational explanation by following her parent's path? Folly, utter folly. But still—

Yielding to the impetuous spirit that had so horrified past governesses but always earned a secret smile from her father, Lissan rose with innate grace. She unhesitatingly moved to the very point at which her father had lowered her mother's feet and began retracing their footsteps.

Before completing a first circuit Lissan wished she'd counted how many times her parents had gone around the circle before falling into its center, but by the time she'd made the second lap it no longer mattered. As if unseen hands were pushing from behind, she stumbled onward at an ever increasing pace until, as if caught by centrifugal force, she was swept along at a terrifying speed. Panicking, she summoned every shred of strength and threw herself free.

Lissan landed on her back—hard! Even the ground's thick green padding was no protection. Her head bounced but her eyes stayed open . . . and widened against the flash of a double-bladed broadsword slashing straight down with deadly force!

Chapter 1

∞

ℛory O'Connor silently led his band of warriors through the ebbing shadows of night and up a heavily wooded hillside. They had tracked O'Brien's bloodthirsty raiders from the burned-out shell of an aging farmer's cottage and meant to wreak vengeance upon the vile curs.

Despite his men's desire to see the deed immediately done, Rory had convinced them of the wisdom in banking the fires of anger the better to see greater punishment inflicted with smallest cost. At his direction, they'd circled around their foes to wait in wooded shadows surrounding an ancient fairy ring in the glade at the hill's summit.

With deceptive calm Rory stood motionless, broad back resting against one strong tree trunk while awaiting the propitious moment to strike back. As lord of the most important among a ring of fortresses protecting Connaught, he was honor-bound to his young cousin, King Turlough, and must defend not only his own holdings but the whole kingdom against forces commanded by the too proud and ambitious king of Munster.

King Muirtrecht of Munster had long claimed the high-kingship of all Ireland, but Turlough, coming into manhood and ever rising in power, presented a danger to that ambition. Intending to weaken his threat, men from Munster harried the borders of Connaught by terrorizing inhabitants, burning farms, and stealing precious livestock.

A snapped twig, a muffled voice earned Rory's immediate attention. He leaned forward, peering through thick leaves and down the slope to where men climbed toward the fairy ring single-file. The rising sun spread its brilliant shades across a morning sky forming an appropriate backdrop for the violence erupting at Rory's signal.

Warriors with raised swords closed in on the summit's newcomers from all sides. Gasps of surprise ending in harsh curses accompanied the fierce clash of blade meeting blade. But as time passed uncounted, the skirmish's initial taunts and blasphemous oaths settled into either grunts of exertion or groans of pain.

Caught in a prolonged and brutal fight with the strong leader of Munster's raiders, Rory lightly whirled to avoid the downward slash of the other's broadsword . . . and froze as it sliced through a beautiful, golden woman inexplicably tumbling at their feet.

Lissan glimpsed blood on the terrifying blade lifting from its deadly attack. That ominous sight jolted her out of shock and into horrified recognition of peril all around. In this glade gone eerily quiet, she was surrounded by men dressed as warriors from a distant past and, despite their broadswords, spears, and daggers, apparently terror-struck to stone.

Too startled for either deep fear or sensible thought, Lissan automatically pushed her skirts demurely down while struggling to sit up. She knew exactly where she'd fallen and yet this long-familiar scene had changed. The ancient oak suddenly seemed half as old while dense forest and thick undergrowth covered ground where there'd never been more than lush grasses and a sprinkling of trees.

"The White Witch. . . ."

Lissan's emerald eyes instantly flew up to the source of

gasped words—the stocky man still standing above and clutching a blade stained with blood as red as his hair. A chorus of fearful voices echoed his epithet even as their frightened sources whirled and deserted the battlefield to flee into woodland shadows. Although clearly the master of one side engaged in this conflict, her assailant followed their lead.

Disconcerted by these extremely odd doings and unaccountably altered surroundings, Lissan struggled to restore some measure of calm and make rational plans. She ought to dash away and rejoin the family waiting in a cottage below . . . but with everything so changed she didn't truthfully know what path would lead her there.

A deep voice like rough velvet intruded. "Are you unharmed?"

"Indeed, yes." Further befuddled to discover herself not so alone as she'd believed, Lissan instantly responded to the Gaelic question in that ancient language learned as a child at her father's knee. "My fall will leave bruises, but it's only my pride that truly suffers."

With the words, Lissan glanced up to meet a penetrating gaze so dark as to seem all of black. It belonged to the raven-haired, stunningly handsome man towering above—taller than any she knew save her golden father and brothers.

While the maiden of sun-gilded hair gaped at him, Rory studied her so long and so well that a wild blush rosed her cheeks. She was dressed in a peculiar gown of amazingly fine cloth such as he'd never seen before. But, despite courageously uptilted chin, it was plainly apprehension that widened emerald eyes of amazing clarity. Surely the White Witch couldn't, wouldn't be afraid of him?

"Once well struck—" Rory calmly probed for a more satisfying response. "Mael O'Brien's blade rarely fails to mortally harm its target."

Cheeks rosy an instant earlier went pale. The broadsword! Sweet Heaven! That it had well and truly struck her was proven by the blood she'd glimpsed on its blade. But how could that be? Heart pounding erratically, Lissan glanced down to a midriff so completely untouched that even the delicate cloth of her morning gown remained whole and unbloodied. No wonder her attacker and the other men had fled in fear.

"Can you account for your deliverance?" Having learned through hard experience that little was as it seemed, Rory was annoyed with himself for instinctively sympathizing with the beauty doubtless enacting a well-practiced charade.

Lissan blinked rapidly against panic roused by the unspoken disdain flowing from a powerfully built interrogator clearly growing impatient. Absently slipping into an action habitually used to busy nervous hands during times of tension, she brushed a cloud of bright tresses back with slow deliberation. Unfortunately, she could no more explain this miracle than she could solve the puzzle of the many abrupt changes in her surroundings or her parents' disappearance.

Suspecting the golden maid's silence was a further feminine ploy to win indulgence by feigning helplessness, Rory flatly demanded, "Who are you?"

"Lissan." She immediately responded, pleased that this question, at least, had a simple answer.

"Like the fairy responsible for those forever-blooming flowers?" As Rory O'Connor nodded toward the circle of blossoms the sunlight that gleamed over black hair was the antithesis of his dark frown. Having long scoffed at the superstitious tales and foolish portents accepted by too many fools, even this mention of otherworldly magic made him uneasy—particularly after this woman's extraordinary arrival.

Lissan's attention flew to the fairy ring she could nearly swear had been trampled by fighting men but now looked fresh and as untouched as she was, despite the broadsword's blow.

"Yes." Lissan's sharp nod sent golden tresses again

tumbling over slender shoulders. "I was named for the fairy in that tale."

Rory's frown deepened. "And from whence do you hail?"

"My home is in London." Uncomfortable beneath a masculine disapproval rarely encountered and never so long sustained, Lissan smiled winsomely at this man unreasonably displeased by answers given as promptly and honestly as she could.

Those responses, however, left Rory more thoroughly and, he was certain, justifiably annoyed with the beauty so confident in her vanity that she blandly confessed what she must know he'd view as a crime. And this she did even while boldly enticing him with an alluring smile to forego his own honor.

"I assume, then"—ice coated Rory's deep voice—"that you were sent by King Henry."

Lissan rightly heard this statement for the accusation it was. These words, however, merely added another layer of alarming bewilderment. After all, Queen Victoria had ruled the British Empire for decades and there hadn't been a royal Henry in a very, very long time.

As a first step toward solving this daunting riddle, but wary of the answer, Lissan quietly asked, "What year is this?"

Disgust for so blatant and foolish an attempt to cloud dangerous issues further deepened Rory's voice as he growled, "The year of our Lord, 1115."

The year 1115? It couldn't be and yet—The image of the broadsword slicing through her body echoed in her mind. She lifted her eyes to meet the stern gaze of the strangely dressed man towering above her.

"Then—" The word caught in Lissan's throat and her forlorn gaze dropped to the hands tightly clasped in her lap. Drawing a deep breath, she forced more words through stiff lips, "Then I have no home in this world."

Rory's black brows thundered together in a fierce scowl.

What did this beauty, this stranger, mean to suggest? That by virtue of her mere presence on his land he was responsible for her? Hands curling into fists, he backed two steps away fully intending to leave the intruder to fend for herself . . . but. . . .

The forlorn droop of slender shoulders cloaked in hair like spun gold stabbed Rory with a sharp pang of guilt. And though he had no qualms about dispatching foes, he'd be a soulless ogre to abandon such tender prey to the vicious beasts of the forest. This admission only deepened his frustration with the muddle Lissan's inexplicable arrival had made of his morn's carefully laid battle plans. That fight had ended not only without a clear winner but with his warriors fleeing as readily as their opponents—a poor position from which to repel the next assault. And he knew all too well that further assaults were inevitable.

Lissan was lost in a glum haze of questions impossible to answer—the greatest of which were how, why, and could she ever return to her own time? Thus preoccupied, she was caught unprepared when a strong hand suddenly seized one of her smaller ones, pulling her up to stand facing its tall, dark owner. Too startled to reason clearly, her wary gaze locked with Rory O'Connor's. At this close view, she realized that his eyes were not truly black but deepest blue and so penetrating it seemed disturbingly possible that he could read her soul.

Rory, in turn, felt himself drawn into fathomless green crystal depths but, as a warrior of courage, fought the lures of a woman who must be either witch or spy. An instant later his skill as tactician reminded him that the best defense was offense.

Swept suddenly full against a broad, muscular frame and held there by arms that seemed bands of steel, Lissan gasped. But even that faint sound was muted by a kiss rough at the outset which gentled into a persuasion stealing her breath and dropping her into a blaze of unfamiliar sensations. Hands uselessly balled into fists failed to land a single blow of protest before she was unceremoniously thrust aside.

Gazing into eyes of green mist, Rory stepped back, while self-disgust hardened his handsome face into a mask of cool cynicism. He had intended to disarm her snares by exercising his own considerable skills as a lady-charmer, but she'd defeated him with lips that tasted of innocence and the stunned expression of a virgin seduced to reckless passion. It was an act. It must be an act—but with it she'd won.

"Follow me," Rory coldly snapped.

"Follow you?" Horrified by her own responsiveness, Lissan glared at the man. "First you assault me and then you have the gall to think I'll obey your orders. I think *not*!"

"The forest is a dangerous place even for an armed man and deadly for a woman alone. There are wolves in these woods. Wolves and wild boar with vicious tusks. And, of course, bands of desperate outlaws and outcasts. All of whom will find you sweet meat for a feast—of one kind or another. That is if you're witless enough to linger here alone and unprotected."

"But if I am the witch you believe me to be, what have I to fear?" Even as Lissan demanded this, her thoughts filled with visions of both the fangs she'd seen on wolves in the London Zoo. And, too, she remembered the crude drawing of a wild boar ravaging its kill. It had been reproduced in the same history book where she'd read about how roving gangs of the angry dispossessed joined dangerous outlaws to make traveling hazardous during the early centuries of this millennia.

For the first time, it occurred to Lissan that her interest in ages gone by, her ongoing attempts to satisfy an endless curiosity about everything from ancient art to the newest scientific discoveries, might have a negative side. The next instant she scolded herself for being foolish when surely every morsel of knowledge would to be useful in navigating her way through the unfamiliar territory of an ancient past.

"So be it." Rory responded after a long pause. While she'd fumed, he had conducted a leisurely examination of the scowling maid. His scrutiny had taken in the full length of her from the mass of gilded hair framing a heart-shaped face down slender, white-gowned form to the dainty slippers as unusual as the rest of her. Now with a sardonic glitter in dark eyes and a mirthless smile, he turned and began striding away.

"No-o-o . . ." Lissan hadn't expected her formidable opponent to capitulate so easily. No gentleman of her day would leave a well-born woman stranded. "I'll follow . . . for now. . . ."

Hearing in her own words an echo of the type of faint-hearted, determinedly frail females she most despised, Lissan cringed. To make matters worse, the wickedly attractive and far too arrogant Mr. O'Connor didn't bother to turn and face her again. Clearly he expected her to be grateful when his pace slowed sufficiently for her to follow through the dense woodland. Annoyance deepened by the fact that gratitude was owed, Lissan indignantly picked up delicate dimity skirts and petticoats to trail behind, ducking under low-hanging branches and stepping over fallen trunks.

When not glancing down to secure firm footing, Lissan pinned her gaze to the tip ends of raven-black hair falling just below the Irishman's broad shoulders. All the while she was fully aware of the towering trees and thick undergrowth making a path known since childhood suddenly unrecognizable. It was the unfamiliarity and new dangers of terrain encompassing the fairy ring that forced Lissan to reluctantly acknowledge she had no choice but to follow the formidable Rory O'Connor's lead.

Yet even as Lissan tagged after a reluctant rescuer, it felt like she'd been dropped into some childhood fairy tale come to life—and feared her destined role was truly that of the apparently wicked witch she'd already been named.

This couldn't be happening! She again refused to accept

this impossible situation. It must be a dream brought on by the grief of her mother's imminent death. No, not a dream but a *nightmare* from which she would surely soon awake.

Lissan instinctively dug the nails of one hand into the palm of the other . . . and winced at the pain. Was it possible to experience such sharp discomfort without waking? Or—horrors—was this reality?

Still irritated at having failed to prevail against the beauty's surely feigned purity, Rory's face was as emotionless as if carved of stone when he stopped at the edge of a clearing.

"This abode has been unused since the death of the woman who last lived here."

At these words, Lissan glanced up to find a tiny thatched building nestled against the base of a hill—in, it seemed fairly certain, precisely the same spot as the one she'd left this morning. And yet this structure had but one level and was even smaller than Daffy's Cottage, something she'd have sworn impossible only the previous day. This was not a dream nor even a nightmare. This was *real*! Lissan struggled to maintain an outward composure while her heart plunged into a sea of panic.

Rory continued while Lissan gaped, "It contains sufficient amenities to shelter you—all save foodstuffs. Those I'll bring on the morrow."

When without a further word the man turned to leave, a fountain of questions burst from Lissan.

"Wait! Tell me who you were fighting . . . and why . . . and will they have followed us here? Am I safe?"

Dark brows arched inquiringly as Rory answered with a mocking question. "Was it not you who claimed that the witch you are is always safe?"

As the irritating Irishman strode away Lissan whirled to stomp toward the small, deserted building with green fires snapping in her eyes and fanning a burning determination to find the way home.

Rory refused to glance back toward the beauty he could

almost believe born of an otherworldly fairy breed but whose questions were surely those of a spy. He couldn't consign her to the dubious mercy of a wolf pack, but neither would he allow her to intrude so far into his sphere that she might learn enough to be of interest to King Henry and a danger to his own.

HAPPILY EVER AFTER—a December bestseller from St. Martin's Paperbacks. Available in November wherever books are sold!

Against the backdrop of an elegant Cornwall mansion before World War II and a vast continent-
spanning canvas during the turbulent war years,
Rosamunde Pilcher's most eagerly-awaited novel is
the story of an extraordinary young woman's coming of age, coming to grips with love and sadness,
and in every sense of the term, coming home...

Rosamunde Pilcher

The #1 *New York Times* Bestselling Author of *The
Shell Seekers* and *September*

COMING HOME

"Rosamunde Pilcher's most satisfying story since *The Shell
Seekers*."

—*Chicago Tribune*

"Captivating...The best sort of book to come home
to...Readers will undoubtedly hope Pilcher comes home
to the typewriter again soon."

—*New York Daily News*

COMING HOME
Rosamunde Pilcher
_____ 95812-9 $7.99 U.S./$9.99 CAN.